A CHAIN ACROSS THE DAWN

A CHAIN ACROSS THE DAWN

DREW WILLIAMS

**SIMON &
SCHUSTER**

London · New York · Sydney · Toronto · New Delhi

A CBS COMPANY

First published in Great Britain by Simon & Schuster UK Ltd, 2019
A CBS COMPANY

Copyright © Drew Williams, 2019

The right of Drew Williams to be identified as author of
this work has been asserted in accordance with the
Copyright, Designs and Patents Act, 1988.

1 3 5 7 9 10 8 6 4 2

Simon & Schuster UK Ltd
1st Floor
222 Gray's Inn Road
London WC1X 8HB

Simon & Schuster Australia, Sydney
Simon & Schuster India, New Delhi

www.simonandschuster.co.uk
www.simonandschuster.com.au
www.simonandschuster.co.in

A CIP catalogue record for this book is available from the British Library.

Hardback ISBN: 978-1-4711-7115-4
Trade Paperback ISBN: 978-1-4711-7116-1
eBook ISBN: 978-1-4711-7117-8
Audio ISBN: 978-1-4711-8059-0

Printed and bound by CPI Group (UK) Ltd, Croydon, CR0 4YY

MIX
Paper from
responsible sources
FSC
www.fsc.org   FSC® C020471

For Presley Luna Barnacastle—Welcome!

ACT
ONE

CHAPTER 1

The air-raid sirens were still screaming, echoing out across the golden sky of Kandriad like some sort of terrifying lament, hollow and vast and *loud* as all hell. The sound bounced off the concrete and the steel of the long-abandoned factory city around us, rolling out over the plains of metal toward the distant horizon still tinged with the faintest blue hints of the dawn.

There *shouldn't* have been air-raid sirens on Kandriad. Not because the pulse had repressed the technology for sirens, but because it had repressed the ability for anyone to conduct air raids at all: flight was supposed to be impossible in an atmosphere this choked with pulse radiation.

Except it wasn't. Jane and I had seen the shadows of the warplanes hurtling over the factory city as we approached by the bridge, dropping bombs and executing amateurish evasive maneuvers to wheel away from the strafing gunfire of the defenders' anti-aircraft weaponry. The planes hadn't exactly been modern spec—prop-driven, combustion-engine relics cobbled together from spare parts—but that didn't change the fact that they *shouldn't* have been able to get into the air at all. Something weird was happening on Kandriad.

Something weird *always* seemed to happen to Jane and me, but this was weirder than most.

"So we . . . knock?" I asked, shifting my weight from side to side, staring up at the massive barred door that was the one and only entrance to the factory city from the south. We hadn't seen a single native as we made our way down the abandoned railway line toward the factory—they were all hunkered down inside their converted city, being dive-bombed by impossible airplanes. The sect wars might have been forgotten by most of the galaxy post-pulse, but on Kandriad they'd never *stopped*, the locals locked in the same stupid conflicts that had led to the pulse in the first place. "Or . . . like . . ." I winced as the sirens came around again; I winced every time. I always *thought* they were finally going to stop as they dopplered away across the distance, and then . . . nope. Still going.

"We should probably wait until they're not having the shit bombed out of them," Jane said mildly, leaning against the railing of the dilapidated bridge and smoking one of her awful cigarettes. *Jane* wasn't fidgety. Jane never *got* fidgety. Taller, leaner, and in significantly better shape than I was, I'd seen her be more collected under sustained gunfire than I usually was making breakfast.

"Do you think that's likely to happen soon, or . . ." I winced as one of the bombers overshot its target, its payload coming down instead on the empty urban district beside the bridge—otherwise known as beside *us*. I was holding a telekinetic shield in place over both Jane and myself, and the feeling of the shrapnel from the blast smashing itself to pieces against what was basically a psychic manifestation of my own will was . . . not overly pleasant. Still, the shield held, and even if it hadn't, our intention shields—hardwired into our nervous systems—would have protected us. Hopefully.

I didn't particularly want to die on a bombed-out hellhole like Kandriad.

Jane waved her hand—and her cigarette—in front of her face, not so much dispelling the cloud of dust that had risen in the wake of the blast as adding to it with her cigarette smoke. "Doesn't seem that way," she said.

"So can we talk about *how* there are warplanes flying and dropping bombs in a pulse-choked atmosphere?" I asked instead. Since we appeared to be stuck out here, *underneath* the falling bombs, that seemed a topic of particularly hefty import.

Jane frowned at that. "I don't know," she said shortly. I almost grinned—despite the nearly-being-blown-apart thing—just because Jane *hated* to admit when she didn't know something, and a part of me was always a little bit thrilled when circumstances forced her to do so anyway.

Still would have traded it for "not huddled just outside a factory door, hoping not to get bombed," though.

"But how—"

"Still don't know, Esa," she sighed, dropping her cigarette butt to the bridge and grinding it out with her boot heel—though it wasn't like there was anything out here to catch on fire. "And either way, we're not likely to find answers standing out here. Go ahead and knock—we've got a gifted kid to find."

"I thought you said we should wait until they *weren't* getting bombed." As if cued by my statement, the air-raid sirens finally cut off, the last hollow howl echoing out over the horizon until it faded into the golden light of the day.

I looked at Jane. She was grinning. I glared at her; that just made her grin some more. She opened her mouth to say something, and I simply held out my hand, forestalling whatever smartassery was about to emerge. "Don't," I told her flatly. "Just . . ." I sighed, and reached for the heavy knocker welded to the riveted steel of the door. "I got this."

I knocked.

CHAPTER 2

In relatively short order, we got a response to our banging. That response was, of course, half a dozen rifles pointed at us from murder holes carved out of the sides of the high wall, but it was a response nonetheless. "Travelers," Jane said, spreading her hands wide to show that she was unarmed—well, to show that she wasn't *holding* a weapon, at least. On a world like Kandriad, nobody went *anywhere* unarmed, and the rifle butt sticking up from behind Jane's shoulder would have just seemed like an everyday necessity to the locals, no different than a farmer carrying a hoe would have been on my homeworld. "Seeking shelter."

"This city is at war, traveler," a voice said from one of the murder holes—sounded like a Wulf, which made sense, since the vaguely canid species had made up about a third of this world's population, before the pulse. "There's very little shelter to be had here."

"Very little to be had out there, either." Jane jerked her thumb behind us, indicating the smoking craters the poorly aimed bombs had blown in the urban "countryside" of what had once been a factory planet.

"How do we know you're not enemy spies?" the Wulf growled. I mean, Wulf almost *always* growl, the sound was just what their muzzles were built for, but I detected a distinct note of aggression in the low-pitched rumble of this one's voice.

"Esa," Jane prompted me, and I reached into my jacket—slowly, as the rifles were still following my every move—to produce a tightly rolled-up scroll. The parchment was as close to what local conditions would have allowed the natives to create as Schaz had been able to make it; hopefully they wouldn't ask too many questions about its provenance beyond that, questions we wouldn't be able to answer given that we'd actually printed it on board a spaceship in orbit, a concept that had receded mostly into myth for the people on Kandriad.

I held the scroll up, where they could see. "Reconnaissance," Jane told them simply. "Aerial photography of the enemy assaulting your walls from the north. Troop positions, fortifications, artillery emplacements—enough intelligence to turn the tide of the fight." Neither Jane nor I really gave a damn who won this particular battle, or even this particular war—whatever conflict it had spun off from, the fighting on Kandriad had long since ceased to matter to the galaxy at large, let alone to the doings of the Justified. What we *did* care about was getting access to the city, and to the gifted child hidden somewhere inside.

"You have planes? Like they do?" The guns were still holding . . . pretty tightly on us.

"Kites," Jane said simply. "And mirrors." *That* was a flat-out lie, but "we took images from our spaceship in low orbit, then smudged them up to *look* like low-tech aerial reconnaissance" wouldn't have gone over nearly as well.

A low sound from the Wulf, not that dissimilar to his growl from before; thankfully, our boss back on Sanctum was also a Wulf, and I recognized the sound of a Wulven chuckle when I heard one. "Kites," the unseen sentry said to himself, almost in wonder. Then: "Open the gate!"

The big metal gates rumbled open; Jane and I stepped along the train tracks, into the interior of the city, where the sentries—Wulf to a one, their rifles still held tightly, though at least not aimed directly at us anymore—watched us closely. Jane handed over the map to their leader, the one who'd spoken. He unrolled it, studied its contents for a moment, then without a word handed it off to one of his subordinates, who promptly took off, presumably for the factory city's command. "It's valid, and it's recent," the lieutenant acknowledged to us, his ice-blue predator's eyes still watching us closely, not as friendly as his words. "I recognize shelling from just a few days ago. Intelligence like that will buy you more than just entry here, strangers. Name your price."

"We're looking for some intelligence of our own," Jane replied. "Looking for one of your citizens, actually. A child, younger than my associate here." She nodded her head toward me; I didn't know how well the local Wulf population would be at gauging a human's age, but at seventeen, I guess I did still have a slightly "unfinished" look, as compared to Jane, at least.

"And why do you seek this child?" the lieutenant asked—not a no. Progress.

"He or she will have . . . gifts. Abilities. We seek children with such gifts, and we train them." All true, for its part. It was simply a question of scale that Jane left out.

"Train them to do what?"

"Whatever is necessary." *That* part wasn't exactly an official piece of the Sanctum syllabus.

The Wulf nodded his head, once. "I know the child you're looking for," he said.

Finally, something going our way for once.

CHAPTER 3

The lieutenant led the way, at least for a little bit, guiding us through the fortifications and the armories and the aid stations and the endless walls—the factory had been remade from a place where things were fabricated to a place entirely structured around war, and it looked like it had seen plenty of the latter.

Beyond the final checkpoint, he took his leave of us with instructions to head toward the "lower wards" and ask around: apparently the maintenance tunnels built beneath the complex, underground, where most of the civilian population lived, safe from the constant artillery attacks and bombing raids. Jane thanked him, and shook his hand—that curiously human gesture, for whatever reason, had spread through almost every alien culture during the Golden Age—and then we went our separate ways, the Wulf sentry back to his post, Jane and I toward the elevators.

We packed onto the massive lifting platform with a group of civilian volunteers covered in dust and stained with smoke, returning from work at the front. The elevator was operated by a clever mechanism of counterweights and interlinked chains: it's always impressive, what people can come up with when they don't have access to the levels of tech that actually *built* the world around them.

As the platform shook to life and began its descent, I looked around me, finding spots in the crowded elevator where I could peek in between the various civilians and out the chain-link cage that surrounded the descending platform. There are various advantages to being short; seeing above the heads of a crowd of people is not one of them. Still, I could make out some of the city passing us by, levels and levels of retrofitted factory turned into districts and facilities and homes. "Is this what it was like?" I asked Jane curiously, not really apropos of anything in particular.

"What *what* was like?" she asked, her gaze still set forward, staring out the cage around the elevator as we were lowered through the factory floors, the spaces once meant for building . . . who knows what, ball bearings or spaceship engines or anti-grav frictionless coagulant, and now retrofitted into armories and schools and churches.

"The sect wars. Your sect wars."

She shrugged, one hand linked into the chain, her fingers tight against the wire. "There were as many different wars as there were sects, kid."

"I know. I get that. I'm asking you if *yours* was anything like *this*."

"Some parts were. Other parts weren't."

"You don't like to talk about it, do you?"

"It was a long time ago."

"But you were—"

She sighed, finally turning and looking at me. "Esa, if you're asking me if I was born in a city under siege, a city like this, the answer is yes. If you're asking me if there was still . . . life, and people trying to *live* their lives, even under those conditions, people trying to normalize the aggressively abnormal until it was . . . just the way things were, then yes. It was like this. If you're asking me if I grew up in a massive factory complex retrofitted into a city retrofitted into the forward operating base of a theater of war, then no. No, I didn't. Okay?"

We were both silent for a moment; around us, the elevator still groaned as it descended, and the civilians sharing the space with us still spoke quietly, though none of them seemed inclined toward raising their voices, either, having just come from the destruction of the front. Finally, I spoke again. "I get that in your hundred and ninety-three years—"

"I'm not a hundred and ninety-three years old, Esa."

"Fine. I get that in your hundred and ninety-*two* years in this universe, you've seen a great deal, and not a great deal of it pretty. I came from a world that I'm not in any rush to remember either, yeah? So I get that. But a home's a home, Jane. It still . . . where we come from still *matters*. You don't get to just . . . turn that part of you off, make it into something else. Your life didn't just . . . restart itself, after you joined the Justified. Or after . . . after the pulse." I'd almost said "after *you* detonated the pulse," which would have been true, but also unfair. Not to mention a *stupid, stupid* thing to say when we were surrounded by strangers, even if we were conversing almost sub-aurally, thanks to our implanted commlinks. "You're still who you were, then. At least a part of you is."

"I'm really, really not, kid." She shook her head again. "Maybe you'll understand when you're older."

I gave a small smile at that. "When I'm a hundred and ninety-one, you mean?"

"Also not a hundred and ninety-one, Esa. We're here." The elevator shivered to a stop; the chain gates slid open, the maintenance tunnels before us as cramped and claustrophobic and silent as the factory floors above had been open and alive. Apparently almost everyone who lived down here was above, either heading to or from the front, or working in the various other areas of the city.

The locals shuffled out, still muted, making their way toward various side passages and the closets and storage rooms they now called living quarters. I mean, I get it, I was used to cramped quarters—Scheherazade's interior was not exactly palatial—but still: it was a tight fit, even to me. Jane stopped one of them, a female Wulf who hadn't shrugged off the armband marked with three diagonal blue lines—the universal symbol for "medic." "We're looking for a child," Jane told her. The medic stared at her face, her bone-deep exhaustion warring with open curiosity at the human asking her questions. "One with . . . talents. We were told to ask down here."

The Wulf nodded, then sighed. "I know the child you mean," she said. "I've . . . tried to help. He lives with his mother, in the subway line apartments. Find the ladders; go as far down as you can; ask around again. Everyone knows who they are. All the way at the edges."

"Do you—can you tell me what the child can do?"

The Wulf stared at Jane for another moment, then shook her head. "It's not my place to say," she answered. "Not my story to tell. Whatever it is you expect, though, prepare yourself for disappointment. It's a sad story. Like so many in this city."

Jane nodded, taking a step backward. "Thank you for your help," she said.

"Of course. Good luck. I hope you *can* help them. They deserve it." With that, she faded into the rest of the shuffling crowd, off to catch some well-deserved rest.

Jane looked at me; I looked back, then shrugged. "At least we know we're looking for a male," I said. "That's something, at least."

"True. 'Prepare yourselves for disappointment,' on the other hand, is . . . less than promising. And the boy still has his mother. That might be . . . tricky."

For whatever reason—most likely the activating trauma that most of the children we were seeking out went through—a substantial percentage of the kids we took back to Sanctum were orphans, more than half, at least. As an orphan myself, I kind of recoiled at the notion that it was a "good" thing, but the truth was it *did* make it easier to convince a child to leave their homeworld—usually the only world they'd ever known—if they wouldn't have to leave parents behind as well. Jane and I had managed it a couple times in the three years we'd been working together, but she was right: it did make things more complicated.

We couldn't offer to take his mother with us, either. That wasn't in our mandate. I gathered it had been tried before, in the early days of Sanctum, with . . . less than ideal results. It wasn't something operatives in our line talked about much—but it had been made very clear to me in my training that, of the things we *were* allowed to promise the kids to secure their co-operation, a place for their parents wasn't among them.

Still, a way off of a world like this one, most parents would want that for their child. That was usually our opening bargaining chip, and as chips went, it was not half bad, especially given the state of siege they were living in now.

We started forward, into the tunnels, looking for a ladder down.

CHAPTER 4

It took us some time, wandering the subway tunnels, asking around about the boy with the gifts, our theoretical cargo—Jane's term, by the way; I kind of hated it, but she used it often enough that it had snuck its way into my vernacular all the same. As it turned out, we needn't have bothered. People were helpful, in a vague enough sort of way—some of them were, at any rate; some growled and refused to speak, others called him a "demon" and made warding symbols with their claws, but a *few* were helpful. Ultimately, though, we could have just wandered the subway at random until we came across the surest possible sign that we were in the right place.

The electric lights in a single section of a subway car were glowing.

Jane noticed it before I did, the difference between the orange glow of sporadic lantern flames and the cold blue flickering of the ancient fluorescents. "Esa," she nudged me quietly, pointing out the light.

"Think it has to do with the planes?" I asked, still keeping my voice low; discussion of the pulse—what was likely assumed to be a universal constant on this world, given that nobody *got* offworld any longer—wasn't likely to make us many friends.

Jane shook her head. "Too localized. Best guess is it's his gift. It *could* be a generator—this world isn't so far down the line that basic gasoline-powered generators wouldn't run—but we haven't seen any others. Plus, I've seen it before: the gift, I mean. A form of electrokinesis. He's a walking, talking fusion battery, and the rads don't affect him any more than they do you. I'm surprised the sect here doesn't have him chained to some of the big machinery above, working him day and night."

I turned to face her. "We've seen mostly decency among them so far," I said. "Even a little bit of kindness, here and there. What makes you so sure they'd try something so awful?"

"Because kindness and decency are the first things to go when the enemy is at the door," she replied. "Come on." She nodded at a figure, staring at us from the door of the subway car, the other Wulf making room around her. "If I had to guess, that's our boy's mother."

We approached the train car, entering the circle of electric light. The female Wulf just stared at us, something tired in her eyes. Jane raised a hand. "We—"

"You have come to try and take my son away from me," the woman said, her voice not . . . accusatory, not exactly, but something else instead. Maybe just tired. Slowly, the claws slid from her fingers, an autonomic reflex, no different than Jane or I getting henflesh if we were spooked. She made no attempt to use those talons, or even *raise* them in a threat or a beseechment— just stood there, staring at us, her eyes almost hollow. Then: "You had better come inside. Please, keep your voices down."

With that, she ducked into the train car, leaving Jane and me no choice but to follow.

The boy wasn't immediately visible; there were a few sheets, strung from the handhold bars above, and we could see a shadow beyond that which *might* have been a child. He seemed to be sleeping. Apparently his—what had Jane called it?—electrokinesis was involuntary; he was running power to the lights above without any conscious effort.

Wish I could do that; using my teke took it *out* of me.

The Wulf woman was folding laundry, refusing to look at us despite her invitation. Inside the train car, under the electric light, I could get a better look at her: there were patchy burns along her arm and the side of her face, where her fur refused to grow. Some injury from the war, possibly? Or just a horrible accident, when her son's powers had manifested? A terrible thing, to be afraid of your own child.

"You have come from beyond the city, seeking a 'gifted' child," she said, still not looking at us, concentrating on her work. "This much the others tell me. Some say that I should let you have him, and be glad: they say you will take him away from this war, and it doesn't matter to where, simply because any place is better than here. They do not actually *care* what happens to him, of course; just that they cannot imagine anyone turning away such an invitation. Others say I should let you take him because he is a demon, and not to be trusted. I have heard this from them before. Still others say I should tear your throats out where you stand—even offered to help. They are not thinking of my boy either, of course: just that they want the minor comforts he can provide. The lights, the air exchangers." She waved a free hand above us, encompassing the minor machinery operating quietly in the subway car's steel. "Tell me: *why* should I let you take my boy? He is my only living son. His life, here, is hard enough; why should I trust that you will not make it harder? All he has in the world is me. All I have in the world is him. Why would I let you take that away from us?"

Jane opened her mouth to answer, but the woman turned to face her before she could speak. "I should warn you," she continued, "think carefully before you speak. I have not entirely cast aside the option to open your veins and abandon you in the deeper tunnels. You are human. We do not know much of your kind, but we *do* remember that you are weaker than we are, physically. I do not think you can raise your guns before I can close the distance between us and end your lives. You are trying to *take my boy away from me*. So I say again: think carefully."

She was wrong, of course; even without my telekinesis, both Jane and I were fast enough on the draw that we could gun her down before she even got halfway down the railcar toward us. But the absolute worst way to start a relationship with our cargo would be to shoot his mother in front of him; that wasn't how we wanted this to go.

"Before I tell you *why* you should let him come with us," Jane told the woman, "there are a few truths that you should know. I will not lie to you. We want to be friends to your son; we want to help him. We cannot do that if his mother tells him never to trust us. Do you believe me?"

The woman looked slowly between Jane and myself, gave the Wulf equivalent of a small smile. "Ah," she said. "Of course. I should have guessed. You are a mother yourself. I needn't have bothered with all the threats, then." She turned back to her laundry; we didn't correct her assumption. "Continue." She was making a big show of being calm, controlled, but I could see the fur jumping near one of the patchy spots on her neck; her pulse was racing through her veins.

"We are not from another sect on this world," Jane told her. "We are not from this world at all."

She simply nodded, not as though she *believed* it, but as though that were a thing she had thought we might say. "And why should I trust you?"

"Look and see for yourself." Jane pulled a small piece of tech from her coat: a simple holographic projector. She waited until the Wulf woman had faced us again, then triggered it on, filling the train car with images of the wider galaxy, making them slide and twist along the metal walls. It operated for only a few seconds—a level of tech well beyond what could last for long on this world—until it burnt out, but the Wulf woman's eyes were still wide as the light faded.

"The pulse—the radiation that keeps the old technology from working here—it has not spread to every world," Jane told her. "There are others where the old technology still runs. We are from one such world. We need your child's help, to *stop* the pulse from spreading to *our* home." Not quite the truth, but close enough that the woman could hear the ring of it in Jane's voice, and just self-interested enough that she could believe it.

"So." With effort, she lifted her eyes from the piece of tech in Jane's hand—burnt out and useless now, but still drawing her gaze with an almost gravitational pull. I don't know if she actually believed, or if she was just pretending that she did, both to us and for herself. Because of what it might mean for her son. "You need my child to help your world. This I can understand—this is not *so* different from what the others said. A world far across the stars, a sect halfway across this one; they are much the same. You also offer him wonders beyond his imagining—some of the others said that, as well. That does not tell me *why* I should let you take him."

"Because," Jane said, swallowing, and even I didn't know what she was going to say next; she clearly had some plan, some play, but damned if *I* knew what it was. "If you do, on our world—with our medicine, our technology— we can help him walk again."

What?

The smile the woman gave was bitter now; even on a Wulf face, I could read that much. She reached over and pushed the hanging sheet aside, revealing her son, sleeping quietly on the seats of the subway car, uncovered. Where the woman had strange scarring on her face and arm, the boy had the same, but at the base of his spine instead.

Ah. Jane had used her HUD to scan the child. Knew about the injury he'd received—likely the same trauma that had caused his powers to awaken.

"You are clever," the woman admitted to Jane, looking down on her son. "I suppose you would have to be, to do what you do. It wasn't a bomb that did this to him, not an attack by the enemy. A chemical spill, instead, in the ammunition factory where I work. Worked. He was bringing me my lunch. Saw the spill, saw me burning. Heard me scream. Do you know what it is like, to a child that young, to hear his mother make a noise like that? An animal noise, pure fear and pain. He just . . . reacted. Grabbed for me. Reached into the flood and blocked the spill with his own back. Pulled me clear, saved my life. As if I needed another reason to love him." She shook her head. "Such a brave boy. And after that, he had taken his last steps. He will never dance with a pretty girl; he will likely never bring one home to meet me. He will never walk again. But after." She waved her hands idly at the lights above, still looking down at her sleeping child.

"All of that is only true so long as he remains *here*, on this world," Jane promised her.

"His spine is twisted—melted. You are telling me you can fix *that*? I think you are lying." She bared just a little bit of fang as she turned back toward us.

Jane shook her head. "Not the damage—not all of it. But there is technology that can . . . attach to him, give him muscles that will react to commands that can bypass the injury to his spine. He will be able to walk again. This much I can promise you. The dancing, the pretty girls—that, I cannot be sure of. But the walking: yes."

"So that is what you offer. A chance for my boy to walk again. To stand just a little closer to the stars above. The stars, where you will take him. Far away from me. I will never see him again. That is the price *I* must pay. The price we *both* must pay. Nothing is ever without a price. This, I understand." She took a deep, shuddering breath. Knelt by her boy's bedside. Shook him awake, gently, as she blinked back the tears rolling down the fur on her face.

"Sho." She whispered his name, and none of the fear, of the hurt, that had just been present in her voice was audible any longer. She would not let him hear it. "Time to wake up, my son. There are people you need to meet. Something . . . wonderful has happened. Sho. Wake—"

Her words were cut off as all of us—Jane, myself, the boy, his mother—were thrown to the ground; the little makeshift apartment had begun shaking violently, and not just the train car, but the tunnel around it as well. There were deep grinding sounds, coming from all around us, like something just outside of the walls, something within the earth and the concrete beyond, was trying to get *through*.

Maybe something wonderful had just happened to Sho—I sure hoped it had. But it sounded like something terrible was on its way as well.

Like the lady said: everything came with a price. The two just weren't always guaranteed to be equal. That wasn't the way the world worked—not any world I'd ever seen, at any rate.

CHAPTER 5

picked myself up, found Jane, who was doing the same thing. Behind her, I could hear the child—Sho—frightened, begging his mother: "Mama, what's happening? Who—*what* are these people? What is—"

"Be calm, now, Sho, be calm. Everything will be—"

"Get outside, Esa," Jane commanded as we got to our feet. "Tell me what's going on."

"Right." I ducked through the open door, the boy's mother's quiet whispers fading away, replaced by the chaos outside the subway car. People everywhere were screaming, running—all in one direction, back the way we had come. So of course I looked the other way.

We were pretty much at the edge of the populated tunnels, maybe even beyond the factory above us, beyond the walls; I'd figured that much. Somewhere past the curve of the subway line, there must have been some sort of collapse, a cave-in, something blocking the access out to the wider world; otherwise there would have been guards, defending an ingress point. At the edge of the fluorescent lights—now flickering, winking in and out, though I couldn't tell if that was because of whatever was happening, or because the boy was awake, his powers fluctuating with his fear—there were a few more points of orange: candles and lanterns. Around them, I could just see it coming: a creeping fog, tinged copper by the small glints of the flame.

Gas.

I ducked back into the rail car. "It's a chemical attack," I told Jane. "We don't have much time."

She nodded; the Wulf woman was already fitting her with some kind of homemade harness, adjusting the straps to wrap Jane's slightly smaller frame. It was probably how she carried her boy around. The woman heard what I said, of course, as did Jane and the boy, but she gave no reaction. Sho, however, was a different story. "We need to move, we need to *go*," he said, pulling himself back up onto his bed with effort, his legs dragging behind him. "The gas—it will expand, fill the tunnels, if they've breached the ceilings beneath the front they'll keep pumping it *in*—"

His mother cut him off—"Sho, be still"—before he could get to the realization the rest of us had already come to. The elevator Jane and I had ridden down in was distant, up several ladders and back underneath the factory proper, not to mention far too small to fit all the people we'd passed on our way here. Even if there were other lifts like them—and we hadn't seen any others, not on our explorations while we'd been looking for the boy—not everyone was making it up to the surface, away from the creeping death approaching. Not even a tenth of them would be able to reach the floors above before the gas expanded to fill the entire tunnel system.

Almost everyone inside the subway tunnels was going to die.

The Wulf sect's enemies above hadn't been able to breach the factory complex's walls, not even with their warplanes, not with all their soldiers and all their guns. So they were targeting another part of the city instead—the civilians, hidden underground, the very place they'd thought they would be safe. Trying to tear out the sect's heart, rather than waste more time and effort trying to push past their defenses.

"We'll have to go *through* it, Esa," Jane told me, even as the Wulf settled her son into the harness over her back. The boy had gritted his teeth, and tears were streaking his face, but he wasn't sobbing anymore. Trying goddamned hard to be brave, instead. I wondered if he'd realized yet what was about to happen to his mother. "Find the breach, get topside again. It's the only way."

I nodded, reaching over to help cinch up the straps around Sho. I lay what I hoped was a comforting hand on his shoulder as I did so, putting my head against his. "We're here to protect you, Sho," I told him in a whisper. "Don't worry about a thing. We've got you now. My name is Esa."

"Esa, yes," he nodded. "Thank . . . thank you. What is—where are we—"

"Just try to stay calm, Sho. Try to focus . . . think about something else. Think about something far away from here. We're taking you to a better place, a better world. But it's going to be scary, getting there." I remembered my own flight, across the face of my homeworld, with Jane and the Preacher, the Pax closing in behind. I'd tried to cover it up, but I'd been terrified. I'm sure he was the same. "I'll be right here with you."

"Listen to the girl, Sho," his mother commanded her boy. "You listen, and you do as she says. She is part of your pack now; she is your sister. She will protect you. She will lay down her life for you, if she has to." She was staring at me as she said it, her amber eyes seeming to blaze in the reflection of the flickering light. I nodded, once. I would.

"Is he tied on?" Jane asked, trying to look behind her, unable to, around Sho's bulk; the effect might almost have been comical, if we weren't all about to die.

"I am . . . yes, I'm good," Sho told her, holding tight to her shoulders. Jane put her wrists underneath his backside and lifted; she was able to stand, even with his bulk, as well as the added weight of all her weapons and ammunition. That was good news. I wouldn't have been able to, and not just because I was smaller; Jane was fucking *fit*.

"You will go now, Sho," his mother told him, stroking the fur around his face. "You will have a better life, a *safer* life, once you are free of all this. And you will remember how much I love you. Always remember that."

"Mother, I—"

"You." The woman had turned her burning glare to Jane now, instead. "I am *trusting* you. Trusting you with my boy. I have no other choice. There is no threat I can make . . . no threat I will be able to carry out, that I can frighten you with. Soon you will be far beyond my reach." Two meanings to those words, hiding the truth behind the hope, for her boy. "All the same. You *will* protect him. Protect him the same as you do your own daughter. From one mother to another, I want your *word*. You will protect him, and you will show him the stars."

Jane freed one hand from the boy, reached out to grip the Wulf woman's wrist. "You have it," she said. "Sho will be safe with me."

The woman smiled, though she was still weeping. She squeezed Jane's arm in return, her claws retracting. "His name is 'Show-no-fang,'" she said through her tears. "He is a good boy."

"Mother, *please*—" the child was begging; she caressed his face once more, then reached under her overturned laundry basket and produced a *giant* fucking shotgun. No wonder she'd been doing "laundry" when we entered.

Okay. So maybe if she hadn't wanted her son to go with us, we would have had more trouble than we thought.

"Go!" she said again, herding us out of the train car—the only home Sho had ever known. The gas was getting closer now, approaching the edge of the electric light, a boil of sick-colored mist, yellow and green and copper-tinged by candle flame. It looked like cancer come to life.

"Esa—" Jane warned, but I was already on it. To think: I'd made fun of her when she insisted we carry gas masks on this mission. I helped Jane get her own mask on, then removed mine from around my neck, pulling out the straps and settling it over Sho's head. It took a little doing to get it over his muzzle, but Justified equipment was designed to fit most of the various species that made up our ranks, and I got it secure after a bit of fiddling.

"Breathe in, breathe out, just like normal," I commanded him, tightening the final straps. "Deep breaths. If you start to hyperventilate . . . don't start to hyperventilate. It'll be all right."

"What about you?" the boy's mother asked me.

"Don't worry yourself," Jane told her with a small smile to me, barely visible through the clouded plastic of her mask. "Your son has his gifts; my daughter has her own."

I nodded, and ran a hand down my face, dragging my fingers through the grease paint that camouflaged my skin as if I were pulling an invisible mask on from underneath my knit hat. A feeling of cold spread from my fingertips, like I was coating my skin with liquid. It was a telekinetic bubble, an old trick I'd learned for dangerous atmospheres; it took effort, keeping it porous enough to let oxygen through while blocking everything else, and I wouldn't be able to use much of my teke while maintaining it, but it would keep me alive in the gas.

"You'll have to take point, Esa," Jane told me, shifting her grip to better take Sho's weight, unintentionally reinforcing her command: with both her hands held behind her, supporting the boy, she wouldn't be able to hold her rifle. "I'll scan, and feed positions to you."

"Got it." I *really* needed to stop being a coward and get a HUD installed, six-hour medical procedure or not. Jane could read heat signatures through the cloud of the gas; I would be mostly blind.

I unslung my submachine gun—I called her "Bitey," had even stenciled fangs under her muzzle brake—and held her at ready position, one finger just outside the trigger guard; with my other hand, I flipped a toggle just above the off-hand grip, and the built-in suppressor mechanism slid into place forward of the barrel. It wouldn't completely silence any shots I made, but hopefully, between the suppressor and the fog of the gas, it would make it harder for any enemies waiting for us to pinpoint my position.

I took a final breath, maybe my last clean one before we stepped into the fog. God, we were really going to do this.

"*Mother*," Sho said desperately, twisting on Jane's back to try and get a look at the face of the woman who had raised him, who had *borne* him, who had fed him and clothed him and chased away his fears and his pain. There was more agony in that single word than others felt in whole lifetimes. I often regretted being raised an orphan. Now was not one of those times.

"Go, my son," the Wulf woman told him, loading shells into her shotgun without looking—her gaze was only for her boy. "Be strong. Be *brave*. Live. There are so many other worlds out there for you to see. Worlds better than this one."

"Mother, I love you—I love you *so much*—"

"I love you too, Sho. I always will. Now go. *Go!*"

Jane took that as her sign; staying longer would just prolong the boy's pain. Not to mention, give a chance for the enemy sect—likely currently widening the breach they'd made to pump in the gas—to get into place in front of us. She started moving *toward* the yellow-greenish fog, and I took my place at her side, my gun held at the ready.

Sho was still twisted around on Jane's back, staring at his mother as she receded away—no different from how she might have seemed if he were on a train pulling away from the station, one of the long-silent cars beside us now. He made one more awful, wordless wail, then buried his face into Jane's shoulder, muffling his sobs; he couldn't see her any longer. The fog had swallowed her whole.

I'd never even asked her name.

CHAPTER 6

We entered the poisoned fog.

It was like stepping into another world, like stepping *out* of Scheherazade's cargo bay, and onto the surface of a planet never terraformed, never meant for our presence. The choking gas was everywhere. Every breath I took drew it in eddies toward me until it was repulsed by the telekinetic mask; I could feel it, wet and thick against my skin like I was wading through slime. It felt like the touch of death, corrosive and awful. Some of that might have been my imagination. Some of it was not.

I kept my gun up. It wasn't like I could shoot the fog, but presumably, if the other sect had found a way into the tunnel to pump the gas in, they were about to follow that assault up with an *actual* assault. Launch their attack on the fortress above through the catacombs of the dead their gas had created.

I couldn't see more than ten feet in front of me, couldn't even see the far side of the tunnel wall. There was just the gas, rolling ever past us as more was pumped inside somewhere ahead. We'd stepped down onto the tracks—it's not as though we were about to be run over by a train car, there hadn't been trains running through these tunnels for a hundred years—and I could count maybe a dozen ties stretched across the concrete floor before those, too, were swallowed up by the yellow-green mists.

The world was silence; even Sho had quieted himself, just a massive pair of golden eyes peering over Jane's shoulder when I stole glances backward at the two of them. Every footstep we took was too loud, as though that sound and that sound alone carried into the distance, further into the swirl of gas.

"Esa," Jane warned. "Heat signatures. Fading. Two dozen paces ahead, up on the access path." I hauled myself up onto the narrow catwalk as silently as I could; Jane and Sho followed below, still on the tracks. I kept moving forward until the forms appeared silently from the still eddies of the fog, like shoals of coral on mist-choked seas. Two Wulf, maintenance workers, it looked like, slumped against the tunnel wall on the same access path I'd taken. They were dying—dead. The signatures Jane was reading were the slow fade of their organs, still giving off heat, but growing colder by the second.

I knelt beside them, shut their staring eyes. I don't know why. I just did. Moved on. I kept to the access catwalk, maybe four feet above the tunnel floor, my boots even in height with Jane's back, slightly behind me. A pin-prick of light appeared in front of me—a candle flame, guttering and sickly in the mist, starved of most of the oxygen it needed to burn. A few tools, scattered below. Must have been where the maintenance workers were ply-ing their trade; they'd staggered backward when the mist had appeared, tried to run. Hadn't gotten far.

"More signatures," Jane said again, the words in my ear on the comm, not audible in the silence of the mist. "Four of them, coming down the tunnel. Armed."

The enemy had found their way through. Not *my* enemy, except now they were; I was in their path, in their way, and they'd shoot me dead, Wulf or not, if they saw me before I saw them. I moved forward, knelt by the candle, and snuffed it out with a teke pinch. Raised up my gun. Hugged the wall and started moving again.

The first soldier appeared out of the mist: masked, armored, down on the railway proper. A Tyll, by build. Patchwork combat armor, but his gun looked deadly enough. I froze in place, raised my own weapon. Let him come. He hadn't seen me yet, in the shadows up on the catwalk—wasn't expecting any-one alive this deep in the gas.

The second form appeared behind him. I wanted to know where as many of them were as possible before I opened fire—the first two had almost moved past me, still looking straight ahead. Any second now, they'd see Jane and Sho, still down on the tracks and back a ways from my position.

More eddies in the mist—the other two were about to make their ap-pearance. I kept my gun trained on the first soldier, my finger slipping inside the trigger guard, even as my eyes were glued on the approach of his companions; my hands shifted almost imperceptibly, the barrel of my weapon slowly pacing the figure I could barely see out of the corner of my eye. The third soldier appeared.

The first called out—he'd seen Jane. My finger twitched on Bitey's trigger. The gun spat three rounds and he went down, tumbling through the fog like a tree felled in the forest, a spatter of teal blood splashing against the tunnel walls, almost glowing like bioluminescence in the mist. I turned the weapon on the second, cut him down as well, ducked low. The third had heard the shots, had seen the muzzle flash, even with the suppressor attached—no gun was entirely without telltale signs of its firing. He was raising a weapon in my general direction, but I'd kept turning Bitey even after cutting down the second soldier, and I had a bead drawn before the next aggressor could find me in the fog. Put three rounds in his chest.

That wasn't good enough—the other two I'd taken in the head, because they were all wearing armor. The third went down, flat on his back, but he was still moving; I could hear him gasping for air, even inside his mask. The shots had probably cracked his ribs, but the bullets hadn't penetrated. I slipped down onto the train tracks, inching toward him, watching the fog for the fourth figure Jane had seen. Nothing. No sign.

I was almost to the man I'd put down; I stepped on the gun that had slipped from his grasp when he fell, the gun he was still blindly reaching for. He'd seen me now—his Tyll eyes, jeweled and wide, were terrified through the plastic of his mask. He gasped a word—something like "don't"—before I drew the knife from my boot and plunged it into his throat, my gun still held on the fog before me, my eyes trained down the iron sights, looking for the approach of the fourth.

The Tyll beneath my knee was trying—and failing—to breathe around the six inches of steel I'd shoved into his neck, his hand scrabbling ineffectually at my arm. His sect had pumped gas into these tunnels, tried to poison hundreds of people: probably succeeded. He had likely volunteered to be the first to climb through the breach, to walk through the dead and the dying with his gun out, to finish what the gas had started. And he thought begging for his life might still my hand.

He wasn't my enemy. I didn't like killing people, didn't like hurting them. I had to *try* not to enjoy killing this one.

The fourth figure appeared in a rush, moving fast—he knew *something* had happened to his friends, but not what. I fired Bitey again. With the gun held one-handed, the recoil carried the three-round burst up, the first bullet catching him high in the chest, the next in his chin, the last in his forehead. He dropped like a stone, and the deadly fog was still again, for the moment.

I was surrounded by the dead—men I'd killed. Nausea fought its way up from my gut, bile rising from my throat—for a moment, the world swam, just from the pure *terror* of it all, the fear that had been coursing through me the whole time. What the fuck had I been *thinking?* I'd forced Jane to take me on this mission—she thought I hadn't been ready, and she'd been right. How arrogant did I have to be to think that I could do this—taking point on a war-torn world, not just my own life but Jane's and Sho's dependent on my actions, my training, my reflexes. I'd fucking *asked* for this. I was scared shitless, and that wasn't changing just because I'd won *this* fight—I was more scared now than I had been before I'd seen the enemy up close. How fucking *stupid* could I be?

I fought the reaction down, forced my body to stop shaking, *pushed* at the fear in my mind until it was locked away in a tight box in a corner, metaphorically speaking. I'd have to open it later—but that was for later. For now: we had work to do.

When Jane and Sho caught up with me I had cleaned my knife, and stowed it; I'd loaded a fresh magazine into Bitey and was quietly filling the nearly emptied clip with new rounds. Jane took a look at the dead around me, nodded once. "Well done," she said. If she could see anything of the near panic attack I'd fought off on my face, she didn't say anything about it.

"Thank you," I replied, stowing the newly filled magazine on the spare-clip hooks dangling from my shoulder holster. I tried not to look at Sho, who was staring wide-eyed at me. Even in a city constantly at war, he'd never seen anything like what I'd just done.

I put that in the "later" box too.

We moved on.

Another couple hundred feet down the tunnel, we found their breach. Jane read the heat signatures first—large ones, not human, but machines instead, their "light" fading as the heat slipped out of them and the pulse radiation ate into their guts. More questions that we couldn't ask, and likely wouldn't ever get answers to: the machines were repurposed mining tools, massive drillheads.

As choked with the pulse radiation as this world was, they should have *never* worked, required cleaner fuel than this world could produce, not to mention intricate electronics to give them life: so how had the sect above managed to trick them into motion long enough to chew a tunnel down to the subway lines? And if there was some sort of defense against the pulse that this sect had somehow figured out, why were the rads busily eating into their tech *now*?

All theoretical, anyway. The bigger problem was the dozen or so heat signatures on the other *side* of the breach, working to widen the newly carved tunnel their dying machines had begun. It was already big enough to allow entrance for their soldiers—the four I'd met and put down farther back in the tunnel were evidence of that. So what the hell else were they trying to get down here? More troops at once? Were they going to storm an entire *brigade* through the subways?

Again—didn't matter. They wanted down, into the subway system; we wanted *up*, out into the open air again, up toward the front lines, as crazy as that sounded. I took a few deep breaths behind my mask, each faster than the last, then I held the final one and slipped my fingers down my face, letting Bitey dangle at my side. Pulled the mask off so that I could focus my telekinetic energy in my hands, instead. Gathered the force just inside my clenched fists, letting it build and build and *build* until it was like my palms were gripped around a pair of tiny, furiously vibrating creatures, digging into my skin to get *out*.

They wanted a wider hole? I'd give them a fucking hole.

I thrust my hands out before me, palms facing the climbing tunnel, letting the force loose with the same motion. The silence of the mist was deepened, for a single moment, all sonic vibration sucked into the release of the telekinetic blast like gravity sucked into a black hole. We couldn't actually *hear* it as my teke battering ram—roughly the size of a train car, and moving twice as fast—hammered its way up the makeshift tunnel, carrying the soldiers inside with it, hopefully until they hit something hard. We only heard the aftermath, collapse and detritus clattering down the concrete.

"Let's *move*," Jane said, pulling herself up onto the platform one-handed,

Sho still on her back. After pulling my teke mask back on, I did the same, climbing into the gas-choked tunnel, climbing up toward the front.

We'd been assuming that the sect above was just pumping gas *down*, into the subway system below, but nope: they'd blanketed the entire front line with the stuff, probably to try and force the defenders back inside the factory walls so they couldn't see the enemy massing their own forces, preparing to send them all underground.

That meant that once we reached the surface, we'd still be blind, but so would they.

We emerged, blinking, into the light of day, what little light there was diffused by the eddying fog, which was more *alive* up here than it had been below, shifting and flowing thanks to the mild air currents on the factory world's surface. The gas pumps up here were automated, unmanned—but still running, less complicated tech than the drilling tools we'd found below. I broke the machines, just because. I doubted it would do any good—they'd already flooded the tunnels—but you never knew.

Maybe, after the lives I'd taken below, I could *save* some lives too. That would be nice.

CHAPTER 7

Now that we were aboveground, Jane activated her long-distance comms, trying to raise Schaz—she'd tried before, when we were in the tunnels, but we'd been too deep, the signal blocked by all the concrete around us. This time, Scheherazade came on the line with no delay.

"We need extraction," Jane said flatly.

"Well, hello to you as well, Jane," Schaz grumbled. I could hear her response through my own comms, Jane feeding the signal to me.

"Not the time, Schaz. We're at the front lines, in front of the factory complex somewhere, hidden in a chemical attack cloud."

"Oh. That *does* sounds unpleasant. Hold on." Schaz went to work, presumably feeding Jane enemy locations and heat signatures from her orbital view, hovering high, high, *high* above the battlefield.

"That train line, there." I couldn't *see* whatever the hell Jane was talking about; again, thanks to my lack of HUD, about all *I* could see was toxic gas and bullet-chewed concrete. But a train line sounded promising. Probably just a continuation of the bridge we'd followed into the city from the south; I thought I remembered something like that from the topographical map we'd studied before Schaz had dropped us off.

"It's cut off from the factory complex itself," Jane continued, still talking to Schaz. "Which means there's not a lot of fighting going on up there—the Wulf in the city must have shattered the support trestle ages ago, to deny the enemy access to their northern gate. How far are we from access, someplace we can climb up?"

"Not too far—half a mile, at most. But Jane, if you *do* manage to get up there, that position is packed with enemy snipers. I can come pick you up, but you'll be under fire the entire time."

"It's not a problem. See the train car, back toward the complex, nearly at the break in the span?"

"The one that's still on the tracks? Sure—it looks like at one point the enemy converted it to a sniper's nest."

"You let us worry about that; they'll be facing the wrong way. We're going to *take* that car, and we're going to get it moving; the tracks themselves are clear. That'll get us past the enemy's forward lines."

"Jane—have you been hit on the head? Esa, has she been hit on the head? That world is *pulsed*; that locomotive's engine requires fusion power to run, and the fusion batteries inside won't *work*."

"We've got an answer to that. Just figure out a flight plan to intercept that train while it's in motion—we won't be able to risk letting it stop, not while we're barreling through enemy positions, so we'll have to transfer from it to *you* as it's moving down the track."

"If you let it go too far—however you're planning to get it started to begin with—there's another break in the bridge, several miles down. Just so you know. That's a long drop to take in a metal box. A metal box that's not, you know, me."

"Understood. Jane out." She switched off her comms, then looked at Sho, who had been following what sounded to *him* like a one-sided conversation with wide eyes.

"Who were you talking to?" he asked.

"Our ship," Jane answered. "She's coming to pick us up."

"Your ship can *talk*?"

I almost smiled at that; the question was . . . familiar, to say the least. I'd asked Jane the same thing, almost verbatim, what felt like lifetimes ago.

"Yes, she can," Jane told him, her voice full of the same poorly hidden annoyance she'd answered *me* with. "Not important right now. You got those electric lights to run, down below, and the pulse didn't burn them out, because the power was coming from *you*, the same way Barious are protected."

"What are 'Barious'?"

"Also not important, at the moment. Do you think you can do the same to a fusion battery, in an old train car?"

He nodded confidently; I was quietly impressed. He'd been through a hell of a day, but here he was, clinging to Jane's back, doing his best to help. "I've activated fusion batteries before," he said. "In the ammunition factory. They don't last very long—a half a day, at most, before the reaction starts to sour and I have to power them down—but I *can* get them running."

"That's all we need. Esa? You got the plan?"

I nodded confidently. "We make our way through this . . . shit . . ."—I waved at the gas cloud around us, and the concrete ruin of the bombed-out surface of the factory world barely visible behind it—"until we can find access to the train line above, probably a ladder up the trestle supports. Then we *climb* that ladder—in full view of all the enemies around us once we breach the top of the gas—and we pray we don't get shot while we're doing it. *Then* we launch an assault on this train car, otherwise known as an enemy sniper position—"

"Quit whining, I already *said* they'll be facing the wrong way—"

"And *then* we get the train car running—if we're not dead by that point, that is—and barrel *past* the enemy lines, theoretically heading toward wherever the hell all these assholes are coming from, so that Schaz can pick us up, transferring from a moving train to a moving spacecraft. Before we run out of train track—and bridge—and come to a much more sudden stop at the bottom of a concrete ravine. That about the long and short of it?"

Sho looked from me, back to Jane. "She makes it sound a lot harder than the thing you said," he told her solemnly.

"She has a bad habit of doing that," Jane replied, glaring at me. "We've got this, Sho. This is what we do."

"Is it?" he asked me.

I nodded, trying to force a confidence into my voice that I *really* didn't feel. We were probably about to get shot at *a lot*. "It is," I told him. "This plan is *kind* of crazy, yeah, but on a scale from one to ten, as compared with some of the other plans we've executed, and survived? It's, like, a four."

"Four is still . . . higher than one. Or two. Or three. I think I would prefer *any* of those numbers to a four."

"So would I, Sho," Jane told him, "but you play the hand you're dealt."

"If this is a four, what would be a *ten*?"

"Once we get clear of all this, remind me to tell you the story of when we stormed a dreadnaught," I told him. "That was, like, at *least* an eight."

"Nine point three," Jane grunted, standing and shifting Sho's weight on her back.

"You only think that because you got shot a little."

"You got *shot?*" Sho asked her.

"All you've seen today, Sho, and you think it's *surprising* she's been shot?"

"Not for the first time, kid," Jane told him, ignoring me.

"They had to give her a new liver," I told him. "She has, like, a machine liver now. And kidneys too."

"Can we stop talking about insane escapades we've pulled in the past, and concentrate on the insane escapade we've got to pull *right now?*" Jane asked.

I shrugged, standing as well, pulling Bitey up into ready position. "It's your plan," I told her.

"Yes, it is. And, as usual, I would *prefer* if we could just execute it, and not stand around a goddamned *war zone* talking it to death."

"Just point the way, partner."

"Down into those trenches." She nodded toward a shadow in the mists I could barely see; I hadn't really noticed them before, but now that she'd named them, I could tell that's what they were—high concrete walls, maybe canals for wastewater, way back when, now repurposed as cover from the firing positions in the factory somewhere behind us. "They should take us most of the way to the access ladder; that way we only have to cross a little open ground to get to it, as opposed to a lot."

"Okay. And how many heat signatures did you read from Schaz's scans down in those trenches?"

"More than a couple. And the concrete could be hiding a whole lot more."

I took a deep breath through my mask; even filtered through my teke field, the oxygen had a bitter tang to it, almost metallic, like rust. Or blood. "Okay, Sho, I might have been wrong. This might be a five instead."

"Esa, just—"

"I know; I'm going."

"We'll be right behind you."

"Good luck!" Sho called out softly. I almost grinned at that. I'd need it. We all would.

CHAPTER 8

I wouldn't have thought it was possible, but the gas was even *thicker* in the trenches than it had been in the subway tunnels, and it was an absolute *soup* compared to the thinned-out variety I'd been dealing with once we'd reached the surface. Whatever this shit was, it was heavier than the surrounding atmosphere, which meant the enemy sect was constantly pumping it out, probably from the bridge somewhere above us—the very bridge we were about to assault.

That was a problem for later. Now, there was just the trench.

We could hear the sounds of fighting somewhere behind us, and *above*, as well, the enemy using the gas attack to launch an assault on the factory walls as a diversion, keeping the sect inside from realizing that the true threat was about to come from below. It all seemed very distant, in the mists—the yellow-green fog and the high trench walls isolating us, making it seem as though we were on an entirely different planet from the world Jane and I had landed on this morning.

I stepped over rubble and debris and the detritus of war: broken guns and mortar craters and torn-apart armor plating. My feet swept through a carpet of loose shell casings like gravel, every step making telltale clinking noises that seemed to echo far into the mist. Every few minutes—not quite *regular*, but close—there was a heavy thumping sound, like a heartbeat, something more felt than heard. I wasn't sure exactly what it was, only that it likely wasn't anything good.

There were very few corpses, from either side. Bullet holes and bloodstains marred the concrete—bloodstains in several different colors, mostly red and teal—but very few actual dead. A part of me shivered away from the implications of that; I doubted, however intense the fighting got, that they were carting the fallen away for proper funeral rites. The more likely implication was that the constant war that raged across this world had given their sect at least a *partial* solution to the chronic food shortages common on a nonagricultural world like this one.

After all, it wasn't exactly "cannibalism" if the enemy's fallen dead were mostly comprised of a different species. Still, elsewhere in the galaxy, fucking *eating* another sentient being was frowned upon, to put it lightly.

"Three, forward. Manning a big gun," Jane whispered through the bug in my ear. I almost jumped out of my skin at her voice—as I moved along the trenches, through the fog of death, it was easy to forget that I wasn't entirely alone, a feeling that wasn't exactly relieved by the fact that, even carrying Sho on her back, Jane was entirely fucking soundless, carpet of debris underfoot or no. A reminder that even after years of training, I still had a long way to go to catch up to her.

I raised Bitey up a little higher, slipping my finger inside the trigger guard. Inched closer to the booming reports echoing down the trench. That was what I had been hearing, what sounded like a heartbeat—the reports of the artillery, a big ground-based gun smashing away at the distant factory walls. We were close enough now that the sound was accompanied by a brief flash of light in the fog, like watching a thunderstorm from a distance and seeing lightning bloom inside the bruised veil of the storm clouds. I came to a curve in the trench; the gun should be just on the other side.

I waited for the next report, when the enemy would be at their busiest, reloading, rearming, preparing their beast of a weapon to fling another round at the thick walls somewhere high above us.

It came, the flash almost blinding, the sound deafening. I moved.

I took all three of the gunners down with quick bursts from Bitey, the shots lost in the fog of war and the general distant chaos in the gas cloud. Reached out with a mild application of my teke and broke the control mechanism for the gun, too. That wouldn't do much good in the long run—and like Jane was constantly reminding me, we weren't *actually* here to try and win this war; getting sucked into a sect conflict wouldn't help us, or Sho, at all—but it made me feel better, just like smashing the gas pumps outside of the breach tunnel had.

In the silence left behind after the big gun was broken, I could hear another sound, a kind of rhythmic chanting, a repeated phrase, over and over again. Many voices, speaking in unison. Jane came around the corner; I frowned at her, tapping one ear with my free hand and then indicating the general direction of the noise. There were three paths out of the gun nest— the way we'd come, a path opposite that one, further along the trench line to the east, and a path leading north, deeper into enemy territory.

The northward path was where the sound came from; I hoped dearly that wasn't the direction we needed to go. Several different experiences with Jane over the last few years had taught me a valuable lesson: chanting is *bad*. Anybody worked up enough to chant in unison is usually planning something horrible.

Jane listened as well for a moment, then raised Schaz again. "Schaz, Jane here," she said softly. "Can you scan radio frequencies, patch into the communications of the sect that's under siege?"

"I can, and already have," Schaz replied, a little petulantly. "Want me to tell you what they're talking about? They're mostly reacting to chaos in the tunnels below their little fort, trying to get civilians out—"

"I want you to wait a few moments, then send a message to them," Jane cut her off. "Do whatever you have to to convince them it's legitimate; impersonate one of their scouts or something. You're reading our position?"

"I am. You're close to the bridge access."

"Good. There should be some sort of structure nearby, a warehouse or a bunker or something. Can you make it out, through the gas?"

"I think I've got it—I can't tell what it is, but I'm reading the location, southeast of you. A container of some kind, maybe a water tank. I can't get heat signatures, though: too much concrete."

"Don't worry about it; we already know how many enemies are inside. Fucking *all* of them. That's their staging ground for the assault down through the tunnels." Oh. Oh, *fuck*. I hadn't put that together. We were currently standing in between the massed might of the enemy sect and their path down into the factory stronghold. The chanting was their commanders, getting them worked up before they started their attack. Fucking *hell*, this was not a good place to be.

"Once we're clear," Jane was still talking to Schaz, "relay that position to the sect inside the city. Have them pound the fuck out of it with their big guns." I grinned at that; probably a savage reaction, but I didn't care.

We weren't supposed to choose sides—the Justified, I mean. It didn't do any good, in the long run. If we'd come at the front lines from the other direction—if Sho had been born into the northern sect, as opposed to the southern one—we would have likely wound up on the other side of this conflict, fighting to break *into* the city, rather than killing off those assaulting it. It was just a matter of luck we'd wound up on the Wulf side of the fighting rather than the Tyll.

All the same, the Tyll sect had used poison gas to kill indiscriminately, and they were about to storm the subway tunnels to launch a cowardly attack on civilians, civilians including Sho's mother, if she was still alive. We'd seen signs that they *ate* the dead, and that they were somehow fighting off the pulse, but only so they could better wage their war. Plus, they'd shot at us, or at least tried to. So fuck them; they could eat hot artillery shells. I'd sleep just fine that night, knowing we'd fucked up their plans to win their stupid little crusade.

"Tell me we don't have to go *through* them," I whispered to Jane. She shook her head, pointed down the eastern trench running along the front instead. I nodded, exhaling with relief, then reloaded Bitey, stepping over the bodies of the dead gunnery crew to take us down the correct route. I wanted as far from the massed assault battalion as we could get, as quickly as possible.

After just a few minutes, something shifted: it might have been my imagination, but I *thought* I could hear new sounds above us—not just the echo of distant gunfire, but a change in the low moan of the constant wind. Maybe even the creak of metal. We were underneath the bridge now, closing on our goal. Sure enough, another few steps forward into the trench, and the trestle supports loomed out of the fog, a wall of metal lattices rising up and up and up, seeming to climb forever up into the sickly toxic atmosphere like a cliff face of woven steel.

"Decision time," Jane said as she came up behind me and saw the trestles as well. "We can keep moving forward—there's an access ladder on one of the support pillars—or we can free climb the trestles themselves."

"One of those things will be easier to do than the other. Especially with you carrying Sho."

"True. But on the other hand, *one* of those things might have snipers in the city watching for enemy movement and an easy kill, snipers who won't be able to tell us from Tyll. We're going to be very exposed either way, but it's significantly less likely those snipers are scanning the trestles themselves for movement."

"Oh. Fuck."

"Hadn't thought of that, had you?"

"Congratulations, Jane, you're very clever in figuring out awful ways for us to get shot. So we free climb, then?"

"I think that would be best. Unless you *want* to take a high-powered rifle round to the back of your intention shield; see if you can hold on to the ladder while that's happening. You could make it into a game. A game called 'Will Esa fall to her death or not?' And also, 'Can her shield recharge before the sniper reloads?' I'd give that one about even odds."

"You're kind of awful sometimes, you know that?"

"So I've been told. Mostly by you. Come on: up and over. I'd like to get climbing—and get clear of where Schaz is going to direct that Wulf artillery barrage—as soon as possible."

CHAPTER 9

I was too short to be a very good climber.

This was just a statement of fact. I was short, even for a human, and humans were short compared to most of the other species—we weren't out and out *small*, like Reint or Reetha, but compared to Mahren or Wulf, we were on the shorter side. And of course, it wasn't like the train trestles had been designed to be climbed *at all*—that's what the ladder access, the access we were currently ignoring, was for—but even if they had been, they would have been designed to be a Wulf arm-span apart, and that was a solid foot longer than my own reach.

All of which was to say Jane was climbing faster than me, and she had Sho on her back. That just wasn't fair. I gritted my teeth behind my teke mask and tried to put just a little more speed into my ascent. I'd long ago given up on actually *competing* with Jane on this sort of thing—not only was she close to purpose-built for athleticism, just *genetically*, she'd spent well over a hundred and fifty years honing her body for this kind of work. Still, I'd be damned if she was going to power through a handicap like "one hundred pounds of furry Wulf adolescent hanging off her back" and *still* hand me my ass.

I climbed faster. The fog was swirling above; we were approaching the top of the gas cloud now. Thank whatever deity. I was thoroughly sick of the world being nothing but yellow-green mist, not to mention holding the tele-kinetic mask in place across my face. As I passed through the last of it and the sky finally opened up above us—the sun still high, nearly directly over-head, the pale gold light of the day making the stretch of the trestle upward seem dreamlike, unreal—I couldn't help it; I looked down.

It didn't *seem* like we were too high up, mainly because of the swirling mist of death that obscured how far we'd already come. The fog just spread and spread, stretching out in either direction, all along the walls of the looming factory complex to our left-hand side. Tiny blooms of light were barely visible in the yellow-green clouds below, gunfire or artillery shells landing.

Even obscured as it was, the front was immense, an insane stretch of violence and wasteland—it was hard to wrap my mind around the concept that this was just *one* battlefield in *one* war between just two of the sects fighting and dying for control of this *one* planet. So much blood being shed, so much pain, and all of it for . . . nothing. Nothing that mattered to anyone, beyond this one lonely sphere in a barely charted corner of our galaxy.

I turned away from the long panorama of the fighting, kept climbing. The bridge rose out of the mists like towers from a sea of fog, stretching on toward the horizon in one direction, shattered and broken in the other, well short of the city walls. Above us, warplanes ducked and dove, making strafing runs against the factory's defenses. We could hear the wailing of the air-raid sirens from within the city, the same sirens we'd heard on our approach from the south. The steel of the trestle shook under my grip as an artillery barrage landed somewhere nearby. I held still for a moment, waited for the shaking to subside, then kept moving up, Jane and Sho just a little ways off to my right.

The lip of the bridge above was approaching quickly now, and we hadn't been shot at yet. Hopefully a good sign. The theoretical snipers in the train car back toward the break in the bridge couldn't see us from their positions— Jane had been right about that—and anyway, they didn't have any particular *reason* to look: we were climbing up from well behind their own front lines. We'd emerged from the subway tunnels already closer to the enemy front than the territory of the sect controlling the factory, and we'd only headed deeper into Tyll-controlled territory from there.

Of course, because we were *almost* there, the end of our climb in sight, that was when the Wulf acted on Scheherazade's warning, and at least a dozen of their big guns fired a massive barrage on the enemy position she'd marked below, *directly* beside the trestle we were ascending.

The factory worlds had been built to last; this bridge had stood through two centuries of war, only breaking away from the factory walls under concentrated effort from the Wulf defenders of the city. Still, there was only so much abuse a structure could take: it was just metal and alloy, after all.

Several of the rivets on the trestles popped free, a terrifying "spanging" sound like bullets being fired. Jane was slightly ahead of me now, and I *saw* the rebar in her hand just pull clean off the structure, still tight in her grip. She had good reflexes, she wouldn't still be alive otherwise: she leapt for the next trestle up even as she started to fall, launching herself upward, but she wasn't going to make it.

I freed my own hand—at least the steel in *my* grip was holding steady—and reached out with my teke, feeling my mask drain away as I did so; hopefully we were high enough that I didn't need it anymore. I ripped the piece of rebar Jane was reaching for free from one side of the trestle, bending it outward, within her reach; she grabbed tight, then scrambled up from there, onto more solid parts of the structure.

For a moment, she simply held stock still, letting her adrenaline rush subside; then, "Thanks, partner," she said over the comms. I could hear her breath coming fast and heavy behind the words.

"No problem," I said, continuing my own ascent. I felt a little bit better about being slower than she was now—if I *hadn't* been a little behind her, I wouldn't have been able to see what was happening. She'd begun climbing again as well; we were almost even on the span. "Ready to storm the train car?" I asked Jane, waving at Sho on her back; he gave me a wan little wave in return, then very *quickly* returned his grip to her shoulder. "Because that's your plan, remember? To storm their sniper positions."

"Most of their soldiers are below us, remember?" she reminded me. "Preparing to storm the tunnels? And also now hopefully buried or torn to pieces by artillery shells. So they likely won't have guards watching their backs— why would they? This'll be easy."

We came over the edge of the bridge, hauling ourselves onto the relatively level concrete surface; looking toward the broken end of the span, I could see the train car—and the occasional flash of rifle fire from inside, as the snipers tracked targets on the city walls.

If we wanted to get that train car moving, step one was getting the enemy snipers *out*.

CHAPTER 10

I hate to admit it, but Jane knows her tactics. The work we did clearing out the snipers' nest wasn't pretty, but it was quick, and it was quiet; most of them never even heard me coming. The one who did got his neck snapped for his troubles—now that I wasn't having to hold the telekinetic gas mask in place on my face, I was back to full combat efficiency, which meant that at close range I was damn near unstoppable. If I did say so myself.

Which I did.

We piled the bodies on the track beside the car—or at least I did; Jane was still carrying Sho, having covered me with her rifle from a prone position down the track while I did the dirty work of clearing out the train—and then it was time for Sho to do *his* thing.

The interior of the car was pretty gloomy, given that the enemy had welded over the windows with steel except for firing slits here or there: it was lit only by a handful of bare bulbs powered by a gasoline generator I could hear chugging along somewhere toward the back, and most of the seats had been torn out, replaced with sandbags and ammunition stores for the snipers.

As Jane and Sho went to work out front, messing around with the battery housing, I moved to the back door of the car and began tossing the ammunition stores outside one by one; the last thing we needed, if we were going to use this rail car to barrel through the enemy positions, was to have it be full of material that would *explode* when we were inevitably shot at. That would end our train ride to freedom real quick.

The gasoline fumes were almost overpowering in the enclosed space; I wondered how people had lived with that smell, when this was their only option for power. I ignored it as best I could and kept working—I had about half of the munitions tossed out the door when there was a sharp "crack," and then a recognizable hum filled the train car, the fluorescent lights hidden by the welded steel flickering to life.

Sho had managed to power up the fusion battery inside the car's engine. We had power.

Sho and Jane joined me momentarily, Jane unbuckling Sho and setting him carefully down on one of the remaining seats. I grinned at him, and did what she hadn't thought to yet—took the gas mask off his muzzle so he could breathe a little more clearly. Jane, meanwhile, scooted underneath the train conductor's control panel, going to work on the wiring, pulling spare bits and bobs from one of the pouches at her belt as she did. Fusion power or not, this machine *was* a hundred years old, at least—getting it running might not take a miracle, but it would require some elbow grease.

"Does she know what she's doing?" Sho whispered to me. "Can we actually get this thing moving again?"

"She knows what she's doing better than *I* do," I replied to him with a grin, going for "incongruously cheery" despite the fact we were in a war zone and still in . . . quite a bit of danger. Sho had said goodbye to his mother just an hour ago, was leaving behind the only world he'd ever known. I could manage just a little bit of upbeat, even if it wasn't usually in my wheelhouse. "I was raised on a world a great deal like yours," I told him, just trying to keep him occupied. "As far as levels of technology go, electrical engineering is . . . not my strong suit, to put it mildly. Plus, Jane's a hundred and ninety years old—she has experience at just about *everything*."

"Not a hundred and ninety, Esa!" Jane called out, her voice muffled on account of the fact that her head was stuck somewhere inside the access panel. Also she may have had something between her teeth.

"For a hundred-and-eighty-nine-year-old, she's also very touchy about her age," I replied to Sho, giving him a conspiratorial grin. That actually earned a slight smile, albeit with shock still chasing the edges—a smile that ended with a cough, the gas fumes in the train car getting to him. I stood, and cut off the power to the gasoline generator, then carefully lifted it out the door with my teke, the wires linking it to the light bulbs growing taut, then snapping; once I'd flung it over the side of the bridge, that was it, that was the majority of the combustible material removed from the train car. The smell improved almost immediately.

We were as ready as we were going to be.

Jane slid out from underneath the access panel, a handful of loose wires held in her mouth until she spat them out on the floor. "Not a hundred and eighty-nine, either," she said.

"Are we good?" I asked her.

"We'll soon find out," she answered, reaching up and pressing the engine primer.

The train hummed to life. It actually jerked forward a bit, like an animal roused from a torporous state, until its brakes kicked in and it settled back on the rails. "We're good," I told Sho. "Just a short train ride and a pickup, and then you'll be up there." I lifted my eyes skyward, indicating . . . well, the roof of the rail car, mostly, but also the sky and stars above.

"And I can leave this world behind for good." Sho barely breathed the words, like if he said them too loud they'd crack and fall apart in his mouth.

"You can leave this world behind for good, and you never, ever have to come back," I agreed.

"Everybody, hold on to something," Jane said from the conductor's cabin. "Based on Schaz's scans, the tracks ahead are *mostly* clear, but that doesn't mean this won't be a bumpy ride—plenty of rubble and detritus that we're just going to have to roll right over."

"And if we hit something you missed on your scans, something we *can't* roll over?" I asked.

"Then the train flips, probably goes right off the side of the bridge, and we all die," Jane shrugged. "If I were you, I'd be more worried about the enemy soldiers we're about to be passing at speed. It won't take them long to realize that this car *shouldn't* be running, and that they should probably be shooting at whoever's inside. Here we go." She eased the throttle forward; the train jerked into motion again, and the bridge—barely visible out the armored windows—started to slide by.

I peered through the sniper slats, watching the bridge rails pass us by outside. "We're really starting to move," I told Sho, squeezing his hand. "Don't listen to Jane about the soldiers outside. They can't see inside, which means they won't know where we are enough to target us. We'll be fine."

"Are you sure?" he asked.

"Sure I'm sure," I lied. I hadn't been Justified for all that long, but I *had* grown up in an orphanage, and I'd done my time as the oldest kid there, the most capable, the one the younger kids turned to when things inside—or in the settlement beyond—got scary. I knew when to lie, and when to tell the truth. This was definitely "lie" territory; if an enemy sniper did get us, we wouldn't feel a thing anyway.

"You said—you said I never had to come back." He was looking out the broken window, and the wind was picking up—I had to strain to hear the words, and not just because of the passage of the train. He was whispering, like he couldn't quite believe what he was saying; at least he wasn't thinking about getting shot. "Would I—once I've paid off my debt to you, would I be able to, though, if I wanted to? For my mother? I mean, if she's . . . if she's . . ."

I frowned at him. "Sho, you're not an indentured servant, you're not . . . some kind of a slave," I said, steering him away from thoughts of his mom— he could mourn later, and *would*, but we couldn't afford to have him trapped in his grief right now. "There's no debt to pay. We're going to take you to Sanctum, they're going to explain some things to you—and hopefully re-pair the damage to your spine, get you walking again—and then you'll be free to do as you wish." More or less. If he *did* choose not to stick around with the Justified, it's not like we were going to hand him a free ship or any-thing: we already didn't have enough to go around, and we weren't *that* altruistic. Somebody would give him a lift out to a populated station some-where, making sure he didn't know the route back to Sanctum, and then he'd be on his own. We didn't exactly have unlimited resources, after all. Though compared to what *he* was used to, it might seem like we did.

"That almost sounds too good to be true." He said the words with a smile, but there was real cynicism behind them; the perils of growing up in a war zone, I suppose.

"Don't worry, Sho—you're going to love it out there. I know I do."

"At this . . . Sanctum?"

"At Sanctum, yeah, but also, just . . ." I waved upward. "Out *there*. A mil-lion, million different worlds, Sho, and all of them with something wonderful or strange, just waiting for us to see."

Meanwhile, Jane had lifted her hand to her ear, triggering a different chan-nel on her comm. "Scheherazade?" she hailed our ship. "We're in motion. Are you on approach?"

"Just starting reentry now, boss," Schaz confirmed. "If I'm going to keep my stealth systems engaged, I'll need to find a glide path high in the upper atmosphere to . . . wait. *Wait.*"

"We're not really capable of 'waiting' at the moment, Schaz," Jane replied. "An object in motion and all that. What's going on?"

"I'm reading—this shouldn't be possible, I don't even know . . . Jane, I'm reading a high concentration of radiological activity, in the heart of the factory city you're leaving behind. Why . . . what could possibly be throwing off *that* much radiation, in the center of a populated—"

"*Everybody down, now!*" Jane screamed the words, dropping to the floor herself. "*Esa, shield! Don't look behind us!*"

I lunged at Sho, pulling him to the floor; he made a startled noise, but didn't resist much—couldn't, not with his legs the way they were. I didn't know what the hell was happening either, but reacting when Jane shouted at me had saved my life in the past. We'd fight like hellcats when we were trapped on board Schaz and both bored, but out in the field, when Jane told me to jump, I jumped. Or dropped, in this particular case.

Jane had pulled herself closer to us, close enough that I could wrap all three of us in a telekinetic shield—she tucked herself over Sho and me both, and I just kept pouring on layers, more and more and more, to defend us against whatever the hell was happening. There had been a level of fear—of outright *panic*—that I didn't often hear in Jane's voice. My ear was pressed against the floor of the train, and I could hear the rumble of the wheels on the tracks below. Just beneath *that* was the sound of my own hammering heartbeat, and Jane's as well, and Sho's, so close I could *feel* their racing pulses through my clothing, through my skin.

Then the steel floor beneath me—all I could see, from my position face-down on the floor of the train—went away; all I could see was *brightness*, an amazing incandescent flash. There was no sound, just *light*. No wonder Jane hadn't want me looking at whatever was happening behind us: I would have been blinded for sure.

What little glass remained in the windows around us all shattered at once as a massive wave of force tried to dislodge the train from its tracks, but amazingly, it just kept *going*, as if, after a hundred years of dormancy, a little thing like whatever the *fuck* was happening back in the factory wasn't going to stop it—it wanted to stretch its mechanical legs, so to speak, and run.

Then sound kicked back in—or caught up—and there was a roar, a howl, like something *chasing* us, not something alive, but something massive, like a wave or a rockslide or a hurricane. Then a terrible groan of shrieking metal— Sho's fingers tightened in mine, but we both just kept staring at the floorboards—and we could *feel* hot wind on our backs, wind we couldn't feel before. Something was ripping at my shield, like a great creature *clawing* at it; I just poured on more and more defenses, adding shielding faster than it could be torn away, until that tearing sensation was gone, and there was only the wind. The wind, and a weirdly *hollow* sensation, almost like a void.

"Mother of gods," Jane whispered. I looked at her; she was staring behind us. I did the same.

The back end of the train had been entirely ripped away. I wasn't sure how the damned thing was still running, but it was. We were still in motion, pulling away from a truly terrible sight: the factory complex, the entire city behind us, was just *gone*, replaced by a rising cloud of fire, blooming out and up from where the city had been, a column of utter destruction topped by something almost like a storm front, the entire stretch of golden sky behind us aflame.

A nuclear blast. Someone had set off a *nuke* in the heart of the Wulf city.

CHAPTER 11

This made no sense. It made no *sense*. The whole reason the sects had been fighting was over control of the factory complex; destroying it gained the Tyll sect nothing, made the entire goddamned *war* pointless. Why would they . . . why would they . . . *how* could they have done it?

Sho was looking at the blast now too. His breath was hitching in his chest, almost hyperventilating, and then he was *howling*, a sound of terrible pain and denial and utmost grief, and he was scrambling along the floorboards as well he could with only his arms until I reached out and grabbed him and held him close, let him howl and scream even as I turned his head away from the sight of the rising bloom of atomic fire that had consumed the sky, turning day into something closer to twilight.

The odds against his mother surviving the gas attack in the tunnels had been slim at best, but he'd been clinging to them all the same. Now, there was no hope, no odds, no chance. She was gone, and he knew it. He wouldn't be able to come back and rescue her, not after we reached Sanctum, not ever. Not until he reached the next life, if there even was such a thing.

I was murmuring something to him as I stroked his fur, but not even *I* knew what I was saying. His howls finally choked off into sobs, and he pressed his face against my shoulder, weeping into my body armor. The train was still rocking beneath us, its interior lit by the horrible Armageddon glow of the blast receding in the distance. I turned to Jane—who had also climbed to her knees—but she was pointing past me, back toward the fiery corona staining the whole atmosphere orange.

"What the *fuck* is that?" she asked.

For a moment after I turned to follow her arm, I thought maybe she'd been hit on the head—even *I* knew what a fission explosion looked like, had seen them in vids—but she wasn't pointing *at* the nuclear fire; she was pointing at something just past it, instead.

Something *emerging* from it.

At first, I thought it was a ship—after everything else we'd seen today, the sudden appearance of a spacecraft, being flown through a ball of nuclear flame, wouldn't have been any more insane than anything *else*—but it wasn't a ship, it was too small for that. Only a speck, but growing larger, gaining. Gaining on us. The farther we pulled away from the mushroom cloud spreading over the industrial landscape, the clearer it became that *whatever* it was, it was chasing *us*, chasing our train. And as it got closer, the impossibility of the thing just kept growing.

It was a *person*. A person in a suit of armor—an exosuit, one equipped with wings and jet thrusters. The wingspan was massive, mechanical—the only species that had natural wings were the Klite, and their six wings were iridescent, more insectoid than bird-like, not like this at all. This was something else, something I couldn't even comprehend, and the image of the dark form, wings spread wide, silhouetted against the rising cloud of flame: it was almost angelic, apocalyptic, somehow terrifying in a way that went deeper than bone, deeper than reason, created an atavistic, whimpering fear at the very heart of me.

Whatever the fuck it *was*—whoever it was—I did *not* want them catching up with us.

Apparently Jane agreed; I was still staring at our pursuer, slack-jawed and holding Sho close, when she unshipped her rifle and opened fire. From a train car in motion toward a target in *flight*: not the easiest shot in the galaxy, to say the least. Still, she managed to land several hits—the approaching *thing* was close enough now that we could see the sparks where the bullets struck its armor—but her target didn't even slow down.

Was it Barious? A Barious's metallic exoskeleton could shrug off rifle rounds like that. I'd never heard of a Barious installing mechanical wings and a flight system before, but it wasn't *impossible*, I supposed. I wished the Preacher were here. She'd know.

"Esa," Jane commanded, reloading her weapon. "Slow it down. *Put* it down, for good."

I nodded, jerking my mind out of its stupor; whatever this was, it was *combat*, and shock in combat will only get you killed. Still holding Sho tight, I reached out with one hand—didn't bother trying to "grab" at the pursuing figure, just put up a *wall* between us and it. As fast as it was moving, suddenly hitting an immobile "object" like that should have spread it all across the landscape.

Instead it just smashed through, like my teke wall had been made of glass rather than the force of my own will, a force harder than steel. It didn't even bother to change course, didn't even shake as it pierced my barrier like it wasn't even there. The backlash of having my teke field destroyed before I had released it actually *snapped* my head backward, like I'd been slapped in the face. I spat blood on the train car floor—that happens sometimes, my system gets overwhelmed, I start bleeding from my sinuses—then went back to glaring at our pursuer, raising up Bitey with my free hand.

Jane had gotten there before me; instead of firing her rifle again, though, she'd managed to fish a grenade launcher out of the handful of weapons the snipers had left behind. She loaded it, raised it up, and fired, all in one fluid motion—if the shots she'd been trying to land from her rifle had been difficult, this one was damn near *impossible*, calculating the arcing trajectory of a much heavier round, fired with much less velocity, against the motion of both her target and the rail car, also taking into consideration the interference from the roaring winds created by both the train's passage and the blast still spreading from the nuclear inferno. Taking a shot like that should have been pure folly, but I'd learned a long time ago never to discount Jane's ability to hit her mark. When Jane wanted something dead, it got dead.

I could actually *see* the grenade as it flew across the blistered sky—it looked at first as if she'd fired it way too far to the right, but that was just her taking the winds into account, and the howling maelstrom yanked the round back on track, an elliptical passage carrying it directly at our pursuer. She was going to hit it dead-on.

Until the figure in the mechanical exosuit raised up one hand, and with a gesture almost *casual* in its disdain swept its clawed gauntlet in the direction of the grenade. The round exploded in midair, a tiny pinprick in the face of the apocalyptic blaze behind it.

I *knew* that sort of motion, the one the figure in flight had made with its hand; I'd *made* that sort of motion. It was exactly how I manipulated my teke. Except whatever the thing behind us had done, it *wasn't* telekinesis—I would have thrown the grenade off course, or knocked it down to the bridge below, not simply set the charge off early.

What in the blue *fuck* was going on?

The pursuing thing slashed its wings together, diving under the midair blast the grenade had left behind, then snapped them open again, still gaining, the blue glare of its thrusters a pinprick of light against the dust-darkened sky. "Schaz," Jane said warningly into her comm. "*Tell* me you didn't get caught in that blast."

"I'm on my way to you now," Scheherazade replied. "From the other direction, thankfully. You've only got a few minutes before you hit the break in the bridge—"

"We've only got a few *seconds* before whatever the *fuck* is chasing us catches up," Jane answered. "Get here, Schaz; *now*. Fuck stealth, come in *hot*. We'll be on the roof." While they were speaking I'd fired Bitey empty at the figure, with little success—unlike Jane, I don't think I even managed to hit it, and even if I had, my rounds were fired at less velocity than those from Jane's rifle: they wouldn't have done any more good than hers did. I just didn't know what else to *do*. "Esa—it's no good," Jane said. "Get Sho strapped in. I don't care *who* the fuck that is—they're not going to be able to stand up to Scheherazade. It's time to get *off* this weird-ass planet."

I could not have agreed more.

CHAPTER 12

The train bucked and rolled underneath our feet as I got Sho tied onto Jane's back again; we were powering through the debris on the tracks, and all it would take was one loose piece of rebar rolling into just the right position underneath the wheels to send us jolting free and smashing over the side of the bridge, but that was the least of our problems.

It took everything I had to concentrate on the buckles and the straps of Sho's harness, to *not* look behind me to see if the . . . *thing* was gaining. Of course it was gaining; it had been gaining before, when we were shooting at it, and nothing had changed. Still, my hands were slick and sweaty as I pulled the last of the knots tight, then squeezed Sho's shoulder once and rapped my knuckles on Jane's body armor, to let her know I was done.

I turned around then, and the thing was still gaining. Because . . . yeah.

I reloaded Bitey and started shooting at it. Again. That seemed the thing to do. Again, it didn't actually have any effect. The thing was close enough that I could actually make out details in the armor now—not just a chunky outer chassis, but one whose lines hugged tight to a body instead, completely unlike any of the other exosuits I'd seen. Those pieces of tech, favored by the security forces on Sanctum, were huge, heavy, unwieldy things, massive slabs of armor that could only be lifted into place with the help of pistons and hydraulics, all powered by a fusion battery. This was almost like a second musculature, tracing the outline of a form that didn't match any alien species I'd ever seen, but that had to be purely ornamental—if it was actually as tight as it looked, there was no way it could have shrugged off the rounds we'd already fired at it. Either that, or the being inside was impossibly thin.

Also, the flying. I'd never seen that before, either.

"Hold on tight, Sho!" Jane shouted over the roar of the wind around us. "Esa!" She pointed her gun at the access hatch in the roof of the train car, long since welded shut back when no one had ever thought this thing would ever get moving again. I gritted my teeth and put a burst of telekinesis through it; it ripped clear, the whole thing, the speed of our passage tearing it free of the car completely. That was a little more than I'd *meant* to do, but I was under a great deal of pressure, and modulating the fine motor control of my teke actually took more work than the big stuff.

With a grace that would have been impressive even if she *hadn't* been carrying an entire adolescent on her back, Jane hung first from the metal plates welded onto the windows, then reached up to grab the edges of the busted hatch, hauling herself up and through, onto the roof above. I did the same—using a burst of teke in lieu of the same level of natural athleticism—and then I was on *top* of a moving train car, and I had a single moment to wonder what the *fuck* I was doing: I had to anchor myself to the metal of the roof with my teke before the wind blew me right the hell off the speeding vehicle.

I was trying to stand on top of a moving train car while being chased by some sort of flying robotic *thing* as we fled the site of a nuclear explosion, heading toward a midair extraction with our approaching starship. My life was . . . strange sometimes, even to me.

Jane had managed to get to her knees, one hand holding tight to a low bar that ran along the side of the roof, the other gripping her pistol even tighter. Based on what we'd seen so far, the bullets from her revolver weren't going to do *shit* to the thing coming after us, but it wasn't like I was letting go of Bitey, either.

We both turned to face back toward the explosion, toward our pursuer. Just in time to see the thing tuck its wings behind it one last time, and dive for the train car.

It smashed into the back of the roof like a missile, hard enough and *heavy* enough to send a jolt through the entire frame, one I could feel even through the vibrations of the train's motion and the howling wind around us. Those clawed gauntlets lashed out and tore into the metal of the roof with a terrible screeching sound, the weight of the armor dragging the figure backward until it anchored, and the thing managed to get to its knees, finally giving us a good glimpse of it.

I hadn't liked the look of it before, at distance, and I sure as shit didn't like it now, up close. The strangely designed armor, more like metal flesh than a hydraulic exosuit; the razor-sharp alloy wings, folded so tightly to the creature's back that you likely couldn't even see them if you were facing it head on; twisting designs, etched or carved into the metal skin like gleaming tattoos, words or ideograms or mathematical expressions in a language I most definitely did not speak, or even recognize.

And the mask that covered whatever face was underneath it. Stylized fangs; a sharp slit of a mouth that wasn't actually an opening, just a raised relief on the metal; the same was true for the wide, glaring eyes, ovoid and strange. Most disturbing of all were the tracks of tears that flowed underneath those reliefs, except I couldn't tell if they were actually supposed to be tears at all, or if they were meant to be flames instead.

The overall effect of the features was purposefully species-neutral; it could have been meant to give the impression of a human face, or Tyll, or a dozen other alien races. There was even the slightest hint of a muzzle that might have made it Reint or Wulf instead. It was as if it were meant to conjure up a demon from *every* culture that it could have resembled.

With another shriek of tearing metal, it ripped one claw free, then sank it into the roof again, closer to us. Did the same with the other. Even in all that heavy armor—and skintight or not, strange alloy or not, it must have weighed a hundred pounds, not even including the wings and the jetpack— the thing was still advancing across the roof, inch by inch, pulling itself toward us. It had no expression, made no sign of its intentions—there was just the grinning snarl, and the scene of utter devastation behind it. It still hadn't *said* a word.

Jane shot it in the face.

The round glanced off the mask without even making a dent, though it did at least snap the thing's head back, making it pause in its relentless forward motion, for just a bit. That gave me enough time to pull my gaze away from the creature and look over the side of the train instead. If bullets weren't going to work, I needed something else to hit it with, something heavier. I frantically scanned the passing roadway beside the tracks, trying to find something that would work—no, no, no, no, no, no, *there*.

I reached out with my teke and an open hand, ripping the snapped and abandoned piece of rebar toward me even as we left it behind, making sure

the arc of its passage toward my grip led *through* the relentless armored figure crawling along the train roof.

The metal pierced through its back like a six-foot-long arrow, bursting
free of its chest until half of the jagged makeshift projectile was sticking out
the front of it. Take *that*, you fucking . . . you fucking . . . you whatever the
fuck you are, you.

There wasn't any blood—not on the piece of rebar, not oozing sluggishly
from around the wound, either. Whatever the hell this thing was, it didn't
bleed.

I hadn't even managed to try and figure out what the hell *that* meant before it raised up one of its gauntlets, wrapped it around the metal shaft driven
through its chest, and started *pulling*.

It was pulling the rebar through itself the way I might thread a needle
through a piece of cloth. It made no sound as it did it—no cries of pain, no
shrieks of rage. The blank eyes of that horrible mask just kept staring at
us, never turning away even as the metal was torn entirely clear of its body,
then thrown unceremoniously from the roof of the train.

There should have been mangled flesh left behind in the wake of the
shaft's passage through the creature's form. There should have been just a
ruin of internal organs and ruptured bone, visible through the large hole the
rebar had carved through its armor. Even if it had been Barious, there would
have been sparking wires and damaged components. There wasn't anything
like that at all. There was just light. A weird, terrifying cerulean glow, like
what was contained within wasn't a *person* at all, but just liquid luminescence
instead, luminescence that wasn't spilling or flowing out of the wound, that
just *glowed* in the center of the thing's broken chest.

I think I actually said "What the fuck," or at least mouthed the words,
but I couldn't hear myself over the wind. I'd seen some weird shit in the last
three years. This still took the cake. It took the cake, and the dish the cake
had come on, and the whole goddamned bakery. Maybe even the whole bakery's *block*.

And that was before the thing lifted up its hand—the same one it had
used to pull the metal shaft free from its body, the other still anchoring it to
the train car roof—and raised it, palm up, toward me. And the metal skin
retracted, and the palm within started to *glow* with that same light.

Whatever happened next, I doubted I was going to enjoy it much.

Thankfully, it didn't happen at all, because at that moment the cobalt glow from the creature's . . . *whatever* was suddenly matched by a piercing line of azure brightness from behind us, a laser that slashed through the back half of the train car, cutting free the section of roof that the creature was clinging to. The thing went sailing free, back down toward the bridge below— then the train was lit by floodlights, and a welcome voice came through the comm in my ear:

"What the hell was *that* thing, and why was he glowing at you?" Schaz asked. "Rude."

I turned—it took some effort to rip my eyes away from the section of track where the roof had smashed down; I doubted that little fall was going to end the whatever-it-was—and saw Scheherazade on approach, her forward lasers still glowing slightly as they cooled. She pulled into a smooth loop, matching the train car's direction and speed, her cargo ramp lowering so that it was *almost* touching the roof. Jane clambered on, Sho still clinging tightly to her back, then both of them reached out to help me do the same.

"Circle back around!" Jane commanded Schaz, one hand clinging to an anchor strap for stability, the other raised to the comm in her ear. "Whatever the hell that thing is, I want to make sure it's dead!"

"Your ship is *awesome!*" Sho cried over the wind.

"Yeah, she is!" I shouted back, grinning. I remembered the first time I'd laid eyes on Schaz too—it had been in similar straits.

The train vanished from beneath us as Schaz cut her forward momentum, then slowly began to arc around; she couldn't match the loop she'd made earlier with us still hanging out of the combination airlock and armory that was Schaz's ramp access. Or rather, she *could* have, but then we would all fall out, and she'd have to pick us up again, if we weren't all dead and splattered far, far below.

"Do you see it?" Jane shouted at me as Schaz's spotlights searched the bridge. I didn't see *it*, but I found the crumpled metal that was the piece of the train Scheherazade had cut free, and I pointed at it; Jane thumped on the last door of the armory lockers with her fist, and the whole thing sprung outward, releasing a massive mounted cannon, a .50 caliber machine gun built onto a swivel rack anchored inside its little hidey-hole.

I had *not* known that we had that.

Jane got herself behind the gun, pulling the bolt back and priming it to fire, the ammunition snaking up into the chamber from a belt line that led back inside Scheherazade. "Do you *see* it?" she asked again, swiveling the big gun around, looking for her target.

I shook my head, still scanning. "No, I—"

"There!" Sho pointed; he was half-twisted around on Jane's back so he could still look. Jane followed the line of his extended arm, as did I: the creature was standing on the bridge, its wings still folded, that single iridescent hole still bored through the center of its armor, where its heart would have been if it had been human. It didn't seem the worse for wear for having been thrown from a moving vehicle, then having half a train roof dropped on top of it.

Jane spun her giant gun on its swivel, aiming down at her target; I started building a teke slam in my fist. Schaz had slipped into hover mode, keeping us about twenty feet above the bridge, and I could actually *smell* the ionization as her rear turret began heating up as well.

Whoever this motherfucker was, he was about to have a real bad day. . . .

A crackling, high-pitched whine filled the comm bug in my ear, like a feedback loop, then a voice, low, mechanical, almost *grinding*, rising from the sonic depths of the interference. *"Her great reckoning will not be so easily diverted. The day* will *arrive—but not yet. Do not doubt your place in the fires."*

That shouldn't have happened. We were using an encrypted frequency.

From where it stood on the bridge, oblivious to the *very* large weapons directed at it, the mechanically angelic creature raised a gauntleted hand toward us, and pointed. Right at us. The implication was clear—it was the exosuited figure that had hacked our comms. Whoever our pursuer *was*, they'd just cracked Justified encryption like it was nothing.

We opened fire. The static still filled our comm channel, the noise almost a kind of laughter, even as the lasers and the giant fucking bullets and my own teke blasts tore through its armor like paper, revealing more of that awful cobalt glow beneath. It didn't matter where we hit it—the chest, the mask, the *wings*—that's all that was inside. Just that terrifying liquid light.

It didn't matter that the thing's armor was cracking apart, shattering and *melting* under the sustained fire; it didn't matter that at this point the thing was more blue *glow* than actual form. It still broke into our comms one last time, and said: *"Her existence is a scream."*

Then the bridge collapsed beneath it under the weight of the barrage and it was gone, falling into the buildings below, lost to the dust and smoke.

For a moment, I simply stood on the ramp, my breath heaving in my chest; I'd put absolutely everything I'd had into that barrage of telekinetic attacks, and I barely even had the strength to stand. So I didn't.

I dropped down to a boneless squat on the edge of the ramp, utterly exhausted. If I hadn't been holding on to one of the anchor straps with my free hand, I might have just kept sliding until I was right back on the bridge below. Not at all my intention.

"Sho," I told our cargo, "don't take this the wrong way, but: fuck your planet. I hate it."

"Try living here," Sho replied with something almost approaching equanimity.

"If everyone's so unhappy to *be* here, can we please *leave?*" Schaz asked. "A pulsed atmosphere like this doesn't get *more* comfortable the longer I'm in it, you know."

"Time to go," Jane agreed, though there was something in her voice—a kind of catch—that I didn't quite trust; it was the way she sounded when she wasn't *quite* lying, but when she had a more . . . distant relationship to the truth than usual. Either way, though, she'd already stowed her big fuck-off gun so she could reach down and give me a hand up, and whatever she was thinking, she was going to keep it to herself, so I reached for her outstretched hand, groaning as I took it; moving was bad. Then again, sitting on the ramp when Schaz closed it would be worse.

I pulled myself into the armory proper, and Schaz started closing her doors, giving us one last glimpse at the just-now-starting-to-dissipate mushroom cloud that was all that was left of Sho's factory city, one last glimpse of his terrible homeworld, where the tens of thousands who had died today would be just a drop in the ongoing flood that was the endless war raging across its surface.

I stood by my statement. Fuck this planet. I was ready to be *off* it.

Schaz kicked in her engines, and I got my wish.

ACT
TWO

CHAPTER 1

Once Schaz had sealed up the outer airlock door, I carefully unstrapped Sho from Jane's back and set him on the low bench that ran along one side of the airlock. He watched from there as Jane and I set about pulling off our gear piece by piece, stowing it inside the hidden armory compartments as we went.

"You two have . . . a great many guns," Sho said, sounding torn between awe and trepidation. "Are the wars just as bad elsewhere as they are on my home?"

"Not everywhere." Jane shook her head, freeing various knives from their sheaths and buckles and ties and attaching them to the magnet inside her locker. "But there are enough places where they *are* that we . . . like to be prepared."

"I've never seen *anyone* who fought the way you did."

"Well, she is a hundred and eighty-eight years old," I told Sho, using a damp cloth to rub at the camo on my face.

"You said something like that before, and I wasn't sure if you were joking or not. Do humans really live that long?"

"Yes, they *can*, but no, I'm not," Jane said sourly. "Ignore Esa. She likes to make a game out of trying to guess my age."

"Why won't you just *tell* her?"

"Because it's good for some people not to have all the answers; they're impressed enough with themselves as it is." *Ouch.* Point for Jane, I suppose.

I'd gotten as much of the face paint off as I was going to with the cloth; I tossed it in the laundry chute—Schaz had a complicated, automated laundry system built into her recyclers, another one of those awesome things about non-pulsed technology that never failed to impress someone who'd grown up doing their washing by hand—and made my way between Jane and Sho, to the inner airlock door, which was still sealed for some reason.

"Hey, Schaz?" I called. "You going to open up for us, or what?"

"In a bit," she replied evasively. "All your complicated gear is sealed away, right?"

She knew damn well it was; she had cameras in the airlock. Why wouldn't she open the door? "Yeah, it is. Come on, Schaz; I want a shower." I didn't *whine* the words, exactly, but I'll admit there might have been a quality to them that might be described as "wheedling." I'd had a hell of a day.

"Who's that?" Sho asked, looking around the airlock. "Is that the *ship?*"

"It is indeed!" Schaz replied brightly. She always liked meeting new people. "Hi, Sho! I'm Scheherazade; you can call me Schaz. I'm your friend! Your friend who's about to spray you with gunk. *Gunk!*"

Nozzles appeared in the walls and the ceilings, and then we were absolutely *drenched* in some sort of horrible-tasting foam, halfway between a liquid and a gel. I *knew* it was horrible tasting because plenty of it got in my mouth, and I was left spitting and gagging, gasping "What the *hell*, Schaz?"

"And why would you think shouting 'gunk' was a fair warning?" Sho moaned, scrubbing futilely at the foam, which, of course, only drove it deeper into his fur.

Jane—who, I couldn't help but notice, had stood stock still through this process, and also had made sure she was near the locker with the towels in it—began cleaning herself off, tossing two more towels to Sho and me. "Relax, kids," she said. "Schaz had to do it; it's procedure."

"*What* fucking procedure?" I could still taste the awful, deep in my mouth. "She's never sprayed us with gunk before! Not even after that . . . that fucking . . . the swamp world, the one with the . . . the . . ."

"We've never been in the fallout zone from a nuclear explosion before, either," Jane said wryly. Apparently done with her gunk shower, Schaz shifted the nozzles over to a mist of water instead, which at least made it easier to get the gunk off our skin. Watching Jane scrub at her hair and Sho go at his fur, I was actually super pleased—maybe for the first time—about my decision a few weeks ago to shave my head. "We just took a bath in extremely harmful radiation. This is decontamination protocol."

"Radiation?" Sho asked worriedly. "That sounds . . . bad."

"It's not good," Jane admitted, "but it's not likely to be fatal, not since we got the decontamination showers active so quickly. This shit"—she nodded at the foam being sucked down by the wash of water into hidden drains under the lockers—"is designed to suck up radiation like a sponge. Scheherazade will eject it out into space before we get out of system, and she'll adjust her lights inside to give us a constant counter-rad bath for the next few days."

"A warning beyond 'gunk' still would have been nice, Schaz," I growled in the general direction of the airlock.

"I'm sorry, dear," she replied meekly. "But the sooner I got it done, the sooner we can get all that nasty radiation *off* of . . . me, and you *know* how I feel about radiation." The nozzles quit with their spray—Sho looked around for a moment, his expression still suspicious, as if he were waiting to see what *other* strange substance Schaz would coat us with next, but when nothing was forthcoming he shook out his fur, still covered in slick patches of foam.

"You'd better have the shower first, buddy," I told him with a sigh. I turned back to the door. "You ready to open *now?*" I asked Schaz.

She slid open the inner airlock without comment.

Jane got Sho into the shower, with instructions to let Schaz know when he was done; that might not be for a while. Not only did he have a great deal of foam to scrub out of his fur, he'd grown up on a world where water was at least a semiprecious resource. It hadn't been quite as rare on my home-world, and I'd still spent, like, half a day in the shower once I realized we had an endless supply of hot water—that it was, in fact, the exact same water raining down over and over again, just drained, filtered, run past the drive core for heat, then spat back at my head.

While they were doing that, I rotated the kitchen into place, mainly to get at the cooling unit so I could dig out some fruit. I was *starving*.

"So," I asked Jane around a largish bite of Klitek marsh flower. "Are we gonna talk about all the *whatever the hell* back there?"

Jane nodded, taking a seat at the table and calling up the holodisplay, Kandriad, the last world accessed, spinning up again. I stuck my tongue out at the glowing map—man, *fuck* that place—but Jane was zooming in, going over Schaz's scans of the factory city. Or what was left of it.

"We're done, Jane," I said, suspicion coloring my tone. "The kid's in the shower. We can stop looking at Kandriad now."

"Thing is—we actually can't," she said, shaking her head, still staring at the map. "That thing that attacked us—you haven't thought it through yet, have you?"

"Thought *what* through?" I neglected to add that what with all the lasers and glowing people and nuclear *fire*, my critical thinking skills had taken something of a back seat to basic survival instinct. It appeared Jane's *hadn't*, even after all that, and I wanted to know what conclusions she'd reached.

"Go at the problem like Marus would," Jane said—still being Jane. No situation so dire she couldn't turn it into a lesson. "See how the puzzle pieces fit together."

I frowned; Marus was one of Jane's oldest friends, another Justified operative—one who'd served with our sect even longer than she had—and if Jane was invoking his name, she meant she wanted me to look at it dispassionately, like a riddle to solve. I took another bite of my flower before setting it on the table and trying my best to think like Marus.

I am cool. I am calm. I am collected. I secretly devour Reetha romance novels because deep down inside I am a great big softy. I am analytical. I break the data down into pieces. I was incredibly proud of Esa on the day she decided to train with a submachine gun, like I do, instead of a big, stupid rifle, like Jane.

"Okay," I said, through a thick wad of marsh flower. "As I see it, we've got three separate questions." Jane was still examining the map, but she didn't stop me—a tacit acknowledgment to continue, so I barreled on, setting the questions up chronologically in my head as I swallowed my bite of sweet pulp. "First: how or *why* was the pulse radiation ignoring some of the tools on the world down below?"

Jane nodded, absently reaching out and stealing my half-peeled flower and taking a bite. "That's the big one," she agreed, ignoring my glare. "The one that means we can't leave, I mean. It's not planetwide." She nodded at the holoprojected map. "In point of fact, it's *so* minimal Schaz's scans can't even pick up the drop in radiation levels; hence why we didn't know about it going in. But even still—even if it's just localized, it was enough to let the Tyll sect put planes in the air, power those drilling machines, and the *implications* of that are just . . ." She shook her head, an expression on her face I didn't often see: something close to wonder.

So I did what Marus would have done: I thought it through.

If there was some sort of "cure" for pulse radiation, even if it was small in scale—could only make complex machines work for an hour or two, at most, in a pulsed atmosphere—what would that *really* change? Communication, maybe—worlds that had been entirely cut off from the greater galactic community would suddenly be able to rejoin it, even if that just meant building a single signal tower in a single square mile that was cleared of pulse rads once a month; worlds that thought the sect wars were still raging, where sects had declared their allegiances to empires long since collapsed, could be shown the truth. Wars would be ended in an instant, almost.

Of course, new ones might begin as well. Predicting the future was a fool's game—if nothing else, the Justified had taught me that, even inadvertently. They'd set off the pulse with the best of intentions, trying to save their homeworld from a planet-destroying superweapon while at the same time avoiding the levels of mass destruction that came with deploying a superweapon of their own, except the pulse had cascaded in a way they never would have been able to predict, and changed the galaxy forever.

So that wasn't what had Jane so excited—her view had always been that war was inevitable. So instead, she was thinking about . . .

She was thinking about the pulse itself, about her role in setting it off. She blamed *herself* for what had happened after; she always had. And the worst of that guilt had always been what had happened to the Barious.

The pulse itself left them unharmed, but their factories—where new Barious were "born"—had gone silent.

A "cure" for pulse radiation—even an incredibly small-scale one, even for just an hour at a time—could it alter that? Reverse that damage, power up the long-silent factories again? Could new Barious be brought into the universe, for the first time in a hundred years?

The Barious were enduring a slow-motion extinction. Even if this only had a *fractional* chance to undo that—Jane was right. We had to learn more.

Goddammit.

CHAPTER 2

O kay—I get it." I leaned back in my chair, and swiped my marsh flower back from Jane. "This is . . . big."

She just nodded patiently—at the thievery and the embarrassingly long time it had taken me to realize what she must have seen the instant we'd first caught sight of those planes wheeling through the golden sky of Kandriad. "So our first question then becomes: what's the scope? What's the scale? How far does this . . . 'cure' . . . reach?"

I stretched across her—keeping my flower held back, away from her pinching fingers—and called up Javier's original scans of the planet from three years ago, reading over his initial findings. "According to Javi, Kandriad *should* have had early industrialization, steam power and coal furnaces, even early gas-powered generators—which we saw a few of—but nothing close to aircraft. He even noted it in his report: 'nothing moving in the atmosphere; the various sects are contained to the factory ruins, the fighting mostly taking place in the no-man's-lands between the various former industrial sites.' Which matches what we saw, *except* for the warplanes shooting at us. And the drilling tools the Tyll sect used to get down into the subway tunnels."

"And the bomb," Jane added dryly. "Nuclear fission should have been off-the-table impossible, *except* for the pulse cure, which leads us to question two: how and *why* did someone detonate a nuclear bomb on the surface below?" She fetched another marsh flower for herself, dropping the peel into the recycler and taking a largish bite of the fruit.

"Not to win the Tyll sect's war, that's for sure," I said. "They were streaming inside—through the tunnels—before the blast went off. Their soldiers died, just like the citizens of the Wulf sect."

Jane nodded. "Which means the question becomes: was it *because* of the pulse cure? Or because of us? Or because of—" She turned, looked at the door to the shower. Because of Sho.

We weren't going to answer that one, not until we had an answer to question three, so I went ahead and put it out there: "And how does all this relate to the armored . . . angry . . . flying . . . *glowing* fella there at the end? Did *he* set off the bomb? If he did, how did he survive the explosion? He came out of that fire like it was nothing, and he seemed to know right where we were, which would seem to indicate the blast wasn't *for* us; if he *was* tracking us somehow—with our comms, say, since he broke right into *those* like they were unshielded—then he would have known we weren't in its radius. Instead, it seems more likely that it was—"

"To cover his tracks." Jane nodded. "To cover up whatever he was *actually* doing on Kandriad. That makes sense. Which means he was there for a reason, and we're back to question two. Sho? The cure? Or us?"

"The Justified have plenty of enemies."

She nodded. "And there are plenty in the universe who would use gifted children for their own ends—which you know, firsthand." I shuddered; I still didn't like to think about what *might* have happened if the Pax had reached me first. "And—obviously—a way to cure the pulse, even in a limited capacity, would be worth . . ."

"Everything," I nodded. "Everything people had, and more."

She frowned at that. "Maybe we're going about this backward," she suggested.

"How so?"

"I think we made a wrong turn somewhere, is all. Your initial theory— which I agree with, by the way—assumes the blue fucker set off the blast, to cover his tracks, to cover up . . . whatever he was after."

"Well, if it wasn't the Tyll, and it wasn't us, it *sure* as hell wasn't the Wulf—"

She nodded, waving me off—she was already there on the reasoning. "But if that's the case," she continued, "*he* was the one who'd found a way around the pulse radiation. It had to have been him—otherwise why would he even *try* it? Why set up a bomb like that at all, unless you knew, somehow, against all logic and reasoning, that the pulse wouldn't stop it? There may not be anything special about Kandriad at all; maybe it was just *him*. If he knew how to set off a nuke on the surface of a pulsed world, maybe he was somehow sucking the rads *out* of the atmosphere, in small pockets, at least—"

"—which cleared the way for the sects down below to suddenly realize some of the dead tech they had lying around wasn't so dead anymore." I nodded, seeing where she was going. "That makes sense. The bomb scarring, the craters from the payloads dropped from the air that we saw coming in— they were new, mostly, the last few weeks, or else very old, from before the pulse. And the assault the Tyll sect was launching, down through the tunnels: that wouldn't have *worked* without the new tech, the drilling equipment and maybe even the pumps for the gas. If they could have done it a decade ago, they would have."

Jane sighed, leaning back in her chair and glaring into the middle distance. "Which means we may have just *killed* the only person who could have answered our questions," she growled. "Great."

I shook my head. "We're missing something," I said.

"We're missing a lot of things," Jane agreed, her tone unhappy. "The 'why,' for starters. He wants to kill us with the bomb—except he chases us out of the fire, so he knows the bomb didn't do it, so maybe not. He wants *Sho*, maybe, but again: he'd been there for weeks, at least—the air raids had been going on for at least that long, so why not make a play for the pup earlier? Based on what we saw, it's not like the Wulf could have stopped him."

That was a grim thought; the thing in the metal mask, wading through the sect soldiers like the spectre of death. Still, it didn't quite square with me. "Don't give him more credit than he deserves, though," I said thoughtfully— another one of Jane's own maxims, deployed back against her. "Even if he was after Sho—maybe he was just like *us*. He knew there was a gifted kid in that city, somewhere, but not how to get at him—it's not like a fucker in a suit of metal armor could just walk up and knock, like we did. And if he started wading through the halls, murdering everyone, the chances that Sho would have *run*, escaped his grasp, before he got to him: pretty high, especially if he didn't know *which* kid he was looking for."

"Fair point," Jane acknowledged. "But it still leaves us with the question: why would someone who *had* that sort of ability, to dissipate pulse radiation— why would they only *use* it to set off a nuclear bomb on a backwater world, to slightly improve the weaponry of a sect war they didn't care about winning?

Why *limit* your ambitions to hunting gifted children, or the Justified, if one of us really *is* who he was after?"

"There's got to be—there has to be a way to . . ." I let my words trail off, running a hand down my face and covering my mouth to stifle a yawn; this conversation hadn't made me any *less* tired. I sighed, still mumbling into my palm. "If we can just—"

"I hate to interrupt the tail-chasing you've got going on," Schaz broke in, "but you should know: there's a ship lifting off from the planet below."

"There's a *what* now?" Jane asked sharply.

"There is. A *ship*. Approaching orbit. From Kandriad."

All of a sudden, I wasn't tired anymore—a jolt of adrenaline coursed through me at Schaz's words, and for a moment, Jane just looked at me, and I looked back, the same impossible thought going through both our minds.

We both stood and rushed for the cockpit at the same time. This wasn't good.

CHAPTER 3

We crowded into the cockpit; Schaz already had the relevant camera feeds at full magnification, Kandriad plastered across the viewscreen. Yep. That was a ship, all right.

It didn't look like any ship *I'd* ever seen—it was twice the size of Scheherazade, who was already largish for her class, but nowhere near as big as, say, a frigate or a cruiser. Its design was rounded, all curves and smooth lines, no hard angles at all. That wasn't super strange in and of itself—not only had the various races all come to starcraft design independently, but plenty of those designs had then influenced and shifted each other during the Golden Age and the wars, meaning there were hundreds of thousands of possible permutations for "thing designed to haul people through the vacuum of space"—but the *look* of it was familiar, in a way I *really* didn't like.

It was covered in the same strange plating our pursuer on the planet below had been, the alloy flowing over the ship like skin over muscle, *moving* and shifting along the craft's chassis as it powered up through the atmosphere toward exit velocity. It almost looked like it was flying—actually flying, like a bird, despite its lack of wings. Like the ship had muscles underneath its armored skin, and they were flexing and stretching as they lifted the ship up through the gravity well.

"But . . . we killed that fucker," I protested; I was almost *offended* by the notion that he might have survived, despite the fact that Jane had just been bemoaning the fact that, in killing him, we might have killed our best chance for answers. "We killed him a *lot*."

"We didn't see a body," Jane growled, taking the flight stick for herself and swapping one of the windows on the viewscreen to a forward perspective, so she could pilot. "If we didn't see a body, we can't assume he was dead."

"We shot him with lasers! We shot him with lasers, and with very, *very* large bullets, and there were very many of them! I hit him with enough kinetic force to bring down a Mahren superpredator! He fell *through* a bridge! Gravity kills everything, Jane. *Everything.*"

"Apparently not." She wheeled the ship away from Kandriad, heading toward the nearest of the world's three moons, a monster a third of the size of Kandriad itself—or at least it had been before it had been cracked nearly in half during the sect wars, and one of the halves had been pulverized into a debris field ringing the intact portion of the satellite.

It was into that very debris field that Jane took us, engaging every single stealth protocol Schaz had as she did, then—once she had us into a stable position, just another part of the slowly circling orbit of the other debris—she powered down as much of the ship as she could.

She wanted to see what the bastard was going to do.

"If we have to go up against him . . ." I murmured, not liking the look of his ship. For one thing, "bigger" carried a great deal of weight in a dogfight—meant more shields, more weapons, more acceleration, though not necessarily more mobility. For another, it was still . . . weird, and we *didn't* know what it could do. Another one of Jane's aphorisms—never start a fight with an enemy who knew more about *you* than you knew about him, not if you could possibly avoid it. We didn't even know what the hell this guy *was*, let alone what his craft was capable of, and he—somehow—seemed to know all about *us*.

"We're silent running; we're instrument cloaked; we're just one more floating, metallic object in a sea of them," Jane said calmingly, though her body language belied that calm: she still had the stick gripped tightly, leaning forward toward the cockpit window, the throttle under her free hand. "He's not going to find us." It sounded more like a hope than a surety.

"He's looking." And he *was*—an oscillating beam of green light stabbed out of the underbelly of his ship, part of what was undoubtedly a whole suite of scanning systems. It swept over Kandriad's first moon—it played across the gray lunar surface like an aurora, then leapt to the second satellite, his ship barely shifting its position as he did.

Our turn.

The scanning laser swept across Schaz's position; once, twice, three times, each time filling the interior of the cockpit with a witchfire green glow. "We are being scanned," Schaz said, somewhat unnecessarily.

"We noticed," I told her; I hadn't realized my teeth were gritted together until that instant. "Did he find us? Or did the stealth tech hold?"

"We'll know soon enough," Jane replied, her gaze still locked on the enemy ship itself, ready to power Schaz up and leap from "hiding" to "fighting" at a moment's notice.

The green sweep of the laser cut off, and for a moment, the strange ship just hung in the atmosphere like a silent monolith—no running lights, no engine flare, it might as well have been a weird piece of forerunner tech, just floating through the void.

Then a flare of . . . *something*, from behind the ship, something *not* the same as the blue blaze of a sublight engine, and it was moving. Moving away from us, at speed, until Jane had to dial up the vidscreen display just to track the thing. A shimmering wave of light spilled from the craft's engines, and suddenly we could see the stars *through* the hull of his ship—he'd made the jump to hyperspace, and we were just seeing the afterimage.

I let out a breath I hadn't known I'd been holding, reaching up to thump the ceiling of the cockpit affectionately. "Let's hear it for MelWill's stealth tech," I said, my voice slightly uneven.

"Schaz?" Jane said, her command voice in full effect. "Get me a read on his escape vector."

"Oh, no," I said. "No, no, no. Jane, that sounds like you're thinking of chasing him. In the litany of bad ideas—you do remember we just dropped half a *bridge* on that guy, right? And the nuclear *bomb* he apparently set off?"

"We *just* talked about how important this could be, Esa," Jane said, still flipping switches above her head, readying Schaz to make the jump to hyperspace, to go after the bomb-dropping asshole.

"We *did*, but I'm asking: what are you planning to do when we *find* him? You want to—what, to capture him, interrogate him?" I didn't like that word, or what it implied, so I rushed right past it. "His ship is bigger than ours—and we *can't* take him on the ground, either, we proved that on Kandriad. Wanting answers for what he did down there is all well and good, but if we don't have a plan to . . . to *subdue* him somehow, we don't have a way to *get* those answers, even if we *can* catch up with him again!"

"It's too big a gain just to let our only lead run off, Esa. Sometimes you have to take risks. Schaz?"

"His vector is locked," she said. "Shall we follow?"

"No!" I stood up and pointed behind me, back toward the living quarters. "We already have our mission, Jane—he's in the shower, terrified and grief-stricken and *completely* unprepared for what the wider universe is actually like. We can't drag him through all of . . . of . . ."

"Didn't work out so badly when it happened to you, did it?" she asked me, a slight grin on her face. I couldn't believe it—she was *grinning* now.

There were a great many things Jane and I shared—things she'd passed on to me as my combat instructor, things she'd passed on to me as my partner, things she'd passed on as a Justified operative. But that thing—the thing that made her *like* danger, that made her *like* going up against something she couldn't possibly beat, that made her *like* pain, just a little bit: that wasn't one of them.

"Go after him." I turned; Sho was done with his shower, and had managed to *pull* himself up to the cockpit using just his arms—was, in point of fact, pulling himself up the handrails so that he could get closer to us. An impressive level of dedication that only served to underline the steel in his words.

"Sho," I said quietly. "We don't understand—"

"I heard you talking." He was panting, a little, from his exertions, but his voice was still firm. "You think the person in that . . . in the other ship . . . is the person in the suit of armor, the one who attacked us on the train. You think *he's* responsible for what happened on my home, and you think you can . . . help people . . . if you track him down. Find out what he knows."

"Yes, but we also—"

"Go after him," he said again, implacable, even as he pulled his frail form into one of the jumpseats in the back of the cockpit. "Find him. Find out *why* he did the things he did. I want to know. I *need* to know."

Jane and I exchanged a look; even though she'd just been the one arguing for chasing the armored what-the-hell halfway across the galaxy, if we had to, she didn't like that *Sho* was perfectly willing to do the same. "Sho, maybe you should—"

"He set off a massive bomb in my home city." Sho hissed the words out between his fangs. "He made sure our enemies were better armed, better prepared than we were. *He killed my mother.*" His golden eyes fluttered closed for a moment; when they reopened again, he'd fought back the tide of anger that had filled his voice, made himself calm again, almost *too* calm, worryingly so. "Go after him," he said again.

I looked from him to Jane; she was looking back at me. I thought back to how *I'd* been, when Jane had pulled me off my homeworld—she was right. I'd survived what came next. Sho would too. If it left him scarred, well: no more scarred than I was. Hopefully.

"Go after him," I echoed the young Wulf boy, and Jane nodded, laying in our course from Scheherazade's calculations.

We made the jump to hyperspace.

CHAPTER 4

The stars poured by the viewscreen until they were a single merge of light, like a liquid flood of illumination—Sho was watching, his face awed. Even after all he'd been through, nothing compared to the first time you saw *that*. Jane stood, and stretched; without comment, she helped Sho out of the jumpseat and back into the living quarters—no real reason to stay in the cockpit, not if we had no idea how long we'd be staying in hyperspace. After some mental gymnastics—could I stand up? Did I even want to? It had been a long, long, *long* day—I followed them both.

Jane was rummaging around in the cold box, Sho installed at the kitchen table; I tapped her on the shoulder, pointing toward the now-freed shower. "Your turn," I told her. Over the years, Jane had spent way too much time alone, and sometimes forgot little things like "a shower after a trip through a war zone is a very good idea." Plus, if she didn't clean up soon, she'd get stains on Schaz's floors, and we'd never hear the end of it.

She just nodded, sticking another peeled marsh flower in her mouth, and made her way into the shower. "You want something to eat?" I asked Sho, taking Jane's place in front of the cold box.

"Please," he said, sounding a little embarrassed that he was hungry, after all he'd been through. It was only natural, of course—the body wants what it wants, and starving yourself won't help you process trauma any faster.

"On it," I said, rummaging around in the fridge again for something more like a meal: Jane and I had a great many skills between the two of us, mostly on Jane's side, but "culinary aptitude" was not one of them. Mostly we lived on prepackaged stuff.

I slid two packets—chosen at random—into the reheater slots, and Schaz started humming merrily as she engaged the microwaves and whatnot. She couldn't cook *either*, but she somehow seemed to think that reheating premade packets that had been prepared and then frozen back on Sanctum *counted* as cooking, and she got weirdly domestic about it.

"Can I ask you something?" Sho asked.

"Sure thing," I said, taking a seat at the counter across from him. That was the *other* reason I'd wanted Jane to shower first—even after a century of ferrying kids back to Sanctum, she was . . . pretty piss-poor at dealing with kids, especially kids working their way through the tectonic shifts in their reality that came with being whisked offworld by an operative of a sect they hadn't known *existed* until Jane showed up.

"I've met . . . very few humans," he said, looking at me carefully, like he was trying to modulate his words, making sure he didn't give any offense. He was a careful kid, our new recruit—much more so than I'd been. I cocked my head, listening, trying to gauge his exact age as I did: I'd say seven or eight, which, for a Wulf child—who matured faster than humans did—would be the equivalent, on an emotional and intellectual scale, of a twelve- or thirteen-year-old human. That made sense—our gifts tended to manifest right around puberty, which hit a Wulf around five or six, and he'd clearly had his abilities for at least a little while, given that his sect had time to figure out how to power things with their furry little battery.

"I wouldn't figure you'd met any at all," I prompted him—everyone we'd seen in the factory city had been Wulf.

"Traders, sometimes, from other settlements. When the war was . . . calmer." Made sense—the population of Kandriad had been roughly divided between Wulf, human, and Tyll, and the various sects couldn't *all* have been at war with each other. "But I've never seen one that had . . ." He motioned toward my head, the gesture almost embarrassed.

I laughed, and ran a hand down my shorn scalp. "Combat efficiency," I told him. "Jane's had a century or more to learn how to fight with long hair— I've only been doing this for a couple of years." That was a *total* lie; the real reason I'd shaved my head had been way dumber. Sounded good, though. "Any other questions?" He must have had thousands, though at that moment Schaz ceased her humming, and the reheater dinged; I pulled the plates out and set one randomly in front of Sho, not even checking to see what I'd cooked. Hopefully something high in protein; Wulf subsisted on a far more meat-heavy diet than humans.

The same dish for both of us: vat-grown beef in gravy, with potatoes on the side. Excellent; Sho wasn't the *only* one who was more than ready to eat. We both dug in, and the conversation paused for a moment—I'd *never* known a teenager from a pulsed world who would let anything get between them and a warm meal, and that included myself.

Yes, I was eating before I'd had my turn in the shower; yes, I was still grime- and gore-encrusted from the fighting and the chaos and the crazy back on Kandriad. No, I didn't care, and Sho didn't seem to mind either. For me, well, it wasn't the first time I'd sat down to a meal looking like I'd just come from a pitched firefight; it wasn't even the first time I'd sat down to a meal when having actually *just come* from a pitched firefight. For Sho, I assumed he'd seen plenty of the like as well, with the front lines of his war so close to his home.

We dug into our food while it was still hot, tearing into the victuals like they might disappear if we let them cool. Even so, Jane finished her shower before we were done, and frowned when she saw we were eating without her. "Thanks," she said, somewhat indignantly.

"You want we should have waited?" I said—or *tried* to say, though the words came out somewhat garbled, given that they were forced around a large mouthful of potatoes.

Jane sighed. "I'll fix something for myself, thanks. For now: your turn."

I pushed my plate away from me, mostly finished—though I made sure to push it *toward* Sho, who had absolutely cleaned his and was staring at the remains of mine like I'd just given him the greatest gift he could imagine—and started toward the shower. I turned, though, before I opened the door. "Hey, Sho?" I said quietly.

He turned, looking up at me with those big gold eyes. "Yes, Esa?" he asked, pronouncing my name like he was trying out the feel of it on his tongue.

"I'm sorry," I said quietly. "For your mother."

He nodded, and then I shut the shower door behind me.

CHAPTER 5

For a moment after I closed the door, I just stared at my face in the mirror: I looked *terrible*. The traces of camo paint that still clung to my dark brown skin gave me a patchy, mottled look, one that came off as *incredibly* unhealthy, not aided by the shadows blooming underneath my wide hazel eyes. Adding to my general "death's door chic" appearance was the fact that I'd picked up a few minor contusions and bruises during the course of our little outing, which was, admittedly, more or less par for the course.

I shook out of my stupor and turned the water pressure over to "high." Let the recyclers work overtime; I needed the soak.

I stood under the spray and leaned against the cool wall, let the water pound against me, and closed my eyes against the pressure. That was the thing about showering after you got out of a combat zone—you tended to decompress in a rush, the warm water telling your body you were safe, it was okay, you could let go of the tension you'd been holding, you could actually start to *process* what you'd been through.

Problem was, I didn't really *want* to process what I'd been through on Kandriad—didn't want to think about the men I'd killed, the expressions on their faces, the feeling and the force behind my arm as I rammed my knife home. I didn't want to think about Sho's mother, standing on the subway platform as the gas approached. I especially didn't want to think about the rising ball of nuclear fire, or the *thing* in armor, the thing with wings, that had soared out of that rising column of flame, the thing we were still *chasing*. Mostly, I didn't want to think about how often I'd felt my pulse racing beneath my skin, the bitter taste of fear in my mouth, or the horrifying, vicious *joy* I'd felt as I'd watched an enemy fall.

Those thoughts came unbidden to my mind anyway, drawn up from the depths by the comforting warmth and pressure of the water.

I didn't know which was worse: that after three years of this kind of work—and no, it hadn't *all* been this kind of work; moments like the peaceable contact we'd made with Sho's sect still outweighed all the scary violence, by a good margin—I was still so *bothered* by all of it, or the fact that, after three years, I still wasn't *as* bothered by it as I felt like I should be.

I'd killed, what, a dozen soldiers today? At least. A dozen thinking, breathing, aware beings, people with their own hopes and dreams and fears, and all that really mattered to me was that they were dead and I wasn't. I got to keep on breathing. They didn't. So fuck them. Those were the stakes.

I was taught early on—well before I met Jane—that the moment you put on a gun you were making a choice to take your survival into your own hands. But that was still better than leaving it in the hands of someone else, someone who might not hesitate to cut down unarmed women or children. People without a fight in them could still die to someone else's. That *was* another one of Jane's sayings. I still don't know if I agreed with it, but I was starting to see that it might not matter if I did, or if I didn't. It was true either way.

I stayed in the shower for a while before I actually started to put effort into cleaning myself, feeding the recyclers with the grit and dust and dried blood Kandriad had left behind. Once I had the remains of the war scrubbed off me, I felt marginally better. I always did. Again—not sure if that was good or bad. Not sure if I should really be able to just . . . leave behind the things I'd done, the lives I'd taken, drawn down the drain just like the gray-and-pink-stained water running off my body. But fuck it. We still had other problems.

At least we had time for showers, and dinners, *time* to decompress. That was the one good thing about the hyperspace voyages: the long travel time meant you got moments to breathe, in between the places you had to be.

When I finally emerged, Sho was still sitting at the table, finishing off what looked like the remains of *Jane's* meal—and he smiled bashfully at me around another forkful of his food. "I ate the rest of your dinner," he told me, as though that weren't patently obvious.

"Share and share alike, brother; that's my motto," I told him. "Plus, we have more." I fished some more fruit from the cooling unit; wasn't really in the mood for hot food anymore anyway, not after so long in the piping-hot shower.

He swallowed his massive bite of dinner, then went for another package.

"Jane told me she wanted to check something out in the cargo hold," he said. "Said she might have a 'gift' for me down there." *That* was interesting—as far as I knew, all we had hidden away in the space beneath our feet were more guns, more munitions. "She *also* told me that the other children at Sanctum— that they all have gifts, like yours, and mine."

I nodded, taking a seat across from him after I'd tossed my marsh flower peel in the recycler. "Like ours, but different, just like our gifts are different," I said.

"And that most of them stay at Sanctum, to train their gifts. She wouldn't say what that meant, exactly, or how, or why. There are many things that she won't tell me. She thinks she's being clever in how she avoids answering those questions—"

"But she's really not." I smiled, faintly. "Yeah, I remember that, too."

"So she . . . discovered you. Rescued you. Like you two rescued me."

"She did, yeah. Three years ago." It felt like a lifetime.

"And did *you* train? At Sanctum?"

"For a little while," I nodded. "Long enough to grasp the fundamentals of my power, and to brush up on all the stuff I missed growing up on a pulsed world; stuff about the galaxy at large, I mean. After that, I figured I was good to go. Most of the other kids—they stay there, find work, find uses for their talents. I didn't figure that I'd been dragged halfway across the galaxy just to sit around that one little corner of it: I wanted to see all the other parts, too. The places in between."

"So that's why you work with Jane? To explore?"

I shook my head. "If I just wanted to explore, I'd work with our friend Javier—he's the cartographer. He goes to the edges of our maps, fills in the blank spaces. Visits worlds we only know a little about, or those we haven't been to in a long time, makes sure what we *thought* we knew still holds true, or to correct what was wrong if it doesn't."

Sho was watching me intently, like I was a riddle he was trying to figure out; I pretended not to notice as I popped another bite of the fruit into my mouth. "So why not *do* that?" he asked finally.

"Why work with Jane?"

He nodded.

"Because she was there when I needed her. Because my world went to hell in a handbasket, and I would have ended up in a very, very bad place if she hadn't found me."

"Like . . . like I would have been caught in that blast, if you hadn't come for me." He was still having trouble talking about it—probably even *thinking* about it—but at least he was trying; that counted for something.

"Exactly," I nodded. "Even worse for me, though, because you would have just been dead; I would have been . . . something else, *made* into something else by the people looking for me." The Pax had wanted to brainwash me, to make me use my gifts to wage their war. I would have still been in there, somewhere, screaming, but gone, as well. I still had nightmares about it, from time to time—what might have been.

"So you were hunted, just like maybe the thing in the armor was hunting for me."

Shit. How had he figured *that* out? "That's only a possibility, Sho," I cautioned him. "We don't know it for sure." But I'd just reinforced the notion that it *might* be, by telling him it was also what had driven me from *my* home. Goddammit. I shook my head, wrenched the conversation back on track. "Point is, I'm not—I'm not doing this because I owe Jane, somehow, and I don't want *you* to think you owe *us*, either. If you want to stay in Sanctum— once we finally make it back there—you should stay in Sanctum; if you want to tell us all to fuck off and go explore the rest of the universe on your own, you should do that instead. Once they fix your spinal bits." I waved another piece of marsh flower in the vague direction of his waist.

"So if you don't do it because you owe her, why do it?" He seemed very intent on getting an answer.

"Because she *saved* me, Sho. And because I can't imagine anything more rewarding out of life than getting to save *you*." There it was, a bold-faced statement answering the question that had eluded me in the shower: *why* was I willing to go through all the violence, all the pain, all the fear? Because it was worth it; that was why. Simple math. "Your talents might make a great deal of difference for thousands of lives in Sanctum, might even help save us from the return of the pulse, and that's one hell of a reward. *My* talents— and the training Jane's given me—make me *uniquely* suited to go back out into the galaxy that tried to grind me to paste, and to pull other kids out of the path of that same thresher."

He swallowed another bite of protein-something, and nodded. "And her?" he asked.

"Jane, you mean?"

He nodded again. I shrugged. "Jane doesn't talk about the past much," I told him. "If she did, I wouldn't bug her about it the way I do. I think she feels like she owes something; I'm just not sure what it is, or who she owes it to. The galaxy, maybe. Or herself. Maybe both."

"She saves people—children—because there was someone she *didn't* save once. Someone she couldn't. Or wouldn't." He said the words with the simple gravity of insight; a guess, sure, but still a pretty damned good one.

I blinked at him for a moment. That was not a possibility I'd ever actually considered. Truth be told, I'd never really asked the question of *why* Jane did this work at all—oh, I'd asked why she'd joined up with the Justified, and gotten evasive answers in return, but I'd never asked why *this* work, why, with her talents, she wasn't in Seamus's security outfit instead, the front lines against an attack on Sanctum. Whatever she'd been before she joined the Justified, it had been something a hell of a lot closer to a soldier than a nursemaid.

He grinned at me slightly, taking in my expression. "Did I say something clever?" he asked.

"Not too bad," I told him, pushing the rest of my marsh flower across the table as a reward. "Not too bad at all." He finished it off in one bite.

CHAPTER 6

Jane eventually emerged from the cargo hold with a goddamned *wheelchair* in tow, huffing and grunting as she lifted it up the ladder from the cargo area belowdecks. Where the hell had she found *that* thing? It was collapsible, motorized—Sho's eyes absolutely *lit* when he saw what it was.

"I know we promised you your legs back, and that *will* happen, Sho," Jane told him, pulling the thing apart. "But obviously, we're not going to be able to take a direct route to Sanctum—"

"Hunting down the thing in the armor comes first." He nodded. "Absolutely."

"Right." She smiled, just a little, liked the steel she heard in his voice. "So until we can get your legs fixed up, I wanted you to at least be able to get around Scheherazade on your own. Esa?"

I nodded, and moved to help him into the chair as Jane held it open. Sho treated the metal contraption—a thing you'd be able to find in most hospitals on every non-pulsed world, and even on a fair bit of them that had received only light doses of pulse rads—like it was an absolute wonder; I hadn't seen a wheelchair in his train car back on Kandriad, either because that sort of thing was too far up the tech tree for his people to fabricate it, or simply because he and his mother had simply been too poor.

He zoomed around in the thing like he was a natural. Thankfully, Scheherazade's interior only had one actual cabin, and all its furniture was modular, meant to be fitted up inside the walls when we weren't using it, so there was plenty of open space for him to get around.

While Sho was busy testing out his new wheels, Jane and I crowded around the kitchen table, Jane reaching to activate the holoprojector, bringing up the star maps of this sector of space. Tracking a ship through hyperspace was relatively easy, provided you had a visual record of their jump—which we did: all you did was calculate the exact trajectory they'd exited the system, then plotted that course out and out and out through the surrounding emptiness between the stars until you hit something of note; there was no such thing as "turning" in the middle of a hyperspace jump.

The problem was, since we didn't know what the hell the armored thing's ship was capable of, we didn't know what its range was, or how fast it was moving—Scheherazade was capable of staying in hyperspace for a week or more, but if he could keep going past that, we'd have to drop out, cool the engines, and hope we could catch up.

"There." Jane reached out, tapped a green dot on the holoprojected map, just inside the red line on his projected course: where we'd have to break off the chase, at least momentarily.

I squinted at the map, opening up the text box of Schaz's database to read what sort of information the Justified had collected on the system. "Not much there," I said doubtfully. "Gas giants, an asteroid belt, a weird nebula at the edge of the system—"

"And that weird nebula's where he'll be headed," Jane said, her voice still confident—whatever it was she knew, it *wasn't* in the Justified's general archives. I swear, sometimes she kept secrets just for the hell of it. "There's a station inside, a former mining asteroid, hollowed out, repurposed."

"And you think he's going there because . . ."

She shrugged. "Process of elimination. There's nothing else on his course *but* that system, and *in* that system, that's the only one thing with any kind of population."

I narrowed my eyes at her. "You said this asteroid had been 'repurposed,'" I said. "Repurposed for *what*? And does it even have a name?"

She nodded at that. "General sustainability—don't worry, it's not like they're building war AI, or anything like that. And the name of the station is Valkyrie Rock."

"What's a valkyrie?" I asked. Even in our shit situation, she smiled at that; my general curiosity always amused her.

"A valkyrie is . . ." She paused, trying to stare at the map and answer my question simultaneously. "It's a thing from an old human myth; a sort of spirit creature that roams battlefields, and takes the honored dead to the afterlife. Only those who fought, and died, as warriors, though; those as strong, or stronger, than the valkyries themselves. And that's the thing about Valkyrie Rock; the inhabitants are . . . they have kind of a thing. About death. Hence the name."

"*What* kind of a thing?" I asked. That didn't sound good. In point of fact, it sounded bad. Very bad. Having "a thing about death" was up there with "a thing about feeding outsiders to superpredators" in terms of unsavory habits various cultures could develop that might have a direct impact on our sanity and well-being.

"They think it's already happened."

"What?"

"They think they're dead; that everybody's dead. They think we're . . . 'living,' for lack of a better term . . . in the afterlife. That this, all of it"—she waved her hand, I guess to indicate, you know, *existence*, though really she was just gesturing at Schaz—"they think it's all a kind of purgatory, a place of testing and punishment. I'm not sure *which* afterlife exactly, but . . . yeah. Valkyrie Rock is a gathering place for those who think they've already died." She turned, slightly; caught my expression, which must not have been pleasant. "It's a big galaxy, Esa," she said, almost defensively. "People believe a lot of strange shit."

"So . . . what does that *mean*?"

Jane shrugged. "So long as we obey their rules, we should be fine. Just— no mentioning the outside universe; as far as they're concerned, Valkyrie Rock is the only 'real' thing in existence, and everything else is just the shadows and fog of the afterlife, there to test them, to trick them. To draw them from the true path."

"And their other rules?"

"I'll go over them before we dock."

"So do you think he's . . . one of them? The armored guy, I mean—is he one of these . . . 'thinks he's dead' people? Cultists? Types?"

She thought about it for a moment, then shook her head. "I doubt it," she replied, taking a sip of her coffee. "The locals aren't *unfriendly*, per se. For a bunch of theoretically dead people. Plus, they don't really give a damn about the outside galaxy, because, again, they think it doesn't exist. So sending out a . . . terrorist, or an assassin, or whatever the hell he was—it's not exactly something they'd *do*."

"So they're not liable to be exactly *pleased* to see him. Or us. Whichever one of us gets there first."

"Well—that depends."

"Depends on *what?*"

"What kind of demon they think we are."

"We're *demons* now?"

"Like I said—nothing else is real to them. Anything from the outside galaxy is just a . . . projection of the afterlife, there to test them, or punish them. If we're the latter, the kind they'd want to appease into leaving them alone, we're golden. If we're the former, tricksters and shapeshifters, there to tempt them into believing this universe *is* real—"

"That's when they kill us with fire."

"About right, yeah."

"Jane?"

"Yeah?"

"What the *fuck* is wrong with . . . with . . . with . . . with everyone?"

She sighed, didn't answer me. Sho, meanwhile, had wheeled up beside us—he was staring at the holoprojection with the same kind of fascination he had for *all* the new tech he hadn't been exposed to on Kandriad. "Why would he be going to a place like . . . like *that?*" he asked, scrutinizing the projection of the nebula Jane had brought up. Apparently, he'd been listening.

I shrugged. "Why would he be on Kandriad?" I asked. "I mean, no offense to your home planet, Sho—"

"You called it a 'shithole' about an hour ago. You also said, repeatedly, 'fuck that place.'"

"Well. Yes. Because fuck that place. Point is, whatever this guy is after— we don't *know* enough to figure out what he wants, why he might be going . . . anywhere, really."

"Hopefully, we'll be able to find out on Valkyrie Rock," Jane shrugged.

"Or he'll be waiting for us when we disembark, and resume trying to murder us."

"Or that."

"Or the *locals* will be trying to murder us, because we're demons."

"Also a distinct possibility, yes, though one we can hopefully mitigate down to 'unlikely.'"

Sho was looking back and forth between Jane and me. "And this is . . . what you two *do*," he said, sounding caught somewhere between awe and shock.

"Pretty much," I agreed.

"I . . . I was kind of hoping the Justified would be *smarter*," he said, sounding more than a little disappointed.

I had to laugh at that.

CHAPTER 7

So: we had our course—chase after the crazy bastard in the weird ship who *maybe* had a cure for the pulse—and we had our destination, a hollowed-out former mining asteroid in the middle of a nebula in an otherwise uninteresting system, populated by a cult of death-obsessed misanthropes who hated the rest of the galaxy.

Just another day in the service of the Justified; time for bed.

Well before she'd met me, Jane had made the decision to convert *her* sleeping quarters—the only separate room in Schaz's interior, apart from the shower and the airlock/armory—into a sort of recovery chamber for the kids she picked up, meaning Sho got his own quarters. Her reasoning was sound: she figured her passengers would need *privacy* more than anything, after being plucked from their homeworlds and spirited away between the stars, that they'd need someplace where they didn't have to put on a brave face for her, or to try and figure out how they were supposed to behave now.

That only became more true if they were dealing with the sort of trauma Sho had just survived. He'd been bearing up well, I'd give him that, but still: he could use some time alone, and he could use some *sleep*. He wasn't the only one.

"Why don't we carry hooch, Jane?" I sighed, changing into my sleeping sweats as she rotated our bunks out of the wall. We'd already settled Sho in his own quarters, and now it was our turn—Jane and I slept in the main cabin, converted into a pair of bunks. "We should carry hooch, just for days like today."

She laughed at that. "Since when do you drink?" she asked me. Then, a heartbeat later: "Seriously, when do *you* drink? You've never done any drinking around me. Who's been teaching you to drink?"

It was almost cute, the rare occasions she remembered she was supposed to be maternal. "Jane, I'm seventeen, I have a drink once in a while, god. I just don't drink with *you* because—how should I put this—you're an *incredibly* morose drunk."

"Who told you that? Marus?"

"Oh, no one *told* me, Jane. I found out for myself. Don't you remember? About a year and a half ago, at that . . . we were at Sanctum, and there was—"

"Wait, was this at that . . . the retirement thing, for TivShall?" She stretched clean sheets across her cot, frowning. "I remember that. Vaguely. I did *not* have too much to drink at that." She sounded vaguely offended by the entire concept, which was too much to bear.

I looked her dead in the eyes, made sure I had her full attention. "Jane, you did," I told her. "You *really* did. You had *so* much to drink, in point of fact, that you sat me down for a monologue about your experiences during the slow-motion demise of the *Ishiguro*. A full *monologue*, Jane. You went on and *on* about the sounds it made as it sank into the crushing atmosphere of some gas giant, about the way the light died as you went down into the depths with the ship. I don't know *exactly* what moral you were trying to get across, outside of 'your early days with the Justified were shit,' but whatever it was, you were *very* intense about it. So, yeah. I'd say you had a *bit* too much to drink."

She paused in the act of pulling off one of her boots. "I do *not* remember that," she admitted, sounding a bit mystified. "I mean, I remember the actual sinking, yeah; I'll never forget that if I live for another hundred years." For a second I was briefly terrified she was going to launch into the entire reminiscence again, but she shook it off and came back to the now. "But I don't remember telling *you* that story, not at *all*. Why would I tell you *that* story?"

"I don't know," I shrugged, "but tell it you did: to me, and to Javier, and to TivShall, and to everyone else anywhere in earshot at the time. Twenty full minutes of bloodcurdling descriptions of asphyxiation and weirdly sexual metaphors about the infinite embrace of death. It still haunts my dreams, Jane. It haunts my fucking dreams. *That's* why we don't drink together very often."

She narrowed her eyes at me. "It's Javi, isn't it?" she asked.

"It's Javi what?"

"It's Javier who's been teaching you to drink."

"Oh, quit clucking, mother hen."

"You're *my* partner; he shouldn't be teaching you his bad habits."

"It's not like I'm littering Schaz's deck with empty beer cans, you know."

"Still. I'm vaguely offended."

"By me, or by Javier?"

"By *you*, obviously. Javi can do what he wants."

I had to laugh at that. "You're more jealous that *I've* been drinking with Javier than that *he's* been drinking with *me*?"

"I'm not jealous, Esa. Just . . . put out."

"Whatever, Jane. I'm just saying, the next time we're at Sanctum—"

"I will track down a bottle of celebratory hooch, yes. I know where Marus keeps a stash of the good stuff."

"Of which you will only allow yourself small doses when we *do* have a drink or two together."

"Don't push your luck."

I climbed into bed; Jane was already in, so Schaz dimmed the lights.

"I *really* told you about the sinking of the *Ishiguro*?" Jane asked me after a moment. "You sure you didn't hear that from Criat or something?"

"Oh, no. I heard it directly from you. Believe me. Not even Criat could give me the kind of detail you were putting into that recollection. That horrible, horrible recollection."

"Oh. Okay. Fine."

"Not really, no."

"Hey, Esa?"

"God, what?" I yawned. I really was ready to get to sleep.

"Good work today."

"Oh." Slightly mollified, I replied: "Thank you, Jane."

"You're welcome."

After a moment, it was my turn: "Hey, Jane?"

"Yes, Esa?"

"You too."

"Thank you."

The long day seemed to stretch out behind us forever, and I was so damned tired I could have dropped into unconsciousness then and there, but: I still had questions, questions about some of the things Jane had said, or implied, down on Kandriad, and if I wasn't going to ask now, I knew I wouldn't get a better chance—god hates a coward, and all that. ". . . Hey, Jane?"

"Yes, Esa?"

"What was your home planet like?"

I could hear her staring at me, in the dark—*through* the dark, even though she didn't have her HUD activated; I would have been able to tell by the glow of her eyes. She didn't say anything, was just lying there, breathing.

"Was it *like* Kandriad? Was it like the factory city, under siege?" I pushed my luck.

"In some ways, yes. In other ways, no."

"That . . . doesn't tell me much."

She sighed; I could hear her rolling over, onto her back. "What do you want from me, Esa?" she asked. Just the sound of her voice, when she said it—it made me sad, like maybe I shouldn't have pressed.

But I was still me, so I kept going anyway. "I want to know what it was like. I figure that would be obvious, given, you know, that's what I asked."

For a moment, I thought she wasn't going to answer, that I'd pushed too far, and she'd just closed up again. Then she just started speaking, like the darkness gave her permission—like if she didn't have to watch my face while she was talking, she could pretend that she was really only talking to herself.

"You went to school in the little settlement you grew up in, right? They didn't have a separate school for the orphanage or anything." I didn't say anything; she already knew the answer, was just trying to ground herself. "Imagine that—going to school—except every week there was some kid whose parent didn't come home from the front; imagine if every month there was some kid who just stopped showing up, not because they'd dropped out, but because they'd been caught in an errant airstrike, or crushed by falling debris, or just shot by an enemy sniper who didn't give a fuck about basic rules of engagement like 'don't shoot kids.' Imagine having to make your way down the front lines just to get a few eggs to eat, or some milk, if there was any to be had. Imagine that being your choice: cross through the trenches and maybe catch a bullet in the head, or starve. Imagine that. Every single day. For years."

"I can't," I said softly. And I couldn't. Just today had been . . . too much.

Beyond too much. The thought of that being *life* . . . it was beyond the limited powers of my imagination.

For a moment, I thought she was done—that she'd made her point, and I'd gotten all I was going to get. That was what normally would have happened—in fact, she'd already told me more than she usually would have. Instead, though, she took a breath, and she just started . . . talking.

"I never bought into my sect's reasoning for the war," she said softly. "Never, not once, even after being raised in it. The elders *tried*—they started us young, indoctrination sessions in every classroom, all vaguely religious nonsense about infidels and heretics and schisms, but I never . . . I couldn't tell you *why* I didn't buy it, I just didn't. But I did hate them, all the same. Our enemy, I mean. I hated them with a pure, almost fulfilling level of malice. They'd defined my world for so long—with their bombs and their assaults and their clumsy attempts at propaganda, broadcast over the loudspeakers and hacked into the terminals—I didn't know what to do *other* than hate them.

"So of course I joined the war, as soon as I was old enough. We all did. The war was all we knew—it was how the world worked, what the world was. Only difference between me and my surviving classmates was I actually *asked* to be sent to the front. I asked for training in special ops. I asked for the recon missions into enemy territory, the sniper assassination details, the last stands against overwhelming odds. Whenever they asked for volunteers, my hand was already up, usually before I even knew what the mission was."

"Why?" I knew the answer—or at least I thought I did—but I had to ask nonetheless.

I could hear her shrug in the darkness. "I didn't care about living much— what did I have to live for? Just more war, more fear, more suffering. All of which I could blame on the enemy on the other side of the front lines. And I *did* care about answering them in kind.

"So. Anyway. Yeah. That's what my home was like, Esa. And if you've ever wondered why the sect wars went on as long as they did, with no end in sight—why they're still raging on worlds like Sho's, to this very day—that's why. It was never about faith, about differing philosophies or beliefs. Maybe when they started, but that point came and went a long time ago. They kept on raging because once you *start* killing each other, it can get goddamned hard to stop."

She didn't say anything else; just rolled over in the dark.

That wasn't what I had asked; she'd never told me that before. I wondered why *now*. She *never* talked about her childhood, ever. Was it something we'd seen on Kandriad? Was it something we'd done, something *I'd* done? Hell, had it been bringing up the sinking of the *Ishiguro* that had done it, a reminder that she *could* open up, once in a while?

Or was it the time she'd spent in the shower while Sho and I were eating, the time *she'd* had to spend going over the faces of the dead?

Maybe Jane and I weren't as far apart as I sometimes thought.

CHAPTER 8

We spent the next few days in our own particular version of domestic-ity: training, reading, slowly introducing Sho to the various modern devices and conveniences that were part of day-to-day life on non-pulsed worlds and starships—not that Scheherazade had a great deal of those, given how spartan Jane kept her interior. Jane broke out her wrench set and re-moved two of the rear jumpseats in the cockpit so that Sho could wheel his chair inside and join us when we were within; she didn't want him to feel like there was a part of the ship where he wasn't welcome, or where we could go to discuss things without him hearing.

Oddly enough, *I* was the one who suggested he also spend some time training on the rear turret—you would have thought Jane would have made the suggestion, but she didn't seem to think Sho was as inclined as I was toward violence. Which—maybe fair, but I remembered Jane training *me* on the guns when I'd come aboard, and having just a *little* bit of control over my fate when we'd inevitably gotten tangled up in a fight: that had helped. Plus, we'd swapped out the old railgun setup for a laser module, and lasers were *way* easier to learn on.

The turret wasn't the easiest thing for Sho to get to, given his condition and the fact that you had to climb down a ladder to even *reach* the thing, but he proved quite adept at it—I guess his mother hadn't spent all her time carrying him around, and he was pretty capable of making his way down without the use of his legs, as he'd shown when he'd crawled all the way from the shower to the cockpit.

Once inside, Schaz called up simulations for him to "fire" at—he wasn't actually firing anything, of course: the turret was incapable of operating in hyperspace. I wasn't even sure what would happen if we tried. Quantum physics was never my strong suit.

In short order he was at least proficient—as far as "massive weapons attached to starships" go, the turret was fairly simple to use, point and shoot, with an overlaid HUD tracking targets and the angles of incoming enemy fire, as well as indicating how much he would have to lead a moving vessel.

You'd think Schaz would just handle firing all the guns herself—and she could, in a pinch—but the truth was, having organic beings do the shooting actually made us more dangerous to an enemy. AI always fired in exactly the same manner, chose exactly the same targeting parameters and threat prioritization; any half-skilled pilot would know how to game those. Having a sentient being at the gun meant that we were more unpredictable, forcing the enemy to react to something beyond AI pattern recognition.

Jane also tried to get some basic information out of him as to his gifts, but unlike me, who'd come to her with my talents mostly fully developed, Sho engaged his unconsciously; things just . . . powered up around him, if they could do so. Schaz actually had to adjust her drive baffles to compensate for the extra juice he was constantly adding to the core. Of course, that meant that if it *did* come to a dogfight—and let's be real; whatever happened on Valkyrie Rock, it almost went without question that *somebody* would be shooting at us—we'd have a hidden advantage with that extra bit of power; our shields would regenerate just a little faster, our lasers' heatsinks would drain just a little quicker, our engines could maintain thrust just a little longer.

Jane didn't talk any more about her past. Sho didn't speak of his mother. I didn't mention all the killing I'd done on Kandriad, or the nightmares it was still giving me. On a ship this small, there were some things you just *didn't* talk about, otherwise they were *all* you would talk about.

Soon enough, we were approaching the end of our cruise, ready to drop out of hyperspace and enter the system with the former mining asteroid full of terrifying cultists who would think we were some kind of ship of the dead. Hooray.

When we were about an hour out from our destination, Jane retreated to the airlock for a moment, then returned with her various cans of camouflage from the armory, setting them all out on the kitchen table. "Just . . . hold still," she told me, leaning in with a can full of glittering gold camo paint—what sort of world had foliage that color, I had no idea, but Jane was always overprepared.

I sat at my chair, trying not to squirm as she set about painting weird designs on my face, meant to make me look more demon-y. Schaz and Sho both chimed in with unhelpful comments as she worked—which was easy for *them* to do, since we'd already decided Sho wouldn't be leaving Scheherazade. It was safer that way. Besides, fur was much harder to apply war paint to.

When Jane was done—and starting to work on herself—I took a look in the mirror; the ultimate design was actually kind of . . . pretty, gold and gray in a sort of tessellating waterfall design. What Jane had been working on for herself was significantly creepier: purples and blues in the shape of dozens of different eyes. It was good work, though—*I* would have confused us with demons, which was sort of the point.

With that taken care of, we all crowded into Schaz's cockpit again as we approached the far edge of our destination system. We dropped out of hyperspace—right into a sort of pulsating veridian fog, already inside the nebula.

"Oh, for fuck's sake," I said, disgusted. "First the gas on Kandriad, now this. Is there . . . have we stumbled into some kind of fucked-up *theme*, here, Jane? Are you doing this on purpose?"

She smiled at that—the effect of which caused a few of her drawn-on eyeballs to seem to wink at me. "Nah," she said, the stick in her hand as she maneuvered us through the gas of the nebula, hopefully toward where we were going: I couldn't see a thing out the viewscreens—beyond "green," I mean. "The universe just hates you."

I sighed. "You might not actually be wrong about that," I said. "After all, I can never seem to—" The witty rejoinder I'd been preparing went unspoken as our destination appeared in the viewscreen.

A massive rock loomed out of the mist, first not there, then *there*, fully formed. It was honeycombed with metal structures and tunnels, like it had been imprinted with circuitry; in several places on the crust large machines sat silent and still, remnants of the mining operation that had once toiled within.

Jane slowed Scheherazade to a stop, just outside of orbital range. Then we just . . . sat.

"What are we doing?" Sho whispered. I understood the inclination.

"We're waiting for the locals to see us," Jane replied, not exactly whispering back, but her voice lower than it usually would have been. "That's only polite, giving them time to decide whether we're dead or demon."

"Shouldn't they have picked us up on scans?" I asked, then felt stupid for asking; of *course* they hadn't, just like Jane hadn't picked up Valkyrie Rock on our own scans. Something about the nebula threw off long-range scanners.

Which *also* meant the strange ship with the armored guy we were chasing could have been *right behind us,* and we wouldn't have known it. Not a comforting thought.

Jane just shook her head. Abruptly, a searchlight cut on, sweeping through the mist from the exterior of the asteroid to focus on Scheherazade. Jane had set a comm channel open; a voice came through, almost sibilant. "This is Charon, operational AI for Valkyrie Rock," it said. Jane frowned at that, but didn't answer. "You are advised to dock at the indicated bay." Our consoles flashed as the AI flagged one of the gaping holes in the asteroid's surface. "Please land your ship, shut down your power, then await the greeting party that will decide your intentions."

With that said, the comms shut off abruptly; not much of a conversationalist, this Charon. Jane was left narrowing her eyes at the viewscreen, not happy about something.

"What's wrong?" I asked her.

"This isn't . . . the AI shouldn't have greeted us," she said flatly. "It should have been one of the priests, with a series of questions to sort out our intent."

"Are you just annoyed that you'd memorized the right answers, and now you don't get to use them?" I asked.

"No," she shook her head, then backtracked. "Well, yes. But not just that."

"You think crazy armored glowing guy is here already?" We *really* needed an actual name to put on this asshole.

"Possible," she allowed. "But if so—if we're right about him setting off the nuke on Kandriad to cover his tracks, he hasn't done the same thing here, and he *could* have: the asteroid is powered by a fusion reactor, and it's not hard at all to convert a fusion reactor into a fission bomb."

"It terrifies me that you know that."

"I know a lot of things that would terrify you. Regardless of whether he's here already or not, though, we're here to find him, which means we need to get on board." With that said, she leaned over the controls again and kicked Schaz into motion, guiding us gently toward the docking bay.

As we got closer, I could *see* the strange designs the cultists had carved into the surface of their home, probably with mining lasers: all sorts of swirls and spirals, tiled frescoes and massive raised reliefs depicting scenes of death and wandering. It wasn't the *most* comforting thing in the world to see as we drifted out of the fog, the muraled surface of the rock looming closer and closer, then swallowing us whole as we entered the docking bay tunnel, the mouth of which had been carved into overlapping rows of hideous gargoyles. As the tunnel closed in around us, it was impossible—for me, anyway—not to look up and notice that the grimacing statuary looked a hell of a lot like teeth, giving the impression of a fanged maw closing around us as we entered the interior of the asteroid itself.

The carvings and designs continued on the inner walls of the tunnel; one by one lights came up, just ahead of our passage, until we'd finally reached a large, circular chamber at the end. At least that was familiar: a docking bay was a docking bay the whole galaxy wide, complete with various hanging machinery and stacks of sealed crates filled with repair materials.

Jane set Schaz down in the very center of the bay—no alarms or klaxons were sounding to alert the natives to an aggressive presence, hopefully a good sign—and we stepped out of the cockpit, letting Sho wheel forward, to the comm station. "If you need to reach us, press here," Jane showed him a button. "But try not to need to. We've got Justified encryption, so the cult won't be able to hear what we're saying, but chances are they'll still know we're *talking*, and that will make them nervous. We don't want to make them nervous."

"I mean, we kind of do, right?" I asked, a little nervous myself. "Shouldn't . . . *shouldn't* demons make them nervous?"

"We want to make them *ontologically* nervous, not 'draw guns and fire' nervous," Jane answered. "There's a difference."

"A difference I might understand if I had any idea what 'ontology' was," I grunted in reply.

"It means . . . don't worry about it. When the priests arrive to greet us, just remember: don't look at them. Don't *speak* to them. If you're asked a direct question, bare your teeth and breathe in, deeply. Let me do the talking."

"Funny how we always seem to default to that."

"Do *you* know how to convince a bunch of cultists that we're demons from the great beyond, sent to test their faith, and further that we're the *type* of demons who shouldn't be trifled with, rather than the type of demons that should be thrown into an airlock and then sucked out the other side? Then further *still*, how to convince them that there *is* a threat coming to invade their home, and we need their help ambushing and *capturing* that threat, so that we can take him alive?"

I took a deep breath, then let it out. "No," I said with a sigh. "No, I do not."

"Well, then. Let me do the talking." She'd unsealed Scheherazade's loading bay as we had that little discussion; she strapped on her revolver and a few knives, gesturing for me to do the same, but that was it for armament. No body armor, no larger guns.

"If we have to defend ourselves, I'm going to feel fairly naked without Bitey," I told her.

She grinned at that. "Then I've taught you well," she said. "Still, if it comes to that, feel free to throw your teke around: that ought to seem fairly demonish."

"Gee. Thanks."

"You know what I mean; quit being a teenager."

"I *am*—"

"I know, it was . . . just get ready." Jane sealed the inner airlock behind us; through the window, I could see Sho, turned to face us in the cockpit. He raised a hand in a wave. I waved back, then turned to face the outer door, fitting my shoulder holsters on and dropping the semiautomatic handguns Javi had given me into the rigs.

"Ready?" Jane asked, one of her hands resting on the butt of her gun; *that* was comforting.

I nodded, taking a deep breath in and facing the outer door. "Ready," I said. Under my breath, I started muttering to myself: "I'm a demon. I'm a demon. I'm a demon. I'm a gray-gold afterlife demon, and I'm here to track down an asshole or devour souls, so you better be willing to help me with the first if you don't want the latter to get *done* to you. The longer I have to wait for the asshole to appear, the more peckish I'm going to grow, so you'd best get ready."

"You don't have to convince *yourself*, Esa," Jane told me—I could hear a smile in her voice, even though I wasn't looking at her. "Just them. I also don't know that a demon would use the word 'peckish' to describe her all-encompassing hunger for mortal souls."

"Shut the fuck up, Jane, let me get into a . . . demon-y kind of a head-space."

"Among other things, I *also* doubt a demon would call themselves 'demon-y.'"

"Just . . . just . . . you know?"

She grinned at that—it never ceased to amuse her when I utterly failed to articulate a thought—and reached out to open the outer airlock.

Welcome to Valkyrie Rock.

CHAPTER 9

It was cold. Why was it so cold? Most species fit comfortably into the same habitable zone of temperatures, and this was an asteroid, an artificial atmosphere; it could be as cool or warm as the inhabitants wanted. So why were they keeping it roughly the same temperature as a freezer?

I rubbed my hands over my arms. "Seriously?" I asked Jane.

She gave a ghost of a smile. "They're dead, remember? The dead don't need heat."

"But I mean . . . they *do*. They're not actually dead." I paused for a moment, and then I couldn't help it; I had to ask. "I mean, they're *not*, right? This isn't . . . we're not . . ."

"No, Esa, they're not actually dead. But they do their damnedest to convince themselves they are." Jane looked around the massive docking bay, her smile gone, replaced by a frown. I got where she was coming from. This was . . . off.

I'd visited plenty of spaceports with Jane over the past three years, and even in private bays like this one, there was usually *some* measure of activity—techs running around making repairs, automated systems humming quietly in the background. Here, there was nothing. Just a kind of stillness, one that could only be described as "funereal."

Of course, I was maybe only thinking that because of the whole "we're all actually dead" thing.

Still, it was . . . off. Weird. Eerie. There should have been *something*.

"How long do we wait?" I asked her.

"Until they're ready to see us," she replied, though she was staring at the locked doors at the entrance just as hard as I was.

"And if they decide they *don't* want to see us?"

"Would *you* want two demons just . . . hanging out in one of your docking bays, unattended? They'll see us."

"Ummmm. Jane?" Since we were both staring at the door, it was hard to miss: not the door itself, but just beside it, near the control panel.

A smear of fuchsia, bright against the cold metal of the wall. Vyriat blood. It led right up to the edge of the door, like someone had been bleeding, reaching for the door controls, then had been dragged away. Likely through the opening, to the other side; otherwise there'd be blood on the floor. Someone had been trying to seal something *out* of the bay, and themselves *in*. Not good. Not a good fucking sign.

"Yeah. I see it."

"Maybe they *aren't* coming to see us. Because maybe they *can't*. Do we have some sort of plan B, here?"

Jane was still staring at that lone splash of color, grim and vibrant at the same time; she reached up to activate her comms. "Schaz?" she asked. "Can you access their systems—hack your way in, get us camera feeds, find out what the hell is going on out there?"

"That's a negative, boss," Schaz replied. "Their networks are firewalled to high heaven."

"Right." Jane approached the control panel—didn't bother punching in numbers, just pulled out her knife and jimmied it open instead, to get access to its guts. She put the blade away, then started digging into the wiring, turning only for a moment to tell me: "Get ready for anything to come through that door."

I nodded, beginning to pull teke energy into myself. "Can I go back inside Schaz, get Bitey?" I asked.

She shook her head, still crossing wires and attaching things to other things that theoretically shouldn't be attached. Look, what do you want, I've already *said* I don't know much about electrical engineering. "We don't *know* that the natives aren't around; they might just be busy," she said. "They'll expect us to wear pistols; rifles would be seen as a declaration of . . . ill intent."

"Jane, you see that, just like I do." I nodded at the bloodstain. "That doesn't say 'busy' to me, that says 'not capable of much at all.' It says 'very bad things have happened here.'" I stepped closer, touched the blood. Still wet. "Very recently."

"Just get ready." She crossed one more wire, and the door slid open.

I was usually happy to be right. This wasn't one of those times.

Half a dozen corpses lay in the access hallway. They had been butchered, the strange, flowing robes they were wearing stained and heavy with the blood of several different species. Many of the bodies had been burnt as well; the heads, specifically. Specifically, and very purposefully. It was as if whoever had done this had torn them apart, then approached each body, one by one, and scorched their faces right the fuck off.

I let the teke pulse subside, and drew one of my pistols instead. Jane did the same thing. "Schaz?" she said into her comms. "Can you get us a route to the central core of Charon?"

"Can do; I've collected mapping data on Valkyrie Rock from your prior visits here. Feeding the information to your HUD." I couldn't see anything, of course, but Jane started forward, moving like she had a purpose—Schaz was already showing her the data.

"Where are we going?" I asked, stepping over the bodies.

"Plan B," Jane told me. "If we can get to the core of the AI running the station, we can reprogram him." Her eyes were darting back and forth as we approached an intersection in the tunnel, scanning for a threat. "Give ourselves administrative access—cameras, door controls, power, the works. That way, we can figure out what *exactly* is going on here, and maybe isolate our . . . friend." We were moving past corpses; "friend" wasn't the word I would have used.

"We're going to brainwash the station AI." For some reason, that made me feel queasy.

"We're going to flip a switch," Jane replied. "We won't change anything else." She peered down the corridors at the intersection, in both directions; more bodies, either way. "Not that he's going to have a lot of use left in him after this, anyway. What's an AI with nothing to serve?"

It was a rhetorical question, but Schaz answered anyway, her voice chilling in its certainty. Or maybe that was just the bodies, making me jumpy. "A ghost," she said, her tone matter-of-fact.

"Thanks, Schaz," I said sourly.

We followed Jane's route into the twisting maze of tunnels, our weapons raised. More bodies, all of them faceless. At least some of them had tried to fight, had weapons lying beside them, shell casings as well. But none of the dead had been killed by bullets. However it was that the glowing monster in the fancy exosuit killed, it wasn't with ballistic firearms.

We'd known his ship might be faster than ours—that he might have arrived in-system hours ahead of us, maybe even half a day or so. But this—this *level* of bloodshed, of combat: it still took *time*. We'd been right on his tail when he'd left Kandriad—this had happened *fast*. Which maybe explained the lack of any sort of alarms. Still, I couldn't wrap my head around how it could have happened so quickly—a whole platoon of soldiers couldn't have left this much carnage in their wake, not in just a few hours.

Unless he was just really, *really* good at carnage.

We came to a more open section of the tunnels, the stone walls spiraling out, high enough to allow several different levels, with catwalks and metal stairs accessing what seemed to be storefronts and apartments on the higher elevations. Just a regular main street, for a death-obsessed cult living on an asteroid in a nebula in the middle of nowhere.

The corpses here had been piled high in the center of the thoroughfare, and burned. The stench was awful. The floor was matted with blood, where the bodies had been dragged from where they fell and tossed onto the bonfire. I'd thought what we'd seen on Kandriad, on the front lines, had been brutal, but it was nothing compared to this.

Whatever strangeness these people had believed in—whatever it was that had driven them out here, to try and stake their claim on a forgotten corner of the galaxy where they could practice their weird shared delusion untouched by the rest of the universe—they hadn't deserved this. No one deserved this. It was tantamount to genocide, wiping an entire belief system out of existence and for . . . *what*?

I had the sinking feeling that it had nothing to do with their beliefs, no different than the carnage on Kandriad that the asshole had exploited, using a war he didn't care about to try and achieve his own goals. Whatever this was, it didn't feel like tactics, like something to do with resources or intelligence gathering or any kind of strategy—it was something *else*, and the people here had just been in the way. Collateral damage.

No different than Sho's mother.

But why the burning? Why the . . . ritual, the debasement? Nothing about it made sense, didn't *fit* into any logic I could summon. It felt like an act of madness.

And we were intent on chasing down that act's executor, deeper in the tunnels of the dead.

That would make us the hunter's *actual* prey. Not a comforting thought.

We moved up to the higher levels of the promenade—another one of Jane's maxims, "always claim the high ground"—and tried not to gag on the lingering smoke from the still-smoldering bodies. We covered each recess in the rock walls as we moved past, the homes and shops where the people butchered in the center of the street had gone about their lives; it was impossible not to notice the bloodstains on the floors, or the smashed-apart doorframes. The thing in the armor had been methodical in his carnage, *precise*, bashing into apartments or shops one by one after he'd taken out those in the main thoroughfare, not *just* killing those in his path, but also hunting down anyone trying to hide from the slaughter.

Like he'd tried to hunt us down, on the train.

"Tell me we're not far now," I asked Jane—almost begged her—as we passed by the corpses themselves, piled high enough that even from the upper level we could still see them rise above the railing of the catwalk. I could have reached out and touched the topmost bodies, blackened and twisted by the heat of the fires. I did not.

Jane consulted her HUD. "We have to cut through a maintenance section, and then we're there," she said. I could tell by her voice she didn't want to hang around here any longer than we had to.

I couldn't blame her.

CHAPTER 10

We cut into the maintenance access tunnels, the walls bare rock supported here and there by girders; this part of the station looked like the actual mine it used to be. Thankfully, it had also apparently been somewhat disused, so it didn't look like the abattoir that the rest of Valkyrie Rock had been turned into.

"Are we going to talk about what we saw back there?" I asked Jane as we made our way through the dimly lit chambers, passing strange designs carved or painted on the bare walls. The mining tunnels continued to alternate between barely touched rock, the natural interior of the asteroid, and the occasional piece of massive tech jutting from the stone, the guts of the machinery that kept the station alive.

"Do we need to?" Jane grunted, pausing at a split in the tunnels. "It's this way."

"The thing that did all this—"

"It's no different from what he did to the factory city. Just on a . . . smaller scale."

"*God*, Jane." Sometimes I forgot how callous she could be. "The people here—"

"If there's anyone left alive on this station, Esa, the only way to *help* them is going to be reaching the AI core and tracking down that motherfucker ourselves." Her voice was almost brittle as she said it, the rage I'd missed earlier—when I'd been thinking she was callous—leaking out around the edges of her words. "So we need to move, we need to—here." She stopped in front of a sealed metal door, incongruous among the rough-hewn rock around us. Again, she jimmied open a control panel, started digging around inside.

I kept watch, trying to alternate between staring back the way we'd come, and down the corridor that lay ahead of us. In a relatively short time—but not as quickly as I would have liked—Jane had the door open; we stepped into a room full of blinking computer systems, rows and rows of data banks. The core of the AI that ran the station; Charon's brain.

"Do you actually know what you're doing?" I hissed at Jane; keeping my voice low just felt like something I should do in here. I wondered if Charon could feel us, trespassing inside his mind like a headache.

"Sure. This isn't the first time I've needed to . . . *convince* an AI to let me access something it didn't want me to." She made a beeline toward a control panel that, to me, looked like all the *rest* of the control panels; she started typing. I stuck my head back outside—still nothing moving, in either direction.

"And we're done," Jane said, stepping away from the console. That had been fast. She paused, then spoke, not to Charon, but to Schaz: "You've got administrative privilege within Charon's systems now," she told our ship. "Can you patch into camera feeds, tell us exactly what's going on in the rest of the station?"

"Can do, boss," Schaz replied. "Let's see: oh. Oh, no."

"You found the glowing guy with the fuck-off armor?"

"I found the glowing guy with the fuck-off armor. He's looking for you two. His ship's docked on the far side of the asteroid from my berth—it looks like he was inside, doing god knows what, but he just came back *out*. He must have had some sort of . . . digital tripwire, rigged up on an access point—we triggered it when I accessed admin status."

"Which means he knows we gave ourselves that status manually," Jane swore. "Which means he knows where we *are*."

"Isn't that what we *wanted*?" I asked, my voice . . . weaker than I would have liked. I wasn't exactly sure it was what *I* wanted, not after seeing the damage he'd left in his wake.

"We wanted to set a trap for him," Jane growled. "That's harder to do when he's busy setting one for *us*."

"He's heading back through the main thoroughfare," Schaz reported. "You need to get out of there, and *not* back the way you came."

Jane paused, thinking. "Does he have administrative privileges as well?" she asked. A good question—if he'd set up some sort of alarm system in Charon's databanks, he might have tried to pull the same trick we had.

"No," Schaz reported succinctly. "I'm listed as the only 'living' administrator on the station."

"How many other 'living' station occupants are there?" I asked.

Schaz paused. "Three," she said.

Jane; myself; the asshole. He'd actually done it. He'd fucking murdered *everyone* on board the asteroid. Hundreds dead, maybe thousands, in just a few hours' time.

Jane shook her head, swallowing back her own horror at the carnage. "Classify him as a threat," she told Schaz.

"Charon's already done that. I'm reviewing the files now; nothing he threw at the bastard worked. Jane—he's had something of a . . . Protecting the people in this station was his only priority. He failed to protect the people of this station. He's well on his way to a serious algorithmic crack."

Jane swore, sulfurously. I didn't know what the hell any of that meant, but it sounded . . . very bad. Being stuck in this station of the dead—the term now significantly more literal than I thought it would be on our approach—with the armored guy hunting us was bad enough; being stuck in this station of the dead with the armored guy hunting us *and* the system AI losing its mind sounded even worse.

She turned and looked at me, raised an eyebrow. "Well?" she asked.

"Well, what?" I didn't know what the hell she wanted from me.

"I'm asking you for ideas."

Well, she didn't do that very often; not a good sign. I thought it through, shook my head. "Direct combat's right out. After what he's done here, and how appreciatively outclassed we were back on Kandriad . . . it's a no go."

"I could rig up the fusion reactor, blow the station."

"Why do you always want to solve things with *explosions*?" I hissed. "How will that solve *anything*?"

"I'm just reminding you of my skill set."

"I know what your skill set is, it's not—" I paused at that, the phrase tripping something in the back of my mind.

"What?" she asked, keeping the rising tension she must have felt—that we *both* were feeling—out of her voice, but only barely.

"'*Don't* fight an enemy until you know their full skill set, not if you can help it.' You taught me that."

"And?" she asked, not doing such a great job holding back the impatience in her voice now.

"Whatever you two are doing," Schaz interjected, "do it faster. He's got your scent—he's headed into the maintenance tunnels. He . . . doesn't look pleased. Or maybe he does. His mask is damaged, and his face is made out of *fire*, just like the rest of him; his facial expressions are . . . hard to read. It doesn't look *good*, that's what I'm saying."

I ignored Scheherazade for now; I already *knew* what was breathing down the backs of our necks, thank you very much. "If we just keep going at him head on," I told Jane, working it out in my head even as I said it, "the only way we learn more about him is when he *hits* us with something new, and ultimately, he'll hit us with something we won't be able to bounce back from, because we didn't see it coming."

"That's . . . what the maxim means, yes."

"So we *need to see it coming*. We need to know what he's got up his armored sleeves. We've got administrative access," I reminded Jane, reaching up to toggle the "mute" on my comms, and gesturing for her to do the same. Frowning, she did so. "Schaz does, at any rate. She can lock the station down, she can *fry* any local ships in the docking bay; they'll be hardwired into Charon already, the same way she patches into John Henry back at Sanctum."

"You don't want to take him on at all." Jane was finally putting it together. "You want to trap him. To turn the whole *asteroid* into a trap."

"And slam the door shut behind us," I nodded. "And in order to do that— to beach him here, without a way *off* this rock—we've got to get to *his* ship."

Jane blinked at me, piecing my plan together, such as it was. "We lead him on a merry chase through the station, slowly working our way toward whatever docking bay that weird craft of his is sitting in."

"Which should buy Schaz time enough to fry out the drive core of every ship connected to Charon," I added.

Jane nodded slowly, still working over my plan in her head. "We break into his ship—should be doable, with Schaz's admin privileges—and see if we can't access his databanks, find out *who* and *what* he is, what he wants. Learn whatever weaknesses we can."

I nodded. "And then, you know: we fuck it right up. Maybe plant a bomb or something. Because fuck this guy. If we can take out his *ship*, it doesn't matter how unkillable *he* is—with the local craft grounded, he'll be stuck here. Then *we* bug out, get somewhere we can get a message to Sanctum, rally the troops, come back with everyone. Like . . . *everyone*. Javier and Marus and the Preacher and Criat and Sahluk and as many combat-trained personnel as we can fit on board our ships; hell, even MelWill will want to poke at this son of a bitch. For a cure for the pulse? The whole of the Justified will turn out to take him on." And in the meantime, he'd be stranded here with only the corpses of the people he'd butchered for company. I saw a bit of poetry in that. Grisly, grisly poetry.

"That just might work," Jane nodded slowly. "We can do even better than that—Schaz can program a broadcast, a quarantine warning or something. Warn off anyone who might get close, so we don't risk some poor bastards stopping in for repairs or something, then getting their ship hijacked and letting the bastard loose."

"You two *really* need to get moving," Schaz put in again; she couldn't hear what we were discussing, not with our comms muted, but she could still *see* us through Charon's cameras. "Get moving now."

"So we're doing it?" I asked Jane. I hoped so—I was fairly proud of the plan. Plus, you know, it didn't involve us actually *fighting* the son of a bitch, so I was happy about *that*, too.

"Not quite. *You're* doing it."

"What?"

"We won't be able to spend enough time on his ship to learn anything— let alone to spite the fucking thing—if he's breathing down our necks. *You're* going to find his ship. Schaz can guide you through tunnels over the comms."

I shook my head. "He has access to our comm channels." That's why I'd muted them in the first place. "Remember? On Kandriad? He broke our encryption without even *trying*; if Schaz tries—"

"Have a little faith, kid." Jane turned back to the console in front of her, typing a flurry of commands in; keying Schaz in on our plan, without broadcasting the information where our enemy could hear it. "Schaz will guide you, but she *won't* say anything about your destination. 'Left right left right straight' will just be soup to this asshole. Besides—he's going to be busy."

I moaned, very softly. "You're not," I said.

She nodded. "Somebody's got to keep him occupied, buy you time—you and Schaz both, you to get to his craft, her to spite the local vessels. I'll engage him, then fade. A running fight. Lead him on a merry chase, one that'll loop me right back to Scheherazade."

"Jane, this guy is—just *look* what he's done around here."

"I'm not some death-obsessed cultist, Esa; I'm not afraid of demons." She raised her revolver; checked that each chamber was loaded, which, of course, they were. "Go. Get moving; get moving now." She stepped to the door, her weapon raised. I followed her through, still hating this plan. She reached out and squeezed my shoulder. "You've got this," she told me.

"Don't you fucking die on me," I swore at her.

"I'll do my best."

"I want better than that; I want a promise."

"Kid, what did I tell you?"

I sighed. "You don't make promises you aren't sure you can keep."

"Stay safe—I'll do my damnedest to do the same. That's the best I can do. Now get going. I've got a date with a motherfucker in armored plating." She was actually *grinning* as she turned her focus back to the corridor that led back to the main thoroughfare, the route we'd taken in. Somewhere between here and there was the asshole hunting us, and Jane was actually *pleased* she was going to get to fight him again, even after the fact that it had taken Schaz hitting the bastard with a ship-to-ship laser blast to put him down the last time.

No matter how much she trained me, no matter how much combat I saw: I didn't think I'd ever get to *that*.

I reached out to touch her—just on her arm, just to remind myself that she was *there*, so that if the unthinkable did happen, I would at least remember doing that—and then I turned, and I ran.

Deeper into the tunnels carved straight through Valkyrie Rock.

CHAPTER 11

I ran in silence through the endless-seeming tunnel system that criss-crossed the interior of the asteroid like arteries through a body. Everything was so still that just the sounds of my labored breathing and the pounding of my heartbeat were deafening in my ears. The rock walls around me seemed unchanging, repeating: the same twisting designs, the same abandoned heavy machinery, the same stripped-out veins of ore. I didn't even need directions from Scheherazade: so far, there was only one way through.

I was almost *glad* to have the silence broken when I heard Jane's voice in my ear, until I realized *why* she was talking. "Hey, fuckstick!" she shouted. "I think I'm a little tired of your attentions. You want something from me, why don't you try asking politely?"

I couldn't hear whatever response he made—if he made a response at all—but I did hear Jane's reply: it came as I entered a chamber unlike any I'd seen before, endless rows of metal racks holding pans of foul-smelling algae. Must have been what the former inhabitants of the asteroid ate for breakfast, lunch, and dinner. "I don't give a damn about what *you* want, you ugly son of a bitch," Jane said. "In fact, I—" Whatever threat or insult she might have issued was drowned out by the roar of a gunshot. That might have meant her enemy had attacked, and she was answering; it might have just meant she shot first, trying to catch him off guard by breaking into her own sentence with a sharp piece of violence.

"Left, then down a ladder," Schaz told me; I veered between the racks of algae, and I could see the ladder she'd mentioned, sticking up out of a hole in the rock floor.

"Well that was *rude*," Jane said, and there was something in her voice I didn't like—something that might have been fear, or pain. "I'll tell you what, why don't we just—" Another gunshot; it seemed to echo as I began my descent, the tight confines of the rock brushing against my shoulders.

"At the bottom of the ladder, go right, then keep moving straight through the next chamber."

"Got it," I answered, forgetting for a moment that *my* comms were muted, that Schaz couldn't hear me.

"*Fuck* you, and *fuck* whatever you might call a mother, and take your fucking *crusade* and your fucking *genocidal tendencies* and you fuck them *both* with a—" Jane's tirade cut off in mid-flow, and there wasn't an answering gunshot this time; I felt fear bloom up through my chest as I hit the bottom of the ladder. Very little could stop Jane in mid-insult.

The corridors were tighter down here; good thing I wasn't claustrophobic. I was on the shortish side, and I still had to stoop—that put me at eye level with a strange maxim, carved into the rock: "Those who await redemption lie beyond." What the fuck did *that* mean?

Still, it was my route; I pressed forward. Still nothing else from Jane. In desperation, I unmuted my comms. "Schaz, what's happening?" I asked.

"Jane's taken the fight into the reactor chamber; it's unshielded, and the radiation is interfering with her comms," Schaz told me. "Don't worry, she's all right. I think. There aren't any cameras in that room." She sighed. "I'm going to have to decontaminate her *all over again* when she gets—"

Another voice boomed out, not just through the comms, but through the speakers built into the girders inches from my head: "*Ad infirmum purificatorio!*" Charon, screaming the words throughout the entire asteroid.

"Oh, dear," Schaz murmured.

"What the—what's going on? Did that AI just shout something in a dead language? *Why does the AI speak a dead language?*"

"Because it was programmed to, dear," Schaz replied mildly. "Charon just vented the reactor's excess heat in the general direction of Jane's adversary. Don't worry about Jane—she should be all right, I've coded Charon to make her survival a priority. Just concentrate on where you're going. You should be about to reach—"

"Oh, you've got to be *fucking kidding me.*" A moment ago, I would have given anything for the tunnel I was in to widen out again—despite my aforementioned lack of claustrophobia, I had been growing more and more unhappy about the ever-tightening passage. Now that it *had* opened up, I would have given anything to crawl back into the confines of the tunnel.

"Yes. That." Schaz said. It took me a moment to force my hand to work, but I managed to reach up and mute my comms, a singular act of bravery, in my opinion. I didn't need Schaz—or Jane, or our pursuer—to hear the noises of sheer terror I was about to make.

"Those who await redemption," my ass. The chamber before me was packed full of the cultists' *dead*. They'd left redemption behind a good long while ago.

The corpses were stuffed into alcoves carved into the rock; they were stacked like cordwood up on the floors; they hung from the ceilings on chains. They'd all been preserved somehow—the smell was intense, but it wasn't decay, something else, drier and more chemical. These weren't mining tunnels any longer—they were catacombs.

Because *of course* a people obsessed with death wouldn't just consign their dead to the void around them like anyone else would. Of course they'd make some kind of *maze of dead bodies* the very heart of their asteroid. And *of course* the path I'd need to take led right through the middle of said maze. That was just . . . that was just how things worked.

If I survived long enough, I wondered if this moment would be my very own "sinking of the *Ishiguro*," a story to drunkenly regale some green recruit with after I'd tied on half a dozen too many and decided to regurgitate my private nightmares all over everyone in earshot. Then I decided I'd be perfectly happy if that were true—because it meant I'd *lived* through this.

I was *not* going to enjoy the next twenty minutes or so. I started forward anyway, pushing my way into the tight corridors lined on either side with corpses.

They were dead; they weren't going to wake up. They were *dead*; they weren't going to wake up. None of the hands I kept brushing up against were going to reach out and grab me; none of their eyes were suddenly going to pop open, a precursor to the army of corpses around me lurching into motion. None of their sunken chest cavities were going to suddenly swell into breath as the dead came back to life, just long enough to attempt dragging me to my own place among their number. Why would they, that would be stupid: the dead didn't need to breathe, they'd just reach for me without even *that much warning.*

Stop it. Stop it. They were dead; they weren't going to wake up.

No matter how much I told myself that, it still seemed almost a guarantee that they *would.* As I pushed my way past the limbs hanging free of the alcoves and ducked under the hanging bodies, I let out a series of tiny yelps and muted curses. It didn't get any better when I passed through what must have been the exact center of the asteroid, and gravity got *weird* for a bit; I was suddenly climbing where I should have been falling, jumping where I should have been crouching, using the alcoves as handholds and crawling over the corpses themselves when "down" suddenly became "sideways," and then "up." Some of the bodies were floating. I did not enjoy that, either.

Finally gravity got its shit together again, and a little ways past that point I saw the exit, another small tunnel, hopefully leading back to another ladder and up the other side. Halfway through Valkyrie Rock; the armored asshole's ship was somewhere above me, in another docking bay, the same as the one Schaz had set down in.

Still no word from Jane.

CHAPTER 12

After the catacombs, the rest of my passage through the bowels of the asteroid was a comparative breeze. Still no word from Jane, though. No more creepy broadcasts in dead languages from Charon, either. Every once in a while I could *feel* tremors through the rock around me, but I didn't know if they were from the normal operation of the machinery that kept (*had* kept) the cultists alive, or if they were reverberations from Jane's fight with the . . . whatever the hell he was, starting to take a toll on the stone itself.

I emerged from the maintenance tunnels in a thoroughfare remarkably similar to the one Jane and I had left behind, only this one was lacking the macabre sight of a stack of bodies turned into a bonfire, a fact for which I was profoundly grateful. "Left," said Schaz, and I obediently turned, making my way toward another docking bay.

"Any word from Jane?" I asked.

"Nothing," she said, and I could tell by the silence that she was just as worried as I was.

More bloodstains in the tunnel leading to the bay; no bodies, though there were shell casings strewn across the floor, burn marks on the walls—the cultists had tried to put up a fight here, presumably when our pursuer had forced his way through the quarantine doors on the docking bay where his ship had set down.

The carnage, the bloodshed—I still couldn't wrap my head around it. What was the *point?* Even if he just wanted to cover his tracks, to leave no witnesses to his passage, he could have set the fusion reactor to blow, just like the bomb he'd set off on Kandriad—why the wholesale slaughter? The cultists hadn't posed a threat; I wasn't sure anything could, not after what we'd seen him shrug off.

The only reasoning I could come up with was one that didn't help much with the cold shivers of fear creeping down my spine: he had *wanted* to do it. He enjoyed it. Reveled in the violence, in the death.

The only person in the galaxy who might hold the key to staving off the pulse, and he was a goddamned maniac.

Didn't matter. I was about to reach his ship, and I was going to cobble together a bomb out of spare parts lying around the bay—Schaz had already used her camera access to figure out how I could do that—and then I was going to blow said ship to kingdom come, and he could contemplate his mass-murdering ways stuck on this rock for however long it took us to rally the troops. After that, he'd be the Justified high council's problem to handle—they could decide his fate.

I passed through the blown-inward docking bay doors, and . . . yeah. That ship didn't get any prettier up close. It was knobbly and distended, weirdly *thin* in some places and bulging in others. The metallic sheen of its strange shielding gave off a kind of hum under the fluorescent lights of the bay; if it hadn't been for the landing struts and the boarding ramp—thankfully, already lowered, likely in his haste to hunt us down—I might have mistaken the thing for some odd metallic comet the cultists had hauled in for study from the nebula around them.

I tried to ignore the ship, sitting like a cancer in the middle of the bay; I worked to build the bomb instead, following Schaz's terse instructions. We still didn't want to give away what we were doing over the comms, so her commands were less "Wire this part into that part, then attach this thing to the other thing" than they were "There. Turn that. That's upside down. No, no, no, no, *right*." It didn't help that being alone in a docking bay with the ship of a monster who was currently doing his damnedest to kill Jane was not exactly doing wonders for my nerves; my hands weren't quite shaking, but they weren't the steadiest things in the world, either.

Finally, the bomb was done, clutched under my arm like a child's toy as I stood at the bottom of the ramp. I took a deep breath, tried to calm my racing pulse. Just ascending into a mass murderer's ship. Whatever was inside, it couldn't be worse than the catacombs I'd already passed through, could it?

Yes. Yes, it most certainly could.

It didn't *seem* too terrible at first—the interior was more of that strange metallic coating, and it was all very . . . *rounded*, no edges here, there, or anywhere, but at least it wasn't decorated by stretched-out, carved-off flesh or anything. It wasn't decorated by *anything*, actually; Jane and I kept Scheherazade relatively spartan, but compared to this, we were decor-obsessed socialites with a deep-seated need to impress anyone who stepped into our home.

That just made it easier to notice the cage, and the body held inside.

It was the only piece of furniture in the living quarters—though "furniture" seemed a woefully inadequate word for bars of cold steel meant for locking up a captive, no cot, no pillow, not even a toilet inside. The corpse was smallish, dressed in the same flowing robes I'd seen on the cultist corpses earlier; even as I approached, I knew what I was going to find.

It was a child—a teenager. A Vyriat, younger than me, about Sho's age—and like the handful of Vyriat peers I knew from Sanctum, her facial tendrils had a green-gold mottling around their base, the hydrostatic muscle groups developing a kind of secondary mutation in the presence of pulse radiation.

She'd been gifted.

Vyriat were the only known species to develop a visual mutation in response to a child being changed by the pulse; in that sense, I was . . . lucky. Lucky I now *knew* why he'd taken her, why he'd been on Kandriad—he was doing the same thing we were, like some fucked-up inversion of the Justified. He was hunting gifted children.

His presence on Kandriad had been about Sho after all. I hoped I wouldn't have to be the one to tell the young Wulf pup that.

I knelt beside the cage, reached in to close the Vyriat's staring eyes. It looked like the thing in the armor had locked her inside, then left her here when we'd triggered his tripwire—she'd been alive, not long ago, was still warm. If only I'd moved *faster*, I could have saved her—it hadn't been the creature hunting us that had killed her at all.

She'd done that herself, with a piece of her robe. Facing abduction at the hands of the . . . thing that had cut his way through the ranks of her friends and family, that had massacred his way through her home, she'd chosen to end her own life rather than learn where he was taking her. I couldn't blame her for it. But god, if only she'd *waited*; how close had I been when she'd made the decision to do this?

I stood up from the cage, a terrible rage burning inside me; I don't know why this was somehow worse than seeing the factory city on Kandriad go up in flames, than seeing all the dead in the halls outside, but it *was*, all the same. Maybe even worse than Sho's mother, making the decision to trust us with her child, knowing she likely wouldn't survive the attack that was coming. She, at least, had died with the hope that her son had escaped: this girl had no such respite in her last moments. She'd died afraid.

The thing in the armor was taking gifted children, *using* them somehow, and felt no compunctions against murdering his way through their families to get to them. Whatever we had to do to him to learn his secrets, to learn how he dispersed the pulse radiation: I was suddenly fine with it. Even if it was painful.

A part of me *hoped* it would be.

I turned away from the dead Vyriat girl—nothing I could do to help her now—and gave the living quarters another cursory look: if I wanted to *get* the thing into the not-so-gentle hands of Justified interrogators, I had a job to do. There was nothing else noteworthy in this part of this ship, so, nursing the low-burning coals of my rage, I made my way to the cockpit.

Same thing there, at least as far as the strange architecture was concerned. More of a "mild depression in the otherwise raised contours of the floor" than a "helm": no flight stick, no pedals or throttle lever or Jane's beloved bank of switches above a pilot's head—just a handful of alcoves in the rocky metallic surface of the ship that seemed to glow faintly when I *wasn't* looking at them.

This place was fucking *weird*.

I was just about to turn and retreat from the cockpit when I saw it: in the glass of the canopy, staring directly *at* me, was the snarling steel face of the creepy motherfucker that had locked the girl in the cage. I actually *felt* my heart skip a beat, and damn near dropped the bomb clutched under my arm; for a moment I was sure that he'd evaded Jane, that he was right outside the cockpit and staring in through the window, and I was going to be trapped on board his ship with him about to come *in*.

Then I realized if that was the case he'd have to be floating, because the canopy was easily twenty feet off the docking bay floor. It wasn't the glowing *thing* staring at me at all—it was just another one of his masks, or rather, the reflection of one in the glass of the canopy, the mask itself mounted behind me, on the cockpit wall just beside the airlock, as if in a place of veneration.

I turned to face it, trying to glare away my fear; the mask just glared right back. Why the hell would he mount it *behind* him in the cockpit? Why wouldn't it be in the living quarters, presumably wherever he kept the rest of his armor? Had he been wearing a mask when he murdered everyone on the asteroid? What did that make this one—his replacement mask? Evil asshole formalwear?

Nothing about this ship made sense. Nothing about this *guy* made sense, if he was a guy at all. The voice over the comms had been vaguely masculine— that was about all I knew.

More to stop the creepy thing from staring at me than anything else, I reached up and detached it from the wall—it gave a slight hydraulic hiss as I did so, and I *really* hoped that didn't mean I'd just set off some alarm system in the rest of his armor, warning him that someone was inside his ship, fucking with his second-best mask. I tucked the terrifying visage into my pouch and backed out of the airlock; Schaz could scan it later, maybe tell us *something* we didn't know.

Okay: where else to check? I made my way back through the living quarters, past the cage with the Vyriat girl inside, then headed aft of the boarding ramp instead, trying to find the ship's drive core, which I wasn't sure I would even—

I found the ship's drive core.

I would say it *didn't* look like any drive core I'd ever seen, but only because I'd only seen a handful of drive cores; even Schaz's was built behind multiple layers of decking, accessible through the hold only in a dire emergency. The few I *had* laid eyes on had just been glowing columns of light surrounded by various important-looking machinery; this one was a kind of *orb* instead, not feeding into anything, just . . . floating, hovering in between spherical depressions in the ceiling above and the floor below.

"You're recording this, right?" I breathed to Schaz. If nothing else, I would bet that MelWill back on Sanctum would love to get her hands on a record of what I'd seen in here, so she could go through the vids millisecond by millisecond and devour the strange tech around the core. And since I was planning on blowing the damn thing to *pieces*, it's not like she could study it when we returned for our captive, either.

"You bet your ass I am," Schaz said. I didn't have a HUD, but my basic gear package was studded with a handful of cameras that Scheherazade could access and download footage from later. Ordinarily I would have been feeding her footage wirelessly as well—we were in range to do so—but if the thing hunting us had hacked our comms, we couldn't risk him being able to access that feed, too.

"Do you see anything?" Schaz asked me, since she couldn't see for herself.

I saw a lot of shit, none of which made sense.

Wait. There.

Another object that didn't make sense, but in a different way, as alien to its surroundings as its surroundings were to everything else.

It was a wonder I hadn't seen it before—well, okay, maybe it wasn't, I'd been too busy staring at the floating orb of fire to notice anything else—but it *did* kind of stand out. Everything else on the ship had those rounded edges, was made of the same metallic material as the ship's coating; the only exception to the rule had been the cage, basic iron bars sort of *melded* into the strange material of the bulkheads. This was the same way: *most of it* was just a computer access port, no different than a thousand others I'd seen on any non-pulsed world, until the wires were sucked into the walls of the hull like the metal had been melted around them.

So: what the hell did *this* mean? He'd set the tripwire in Charon's systems, so he was plenty capable of interfacing with traditional technology—did this mean he had accomplices, people who'd need to use more traditional data storages than . . . than . . . than however the *fuck* he stored information otherwise?

Worry about it later. I dug a remote storage drive out of my pockets, then tapped one of the cameras, the one on my shoulder; I had to risk triggering the feeds so Schaz could take over: I sure as hell didn't know how to download data from . . . wherever the hell those wires led. Hopefully Jane was keeping our pursuer busy enough that he wouldn't notice the new signal. Hopefully Jane was *alive* to keep him busy.

I held the drive up to the camera transmitting to Schaz; the tiny pinprick of light on the exterior of the plastic clicked to green. Schaz had a wireless signal—she was operating the drive now. I plugged the device into the port, then poked around for someplace to set the bomb.

We didn't have the time or the materials to make any sort of wireless receiver or timer, so we'd decided on a dead man's switch instead; I settled for resting the explosive right up against the core, then held the trigger depressed with my teke as I backed away slowly. I waited a tense moment for the light on the wireless drive to click over to green again—finished downloading—then bent to retrieve the device and booked it the hell out of the ship. At least this way, the Vyriat girl would get one hell of a funeral pyre.

I didn't actually know what the range limits of my telekinesis were. It seemed like we were about to find out.

CHAPTER 13

I felt my teke start to slip as I passed through the doors to the docking bay; I started running after that. Once the switch triggered, I'd still have a few moments as the chemical mixture that made up the bomb started to combine—of course, given how terse Schaz had been forced to be over the comms, I didn't know if those moments would last ten minutes or ten sec—

The blast picked me up and *threw* me against the far wall, my intention shield absorbing the impacts from the half a dozen pieces of shrapnel that had come whistling down the corridor like bullets made of razors. I hit, hard, then hit again as I landed.

Ow. Being that close to an explosion *sucked*.

"That didn't look fun," Schaz commiserated as I tried to pick myself up, and failed. Maybe just another moment, lying on the floor, gasping for breath.

"Oh, no, it was grand," I wheezed back. "You should try it sometime."

"I do it *all* the time, remember? Remember all the space battles we've been in?"

"Oh. Right."

"I'm just saying—the *next* time you prioritize some distant target rather than an incoming missile, arguing that 'Schaz's shields can take it,' I want you to *remember* this moment. Remember how much it rattled you, and how hard it was to think, after. Fair deal?"

I exhaled something that most definitely weren't actual words, just a kind of wheeze.

"Fair deal," Schaz agreed, mostly to herself. In the process of making obscene gestures in the general direction of her docking bay, I at least managed to get to my knees.

My comm crackled to life. "Esa, was that blast what I think it was?" Jane asked. Thank god—she was alive.

"Where the hell have you *been*?" I coughed, using the wall behind me to lean against as I tried to stand. "And also, yes."

"I didn't want to give away my position by using the comms; he's been chasing me all across this asteroid. Schaz, double check, but the route from her position to you along the main thoroughfare *should* be clear; as soon as he heard that blast, the asshole booked it toward the tunnels, so he's coming at her from the interior."

"Clear," Schaz agreed tersely—she must have been scanning her feeds, looking for the glowing bastard, but the cameras were patchier in the maintenance tunnels, as I well knew.

"What . . . what does all that *mean*?" I asked, still a little fuzzy from the "mostly being blown up" that had just happened.

"It means *run*," Jane growled; I could tell from the way she clipped her sentences that she was already doing the same.

Starting a full-out run from a dead stop is hard enough—starting a full-out run from a dead stop after you've just suffered a mild *being blown up* is not one of my favorite things in the world, as I was just learning. I did it anyway.

The lights in the tunnels were shutting off behind me, one by one, leaving a sea of darkness in my wake. I didn't know if Charon was doing that, or if it was something else; I just kept running. Every step I took, another shadow fell across the floor before me. And somewhere in the deep center of the asteroid—maybe passing through the catacombs even now—our enemy was coming.

If he knew that I'd just blown up his ship, he was probably going to be *pissed*. If he'd figured out we'd fried all the *other* ships on board the station, trapping him here once we escaped, he was going to be even more so. That thought gave me a savage kind of joy—a petty vengeance in the face of all he'd done, but fulfilling, even so—and it helped to push my speed up just a little bit higher. How much farther was it, anyway? How much farther—

I saw Jane, pelting down the corridor toward me; she'd passed the entrance to Scheherazade's docking bay, trying to reach me before our pursuer did. I grinned when I saw her—put on just a *little* more speed.

That may have saved my life.

Jane slowed to a stop, drawing her pistol and firing in a single fluid motion; I saw her do it and just *reacted*, threw myself into a slide just as a sizzling bolt of energy sang over my head, right through the place where I had been, close enough that the passage of ionized atmosphere made the fine hairs on my arm stand on end.

I couldn't help myself: as I came to a stop, I turned.

Our enemy had shed his armor somewhere along the way—or Jane had torn it off him, piece by piece. Now, he was just a shining, glowing figure, a being made purely from azure fire. Four limbs, a chest, a head, but beyond that, nothing: a terrifying spectre of energy and flame, his face like a void.

And he was closing the distance.

Jane was still firing, but her rounds weren't doing any more good than they had when he'd been wearing armor—I actually saw one of the bullets get close and vanish in a burst of sparks and metal shards; he was *melting* the rounds before they hit—and he was still stalking forward, his hands out at his sides, light spilling between his fingers, glowing brighter.

"*You cannot silence the coming scream,*" he growled, the words seeming to come from everywhere and nowhere—because they were *still* coming from my comm, despite the fact that he was close enough that I should have been able to just hear him. He wasn't *speaking* at all, just . . . transmitting. "*You cannot escape the fire, nor the fall. Purification is your destiny. Purification is the destiny of*—"

"*Go!*" Jane shouted at me, emptying the chambers of her revolver of dead casings and slipping a new cartridge in even as the cylinder spun. It was a fancy trick, and it wasn't going to make a damn bit of difference—her bullets weren't even fazing him.

Except when she aimed next—pulling the hammer on a still-spinning cylinder, five-to-one odds it had stopped on an empty chamber, but this was Jane, there was a bullet under that hammer as sure as I was breathing—she wasn't aiming *at* the stalking figure of blue flame: she fired instead at a transformer clinging to the rock wall between him and us, a transformer that gave off a shower of bright sparks into the darkness when her single bullet smashed it open.

And once she'd damaged it, Charon seized control.

A torrent of blazing energy filled the hallway, making a shield of crackling lightning between us and our enemy, but he'd seen what we were trying to do, and he threw one last attack before the wave of electricity cut off the tunnel—an orb of glowing blue flame that *just* made it past Charon's impromptu electric fence.

It was aimed straight at Jane.

She was flat-footed; even if she'd wanted to dodge, she wouldn't have time. Intention shield raised or not, that much energy would cook her where she stood. I don't know *how* I reacted, but I know *why*—I'd thought I was going to lose her once, and I'd vowed then and there that I'd never risk that again.

So I reached out with my teke, and I *grabbed* at the ball of lightning with my mind.

It was a bad idea.

It was a *horrible* idea.

It wasn't really an *idea* at all, just a thing I did, somewhere in between seeing the projectile of burning energy and tracing its route to its target in an instant. If I'd *had* time to think about it, I never would have done it—my teke functioned as an extension of my brain, just like my *hands* were an extension of my brain. I couldn't manipulate pure energy with telekinesis any more than I could reach into a fire and grab the flame. I did it anyway.

It felt like *burning*. Inside my skull.

I held on. It was aimed at Jane.

I tried to scream; no sound came out, replaced by a whisper of smoke from my nostrils and my throat. I really *was* burning, no different than if I *had* reached out and grabbed the fire—the energy leaping from the projectile to me, tracing the path of my teke back along the same quantum channel I used to control it, trying to fry my mind from the inside out.

With more effort than I'd ever put into anything, *ever*, I *pulled* at the ball of fire, I *yanked* at it, I used every ounce of energy I had to jerk the thing out of position.

I felt it shift, just a little, and then I was collapsing; I was done. I started to pass out.

But just before I did, I saw the ball of circular lightning pass Jane by, just an inch or so to her left. I'd fucking *done* it. It had been monumentally stupid, but I'd done it anyway.

Then the world went to black, and I don't think that was just Charon cutting off the lights.

ACT
THREE

CHAPTER 1

When I finally clawed my way back to consciousness I found Sho staring down at me, his big unblinking eyes amber wells of concern. "How do you feel?" he asked.

I made a kind of whimpering groan as response. I didn't feel quite up to speech just yet. God, everything . . . everything *hurt*. What had happened to make me feel this way again? What had I *done* to myself?

Oh. Right. I'd reached out and grabbed an energy blast carrying enough megajoules to fry something ten times my size. That had been stupid of me. Still—I'd saved Jane. I think.

I tried to sit up; when I failed at that, I settled for looking around instead. I was on board Scheherazade; by the thrum making its way up through the medbay's table, we were in hyperspace. "How long . . ." Hey, I could actually manage speech. Good for me. Granted, I sounded like someone ten times my age—someone ten times my age who had managed to smoke three packs of cigarettes a day—but still. Speech. That was progress.

"Not long." Sho shook his head. "Jane carried you off of the asteroid, strapped you down, then got us out of there. Half an hour or so, no more. When I asked what happened to you, she said you had been very brave. And also monumentally stupid."

"Yeah, that . . . that seems fair."

"Esa—there was smoke coming out of . . . you were *leaking* smoke. Out of your mouth, your nose, your tear ducts. I helped Jane lift you up onto the table; you were *hot* to the touch. Not just warm—scalding."

The use of my gifts was still more "magic" than "science," at least to me, but apparently whatever bond let me reach out and manipulate objects with telekinesis, it was *also* a conductor for energy. Great. I'd *mostly* known that—a few similar experiments back on Sanctum had taught me *not* to try and shield myself from laser fire with my teke, if nothing else—but I'd say I'd just definitely confirmed those suspicions.

"And the asshole?" I rasped.

"As far as we know, still stuck back on Valkyrie Rock," Sho said, before smiling grimly. "I find a certain poetry in that."

"That was the plan." I tried to sit up again, succeeded this time. Yet more progress.

Unfortunately, it also brought me to Jane's attention: as Scheherazade's interior swung into view, I found her glaring at me from the kitchen table. I had not been aware she was sitting nearby, listening in—I'd thought she was in the cockpit. "What the *hell*?" she asked, with no preamble.

"Good to see you survived, Jane," I said, rubbing the back of my neck. Just . . . everything hurt. Every motion, every action, every *breath*. "You're welcome, by the way—"

"Don't give me that bullshit," Jane growled. "You reached out and *grabbed* an energy projectile with your telekinesis. Couldn't you have *guessed* that wouldn't have ended well for you?"

"It would have ended worse for you if I hadn't," I glared back, or tried to, anyway. It was harder when she adamantly refused to stay in focus. "I'm sorry you had to drag me back here *slightly* overcooked, but I figure that's better than me trying to drag your charred *corpse* back on board." I ran a hand over my scalp, and coughed. Honestly, I was a little surprised there wasn't a small puff of smoke when I did.

I didn't think it was possible, but Jane's eyes had narrowed even more. "Esa?" she asked.

"Yes?"

"You know, you never told me *why* you shaved your head." She'd noticed my guilty gesture. Crap.

"That's true—I didn't, did I?"

She took a deep, shuddering breath, her hands wrapping around the table's edge. I was fairly sure she was counting to ten in her head. If she *was*, it didn't appear to help. "Esa?" she asked again.

"Yes?" Okay, admittedly, I was just being a pain in the ass at this point, but would it have killed her to say "thanks"?

"Did you shave your head because you *tried* something back at Sanctum? Something that caught your *hair* on fire?"

"Put that together all by yourself, did you?"

"God . . . god *damn it*, Esa."

"What, Jane, what? It *worked*. It worked, and now we know that it *can* work, and that means—" I paused, looked her up and down for a moment, and then it was my turn to narrow my eyes as I reached certain conclusions of my own. "Jane?"

"Yes, Esa?" Her voice had mostly come back to level.

"Your boot seems to be . . . somewhat *charred*. I couldn't help but notice, because *half your pants leg is gone*. Jane—did you try and *kick* the glowing being made of energy? Is that a thing you tried to do?"

She shrugged. "It seemed better than the alternative, which was letting him grab me."

"Yeah? And did it work?"

She pulled her shirt down from her shoulder; an almost-perfect handprint—six fingered—had been seared into her skin. "Not as such, no," she admitted.

I couldn't help it; I had to laugh at that. I mean, I didn't do it *well*—it turned into more of a cough—but still. Meanwhile, Schaz was making noises of concern: apparently Jane had been too busy getting *me* strapped in and getting us off the asteroid, and she hadn't so much dealt with any of her injuries. With a groan, I slid off the table, and patted it so that Jane would take my place. I had to balance on Sho's wheelchair to make it over to the kitchen counter.

Jane stripped; she'd been downplaying the cost of her own little adventure. She had a dozen small burns, at least, plus a handful of lacerations, most deep enough to still be bleeding freely. It was kind of a wonder she was still standing. Then again, I'd fought the bastard for forty seconds and nearly cooked my brain inside my own skull; she'd fought him—or at least kept him off of me—for nearly forty *minutes*. Surviving that at *all* was damned impressive.

"Is the course locked in?" I asked Jane.

She nodded as Schaz lowered one of the medical arms toward her, complete with a dripping sedative needle. "Yep," was all she said.

"Great. Grand. Where the hell are we *going*?" As I recalled, the next step in our little ad hoc plan had been to get somewhere with a broadcast antenna, where we could signal Sanctum for help—but I had no idea where that was.

"Jalia Preserve V."

Well, that told me fuck-all. "And where's *that*?"

"Where we're going. Hopefully I'll be awake before we get there."

"And if you're not?"

She waved in my general direction. "Make something up," she told me.

Then Schaz plunged the needle into her arm, and she was *out*.

I looked at Sho; he looked back at me. "I don't suppose she told *you* anything about this place?" I asked him. Mutely, he shook his head. "Oh," I replied, a little disappointed. I mean, no, I hadn't *really* expected Jane to fill Sho in after she hadn't done the same for me, but still. Would have been nice. I sighed, and stumbled my way to the cold box. I could *really* use something nearly freezing to drink right about now.

I dug something out, then turned to find Sho still staring at me with wide eyes.

"Yes, Sho?" I asked, pressing my cool drink to my head. I think it was some form of juice, but I cared less about the contents than the simple fact that it was *cold*.

"You just nearly *died* using your gifts to fight off a being made of energy. You were still *smoking* when she hauled you in here."

"You mentioned this already."

"And she—she went through all of *that*," he gestured vaguely in Jane's direction, still zonked out on the table as the arms began to administer their treatments, "and she still made sure to get you back here. Don't take this the wrong way, but you and Jane *may* be two of the *scariest* people I've ever met."

"Only to our enemies, Sho."

"I know; I get that. It's not that *I'm* scared of you, it's that—"

"I get what you're saying." Watching Jane and the Preacher defend us against the Pax for the first time, I'd felt the same way: I hadn't known combat could even be fought on that level. My prior experience was all watching the natives of the settlement where I grew up take potshots at bandits with barely functional rifles.

"My point is—you two are badasses, absolutely."

"I would say 'thank you,' but I'm pretty sure you're going to qualify that statement with another one in just a bit."

"This . . . thing that's after us—"

"Hopefully not after us anymore; hopefully stuck on that rock until we can show up to pry him out of there with a goddamned army."

"Even so . . ." He looked . . . worried. I couldn't blame him. The two "protectors" his mother had handed him to, the only two people he knew in the wide galaxy, were exactly 0–2 against the threat we'd just contained. Oh, we'd locked him up, but we'd nearly *died* doing it. Jane and I were dangerous. That thing was . . . worse.

"Even so, nothing," I said firmly, faking a confidence I didn't feel. "We trapped him; we won this round."

"You were almost on *fire*."

I shrugged. "A win's a win."

"It doesn't *feel* like we've won anything. The people on my homeworld— the people on that asteroid . . . it doesn't feel like we've won anything at *all*."

Great. Way to poke a hole in my incredibly delicate ego booster, Sho. "No, it doesn't," I agreed. Behind Sho, Schaz's medical arms whirred in quiet motion as she stitched and patched and coated Jane. It was hard to call anything a win when both Jane and I had come out . . . significantly the worse for wear.

Sho looked around Schaz's interior. "So . . . what now?" he asked.

I shrugged, cracking open my juice and taking a drink. "Wanna play cards to pass the time? We can play Vyrene High-Pass."

"I don't know how to play that."

"We can play Vyrene High-Pass for money."

CHAPTER 2

We didn't wind up playing cards. What we *did* wind up doing was studying Schaz's data banks for information on Jalia Preserve V; if we were going to reach our mysterious bolthole before Jane woke up, I wanted to know significantly more than I currently did, which could be summed up as "Jane thought maybe it had a high-powered broadcast tower." As reconnaissance went, that was . . . not exactly a full report.

Unfortunately, Schaz didn't have much to give us either. Justified operatives had never *been* to Jalia Preserve V, which meant all Schaz had was second- and third-hand information bought from various map-data packets Jane had picked up from various data-brokers, most of it decades old, *all* of it completely unreliable, and sometimes even conflicting.

Still, we got at least a patchy idea of the world we were about to descend toward: pre–sect wars it had belonged to a rich monarchical sect, the Jaliad, who had set aside dozens of livable worlds for the private, personal use of their ruling class, a few light years away from the star systems they controlled. Jalia Preserve V had been one such world, terraformed to precise specifications, then painstakingly populated with flora and fauna from across half a dozen different spectrums of life: forests from the Reetha homeworld, living crystal colonies from the Mahren planets, all sorts of different predator and prey species from the human and Reint and Wulf homelands, some segregated by continental divides, some mixed together, just to see what would come out on top, like a forced evolutionary experiment.

The point hadn't been scientific research, though—it had been a kind of retreat for the monarchs of the Jalia and their chosen retainers and sycophants. Basically, a nature preserve for the rich to go vacationing in, somewhere they could while away their hours far from the teeming masses they were meant to serve, spending their time sightseeing or hunting or just screwing around in the elaborate private villas dotting the world.

There was very little information about what had happened to the planet *after* the sect wars had broken out. The Jaliad ruling class itself had been toppled fairly early on in a grisly coup—Scheherazade's databanks had information about something called the "Display of the Bloody Angels," which I very specifically did *not* open in a new tab to learn more about—and infighting within the population on the Jaliad homeworld had led to Jalia Preserve V pretty much falling off the map.

According to several of the data-broker reports, there were still automated defenses set up in orbit and on the world's surface; if someone wanted to claim the world, they would either have to be a distant blood relative to the former Jaliad monarchs—which, given that the ruling families had been torn out branch and root by their justifiably pissed-off subjects, seemed unlikely—or they'd have to come with a couple of dreadnaughts, and be willing for those craft to take a beating. Apparently nobody wanted a fancy nature preserve that badly, or at least nobody who might have had any idea it existed did, because the world was still spinning all on its lonesome, which was impressive, given that it was non-pulsed.

The only *other* way to descend safely into the atmosphere of Jalia Preserve V would be if one had access to the *codes* for the defense network, which Jane unaccountably did. There were no notes in her files on the world about *where* she'd retrieved those codes; a constant, low-level paranoia was a hallmark of Jane's personality, forged in her twin lives as a sect soldier and a Justified operative, and some things she just kept to herself, not even trusting them to Scheherazade.

Still, I understood Jane's reasoning for selecting the Jalia Preserve as our broadcast world: as far as the databanks told us, it was unpopulated, *and* it was non-pulsed, which meant the Jalia monarchs may have left behind broadcast towers we could use to get our signal out, towers that wouldn't have been reduced to uselessness by pulse radiation. We could send out the signal, then set down on some spectacular vista, nurse our wounds, and let Schaz decrypt the data I'd pulled out of the blue fucker's ship—I'd asked, and it was cooking away merrily in her background processes. Then, all we'd have to do was wait for the cavalry to arrive. Preferably somewhere with a beach. I'd never seen the ocean.

Sho and I crowded into the cockpit when Schaz announced we were about to drop out of hyperspace; there wasn't actually any difference between what we'd see out the window and what we'd see if we'd just pulled up the forward camera views on the holoprojector in the living quarters, but somehow it felt more *real*, seeing the system splashed over the slightly curved screen ahead of the pilot's chair.

Perhaps unsurprisingly, given its lineage, Jalia Preserve V was an incredibly beautiful world, its atmosphere stained with the lightest of violet tinges, as if some clumsy godling had spilled pale pastel ink in shades of lavender and orchid into the sky. The continents below—peeking through slightly vermillion-tinted cloud cover—were lapped by pristine turquoise seas, and the varying foliage covering the landmass shifted in waves from deep greens to bright oranges to glittering golds. The entire edge of the visible hemisphere gave off a light blue sheen, thanks to the glow of the massive star at the center of the system.

And because none of *that* was pretty enough for the long-deposed rulers of the Jaliad (who I was beginning to gather wouldn't have ranked "understated" as their favorite form of decor), the planet was encircled by a spiraling Möbius strip of rings, coiling and feeding into themselves like a lithic river of cosmic sediment. Whether the world had come that way, or the terraforming engineers had painstakingly engineered the gravity of the planet's orbit in order to *generate* that delicately twisted ribbon of broken stone and ice, I had no idea. The universe was a place of marvels, after all—whether forged naturally or willed into being by sentient creatures, they were wonders all the same.

"Oh, *wow*," Sho breathed, staring at the awesome spectacle of wonder ahead of us.

I nodded mutely. That about said it all. As one of the four moons rotated toward us, I could see where the Jaliad ruling class had fucking *carved their family crest* into the lunar surface in a massive, miles-wide art installation, where it would doubtless reflect the azure light of the system's sun and shine down on the world below, a glowing reminder of their wealth and their legacy and their history.

Rich people were fucking *weird.*

"Beginning our descent," Scheherazade announced. "Jane laid in a very precise vector I was supposed to follow in the event that she was . . . unavailable for our approach."

"You mean like 'snoring off a sedative in the medbay' unavailable?" I asked wryly.

"Quite," Schaz agreed, the planet dipping toward us in the viewscreen.

"I don't suppose *you* have any idea why she'd want us to descend to a specific spot on this particular world," I asked.

"None whatsoever!" Schaz replied cheerily. I was going to ask her to elaborate—though how she would have elaborated on "none whatsoever," I really wasn't sure—but I got distracted as Schaz's cameras picked up the floating defense platforms in orbit, absolutely bristling with guns. Somewhere below us, the anti-orbital cannons would have perked up as well, tracking our passage toward their fiefdom across that lovely pastel sky. Just the thought of those giant cannons being trained on our little ship made my gut tighten involuntarily.

"Have you transmitted Jane's access codes to the defense net yet?" I asked Schaz.

"I *knew* there was something I was forgetting!" Yes, she still sounded cheery when she said that. I don't know *why*—it's not like she would have survived either, if that defense network had decided to wipe us out. Wouldn't *that* be an anticlimactic ending to our latest adventure; burned out of the stars by a long-dormant anti-orbital cannon protecting the territory of a long-dead monarchy just because Schaz was occasionally *absentminded.* "Codes transmitted now," she said. "We're all clear!"

I didn't respond to that at all; I was too busy trying not to have a heart attack. The staving off of my inevitable demise wasn't *helped* when Schaz's speakers came to life, blaring a blast of brassy fanfare. "Welcome to the Jalia Preserve V, Duchess of Ancraid," a bright, Reetha-accented voice followed the off-putting music. "Your *dacha* is undergoing maintenance—"

"If I'm scanning along that suggested flight path correctly, her *dacha* has fallen off a cliff and into the sea," Schaz interrupted snidely.

"—so I'm going to redirect you to one of your family's common holdings. If you'd like to change this flight path—perhaps to the Baron of Levighal's alpine villa; I know you've enjoyed your time there in the past—please just let me know, and I'll—" I reached down and cut the transmission off. Even if the Jaliad ruling class *had* been wiped out by their own subjects for being resource-hoarding assholes who spent their money *carving things into moons* rather than feeding their people, there was something unaccountably sad about the thought of the defense net's controlling AI just waiting for another arrival of the ruling family it was meant to serve, a family that was never going to return.

"Good." I turned; Jane was awake, and standing in the doorway. She looked . . . well, not "better," given that she was covered in bandages and healing foam, but at least steadier on her feet. "We're here."

"The Duchess of Ancraid?" I asked her, raising an eyebrow.

She shrugged, stepping between Sho and me to take her seat in the pilot's chair, still moving somewhat gingerly. "Don't ask me—I didn't steal the codes." Instead of taking the stick, she opened another comm channel, reaching for the microphone. "Mo, if you're near your radio," she said, "put out the good china; you're about to have visitors." That was it—that was the extent of her communication before she leaned back in her chair. "Schaz, loop that message," she ordered.

"Mo?" Schaz asked, her voice excited, as if someone had just told her we were getting a *puppy* on our next rotation to Sanctum. I mean, a puppy other than the Wulf adolescent currently on board. "*Mo's* down there?"

"If he hasn't been eaten, yeah." Jane nodded.

"You've known where he is for . . . for . . . for *however* long, and you didn't *tell me?*"

"Remember when you were secretly receiving messages from Javier behind my back? Remember when that could have gotten us *exiled?* No, Schaz, I didn't tell you."

"Oh." She mulled this over for a while. "What's he been doing?"

"It's Mo. Looking for God, I suppose. And likely failing to find Him."

Sho leaned into me. "Who's Mo?" he whispered.

"I have no idea," I whispered back. "Jane's a hundred and eighty-seven years old, after all; she's bound to have some acquaintances she's never mentioned."

"I'm *not* a hundred and eighty-seven, Esa." Jane raised her voice. She had very good hearing. Also, Sho and I were barely five feet away.

"Fine. One hundred and eighty-six. It's not becoming of a woman your age to get so defensive, you know."

CHAPTER 3

Schaz kept us on our current, Jane-mandated approach as we waited for a response to my partner's message, the different landmasses and changing climate zones of the various preserves below meaning the view out the window changed nearly every time I looked. "So you're not going to *tell* us who Mo is," I said to Jane.

"You'll find out soon enough," she shrugged.

"Again—unless he's been eaten."

"And if he's been eaten, it won't matter. We'll just set down somewhere, and avail ourselves of the—"

The comm crackled to life. "Jane?" A voice, deep, like a thrum through stone; a Mahren. "Is that really you? Finally come to visit after all these years?"

"You know me, old man, I'm all about diligence," Jane replied; she was smiling. I figured that was a good sign.

"Otherwise known as you're in deep shit, and this is literally the only place you have to turn."

"Maybe I just wanted to check on you, make sure you haven't gone senile in your old age."

"So you're in *really* deep shit, huh?"

"Yep."

"I'm sending Schaz a flight path; I've moved camp since I last sent you my coordinates. Hello, Scheherazade."

"Hello, Mo. It's good to hear your voice again." Schaz sounded . . . almost *girlish* as she responded.

"You as well, my dear."

"Schaz is running a deep decryption program, Mo," Jane said. "I'd like to let her engage soak protocols to speed up the work. I take it you're by an ocean?"

"You know me too well. That flight plan will set you down in a clearing a few miles away from the shore, but she can reach the water regularly from there. I'll hike out to meet you and see you when you set down."

"You don't have to do that, Mo."

"Sure I do. You'll never find me otherwise. Unless something has drastically changed in the last half century, you were always a fantastic urban scout, and fairly shit at wilderness pathfinding."

I snorted a laugh at that; Jane turned a mildly annoyed glance my way. "You are." I shrugged, then turned to Sho. "She is."

The comm crackled to life again. "There's someone else with you, Red," the mysterious Mo said. I had no idea why he called her that—there was nothing "red" about Jane at all, and I'd never heard anyone *else* call her that before. "You haven't come to kill me, by any chance?" He didn't seem perturbed to be asking it—he might as well have been politely inquiring if she'd brought him some extra cinnamon or other basic household goods, because his supplies were running low.

"Come on, Mo," Jane replied. "If I was here for that, I wouldn't let you see it coming. I owe you that much."

"Fair enough. You always were a good girl."

Jane smiled at that. "Except when I wasn't."

"Except when you weren't. I'll meet you in the clearing; looking forward to meeting your friends there. Mo out."

Jane shut off the comms, leaned back in her chair, still staring out the viewport, not really looking at anything in particular. Schaz gave a lurching shift as she matched the new flight plan, dipping us closer to the landscape below.

"You're really not going to tell us who this guy is, are you?" I asked Jane. Without waiting for her response, I turned to face the living area instead. "Schaz? Will *you* tell us who this guy is?"

"He's Mo," she replied simply.

"Yeah, I'd figured that much out for myself, thanks."

"He's—he was Jane's—"

"Leave it, Scheherazade," Jane said. "Let her put it together for herself."

I stuck my tongue out at her. "Another test?" I asked.

"Another test," she nodded, standing up from her chair. "I'm going to make myself a cup of coffee."

"You're nervous," I said, almost awed at the concept, even as I unbuckled my flight harness and followed her, pushing Sho's wheelchair along with us. "You're *nervous* about meeting this guy again after . . . however long."

"Not nervous. Maybe a little excited."

"Plus, there's always the possibility that he's gone crazy," Schaz put in. "He has been alone for a *very* long time."

I frowned at that. "Jane, if we have to fight a rampaging Mahren, I'd rather we just set down someplace *else*, thanks. Mahren are *very* hard to kill."

"Mahren are the big rock people, right?" Sho asked. "We didn't have any of them on my homeworld. Or at least, not that I ever met."

"Big rock people," I nodded. "Stupidly strong, very long-lived, naturally resistant to ballistics. And energy weapons. And fire. And pretty much everything else."

"He hasn't gone crazy, Schaz," Jane said, pouring herself a cup of coffee. "Isolation was always where Mo thrived."

"A trait he passed—"

"*And* if anyone can put together . . ."—she waved a hand in the general direction of the holoprojector, meaning "all the weird shit that had happened to us over the past week or so"—"it'll be Mo. He's forgotten more about galactic esoterica than the four of us combined will ever know."

"That's a nice word for the invulnerable energy monster that's trying to kill us." I nodded. "'Esoterica.' I like that."

Jane took a sip of her coffee, wrinkled her nose at how hot it was. She was weird like that. "Why don't you two go back into the cockpit?" she suggested. "Keep an eye on our descent; take in the sights. Jalia's a very . . . interesting-looking world."

"Come on, Sho." I spun his chair around by the handles, pointing him back at the cockpit. "Jane wants some time alone."

"Because she's nervous?" he asked.

"Because she's nervous," I confirmed. "After all, at a hundred and eighty-five, it takes her a minute to collect herself."

"Not a hundred and eighty-five!" Jane shouted after us. "Not a hundred and eighty-six, either! Or a hundred and eighty-four!"

I grinned, and wheeled Sho into place. We were passing over a vast plain of shimmering grassland; on the viewscreen at magnification, we could make out herds of . . . something down below, massive beasts with armor plating and three protruding tusks. "What are those?" I asked Schaz.

"Talmisau, from the Klite homeworld," Schaz told us. "Very important in Klitek mythology—beasts supposedly possessed of vast, ancient knowledge."

"And those smaller . . . things, running with them?"

"Giraffes, from the human sphere. Apparently the two species have reached a kind of symbiosis." She shifted the view; we watched the herd approach a massive tree, growing all on its lonesome on the sweeping savannah. The larger talmisau grazed on the foliage well above the reach of the giraffes, which had the possibly unintentional side effect of their razor tusks slicing some of the other branches free, dropping them low enough that the giraffes could get to them.

"Beautiful," Sho breathed. I wondered when the last time he'd seen wild animals had been, if ever. Beyond rats, and other vermin. My homeworld had been the recipient of a fully functional—if mostly domesticated—Tyll ecosystem, for reasons no one had understood anymore, and even I found the sight of the great beasts below pretty impressive.

We passed over a sprawling estate on the savannah; Schaz saved the image, and expanded it for us to peruse. "A hunting lodge, most likely," she explained.

For some reason, that struck me as sad—almost pathetic. There was a note of something like disgust in my voice when I said, "So the nobles of the Jaliad could shoot the talmisau, and the giraffes. For sport."

"And whatever else is living out here. I doubt they *just* introduced herbivorous species. After all, hunting things that aren't hunting you back wouldn't seem the *most* exciting pastime. Not that I'd know."

Sho smiled. "You don't consider yourself a hunter, Scheherazade?"

"Not of animals, Show-no-fang."

We settled in to watch the planet pass beneath us; in short order we were a shadow above a desert of sandy canyons, then above a network of *almost-natural-seeming* rivers that formed a design when viewed from high enough up, and finally we cruised just over a breathtaking vista of snow-capped peaks—likely where Lord Levihoo's alpine villa was located, a suspicion that was confirmed when we passed something that looked like a castle out of a fairy tale, all sweeping, lonely towers and wide, now-broken windows and other architectural features that would be absolutely horrendous if the position came under siege, otherwise known as the entire *point* of a castle.

"So *much* wealth here." Sho sighed. "And so little on my home. If the ruling class of the Jaliad had held back the money required to build just *one* of these palaces, I wonder: how long would that money have fed my sect?"

"Assuming that—if they felt such a philanthropic urge—they could have even *gotten* it to your sect," I reminded him. "The pulse aside—and the fact that the Jaliad rulers were all dead well before you were born aside—if some foreign sect had just showered cash over one group on your world, how would the others have reacted?"

"They would have banded together to destroy us," he admitted sadly. "Before we used it to grow more powerful than any of them."

"And then gone right back to destroying each other when that was done," I nodded. "Money didn't keep the Jaliad monarchy alive once their people started to revolt, either. I've always thought that cash doesn't solve nearly as many problems as rich people seem to think it might."

"Says someone who's never had any," Schaz reminded me.

"There is that. And it's more than likely true that I only *tell* myself that so that I don't get *too* angry at stupidly wasteful people like the Jaliad." I nodded at the viewscreen, and the image of the fairy-tale castle, still spinning on the mountaintop. "After all, it was bad habits like *that*—how they used their money, their power—that led to their *very* bad ending, ultimately."

"So if you had money—"

"I would build a solid-gold statue of myself and force everyone to worship it." I grinned at him. "Power corrupts, and all that. I'm gonna die eventually, anyway; might as well die at the hands of an angry mob jealous of the stupidly awesome lifestyle I've lived for however long I could get away with it."

"It wasn't jealousy that ended the Jaliad." Sho shook his head. "It was the broken promise. 'Let us rule you, and we will keep you safe.' And then the sect wars came, and they couldn't."

I sighed. "You're kind of a downer, you know that, Sho?"

"I know."

CHAPTER 4

We crossed over an ocean before we approached our destination, the turquoise waters below broken by the swells of whitecaps rushing toward the distant shore. In the distance, I could see what I thought was *maybe* a broadcast tower, one we could use to send our signal—but given that this world had been designed by aesthetic-mad egomaniacs, it was all whirls and spirals and may have been a purely decorative thing, serving no real purpose at all beyond shouting "We have money, and lots of it!" to anyone who might come across it.

Jane reentered the cockpit and took the stick when it was time to set us down; the "clearing" her friend had indicated as a landing zone was tricky to get to, because of course it was—underneath a rocky outcropping covered in flowing vines that would keep us from being seen from above, despite the fact that anyone *looking* for us from above would have had to deal with the defense network in orbit. I scanned the camera feeds, but I didn't see anyone at the edges of the open area. "I think we beat your friend here," I announced.

Jane took a cursory glance at the screen. "No, we didn't," she said, then went back to setting us down.

We both grabbed our basic gear bags, Sho already impatiently waiting for us in the airlock, his fingers beating out a drumbeat tattoo on the grips of his wheels. I could understand the impulse—it was a terribly pretty world, and unlike us, he hadn't gotten to disembark on Valkyrie Rock, so he'd been cooped up inside Scheherazade for over a week. Granted, he also hadn't almost been *killed* on Valkyrie Rock, so I figured it was a fair exchange. "Am I taking my guns?" I asked Jane.

"I don't know, Esa," Jane shrugged, strapping on her revolver. "We're going to be a couple miles away from Scheherazade, for a few days at least. We're going to be meeting somebody you don't know at *all*, plus there's always the off chance we'll run into someone else down there, and when *that* happens, 'someone else' almost always wants to kill us. So: *do* you want to take your guns?"

I took my guns.

Schaz opened her airlock and lowered her ramp; immediately, the smell of the jungle beyond us entered the cargo area, thick and alive. There was a kind of iridescent glitter to the air, some sort of pollen, I think, put off by the thick blue trees that grew from the rich soil. I scanned the edge of the jungle—what little I could see through the hanging vines—but I still couldn't place Mo. "Are you sure your friend is here?" I asked Jane again.

"Yep," she nodded, descending the ramp. Sho and I followed, and then suddenly, there he was: a huge Mahren, standing just inside the vines. I had no idea how he'd done that—I'd *just* looked there, and he hadn't been visible. And it's not like he was *small*. Even for a Mahren he was a big fella, nine feet tall and nearly as broad through the shoulders as Jane and I standing next to each other would have been. His rocky skin was roughly the color of limestone, and like all older Mahren, male or female, he had a heavy "beard" of crystals extending from his jaw, pale green and translucent.

"Hello, Red," he said to Jane, his voice a deep bass rumble somewhere in the earthquake range. As he shifted, I could see the stock of an old rifle poking up over his shoulder—this wasn't a pulsed world, he wouldn't *need* a gun that old, but I had a feeling that was only the start of the strangeness about this particular Mahren.

"How's it going, Mo?" Jane returned his greeting, taking a step forward. "Any closer to finding what you're looking for?"

He shook his head. "It's not the end of the journey that defines me," he told her. "It's the search."

She took another step closer—there was a strange current running between them, something *almost* like violence, but maybe I was reading it wrong—and then she reached out, and she hugged him.

I don't think I'd ever seen Jane hug *anybody*. I'd seen her make out with Javier, and I'd seen her shake people's hands, but she really wasn't the hugging *type*.

So, yeah: not violence after all.

He hugged her back, one-handed—and very gently, so he didn't crush her into paste—and she stepped away from him, grinning. "I've missed you, old man," she said.

"And I've missed you," he told her, then nodded at Sho and me. "Introduce me to your companions."

She turned back toward us. "Mo, this is Esa, my partner, and Show-no-fang, called Sho. He's our current passenger, en route back to Sanctum."

"It is good to meet you both," he nodded. "My name is Mohammed ibn Abdullah ibn Ghaluk. *As-salāmu 'alaykumā.*"

Thankfully, I'd taken a comparative religions course as part of my studies—usually conducted in hyperspace between jobs—and I returned the traditional greeting. "*'Alaykumu as-salām.* I didn't know there were that many Mahren Muslims out there."

"There are not," he laughed. "Long ago, I was a member of a sect that converted. Of the dozen most popular religions in the galaxy, five of them come from human culture. I've always found that a fascinating contribution, often overlooked when it comes to the impact of your race: you are *very* good at religion."

"Also very good at killing each other," Jane added sourly. "I think the two might have something in common."

Mo arched a crystalline eyebrow. "Jane has never approved of my faith," he told us, speaking as though in confidence, despite the fact that Jane was right there. "She has never approved of *any* faith, actually: a holdover from her youth. Don't let her cloud your mind, young Esa. She approaches life in a very . . . singular manner, but it is not the only approach that is available to you."

I grinned at him. "You knew Jane in her youth, huh? Mo, my man, I think I might have some questions for you."

"All right," Jane cut that one off. "We should get moving. Mo, I'd imagine you have a camp somewhere."

"Yes; this way," he said, leading us through the vines, into the great rising forest beyond. "If you're wondering how I know Jane," he said to me, holding up the canopy of vines so that Sho could wheel under them, "the easiest way to put it is that *she* was my *you*. I was her partner for many years, after she first joined the Justified."

"*Were* you now?" This was fascinating enough that I barely paid attention to the breathtaking sight of the twisting blue trees of Klitek extraction, twining and knotting themselves together into the jungle canopy above. "I don't know that she's mentioned you before." I paused, a vague memory coming back to me. "Well, maybe once."

He laughed at that. "The sinking of the *Ishiguro*, yes? Well, I can't blame her for telling you that story, even if she's not *supposed* to mention an old exile like me to her impressionable pupil. That was an . . . *impressive* day."

"So if *you* were *her* partner back then—"

"Think about it this way, Esa," Jane interrupted me. "How much of what *I* know about combat do you know?"

"I guess . . . around thirty percent, maybe?"

She laughed. "That's cute. But for argument's sake, we'll pretend it's actually true. If you know thirty percent of what I know, what I know is thirty percent of what Mo knows—not counting whatever he's picked up out here on the fringes. I trained you; he trained me. Once I joined the Justified, anyway."

"So why are you out here?" Sho asked the large Mahren. "I mean—I don't mean to pry, I'm not . . . I mean, why *here*?"

"After many years of life as a . . . soldier"—the pause before he said the last word was barely noticeable, but it was there: whatever Mohammed had been when he served the Justified, "soldier" was not the first word he would have called it—"I experienced something of a . . . crisis of faith. As I said, I was raised in an Islamic sect, far away from the wars and the chaos. Our world was . . . a backwater, perhaps, but not unlovely, in its way, and we lived in peace and contentment. Until our enemies came." He paused for a moment after that, just kept pushing his way through the jungle, finding a rough path, making sure we couldn't see his face. "Afterward, I joined the Justified; afterward, I no longer believed. For years, I served, many of them alongside Red. Then my second crisis of belief, and I came to question whether my service—and more crucially, *how* I served—was actually how I should find purpose in my life. The moment I walked away was the moment my faith returned."

"And it's still hanging around, I see," Jane said, like she was talking about some form of social disease rather than a spiritual well of faith.

"It comes and goes," he shrugged. "When I find that I believe, that I *have* believed, every day for a year, all the way to the deepest chamber of my heart and the very crown of my soul: on that day, my journey will be over."

"And today?"

He grinned. "Today Allah has brought an old friend to give me relief from my isolation. Yes, Red—today I believe."

"But why *here?*" Sho asked again. "I mean—I'm assuming you have a ship somewhere, that you could have gone anywhere in the galaxy. This world is . . . beautiful, but it's also—you mentioned your isolation. Do you not get lonely?"

"I do," he nodded, effortlessly lifting a massive fallen tree trunk out of our path so that Sho could wheel under it. "But it is also . . . easier, to listen for the true voice of God, when I am not surrounded by other clamoring distractions."

"I don't think I ever clamored," Jane frowned at him.

"No, you did not," he agreed. "But your actions spoke very loudly indeed."

"It's been five minutes, Mo—can we *not* argue about religion? At least not for a little bit?"

"*I* have never been the one arguing, Jane." He paused, then, holding up a hand for silence. In a clearing before us, a half dozen creatures had gathered, grazing on a patch of violet foliage. I'd never seen their like before: strange quadrupeds with short, tawny fur, some with twisting antlers, some without. Mo quietly unshipped his rifle, but before he'd brought the scope to his eye, something spooked the creatures, and they fled deeper into the shadows of the azure jungle, bounding on spindly legs at a surprisingly fast clip. "A pity," Mo murmured. "I should have liked to have offered you fresh meat for dinner tonight."

"What *were* those?" I asked, still almost holding my breath, despite the fact that the animals were long gone.

He turned to smile at me as he stowed his rifle again. "You were not raised in a human biome, I see. They are called 'deer,' a herbivore from the human homeworld. That is the other reason I have chosen this particular world to continue my search for the quiet voice inside myself: plentiful game, clean water, somewhere I can support myself."

"And an automated defense system in orbit that ensures you remain uninterrupted in your meditations," Jane added dryly.

"And also that, yes," he nodded. "So: now that you know why *I* am here, why don't you tell *me* what brings you to my door?"

"Mo, old friend: that is one hell of a story, and not a short one."

"We have some time until we reach the beach, and my abode; would you prefer to wait until we have reached what little comforts I can offer to begin telling it?"

"We've trapped a crazy fucker made of glowing blue fire on an asteroid where he murdered everybody, and now we need to signal the Justified to come take him away because he might have a cure for the pulse," I said. Jane looked at me; I shrugged. "What?" I asked. "Not everything has to be a production, you know. Red."

"*Don't* call me that."

"A glowing being of fire. Hmmm." That "hmmm" was somewhat hopeful; he didn't sound like he was at all thrown by the concept. Then again, I didn't get the impression Mo was thrown by much—he hadn't even reacted to the "cure for the pulse" bit.

"Pure energy, actually," Jane clarified.

Mo turned to his former protégé. "And would that explain the damage you've done to your foot?"

Jane grinned, just a bit. "Yes, Mo—I tried to kick a being of pure energy, right between its legs. Turns out, in case you were wondering: no. That's *not* where he keeps his genitals."

Mo laughed at that. "All right. So where *does* a being of pure energy keep his genitals?"

"Hell if I know. Not any of the other places I kicked him either."

"Red. Didn't I teach you not to try a damned fool thing twice?"

"You may have taught it," Jane shrugged, "I sure as hell never learned it. Or managed to pass it on." She gave me a hard look as she said the last; I ignored her, and kept pushing my way through the vines that covered the path.

CHAPTER 5

Jane elaborated on our recent adventures as we made our way through the forest; Mo listened, but said little, nodding occasionally—though he did ask Schaz to transfer the video of our various encounters with our pursuer over to his network, which meant that regardless of the monastic, isolated life he had chosen to live, he still had access to a certain level of technology in his camp.

Where *that* was, I still had no idea, but he led us unerringly through the forest; the going was rough with Sho's wheelchair for a bit, until we came to an overgrown path that might once have been an actual road. I think it might have been paved in platinum once. At least the Jaliad monarchy had been consistent in their profligacy.

Finally, we could hear a sound like distant thunder, echoing through the massive trees. We were nearing the shore—the ocean. I couldn't help it; I pushed my way past Jane and Mo, throwing a grin at Sho as I did, and then I was just *running*, moving as fast as I could toward the light of the beach ahead, clear of the shadows of the jungle. I'd never seen a real ocean before.

It was just as gorgeous as I'd expected.

I just stood there for a while, my boots half buried in the white sand, looking at the *vastness* of it. It shouldn't have seemed so big, not after I'd spent the last three years traversing the immensity of the void, but it did. It wasn't just the size of the endless blue horizon that spread underneath the mimosa-colored sky; it was how *alive* it was, an endless ecosystem of water, the liquid flowing and rolling like a living thing, waves crashing and retreating, over and over again.

When the others arrived, I turned wordlessly, and knelt so that I could embrace Sho. He was crying as well. He'd never seen a sea either; his home had been nothing but near-infinite fields of metal.

I wiped the tears off my face and grinned at Jane. "Can I go swimming?" I asked her.

She frowned. "You barely know how to swim," she reminded me.

"I do! I do too! Criat taught me!"

"Criat's a Wulf. He can barely dog paddle." She actually said it with a straight face. "We don't have any idea what the currents are like in there, Esa. You could be carried halfway to another continent in a heartbeat."

"Actually, the currents are fairly mild," Mo put in.

"See?" I pointed at my new best friend.

"How would you know?" Jane rounded on Mo. "*You* can't swim either. Mahren don't swim, they sink."

"I go fishing," he shrugged. Then he grinned at Jane. "This is new, you know: this maternal, protective instinct. I think it suits you." She glared at him. "Shove it?" he guessed. She just nodded. I laughed.

"Come on." Mo nodded down the beach, where we could make out his "camp"—a complex of tile-roofed villas stretching out from the beach and onto a system of piers built out over the water. Most of the paint had been worn away over the centuries, and a few of the outlying buildings had collapsed into the sea, but it was still recognizably a pleasure palace built for and *by* the superrich—or, more accurately, by their army of contractors and servants, I suppose.

"You know, I always found the poverty you were willing to endure in your search for your God inspiring," Jane told Mo, her voice deadpan dry.

"What? The Jaliad left behind a perfectly usable beachside complex, and you expect me to just ignore it and build a hut out of thatched grass in its shadow instead? Come on—let's get you settled. You can set off for the broadcast tower in the morning, and after that, you'll have to wait for a reply as Schaz runs her decryption—you're likely to be here for a while."

We trooped down the beach toward Mo's seaside paradise; I took off my boots to feel the warm sand between my toes. The waves rolled in and receded with an impressive regularity, the bright light of the blue sun in the sky reflecting off the equally blue waters, the faint lavender tinge of the atmosphere the only break in the otherwise monochromatic color scheme of the seaside-blue sun, blue sea, blue jungle.

There was a ramp leading up to a loading door on this side of the complex; Mo effortlessly pushed Sho's wheelchair up that as Jane manipulated a set of impressively unrusted chains to raise the door itself. All the metal in the villa must have been treated with some sort of anti-rusting agent, to hold up for this long right next to the salten sea.

Mo continued to push Sho inside, but Jane turned back toward the jungle, looking at the horizon, and I hung back with her. "Schaz?" she said into her comms. "We've made it to Mo's villa; we're good for now. Go ahead and engage your soak."

"About time," Schaz sighed. "Do you need anything else? Overclocking the decryption algorithms may leave me out of communication for a bit."

"Just stick your head up every once in a while, check in," Jane told her. "Otherwise—have fun."

"I do kind of love this," Schaz admitted. "I mean, from a utilitarian standpoint, it *does* serve a purpose, but—"

"Enjoy."

"What the hell is happening again?" I asked Jane. She just nodded at the horizon over the jungle—the direction we'd come from.

"Just watch," she said.

I heard something in the distance, growing closer, fast, then Schaz appeared over the tops of the trees, and through the comms I could actually hear her, unmistakable: "*Whee!*" she shouted as she sped overhead, headed out to sea. She did an impressive loop—then plowed directly into the ocean, diving into the depths.

I sighed. "Even Schaz gets to go swimming," I complained to Jane.

Jane laughed. "She's not *swimming*, Esa," she told me. "She'll go as deep as she can, to where the water's coolest, almost freezing, and she'll expose her data core to that cold. It'll help with the decryption—she'll be able to work longer, faster, without risking an overheat. It also means the hyperdrive won't have to cool for nearly as long, once we get into the atmosphere."

"She *still* gets to go swimming," I said, then paused. "Wait. If the plan was for Schaz to do . . . that . . . anyway, why the hell didn't she just let us off right beside Mo's villa? Why did we have to hike through all that damned jungle?"

"Partially so that we could know where the clearing was, where Schaz would be staying when she's not running the decryption." Jane shrugged. "She will have to stop every once in a while to let her drive core recharge.

And partially for Mo's benefit, so he could get a read on us before revealing where he lived."

"To give him a chance to decide if we really were here to kill him, you mean."

"Yes."

"But he's your friend."

"He's also former Justified. He knows how we view exiled. His parting ways with our sect wasn't quite as . . . *mutinous* . . . as Javier's was, but he still walked away with knowledge that could be very dangerous in the wrong hands. He has a perfectly valid reason to be a little wary of us tracking him down again, even after all this time."

I paused, still staring out at the ocean—I thought I could just *barely* see bubbles, breaking the surface, above where Schaz was currently sinking. "But he still trusted you enough to tell you where he was. You said you'd never been here before—he must have told you, and passed along the key to the defense network, too." She nodded in confirmation, looking out at the ocean with me. I sighed. "So he trusts you, but he still thinks you might have come to kill him. At least now I know where you picked up your paranoid tendencies from."

She started to respond one way to that, then shut her mouth, rethinking it. "Maybe," she said finally. "But maybe those 'paranoid tendencies' are why we're still alive, Mo and I both. Maybe *you* should try and pick some of those up yourself."

I thought about that for a moment, then shook my head. "If I hadn't seen you—or Javier, or Marus, or the Preacher—for nearly a hundred years, and you came knocking on my door: no. I don't think I could fear you. I don't think I'd want to be the person who could do that."

"It's not fear, Esa. It's . . . awareness."

"The reason he's all alone out here isn't *just* because it's part of his search for God, or whatever. It's also because he can't trust *anyone* anymore. His mind—his experience, the years he spent as a Justified operative—won't let him. Or am I wrong?"

She shook her head. "You're not wrong."

"I won't live like that, Jane."

"Then you may not live long. Come on inside." We stepped into the former Jaliad villa—now Mo's stylish seaside retreat. The interiors were significantly more dilapidated than the exterior; the walls and the roofs and whatnot had been built to last, but the decorations inside had been expected to receive constant maintenance and upkeep from a likely small army of servants, servants who had vanished at the same time the Jaliad monarchy had. The frescoed floors and muraled walls were chipped and damaged; chandeliers had dropped and broken and been shoved unceremoniously to one side.

There was still light, mainly from the large windows and skylights built into each room—the fixtures must have been made of the same stuff spacecraft portholes were crafted from, to have stood up to hundreds of years of exposure to the elements—but little to no electricity, until we came to the interior dining hall where Mo had set up a small operations area, full of networked computers and ad hoc equipment he'd cobbled together.

"I just realized—*you don't* have a ship," I told him. "At least, not one we've seen."

He shook his head. "I came here with a group of pirates, seeking treasure," he said. "I knew about the defenses, of course; they didn't."

"And you didn't warn them."

"And I didn't warn them. I didn't make them *choose* larceny and murder as their occupation, after all. I ditched out in an escape pod shortly before the automated defenses cut them to pieces."

"You came here, knowing the chances that you'd ever leave would be . . . remote, at best."

"I needed someplace quiet, to contemplate my deeds, to meditate and study. It seemed a very good fit. Making my passage here a one-way trip seemed . . . *dedicated*. At the time. Besides. If I'd truly needed offworld, I could have reached out to Red." He nodded at Jane. "She would have come and picked me up."

"Maybe." Jane made a show of considering the possibility. "When I'd found the time. This one keeps me pretty busy, you know." She nodded at me.

"You would have come," Mo shrugged, seeing right through her little act. "Come—I'll show you to some of the undamaged sleeping quarters. Most of them belonged to the maids and the cooks and the mechanics and other various staff, rather than the wealthy that kept this place for their own amusement; I think there might be a little poetry in that."

CHAPTER 6

When I was done stowing my gear, I took a brief exploratory tour of the complex—another one of Jane's mantras: "Always have three exits," an important rule in a place as big as this, a maze of servants' quarters, kitchens, living spaces, with balconies and walkways connecting the upper floors, most of which only led out to the ocean. My curiosity satisfied for the moment, I returned to the dining room where Mo had set up his equipment.

The big Mahren himself was still sitting at the table, staring at the vidscreen, watching the recordings from our body cameras, studying our encounters with the strange being pursuing the gifted children. He must have watched them several times; there wasn't all *that* much footage to go through.

Still, he was riveted—all his attention devoted to the screen, not even acknowledging my presence as I entered, though just like with Jane, I knew *he* knew I was there. He simply wasn't *saying* anything, not drawing any conclusions. At least, not that I could tell.

"You know who he is." Jane had entered just after me; she read her old mentor like a book.

"I know *what* he is," Mo temporized, reaching up to pause the vid. I moved around behind him, so I could see what he was looking at: the interior of Valkyrie Rock, the being of blue flame stalking us through the tunnels, its hand raised, about to fire an energy pulse. It must have been from Jane's camera—it was the same attack I'd barely saved her from, by reaching out and manipulating the energy with my teke. And nearly killing myself in the process. "As do you. Or you should, if I taught you anything."

"Well then, you sucked as a teacher, because I have no idea, Mo. Come on. No games." Jane pulled up a chair across from him; she didn't need to see the feeds.

Mo leaned back, still studying the figure on the monitor. "He's a Cyn. That part is fundamentally clear." I felt like there should have been a thunderclap or something after his statement—after all this time referring to him as "the guy in the armor," we had a species, at least, to go with the lack of face—but the truth was, I only barely knew what a Cyn even *was*.

"That's not possible." Jane said the words flatly—no affectation, just a statement of fact, like the star beyond the window was blue, or she could make a sniper shot at a thousand meters.

"It's self-evident." Mo gestured at the vid. "The Cyn are the only beings that don't breathe oxygen; the only beings capable of surviving in deep space for extended periods of time; the only beings that don't use carbon as the basic building block of their biology, their molecular structure."

"It's a long fucking jump from 'non-carbon-based life form' to 'being made up of energy.'"

"It tracks. The Cyn were always . . . viewed as different by the other species. Fundamentally. The old texts talk about them in terms—I think 'awe' might be the closest descriptor. We have very few records from the Golden Age, from before the sect wars. We know very little *about* the Cyn."

"I still think 'they fucking *glowed*' would have showed up somewhere in the old records."

"Maybe. Maybe not. What *do* we know about them? Nothing for certain, outside of the fact that they were *fundamentally* different from the other sixteen species, Barious included."

"We know they vanished. They fucked right off, disappeared off everyone's radar, off the edge of every map. Well before the pulse, well before . . . How long has it been since anyone's seen one? Five hundred years? Six? Longer?"

"Long enough for the fact that they're made of fire to pass into myth and legend, I'd say."

"Mo—it's just not possible. Where have they *been*?"

"I don't know." He didn't sound pleased about that fact. "But think about it, for just a moment. A being made of energy—what would they consume? For sustenance?"

She shrugged uncomfortably; conjecture had never been one of Jane's strong suits. I wished the Preacher were here. I didn't know what the hell they were talking about, but it didn't sound good. "More energy, I suppose," she said. "That's the only reason anyone consumes anything, really."

"And what do we call the *transmission* of energy, in wave or particle form? In organic biology, the energy we consume is called 'caloric'; in a being *made* of energy, though, it—"

"Mo, this really isn't time for a goddamned physics—"

"Radiation. I'm saying it eats radiation."

That bit I understood. "It eats *pulse* radiation," I said, the implications making my head spin. "That's how—the warplanes, on Kandriad, the nuclear blast—that's how they were all possible. Because that fucking thing *ate* the pulse radiation that stopped the tech from working."

"Okay. Maybe. *Maybe* that tracks," Jane said. If it did, it was . . . a complication, to put it mildly. What were we going to do, *chain* the asshole to some Barious factory to try and see if it would start working again? Pushing past that idea, though, Jane leaned forward in her chair. "It's still a fucking leap to call it a Cyn."

"Which is more likely? That it's the long-lost seventeenth species, the one we *know* was different, on a basic, bedrock molecular level, than all the others? Or that it's some *new* being, discovered or somehow *manifested* in this dark age we live in?"

"All right—time the fuck out." I rapped on the table to get their attention. "Back up. Remember that I didn't grow up with any of this nonsense—"

"Neither did we, Esa," Jane said, something almost amused about the tilt of her mouth. "The Cyn have been legend since long before I—or even Mo—was ever born."

"Still, you know what they are, theoretically, at least. Sho and I"—I gestured to Sho, who had just wheeled in, parking his chair at the edge of the table and listening in with interest—"we've got no clue what the fuck you're even *talking* about."

Jane took a breath, then nodded. "You're right. I'm sorry." She looked over to Mo. "Where to start?" she asked.

"At the beginning," he replied. "In the Golden Age, there were fifteen species, all of whom reached space flight and hyperdrive technology at roughly the same time, 'same' here having a relatively broad definition. Despite the fact that they all evolved independently, many have argued for the hand of some greater force in that massive cosmological coincidence—if not a deity of some kind, watching over the galaxy, then a progenitor race, like the long-lost species that built the Barious."

I frowned. "I've always heard that there were *seventeen* species that made up the sentient beings in the galaxy," I said. "Why only fifteen?"

He lifted two fingers, then dropped one down. "I'm not counting the Barious—they were *made*, as I said. They didn't evolve. They hibernated, instead, until the Reetha woke them up again. The *second* species I'm not counting are the Cyn. The outlier that proved how strange the coincidences between the other species were. All the others, even Barious, were carbon based, required the same basic elements to survive—caloric energy, hydration, even the same rough pressure and atmosphere, namely a high oxygen content. The commonalities extended beyond even those: similar gravitational forces on their homeworlds, *close* to similar orbital periods, day-night cycles, even basic social structures."

"So where do the Cyn come in?"

"As I said—outliers. They evolved at roughly the same rate, in roughly the same instance, cosmologically speaking, as the others, but shared *none* of the other commonalities. They don't breathe oxygen; they don't breathe, period. Their biology is *not* based on carbon: that much we know for a fact, based on what few records from the time survive. Beyond that, everything else is conjecture and theory."

"A wild guess," Jane added.

He reached up, rocked his hand back and forth. "A guess, yes, but less wild than 'educated.' As you've seen"—he nodded at the vids—"the being pursuing you does *not* share the same commonalities the other sixteen species do. It's not much of a stretch to suggest that this creature's biology is based, again, not on carbon—or even matter—but on energy, instead. Living energy. It's just a quick hop from there to suggest that they didn't survive, thrive, on their homeworld—wherever that might have been—by manipulating *matter*, the way the other species did; instead, they learned to manipulate *energy*. It wouldn't be unrealistic for them to have invented fusion before they invented flight. *That* is why I believe . . . *consuming* . . . the pulse radiation would be as natural to him as breathing."

"It's also why our weapons don't affect him," Jane ran a hand down her face. "Ballistic kinetic energy, the heat energy of lasers, even—when he trig-gered the grenade I shot at him, back on Kandriad. He just activated the dormant energy of the explosive."

"All right, but where the hell did they *go*?" I asked. "And *why*?"

"No one knows," Mo answered. "Maybe they did, once, but those answers have long been lost. They just . . . vanished from the face of the galaxy."

"Marus . . ." Jane shook her head, collected her thoughts. "He used to say that it was a commonly held belief—among historians, I mean, the few people left who studied the old eras, the time before the pulse—that the sect-war era started with something called the Valerina riots, and the Barious suppres-sion that came after. That *those* were the first shots of the wars, even if they didn't know it at the time. And maybe they're right, in the terms of that's where it *began*. But the faltering of the Golden Age and the beginning of five hundred years of fighting weren't actually the same moment; we just tend to conflate them, to think one led *directly* into the other. Marus said—and he'd know, he studies history, he has to—he said that the riots and the suppres-sion came a century *after* the actual end of the Golden Age. He said *that* came when the Cyn abandoned the rest of us."

"Why?" Sho asked quietly. He wasn't asking why the Cyn left, this time—he was asking why Marus thought *that* moment marked the end of the Golden Age.

"Because . . . because it was the first time a conflict arose that couldn't be settled, couldn't be worked through with diplomacy or negotiation, compro-mise or social understanding. The underpinnings of that dying era. It was the first time we failed to live up to our potential. The Cyn didn't get what they wanted—whatever the hell it was—so they just . . . left, up and left, and there went the idea that it was even *possible* for so many disparate groups of people to always find common ground."

"So the Cyn wanted something the rest of the species wouldn't give them, and they fucked right off." I nodded. "Okay. I understand so far." I leaned forward, pointed at the monitor. "But how the hell does that explain *him*? Why would the Cyn reemerge *now*, and why on someplace like Kandriad? Even if they are capable of eating pulse radiation, it's been over a century since the pulse began. Why . . . why us, why fucking *hunt* gifted children across the cosmos? What does it *want*?"

"Why are you so sure it's hunting the gifted?" Sho asked. I grimaced; I hadn't told him about what I'd found in the Cyn's ship. I didn't know if Jane knew, either, though Scheherazade might have told her—she'd been watching through my cameras, after all.

"My question is just—what does it *want*?" I said.

"That's the part that worries me, yes." Mo nodded.

"Oh, and the notion that it might be a *Cyn* doesn't?" Jane raised an eyebrow.

"That's bad enough, yes," Mo agreed, "but as I said: it's not just *what* he is—he might be—that makes him a threat. It's *who*." He nodded at the screen in front of him. "Being a Cyn makes him hard to kill, yes. Makes him very . . . capable. But look at him. Look at his face." He *did* have one, just barely: the faintest hint of features in the flickering flames that made up his being, frozen in the static of the monitor. I didn't like what I saw there.

"We still don't know what he's after," I said quietly. "Even if it *is* gifted kids . . ." We didn't know what he *wanted* with us.

"No," Mo agreed, "but we know *why* he's after them." He nodded again at the screen. "Listen to what he's said, what he's *told* you, the words he spoke: of a 'reckoning,' a 'destined day,' a 'purification.' That face . . . that's not someone fulfilling a contract, or fighting for survival. *That*"—he reached out and tapped the monitor, making the image flicker for a moment—"that is a zealot. And *that* is what makes him dangerous. A man who speaks as though he holds God's own authority over someone else's life: he will be relentless, unstoppable, unwavering in his belief that he, and he alone, walks a righteous path." Mo shook his head, still staring at the image, frozen on the screen. "Death will be the only way to protect yourself from him. Yours, or his own. Attempting his capture is a fool's game."

"You're a believer, Mo," Jane said quietly. "I wouldn't think you'd excoriate someone else for being the same."

"A believer, yes—on some days," he agreed. "But not *that*. Never that. Of all my failings, possessing the arrogance to presume that I *alone* know the will of God, that I *alone* can be trusted to carry out His commandments; that all my actions, no matter how horrific they may seem, will be forgiven— will ultimately be *justified*—because of my faith . . . That level of belief is something I have never come anywhere near. And when I pray tonight, I will thank Allah that that is so."

We all had crowded around the monitor by this point—even Sho, in his chair, even Jane. We all stared at that barest hint of a face in the swept-up flames that made up the Cyn's head—now that Mo had said what he saw, I couldn't see anything but. A determination, a level of *commitment*, that went beyond survival, that may well have sailed right past sanity. Whatever it was the Cyn wanted, nothing was going to stop him from getting it.

And yet he may well have held an answer to the pulse. *Could* the Justified negotiate with him, learn from him? After what he'd done—did I even *want* them to? "You cannot escape the fire, nor the fall." That was what he had said. And he was going to *drag* us to that fate if he had to kill half the god-damned galaxy to get us there—*that* was what he meant by "you cannot escape." He meant that once he'd decided to kill us, it was inevitable, our destiny, his and ours both. Our deaths were *meant* to be.

"So do you believe right now, Mo?" Jane asked her mentor quietly.

"In this moment? Looking at what faith has twisted this . . . thing into?" Mo shook his head gently. "No. No, today, right now, I do not believe. But *he* does." He nodded again at the figure of flame on the screen. "And he does not have days of doubt."

CHAPTER 7

Dinner that night was a subdued affair, despite the fact that it was excellent—I guess living primarily off whatever fish he could catch in the ocean beyond his villa had given Mo plenty of time to practice his piscine-related culinary skills. Tasty fish curry aside, though, the conversation about the Cyn—and the nature of his hate—was fresh in everyone's minds, which tended to put a damper on their appetites.

Except for Sho. The discovery that our enemy was a member of a long-lost species even more powerful—and more dangerous—than we might have imagined notwithstanding, nobody ate like a Wulf adolescent.

After we'd finished up our meal and night began to fall, Mo went off to pray, Jane went off to prowl the grounds, Sho went . . . somewhere, I'm really not sure, and I stayed right at the big dining room table, having set up an acetylene torch on the fancy inlaid wood in front of me, terribly out of place among the finery and the delicate decorations. I stared into its flame for a moment, the only light source in the room other than the glow of Mo's monitors and the moonlight falling from the windows.

Regardless of the fact that we had *this* Cyn trapped on Valkyrie Rock, where there was one zealot, there were more. That sort of focused hate didn't just spring fully formed from the void; there was a *belief* out there, a dangerous one, and this particular Cyn was only a . . . a *symptom* of it. For all we knew, the whole damned race believed like he did. If I was going to learn to take on more of his kind, I was going to have to learn how to manipulate energy, just like they did. That was . . . that was just a fact.

I'd proven I could *do* it, back on Valkyrie Rock—I'd shifted the angle of his attack, just a little, but enough. Now I just needed to learn to do it *without* melting my brain. And, as Jane had taught me, the only way to get better at a thing was practice.

I reached out with my telekinesis, and tried to lift the flame free of the torch.

Ouch.

It felt as though I were grasping the fire with my bare hands, thrusting fingers deep into the flame, except it was my *mind* that was burning, not my palms. I growled soundlessly, snorted—hopefully not smoke—and tried again.

Ouch.

The goddamned fire didn't even budge before I had to withdraw my "touch." It might have been wiser to start with something less . . . energetic—a candle flame, rather than a welding torch—but I was afraid that I'd simply crush the wick rather than *actually* manipulate the fire. Plus, plunge into the deep end and all that. I'd shifted the flight path of a ball of primal energy made up of . . . whatever the hell the Cyn was actually made up of, or summoned to his being, or whatever: I could do *this.* I could do a simple torch flame if I only—

Ooouchgoddammit.

Dejected, I threw myself back into my chair—I had been leaning over the welding torch, like I was trying to will it into submission with body language—and glared at the hissing finger of flame, completely unaffected by my efforts.

"It is good to try." I looked up; Mo had returned from his prayers, was watching me fail with something almost like amusement on his craggy face. "But do not try so hard you convince yourself what you are learning to do cannot be done."

"I *know* it can be done; I've done it," I growled, putting my hands on either side of the torch as I prepared to try again. "That's the problem. I know it *can* be done—I just have no idea how I actually *did* it." I tried again, trying to focus on the light from the flame, rather than the flame itself; pictured my teke not as hands, like I usually did, but as a cool wind, lifting the flame up, raising it off the flow of gas and floating it—

Ouch!

At least this time the flame had bobbed off its nozzle, just for a moment. I think.

I stuck my tongue out at the welding torch, then looked back to Mo, giving my "burns" a little time to cool off. "How were your prayers?" I asked politely.

"Good, thank you," he said, pulling up a bench beside me—the metal creaked under his weight, the furniture designed for several members of the Reetha aristocracy rather than a single, massive Mahren soldier. "I always find it calming, praying whilst looking out at the ocean. Such a large thing, one that makes me feel so small beside it."

"You said earlier—after we looked at the video, after you saw the . . . thing . . . that we've been facing—you said you didn't believe, not today. But you still pray."

He nodded. "Just because I may not believe *today*, little one, does not mean that Allah does not believe in *me*. I pray for guidance, so that I may help you find your path. If that guidance comes, it will be *because* I prayed—either through the will of Allah or through my own." He nodded at the torch flame. "Imagine your mind is coated in something that makes it fireproof—as if the flame is raging in, say, Scheherazade's interior, where nothing can actually *stay* on fire for long."

I tried that; it actually worked, a little. That is, I managed to *visibly* pull the flame off the nozzle of the torch before—

Ouch ouch ouch ouch—

—I had to drop it, like a match that had burnt down to my fingertips. Mo reached over and shut off the torch for a moment, letting it cool. "You're trying because you *want* an end result," he suggested. "But wanting a thing is not enough to make it so. You need to try because you *can*, and that is all. In the early days after the pulse, as we realized what was becoming of the next generation—after Jane and I finally returned to the Justified, after our years in the wilderness—training them in their gifts was as much about intuition and guesswork as it was about control."

"She never talks about that time," I told him, taking a drink of water so that I could measure my words carefully—if I wanted to know more about Jane's past, here was a golden opportunity, but I also didn't want to *trick* Mo into saying something Jane wouldn't want him to say, either. "It's like, in her mind, the Justified have always been what they are today."

"Jane does not like to think about the past. And for good reason. There are monsters there, for her."

"There are monsters today, too. We've got one locked up on an asteroid."

"Forgive me; I misspoke. The monsters in the years before and after the pulse—the monsters in Jane's memory—are not just those that have pursued her. Some of them *are* her, as well. I was with her, on the mission to set off the weapon that became such a great curse upon our galaxy. I was with her afterward, as well, when we found ourselves stuck on an enemy world, when all advanced technology ground to a halt. A dozen operatives went on that mission. Only Jane and I remained when we were finally able to get off that world, three years later. The things we had to do, to survive that chaos; many of them were not . . . pleasant."

"So is that . . ." I sighed, and threw caution to the winds. "That's one of the things she doesn't talk about. She does what she does *now*, finding kids like Sho, kids like me. But obviously that's not what she did *before* the pulse, because that wasn't a thing that needed doing—there were no kids like us, not back then. Setting off the weapon, infiltrating enemy territory to do so—is that what you guys *did?*"

He nodded. "That's what we did, for the most part; that's even how Jane and I met. I was a different man back then. Angrier, more . . . *assertive* in my beliefs of right and wrong. I ran counter-ops for the Justified, small squads with a great deal of latitude, put together to neutralize threats before they could fully coalesce against us. I recruited Jane right out of one of those threats, one of the sects preparing to harm us, though they themselves did not know that's what they were doing. I used her to destroy them. More accurately, to make them destroy themselves. I turned her against her own people, for the greater good. What I *thought* was the greater good." He had been staring into the middle distance as he spoke; now he shifted his gaze to me and lifted a rocky eyebrow. "I take it you did not know any of this."

Mutely, I shook my head.

"What we did, what *I* did, was necessary—I still believe that—but it was also . . . very cruel." He reached over and triggered the torch again, stared into the flame. "That was part of why I left your sect, despite my belief that they remain the best hope for saving this galaxy. After the pulse, I knew they *needed* to exist, that if anyone could respond to the threat that had been un- leashed, it would be those who unleashed it; but I *also* knew that I was no longer the man to ensure that existence.

"Jane felt similarly, I believe, but she still thought she owed something, despite what joining the Justified had cost her, initially. So rather than leave when her mentor did, she soothed her conscience by taking on a different duty instead: rescuing children, many of them in even worse situations than she had been when I found her. Penance, penitence, protecting the innocent from the harsh galaxy around them."

"Well," I shrugged, turning back to the candle flame, "that explains why someone who doesn't actually seem to *like* children very much volunteers to work with them." I closed my eyes—*felt* with the edges of my teke instead, until I surrounded the candle flame. Lifted. I could feel it come up, blissfully pain-free for a moment, then—

Ouch.

I opened my eyes again, glared at the flame. Mo laughed, softly; I transferred the glare to him. "If this galaxy is so harsh," I asked him, "why do you believe at all? Why even try? Why *look* for God, if He's the one responsible for this mess we're in in the first place?"

"I do not have to *try* to believe in order to have faith, Esa," he told me. "Living beings—even beings like the Cyn that hunts you—are hardwired to believe in *something*, whether that might be religion, reason, an ideology. Belief is simply what we do. Yet that same *need* for faith—that same desire to have our beliefs proven out, to have others share them—is what created the sect wars in the first place."

"'For me to be right, that means someone else must be wrong.'"

"'And I must convert that person to my way of thinking, by the sword, if necessary, because believing differently than me makes them a threat, somehow.' Exactly. I think there *must* be another way; there must be a reason we *want* to believe so badly, a reason we were given this . . . blessing that we turned into an excuse to indulge our baser instincts. Something other than our reach exceeding our grasp. Jane thinks it's all just nonsense, an indulgence—that thinking creatures invented belief purely as a way to justify our deep-seated need to dominate, to kill. I have to believe in better angels than that."

"You don't think we need to fight?"

"Doesn't the mere existence of the Golden Age prove that we do not?"

"Yet you still think we *should* fight, against those who would harm others."

He nodded again. "Because there are those who, whether because of who they are or what they have done, will never give up their cause to dominate and control others. Whether they are doing so because of belief or something else—does it really matter, in the end? Does faith allow evil people to do evil without fearing retribution, because if their god is with them, their every action *must* be right? Or would evil people *always* have done evil, and merely use faith to condone their actions simply because it is near at hand?"

He shook his head. "I say a killer will always kill, no matter if they do it for a flag or a coin or a benediction from a distant god. Evil will always *be* evil; it is those who would do *good* that must constantly examine their actions, to make sure that what they are doing is truly taking the nobler path."

Still listening to Mo's words, I reached out *fast* to the flame; tried to *trick* it into thinking I wasn't going to grab it again. Yes, I was that desperate. I managed to tear it off the nozzle of the torch, but the motion was too much for the dancing flame, and it snuffed out. I sighed, and relit the damn thing. "So that's why you left the Justified. Because you were no longer walking a noble path."

He nodded. "Their cause was still noble. But I was not."

"And now you . . . what? Seek isolation, seek atonement? How can you atone if there's no one around for you to help?"

He smiled. "You found me, didn't you?"

"Because Jane knew where to look."

"I seek the voice of Allah, little one. I believe when I can truly hear Him in my heart, then He will tell me what I am meant to do next."

"And if you *never* hear from him again?"

"Then that, also, is His will, and I will be called to judgment to account for all that I have done, right or wrong, good or bad."

"And in the meantime, you just . . . wait?"

"I hunt, and I fish, and I think. I spend my evenings on the balconies or out on the deck"—he nodded at the windows—"talking to old friends."

"But . . . you're all alone here."

He shrugged. "Well, most of my friends are dead. Don't worry—they don't usually talk back." He tapped the side of his head. "Just up here. Also, Esa?"

"Yes?"

He nodded, at the flame of the torch. Which was hovering just a few inches from the nozzle.

I'd done it.

As soon as I *realized* I'd done it, of course, it scorched the *shit* out of me. *Ouch. Fuck!*

CHAPTER 8

In the morning Sho and I set off for the broadcast tower, with Jane's prerecorded message—complete with the video footage of our engagements with the Cyn, the data Schaz was still deciphering, and notations from both of us for Criat to scour—tucked into my pouch.

The tower was the same structure I'd seen from the air; it was a few miles up the beach, but the day was gorgeous—of course it was; we were on a nature preserve for the super rich, "an utter lack of nongorgeous days" had probably been in the design document of the original terraformers—and the sand up the beach was firm enough that Sho's wheelchair had no problem gripping it. I'd been the one to suggest that Sho and I handle sending the message, to give Mo and Jane a chance to catch up as well as to let the two of us get the lay of the land.

Plus, there was that conversation we needed to have, gifted child to gifted child, survivor to survivor. I wasn't looking forward to it, but like I was starting to learn from Jane: when you had a hard thing to do, the best thing was usually to just . . . do it. Letting it fester would only make it worse.

"Sho," I said, trying to find a way to start. We'd been heading up the beach in peaceable silence for the last little bit—or at least, *Sho* had seemed peaceful; I'd been looking for a good way to tell him what I needed to tell him.

"Yes, Esa?" he asked. I stopped walking for a moment, stared out at the ocean. Just . . . *do it*, dammit. Just be brave. If it were you, *you* would want to know.

"I need . . . I need to tell you something."

"You found something. On the Cyn's ship. Something that means . . . something that told you he really *was* on Kandriad hunting gifted children." I turned toward him, my eyes wide—how the hell had he put that together?

The answer was simple: he was *smart*, and he thought things through, and he was observant as all hell.

He took my surprised reaction as assent—there was that observant nature again—and nodded, something incredibly painful, almost bitter, in the sharp jerk of his head. "I thought so," he whispered. "Which means what happened . . . what happened to my city . . . what happened to my mother . . . it was because of me."

"*No.*" I said the single word as forcefully as I could—so forcefully, in point of fact, that a puff of sand was kicked up from the beach, my teke reacting to my ironclad sense of negation. "What happened on Kandriad was because of the Cyn, Sho. It was because of *him*. You didn't choose to be born the way you were, and you certainly didn't choose to be *hunted*." I'd been through much the same thing, when Jane had found me—blamed myself for the Pax razing my hometown. I was determined to help Sho through the same thing I'd suffered, the same self-doubt, the same self-hate.

"What did you find?" he asked me, those big gold eyes staring up into my own.

I knelt in the sand, the ocean behind me, so I could look him in the face. "A girl," I said sadly. "A Vyriat girl, younger . . . younger than both of us, I think. He'd . . . locked her in a cage. She saw her chance to escape from him, and she took it."

"'Escape' from him? You mean—"

I nodded. "She only saw one way out of his grip, one way out of . . . whatever it was he wanted her for. And she took it."

He looked away from me then. "I wonder if I could have done the same," he said.

"You didn't have to. You didn't have to *make* that choice, Sho."

"I know I didn't. Because of you." He looked out, reached up with one paw to touch my face. "Thank you, Esa."

I nodded, once, the motion making the pads of his paw rough against my skin. "The Cyn is the one to blame for this, Sho. Not the pulse that gave us these gifts, not the Tyll sect on your homeworld leading the attack—that motherfucker we've got locked up on Valkyrie Rock, *he's* the one that did this. You get that, right?"

"I get it," he said, looking away from me then, out over the ocean, and, looking at his face, I think maybe he *did*—but I didn't see any hate there, no rage, just a kind of . . . all-encompassing sorrow, a sadness that extended even toward the Cyn himself, for what his beliefs had made him. "I just wish I didn't."

I let the silence sit for a moment, until I thought it had sat long enough. Then I reached out, gently, and turned his face back toward me. His eyes were full of tears.

Forced to look into my eyes, he was forced into speech, too. "I blame him for it, yes," he said, something so . . . so *small* about his voice then. "But I don't know what . . . My mother. She was in the tunnels . . . she may have gotten out. She may have gotten *up*, climbed higher into the factory. And then came the blast. Esa, I . . . I don't know which one to wish *for*. I don't know whether or not to wish she died in the gas, or in the fires. I don't know which would be more *painless*, which would . . ." He choked back a sob; I put my hands on either side of his neck, touched my head to his, and let him cry.

Good. Let him blame the Cyn for that, for the impossible choice he was facing, for the cruelty that left him wondering *which* death the woman who had raised him had faced. They were both on the head of the Cyn, either way.

He stopped crying after a while. I'd been crying too—I'm a bit of a cry-baby, really; someone *else* starts crying, *I* start crying, it's a mess—and for a moment, we just looked at each other, me kneeling on the beach, him still in his chair. "I can . . . despise the Cyn for what he did," he said finally. "For making my mother face that choice. It's easy. But Esa?"

"Yeah, Sho?" I sniffed; *he'd* actually stopped crying before I did.

"I'm glad you found me. Even if it *hadn't* saved my life . . . I'd still be glad. So . . . so thank you."

I smiled at him, managed something like a grin. "You're welcome, Sho," I told him. "I'm glad we found you, too."

We headed farther up the beach.

The tower wasn't much farther—a twisting spire of delicate construction that rose twice as high as any of the nearby jungle. The looping crescents of blue and gold that made up the helix at the center of the thing hadn't been weathered at *all* by over a century of rainfall or sand or salt or the other forces of natural entropy; I had no idea what the damned thing was made of, but at least it was a good sign that the thing was still *capable* of sending our message.

"Think it'll work?" Sho asked, bringing his wheelchair to a stop and staring up at the tower. We were both trying our best to pretend like we hadn't been bawling our eyes out less than an hour before; were mostly succeeding, too. "It likely won't have power after so many years."

I shrugged. "Well, that's why I brought a rolling fusion battery along."

"You did? I didn't see you—*hey!*" I grinned back at him—I'd always *wanted* a little brother to play stupid jokes on; maybe later I'd try to braid his fur— as I started sauntering toward the base of the tower, the structure casting a long shadow down the beach even as it rose up to intersect with the planetary rings soaring in the sky above.

There was no door to let us inside of the structure, no actual "interior" at all, just a canopied overhang above a small access monitor—because god forbid the Jaliad actually got *rained* on if they wanted to send a message offworld. Though come to think of it, they probably just dictated the messages in the comfort of their palatial estates, and sent a servant to actually do the broadcasting. The rising tower was incredibly intricately designed down to the smallest detail, like a piece of delicate artwork soaring into the sky, and had only ever meant to be seen as they flew past.

I wasn't even beneath the overhang yet when the screen snapped to life; I looked back, and sure enough, here came Sho, bringing the envelope of his gifts with him. *That* was good—if I'd actually needed to rewire the thing, we would have had to make tracks back to Mo's villa and admit defeat. Unless *Sho* knew how to rewire a broadcast antenna, which was . . . doubtful, given the level of tech on his homeworld.

I fitted Jane's message into the slot and punched in the Justified encryption code and the coordinates of Sanctum. Sho was staring upward at the tower as I pressed the broadcast button—I think maybe he was expecting a burst of light or something—but there wasn't anything to *see*; the broadcast was invisible. All the same, the message had gone out, heading toward the Justified, and every one of our ships it passed would *also* get an alert: there was a

Justified operative in trouble, all hands on deck, haul ass and save the day, "Code Red" or whatever.

One of these days I should . . . I should probably learn the actual code names. Might be important.

CHAPTER 9

The message was sent; Schaz was merrily bubbling away under the surface of the sea, working on the decryption of the data and the analysis of the mask I'd nicked from the Cyn's ship; the Cyn himself, the fucker, was still trapped in the abattoir he'd made of Valkyrie Rock. We had nothing but time.

Our days spent in Mo's villa—or rather, the Jaliad villa Mo was squatting in—quickly fell into a certain pattern. Mo would go out in the morning to hunt, or else sit on the upper levels of the villa's decks to fish, watching Jane and me training along the beach, while Sho did roughly the same in the shade of the villa, trying to learn how to *actively* manipulate the fusion energy he gave off in waves. Jane had something against enforced idleness, and after three years, I'd grown to appreciate that fact: if we had nothing else to do, we trained.

We'd break for lunch—usually leftovers from the night before—and then I'd practice channeling energy through my telekinesis, while Jane would take Sho and try to walk him through his progress during the morning. Both of us had incremental success, though it always came hard earned: Sho always looked worn out and frazzled when lunch rolled around, and I had to shave my head again after the stubble that had been slowly taking over my scalp decided to catch fire on a bad day.

Still, we were making progress. By the end of the week, Sho could generate an electric current out of thin air, a current he would then lash at me: I could hold off his attacks at the very least, and once or twice I managed to siphon off enough energy to gather it up in a teke spike and toss it back at him—though I aimed for the beach beside him, not for Sho himself: he hadn't gone through any defensive training yet, and we didn't have the facilities here to implant an intention shield into his neck.

The evenings were for relaxing, or being as relaxed as any of us got: two old soldiers, and two teenagers doing their damnedest to adjust to having superpowers. Or in my case, trying to do new shit with *old* superpowers. I'd just been starting to get a handle on using my teke in combat, and now this new wrinkle came up.

One night, Mo and Jane were trading war stories on the deck—not stories about when they'd worked together, unfortunately, more "what's the craziest thing you've fought since we went our separate ways"—and I wheeled Sho off to bed. When I came back, I paused by the door. I wasn't *trying* to eavesdrop, per se; Jane and Mo were just deep in conversation, and I didn't want to interrupt them.

Also, I wanted to eavesdrop.

Mo was speaking as I made my decision *not* to approach. "How much longer are you going to keep this up, Red? You've fought your wars."

"There are always more wars, Mo."

"And always new blood to fight them. The girl's good." That was nice to hear.

"She's not as good as me." Well, okay, but still.

"She's not what you were when you were her age, no. But that's not what I meant. You and I . . . we're compromised. And I don't just mean the pulse; I don't just mean the decisions we made, with the Justified. From before that, even. When I say she's good, I mean she's *good*, Jane. She'll be able to find ways . . . solutions . . . we never could. She's not a killer. Not at heart."

Jane sighed, shifted in her chair. I drew back, farther into the shadows. "You're right," she said, staring up at the rings that split the night sky.

Mo shrugged. "I've always been able to read people."

"I mean about me, old man. Esa too, but mostly . . . I'm getting old, Mo."

"Ah, you look fine. I meant more how long did you *want* to do it; wasn't asking how long you *could*. I'm a hundred years older than you are, and I'm still kicking."

"You're Mahren; you've still got a ways to go on your natural lifespan. I'm well past mine. It's just nanotech and synthetic . . . everything, holding me together now. Humans just weren't meant to live this long. I certainly never was. When I was Esa's age, I never dreamt I'd see my next decade, let alone a century or more.'"

"Then retire. Scoop up this Javier of yours, find some forgotten world somewhere, live out what's left of your days. Take up fishing, basket weaving, whatever. Just don't take up a gun again."

"You've still got your guns."

"But I don't have your ghosts. The Justified made me a killer, Jane. For better or worse—"

"They didn't have to *make* me anything. I know. I was already . . . by the time you found me—"

"You needed training in a lot of ways. Never in that one."

I think Jane almost smiled at that; I could hear it in her voice. "Was I really so feral?"

"It's a question of degrees," Mo shrugged. "I just had to remind you that you were a person, underneath all the rest. She's doing the same thing—the girl, I mean. And *that's* why you feel old, Red. It's not because you're failing, or fading. It's because for the first time in a long time, you've got someone around to remind you that you have more to offer than death."

"And also because she's seventeen, and I'm . . . not."

"And also that, yes." Mo sighed, shifted in his chair. "Do you remember the story of Aeliadh Hill, Jane? I told it to you, when you were young."

"Where the last of the great Vyriat knights made their stand, defending the last library, before the Vyriat Dark Ages descended. Yeah, I remember. They died, to a man. And their cause was lost."

"Their *war* was lost; not their cause. After, they became legend, their story told, over and over, a reminder *during* the Dark Ages of what the Vyriat could become. My point is: you're not there. Not yet. Your story doesn't have to end like that, even if that ending for them was a beginning for someone else. They fought to the last because they had no other choice. You shouldn't go *looking* for your Aeliadh Hill. That's all I'm trying to say. You've still got a good fight or two left in you."

CHAPTER 10

We kept training, and we kept waiting: for Schaz to finish her decryption, for some sort of message to arrive from Sanctum. Mo's hospitality had its limits: he had point blank refused to let us offer up Jaliad as a staging ground for our second assault on the Cyn's prison, had refused to let us tell the Justified where we were at all. That meant we were waiting to hear that Sanctum was sending other operatives to Valkyrie Rock, and once we did, we could join them there.

After another round with Sho, I lay exhausted and panting on the warm wood of the deck, my sparring partner in his wheelchair beside me. "It feels like I'm lifting this whole place with my legs," he moaned, just as worn as I was. "You know—the legs that *don't work*."

"Jane always says, 'if something comes easy, you're doing it wrong.'" I closed my eyes against the bright blue glare of the sun as it descended down toward the ocean, making its way through the twisting ribbon of the planet's rings, light shining through the gaps of the orbit-clutched sediment.

"I'm not saying it should be *easy*, just that I wouldn't mind if it was just a little *less hard*," Sho replied. I grinned at that, but said nothing. "Hey—there's Mo."

I sat up, shading my eyes against the sun. Mo was indeed emerging from the forests, but unlike most afternoons, he didn't have some exotic beast for us to eat hefted on his shoulders. He was moving fast, instead. Fast wasn't good.

"Something's up," I told Sho, slipping off the edge of the deck and dropping to the sand below. "Get inside the house." I didn't wait for him to do so—though I did hear the motorized hum of his wheelchair as he started moving—I just set off running, heading toward our host, already building a teke field in my hands.

Watching a Mahren run was like watching a never-ending rockslide; he was really booking it. I put on a little extra burst of speed as well, until I was within shouting distance, and he started waving his arms. "Go back!" I could barely make out the words he was saying. "There's something—a reading, on my radar! Check the monitors!"

I turned on a dime, started sprinting back toward the villa. Exhausted or not, I closed that distance in a quarter of the time it would have taken me at a walk: my constant training with Jane paid dividends. I hauled myself back up onto the deck and darted inside the open doors, making for the dining room, where I found Sho and Jane already gathered around the pile of seemingly random tech that was Mo's early-warning system.

"It's a ship," Jane confirmed as I approached. "Its systems are stealthed; we don't know anything more than that."

"Relative size?" I asked.

"Smaller than Schaz by about half."

All right—at least it wasn't the Cyn, somehow escaped from Valkyrie Rock and out for revenge. Or, scratch that: at least it wasn't the Cyn somehow escaped from Valkyrie Rock still in his possibly Cyn *ship*—if he *had* made his way off of Valkyrie Rock, it was entirely likely his vessel hadn't been salvageable, and he'd hijacked some other craft to take him this far, something we'd missed when Schaz was spiking all the other vessels on board the asteroid.

"It's slowing down," Sho said, still glued to the monitors. He turned to look at Jane and me, fear in his eyes. "It's definitely making for us."

"That tears it; I'm headed for the roof," Jane said, grabbing her rifle from where it was leaning against the wall.

"Can you raise Schaz?" I asked. Jane was good with her rifle, but a spacecraft would be armored, heavily shielded: a handheld weapon wouldn't even make a scratch. I *really* wouldn't have minded leveling the playing field with our own ship at this point.

Jane shook her head. "You should have seen her dive, just an hour or so ago," she pointed out. I *had*, I just hadn't thought about it. Goddammit. We were on our own.

"Go," I told her. "Take up position." I had an idea. "Sho, come with me."

"Where are we going?"

"To take our new abilities for a test drive." Sho obediently wheeled after me as I made my way through the halls of the villa to a ramp leading up to the second floor; we crouched just inside a shuttered window of one of the outlying buildings, that side of the structure in shadow thanks to the sun being past its zenith somewhere behind us. I opened the shutters and looked out over the beach, Sho just behind me, already building a current.

There was nothing moving on the sands, nothing moving in the trees beyond the natural shift and sway of the leaves as the ocean breezes passed through them. Mo must have already made his way inside—he wasn't visible, though I could see his tracks in the sand. The shadows of the rings made ribbons of shade across the beach; I sat in a crouch and held up one hand, my palm flat, creating a kind of . . . *vessel* in my palm, just like I had during the training Sho and I had been engaged in a little bit ago.

"All right, Sho," I told him. "This is the real thing, now. Give me a slow trickle, just a little bit." In my left hand, I formed a teke spear, the "weight" of it offsetting the sphere in my right. As Sho fed his current to me, I fed it into the sphere, and kept the other weapon at the ready as well. If it really was the Cyn that came setting down on the beach, he'd get the sphere full of energy; ballistic weapons didn't seem to threaten him, but he *had* been contained by the burst of lightning from the shattered transformer on Valkyrie Rock, so at least *some* forms of energy had an effect.

If it was anyone else—and they were threatening—they'd get the spear. The "thrown" weapon wouldn't likely kill them—my fine control over my telekinesis didn't extend to giving sharp edges to my projectiles—but it *would* put them on their ass long enough for us to figure out who the hell they were, and what they wanted here.

I felt Sho's energy climbing over my skin like a line of hot ants. Grimacing, I kept feeding it into my sphere, a single mantra passing through my mind: *Please don't catch on fire. Please don't catch on fire. Please don't catch on fire.*

The ship appeared, matching its course to the rising arcs of the planetary rings—meaning we *couldn't* make out its form against the shadow. Clever captain. The sphere in my palm was slowly filling up with energy, like a cup filling up with water; I had about as much as I could hold, so I whispered "enough" to Sho, and he cut the flow.

Now I just had to kneel there, holding it, like a glass ball full of molten fire. Fun times.

There was something familiar about the whining of the ship's engines, but I couldn't quite place it. It was definitely slowing down now, almost coming to a stop, hovering—but not quite setting down—over the beach where moments ago Sho and I had been training. As it descended, its form became clear, and I realized where I'd seen it before—

"Don't shoot!" I shouted through my comms at Jane; I could only hope Mo was close enough to his comm station that he could hear me as well. "It's a friend!"

The ship's ramp opened, and a form stepped out, making the twenty-foot drop from the craft to the beach with the kind of nonchalant disdain for gravity that only a species made entirely of metal could manage: a Barious.

"Got your message!" the Preacher shouted at the villa, raising one hand to shade her eyes from the sun. "You were supposed to be back in Sanctum days ago; what the *hell* are you doing out here?"

CHAPTER 11

I didn't know what to do with the orb of crackling energy Sho had fed me, so I wound up just hucking it as far out to sea as I could, where it made a lovely waterspout.

There were introductions all around after we all descended to the beach: Mo, the Preacher, and Sho all very politely pretending like none of them had been prepared to kill the other just moments before. It turned out that, since we'd been overdue to return to Sanctum, the Preacher had *already* been on her way to our last known position—Kandriad—when she'd encountered our message; she did that sort of thing, she was *way* overprotective.

From there, she'd tracked the signal back to its origin, rather than heading directly to the rally point we'd set for the Justified, like the message stated she should: for all that the Preacher was *with* the Justified now, she didn't really consider herself a member of the sect, and so considered Justified commands more of "polite suggestions" than anything else.

She'd made her way past the war satellites thanks to what she called a "conversation" with the Jaliad AI; I had to wonder if that conversation hadn't involved the Preacher hacking her way into the Jaliad defense network and writing her own ticket as a long-lost member of the very, *very* dead monarchy. There were very few networks in the galaxy that could stand up to a determined Barious when it came to hacking or decryption.

"A Cyn." The Preacher shook her head, sitting at a table on the deck that stretched out from the villa over the sea. "It's . . . hard to believe."

"But not impossible," Mo put in. "They went *somewhere*, after all."

"So did our creators," the Preacher said mildly. "It's not as though I ever expected *them* to show up again. And you have no idea why he's trying to capture gifted children? Are there . . . specific gifts they have, some sort of further criteria? Something to do with energy, perhaps? Which—well done, by the way." She nodded at me. "Your gifts are coming along well." Then she frowned. "Also, what happened to your hair?"

I rushed past that part. "You seem less . . . *thrilled* than I'd thought you'd be, Preacher."

"About what? The fact that you think this . . . *being* . . . can consume pulse radiation? About the fact that the key to the survival of my people—my *species*—might lie in the hands of some sort of carnage-happy predator who has been *butchering* his way across the galaxy? You expected I'd be *thrilled* by that?"

"I mean . . . 'enthused,' at least?"

"I'll be 'enthused' when we learn how to *reproduce* what he is capable of—divorced from his rampages of death." That was fair, probably.

"I said this to Jane, and I'll say it to you as well, just so there is no confusion," Mo put in, his words directed at the Preacher. "Trying to take this . . . creature alive . . . will not be possible. Containing him on the asteroid was one thing, but getting him to the point where you can study him, interact with him—I would not suggest getting your hopes too high on that measure."

The Preacher narrowed her eyes at him, her irises dilating in a spiral like a camera lens. "My lack of 'enthusiasm' aside, that thing may well hold the answer to the question I've been studying for a century, Mohammed. Whatever *risks* are involved—"

"You misunderstand," Mo told her. "I'm not saying it will be *difficult* to take him alive, I'm saying you *can't*. Not if he doesn't want you to, and he *will not want you to*. You're focused on what he *is*—a being made of energy, a Cyn, something that eats away at the pulse. You're forgetting *who* he is; namely, a zealot, a believer, one seeking a kind of . . . rapture through his violence. Even if you were to attempt to transport him back to Sanctum, back to your scientists, he can *manipulate* energy. That sort of manipulation starts from within."

"You think he'd snuff himself out rather than fall into our hands." Jane nodded, leaning back in her chair. "That tracks. For all we know, he may have done so already."

"For what he's offering—for what his *existence* offers—we have to try," the Preacher said stubbornly. "There must be some way to . . . incapacitate him, to prevent him from—"

"You honestly don't understand, do you?" Mo shook his head. "You're not getting the old galaxy *back*, Barious. These are the worlds we have now, pulsed or not. We must make our peace with that."

"Easy to say, coming from a species not barreling toward extinction." The Preacher glared at him.

"We've got time, still," I interjected, trying to cool tempers all around. "Time to think up our best approach. He's *stuck* on that asteroid, so unless he *has* . . . snuffed himself out—in which case, we can't do a damn thing about it anyway—*we* have the advantage." I turned to Jane. "Has Schaz made any headway decrypting the drive I managed to copy from his systems? Or pulling apart the mask?"

"Not the last time I spoke to her, no." Jane shook her head. "That was an hour or so ago, this morning, before she dove back into the deep."

"What's all this?" the Preacher asked.

"When Esa broke into his ship to plant the bomb—"

"You let *Esa* do that? Alone?"

"We didn't have a hell of a lot of choice, Preacher."

"I can take care of myself, you know," I told her, a little stung.

"You're a child."

"Not for a while now, actually," I shot back.

The Preacher and I glared at each other for a bit; we always seemed to wind up doing that. For a being with theoretically perfect recall, the Preacher always seemed to have a bit of a blind spot for my capabilities. No matter how often I proved that I could take care of myself, she always seemed to want to treat me like I was made of glass, a fragile, delicate thing that needed to be protected at all costs.

When I felt like I'd glared enough to make my point—the Preacher could glare all day without moving a muscle, but I was just human, I'd get tired eventually—I turned back to Jane. "Did Schaz say how much longer it would take?" I asked. "Maybe there's something in those files, something about the mask, something that can tell us . . . I don't know, but something we *don't* know now."

"Just that she wasn't particularly close," Jane said mildly, pretending like the Preacher and I hadn't interrupted the conversation to just stare angrily at each other for a little bit. "The systems the Cyn used are almost entirely foreign to her—almost, but not quite. That means it's taking a great deal of work." I thought of the strangeness of the drive on board that alien ship—the only piece of tech I'd even vaguely recognized, wired into foreign systems with a definite lack of delicacy. "Almost, but not quite" sounded about right.

The Preacher stood, her hands still on the table. "When she resurfaces, have her give me access to the network on which she's running her decryption algorithms," she said.

"She's not going to do that—she's not doing it on a network at all," Jane told her. "Our encryption's been hacked one too many times lately."

"So have her come here, and let me on board." The Preacher didn't actually have any teeth to grind, but her jaw was still tensed, as though she were still *trying*, very, very hard. "I have much more advanced intrusion packages than your shack . . . than Scheherazade." Oh, good. If the Preacher reverted to referring to any non-Barious AI as "shackled," she and Jane were really going to fight, and I don't mean that in a "shouting match" kind of way. Barious or not, I didn't know if that was a fight the Preacher was going to win. "In the meantime, I need to speak to you. In private." She was still glaring daggers at Jane; great. It looked like they were going to fight anyway.

Without another word, they stalked off into the villa. "So that's another Justified," Sho said. "She seems . . ." He groped for a term, probably looking for one that didn't include a rude phrase or two, for politeness's sake.

"Yeah, I know," I sighed. "But she means well." That was part of the problem.

"You think they're fighting about you?" Sho asked.

"Well, they're sure as hell not fighting about *you*," I replied. "You might not have noticed, but the Preacher doesn't really *care* who she offends."

"Unless it's you. So they're *definitely* fighting about you."

"That would be my conclusion, yeah."

"They seem to have gone into one of the upstairs rooms," Sho said. Then, with something like a grin: "I've noticed over the last few days that there's a central maintenance area for what used to be the villa's climate-control system. If you're in there, you can hear someone speaking from almost anywhere in the main villa, through the ducts."

I grinned in return, standing from the table. "You just happened to notice that, did you? Want to show me where it is?"

"I should probably stop the two of you," Mo said mildly. "To protect Jane's privacy, and all that."

"But you're not going to, are you?"

"No, I'm not. Jane *is* teaching you spycraft, after all, or at least she's meant to be. Gathering intelligence is part of your education. Have fun snooping."

We went to do just that.

CHAPTER 12

Sho and I made our way through the servants' quarters to the maintenance areas—Mo hadn't cleaned these rooms out, probably because he couldn't even *fit* back here; the Jaliad had been Reetha, after all, and the vaulted ceilings and wide open spaces of the villa proper notwithstanding, the Reetha were a small people. We ignored the detritus of lives long abandoned and squeezed into the climate-control access area, where we could hear Jane and the Preacher, clear as a bell, their voices echoing through the ducts.

Of course, we probably could have heard them from *anywhere* in the villa; their "private conversation" had already moved into shouting territory.

"Have you taken a *look* at her lately, Jane? Have you seen what she's *wearing*? Body armor and combat boots; a full set of—"

"Oh, I'm so fucking *sorry*, Preacher, I'm only training her to keep herself *alive*; if I had known her sartorial education was more important than—"

"She's bruised, just—*everywhere*, she has blood under her nails and all over her clothes—has she even taken a *shower* since you got here?" I felt a pang at that; I actually hadn't. I mean, I'd *tried* to go swimming, but Jane had stopped me. "She doesn't *belong* out here, Jane. She doesn't—"

"What do you want, Preacher? You want me to keep her locked up at Sanctum, stuck in classes with the rest of the next-generation kids?"

"*Yes*. That's exactly what I want. That's what's *best* for her, Jane, even if you can't see it—"

"She made the choice to come out here, Preacher. *She* did, not me."

"You agreed, and you should have known better—you should have known what taking her out here would *do*. Just *look at her*. She's wearing *guns*, Jane—multiple guns, including those fucking pistols that your petty criminal of a boyfriend gave her; what the hell kind of a birthday gift is that for a seventeen-year-old girl?"

"Don't try and drag Javier into this; he's done more right by her than—"

"Pistols and submachine guns and *knives*, Jane. Even here, where she's supposed to be safe. What kind of life are you giving her, where she never feels *safe?*"

"Better that she doesn't *feel* safe and actually *is* than she *feels* safe when she's not and that gets her *dead;* better that she—"

"Those *aren't* the only options; stop pretending like they are! There are safe places in this universe; Sanctum is one of them, where she belongs! And you don't think that—"

"Tell me something: what's safer, in the long run? A thing made of glass, locked behind a steel cage? Or a thing *made* of steel, that can actually defend *itself?* She's not suited for classrooms and medical suites, not any more than—"

"Oh, stop projecting your own insecurities on her, Jane. You're the one who can't bear to stay in one place; *you're* the one who can't bear to look at yourself in a mirror. Your sins aren't hers, and she shouldn't have to carry the weight of them."

"I'll say it again, and I'll *keep* fucking saying it: *she* decided to do this, to do *good*, rather than just sitting around and—"

"She's seventeen, she was barely *fourteen* when she made that decision, and you're acting like she's a full-grown adult! She's not *capable* of deciding what's best for her, that's *why she's still a child!*"

Jane didn't shout her response; instead, her words were low, low enough that Sho and I had to strain to hear, her voice threaded with real rage and something that was almost malice. "You look at her and you see the infant you stole from the station where she was born; you see the toddler you *gave away*. She's grown since then, Preacher. You just weren't around to see it."

A deep, shuddering breath—from the Preacher, who didn't need to breathe. Jane had touched a nerve. "I understand, Jane, that where *you* were born, the people around you had more use for weapons than for little girls, and so that's what they *made* you. I understand that you never had a chance to be anything different. Sanctum is *better* than that; the Justified are better than that. They're *meant* to be—that's the whole point!"

"The point is to do *good*. She can do more good out here, with me— without her, I never would have gotten Sho out alive, never would have gotten him off of Kandriad. That's the point. She saved me in that factory, and again on Valkyrie Rock; she's saved *me* a dozen times more than I've saved *her. That's* the point. She's *good at this,* Preacher; I don't know why you can't see it."

"She may be *good* at it, Jane—and if she is, it's because of your training, I'll grant you that—but it's not who she *is.* It's what you're *making* her. She is *not* a soldier, not at heart. She is *not* a killer. You look at her and you see someone becoming something . . . something dangerous, something violent, and you're *proud* of that fact—"

"I am; I damn well am! She's learning how to keep herself *alive*—"

"She's killing herself, bit by bit! Every time you haul her back to Sanctum from some godforsaken rock somewhere, she's *different,* Jane, and not in a good way, no matter how much you might suggest otherwise! Your 'training,' your *world,* it's killing her! You just can't see it because *impressing* you is so goddamned important to her that she *makes sure* you can't—that you can't see through the brave face she puts on! You can't see that—"

"*Of course I can!*" Jane roared the words; both of them were stunned into silence for a moment by the vehemence behind them. "Of course I can," Jane repeated, softer this time. "You think I don't know, Preacher? You think I can't *see* how the lives she's taken haunt her? How every single *one* haunts her? No, Preacher. I can see. You're right—she's not like me. She gets that there's a cost; a cost paid not just by those she puts down, but one that comes from inside her as well. It took me way too long to realize the same thing. But ignoring that cost—doing the hard thing *anyway,* and making sure that *you're* the one that pays, not someone else—*that's* the right thing to do. *That's* what I'm teaching her."

"And ruining her, in the process. Why isn't *she* worthy of your protection, Jane? Why isn't she—"

"Because she's capable of protecting others, Preacher. Because she's *stronger* than me. Because she can bear that cost, better than I can. In the long run."

"So she eats your sins. That's how it is."

"There's no life without sin, Preacher; *that's* how it is. Finding a way to deal with what that means—learning how to stomach the . . . wrong living sometimes requires—that's *part* of what staying alive means, in this galaxy, in what it is *now.* And that's *how* you learn it—by putting on a brave face, wearing that mask until it's *not* a mask anymore. You learn it by pretending it doesn't bother you until . . . until it just doesn't anymore. At least not as much." Jane sighed, more exhaustion, more weariness, in that simple noise than in any of her shouted words.

"You remember you're talking about murder, right?" There was spite in the Preacher's words, but also kindness, too. Or at least grief.

"I'm talking about survival, Preacher. There's a difference."

"But can you still tell where that line is drawn? Have you *ever* actually known? And now you're teaching her to erase it, just like you learned to do. Just like your sect taught you. The sins of the mother only stop being passed down when the *mother* puts a stop to it, Jane. It's not the child's duty. It's not her weight to carry."

"Neither is your redemption, Preacher. We're neither one of us her mother. And who's fucking fault is *that*?"

For a moment, I was entirely sure the next thing we'd hear would be the Preacher throwing Jane through a wall. I think it came damn close. Then the moment passed, and the next after that.

"I'm sorry," Jane said quietly, finally, a real apology in her voice. "You didn't deserve that. But you don't get to make decisions for her, not any more than I do. All we can do is try to keep her safe. She's the one who gets to decide what that means. It's her life. Not ours."

"And if you have to sacrifice a part of her, in doing so?"

"She's paying the cost, Preacher. Like you said. If she thinks it's too high, she'll stop paying it. It's that simple. And it's *her* choice. I'm gonna walk away now. We've already said more than we should; things we both will likely end up regretting. For what it's worth—again—I'm sorry."

We heard the sound of a door shutting, and then that was that.

Sho and I stepped out of the maintenance area; I sat on one of the hard cots the servants here had slept on, undecayed by the simple fact that it had never been made of soft enough material that it was at risk of decay in the first place. I didn't say anything for a while.

"I'm sorry I suggested we listen to that," Sho said finally. I looked at him and shook my head, brushed tears away from my face.

"They're wrong," I said, as much to myself as I said it to him. "Helping people, doing what Jane and I do—it's *not* turning me into a monster."

"I don't think you're a monster," Sho told me, wheeling closer so he could take my hand in his paw. "I could never think that. You saved me, Esa. And I know . . . I know you would have saved my mother, too. If you could have."

"But I couldn't. And Sho—I didn't even *try.*"

"You did what good you could, with what options you had available. That's all anyone can ask. Your Sanctum—no matter what the Preacher says, how *good* it's supposed to be—they wouldn't have let my mother in, would they? She never had that option."

"But we could have at least gotten her *out*—"

"There were only two masks, Jane. To protect us from the gas. You could barely make one for yourself; you couldn't have managed another. No matter how much pressure the two up there are putting on you, there are boundaries to what you can do, limitations. Asking you to reach beyond them, expecting you to . . . it's cruel. I wonder if they realize *how* cruel. Only a fool thinks he has no limits."

"And only a coward never tries to reach beyond them." I'd forgotten who'd taught me that. Criat, maybe.

"You didn't kill my mother, Esa," Sho told me, something like finality in his voice. "Not any more than I did. *You* made sure I knew that, and what you said is still true: it was the Cyn. All of it, him. The rest . . ." He shook his head, then gave me something close to a smile. "Now come on. After being cooped up in that closet with you, I can tell you that your Barious friend is *absolutely* right about one thing." He wrinkled his muzzle at me. "You really *could* use a shower."

CHAPTER 13

It rained that night; I hadn't thought the world was capable of rain, thought maybe the flora and fauna fed off of some sort of buried irrigation system instead, but apparently the Jalia monarchy liked variance in their weather. At least the atmosphere matched my mood.

It wasn't any quiet drizzle, either—we were still in the tropics, and when storms hit, they *hit*. It sounded like something alive, pacing outside the villa's walls, the thunder crashing and the wind roaring and the downpour making a constant drum on the roof and on the ocean outside.

I couldn't sleep.

Finally I gave up, tossed off my blanket and crawled into my clothes. I padded through the long-emptied halls, past ancient sculpture designed to represent who the hell knows what, until I stepped out onto the deck overlooking the sea, and stood just under the eaves of the roof, looking out into the downpour.

The crimson flashes of lightning stretched from cloud to cloud, giving the storm a violent vermillion tinge that almost made me queasy. The seas were lashed into chaos, tides and waves and wind all working against each other, making whirlpools and walls of water I could barely make out in the dimness.

I took a breath and stepped out into the rain. Let it wash over me.

It didn't matter what the Preacher said; Sho was right. I wasn't a monster. I was trying to do good. And whatever this galaxy threw at me, I could *take* it. I wasn't some child, ready to shut her eyes and try to look away as the *real* monsters reached for her from the dark, able to do nothing as their claws caressed her skin: I would fight and claw and fucking *bite* if I had to, to stay alive, to do what needed doing.

But I wasn't stronger than Jane, either. I didn't have her training—I hadn't come howling out of a world at war, full of grief and rage at all the wrongs that had been done to me. I didn't enjoy fighting, not really. It felt good when I was alive, when I *survived* against impossible odds, and it felt good to *do* good, but the fighting itself; that wasn't what made me, me.

I wasn't their fucking messiah; I wasn't their chosen one. I wasn't going to save either of them. God damn them both for putting that weight on me. I hadn't *made* the Preacher choose the paths she had, choices that had doomed my parents, choices she now felt wracked with guilt over; I hadn't made Jane into a tool for violence, hadn't made her so that violence was always the first option she reached for.

Whatever was coming next—whether that was dealing with the Cyn, still trapped in the halls of the dead on Valkyrie Rock, or whether this galaxy was going to throw something *else* at us, something horrible and new, or maybe even something beautiful—I'd meet it as *me*. Not as the Preacher's delicate hope for the future, and not as Jane's soldier-in-training. If they wanted to hold me to two completely different standards, they could try all they wanted: the only standard that truly mattered was my own.

What that *was*, I was still evolving. And that felt right. I was, after all, just a child. Like they'd pointed out, repeatedly. I didn't have to know everything—I didn't *have* to have everything figured out. There'd be time enough for that. Assuming I survived that long.

I pulled myself up onto the railing of the deck, and never mind the storm. I just perched there, staring out at the lashing sea, let the rain pour over me, and let myself not care. It was just water, falling from the sky.

I sat there until morning.

Mo emerged from the villa to say his prayers; when he was done, he brought me a cup of coffee, and together we watched the sun begin its rise. The storm had broken just before the dawn had begun; the storm clouds had drifted away, no longer heavy with the red-streaked signals of the thunder, and we faced the unbroken empyrean vastness of lavender watercolor wash above, varied only by the twisting ribbon of the planet's rings, those impossible Möbius strips of billions upon billions of pieces of stone and crystal and ice. They rose up from the horizon like some distant tower thrust up from the sea—or maybe the supporting suspensions of the sky itself.

As the sun rose, making its way past the rings, the glowing blue orb was bisected by those bands of orbital stone, the descending light reflecting off the shimmering detritus. The rings themselves were a shadow across the azure circle of fire, drawing a line taut over the horizon as if they were a chain across the dawn, trying to hold the rising sun in place, trying to stop the new light from spreading over the surface of the calming sea. But nothing could stop the day from coming—not even a metaphor.

"Thanks," I said to Mo, taking the coffee cup from him.

"Of course," he said. "I heard that *you* overheard a conversation last night that you might need some recovery from. Coffee works as well as anything as an agent of respite."

"Sho?" I asked, smiling slightly, still staring out at the sun's new light, shining down through the tiny—and also huge—gaps in the rings.

"Sho," he nodded. "That boy gossips like a grandmother on market day."

"Any advice?" I asked him.

"You'd ask the advice of a man who's spent a century looking for God, and hasn't found Him yet?" he asked mildly.

I took a sip of my coffee. "Sure. At least it means you haven't been fooled."

"Or maybe I *have* found Him, and I just fooled myself into thinking I hadn't. Sometimes not knowing something is better than knowing, in its own way. Or at least easier."

"I don't think so." I shook my head. "I think if you'd found God, you'd know." Just like once I found the person I was supposed to be—not just the person the Preacher or Jane needed me to be—*I'd* know. I wasn't there yet. But I was trying.

"I suppose. Otherwise, I couldn't really be said to have 'found' him, could I?" Mo took a drink from his own coffee cup.

"So I'll ask again: any advice you want to give?"

"Plenty I *want* to give," he said, taking a look at me. "But that's just me being an old man, one who wants to feel useful. None I think you actually need. It seems you've come to a few conclusions on your own, sitting out here in the rain for hours. Plus, I think you've already got two too many people telling you who you're supposed to be; that's part of the problem."

"And you're not going to say that I should just listen for God instead?"

"I think if you can hear *yourself* through the din of their voices, Esa, then you are already hearing Him, quite well. *Alhamdulillah.* That is something of a minor miracle in and of itself."

I smiled at that, shaking my head softly. "What was Jane like?" I asked him then—it seemed like a change in direction, a non sequitur, but it wasn't, not really. "When she was asking *herself* these sorts of questions, I mean—when she was my age. You knew her when she was that young, right?"

"Yes," he nodded. "But I don't think I should tell you very much. She wouldn't want me to. And unlike our young Wulf friend, I am not a gossip. Besides: we have both changed, much, since then. I made *different* mistakes when I was trying to teach her than the mistakes she is making now, with you. There might be some good in that, some hope for the future: the mistakes *she* is making are . . . much less severe than the ones I made with her."

"You took her from her sect. You said that the other night."

"I didn't just take her, little one; I *used* her, like firing a bullet from a gun. Gave her the tools she needed to tear them down, and then let her see, in a way she'd always been blind to, exactly what they'd done *to* her. I knew exactly what she would do with that knowledge, with those tools; I knew what she had within her. And I was right. When she was done, that sect was no longer a threat to the Justified. Or anyone else. Or anything at all, really." He stared out at the ocean; listened to the sound of the water, lapping against the beach. Or listened to something else, in the halls of his memory, but what it was, I would never know. "As I said"—he shook his head finally—"it was not my proudest moment. I had turned my face from Allah during that time, and did many things I have since come to regret."

"And taking Jane from her people—that's one of them."

"No. *Using* her, yes; I regret that. But she was always better than they were. She did not belong with their simple dogma, their dangerously reductive creeds. I have no doubt that I gave her a *longer* life with the Justified than she would have had otherwise, a life where she could do more good. Was it actually better—is it *better* to be shown the truth of the lie, even if the lie is a comforting thing?"

"Yes," I said, immediately. I didn't even have to think about it.

He smiled at that. "It is good to hear you say so." He turned from the railing—could evidently hear something I couldn't. After a moment, it became clear to me as well: the sound of a ship's engines, firing up. "Ah. It appears the Preacher has finished her consultation with Scheherazade. Shall we go find out what they have to say?" He offered me a hand; I took it, and hopped down off the rail.

"Hey, Mo?" I said as Schaz lifted off from the beach and disappeared toward the jungle, heading back to the clearing where she was making her berth.

"Yes?"

"She misses you, sometimes. I didn't know it was you she was missing before I met you, but . . . I think it's true."

"As I miss her. But our paths through life took different roads; that is the way of it, at times. Still. I am glad she came to see me. It has been good to speak to someone who knew me when I was a worse man, and can still abide my presence."

"Despite the fact that she thinks your search for God makes you a crazy person."

"Despite that, yes. Not one of us is perfect, little Esa. And Jane even less than most."

CHAPTER 14

W ell, that was a great deal of work for nothing," Jane was saying as we entered the dining hall, her voice drier than a desert.

"Not *nothing*," the Preacher replied, some asperity in her tone; at least they weren't yelling at each other again. "Just not as much as we might have hoped."

Jane looked up as Mo and I approached; Sho was wheeling in from another room as well. "The Preacher finished decrypting the drive you took from the Cyn's ship," she told us. "Apparently, most of it is in some kind of ancient language, one neither of us has ever seen before. It's not a problem of decryption, it's one of translation."

"May I look?" Mo asked. Jane nodded at the screen, and let him take her place at the chair; he stared for a moment, then shook his head. "It must be an ancient Cyn text," he said. "I don't know of any way you *might* translate it; I'm sorry. Maybe one of the lost Golden Age core worlds, perhaps a museum or an archive there . . . that's all I can think to suggest. And of course, 'lost' is the operative term there."

"The longer we leave that . . . thing . . . locked on Valkyrie Rock, the longer it has to find a way to escape," Sho shook his head. He turned toward Jane. "Have we heard anything from your friends?"

"The Preacher was already on her way toward us when she intercepted the message," Jane replied, running a hand through her hair, obviously a little frustrated herself with the enforced idleness—of all the traits Jane had picked up from Mo, "an excess of patience" was not one of them. "It hasn't been long enough for it to actually *reach* Sanctum yet, let alone for the rest of the Justified to mount a response."

"It's not like there was *nothing* useful on the drive, though," the Preacher interjected. "There was *this*, tucked away in the data." She tapped at one of

Mo's many keyboards, bringing up an image on one of the screens. "It's a map of the galaxy." No shit—even I could tell that for myself.

"We . . . already knew what the galaxy looked like, Preacher," Mo said doubtfully, clearly *trying* not to give offense, but, like me, not really sure where she was going. "Most of us, at least." He smiled at Sho, who gave him a tired smile in return.

"Yes. Obviously. But this map is marked, keyed." She bent over, typed in another few keystrokes; suddenly there were highlights and markings on certain systems. "Different worlds—most of them settled—annotated in the same script—"

"Which we can't read," Jane reminded us all, unnecessarily.

"—and *also* time stamped." The Preacher glared at her, finally getting to her point. "Based on the entry for Kandriad, it's a record, a travelogue of sorts. There are blank spots—spots where his ship *wasn't* inputting data, where he headed 'off-grid,' so to speak—but of the worlds he *did* visit . . . there must be some sort of correlation, a pattern of some kind—"

Jane retrieved the keyboard from the Preacher, started flipping through the galaxy, seemingly at random, jumping from entry to entry down the list of worlds the Cyn had visited. "Dead ends," she said quietly, mostly to herself.

"How's that?" Mo asked her.

"A handful of these worlds—I've visited them, as well. Esa and I both, in our official capacity. Esa, here: Nellioc—"

"That sucking waste of time? The swamp world, with the . . . the . . . the leech things, the horrible leech things? Where we found—"

"Where we found absolutely nothing." Jane nodded. "No sign of the next-generation child our intelligence said was supposed to be there. Some of these others, I've heard them mentioned in briefings, from Criat. They're all false positives."

"Because he got there first," Sho said quietly. "Because he had already *found* your 'next-generation' child. And taken them."

"How far back do they go?" I asked. "How long has he been . . ."

"Doing the same thing we have?" Jane asked, something brittle in her voice. "Tracking gifted children, pulling them off their homeworlds? Quite a while. Here." She reached across the Preacher, tapped her own set of commands in, focusing on one world in the Cyn's timeline, several years back, a world I recognized immediately when she pulled it up on the screen.

"My home," I said, my breath catching in my chest just a little bit.

Jane nodded. "He visited less than a month after I took you away."

"I hope he had fun, fighting his way through the Pax occupation." I couldn't help it; my voice was a little sour. There was something awful about the idea of the Cyn and the Pax killing each other off, each trying to kidnap me.

"Wait—let me see that." The Preacher shouldered Jane aside again, her fingers dancing over the keyboard; Jane gave her a sour look, but let her do her thing. Dates and worlds spun past on the screen—whatever the Preacher was looking for, it was way, way back.

"*No.*" And apparently she'd found it, and didn't much like what she'd found.

"Katya? I've never even heard of that system," Jane said, looking at the corner of the galaxy map the Preacher had pulled up. "I mean—there's nothing there. A handful of gas giants, no habitable worlds, not even—"

"There *was* something there—once," the Preacher said, bitter. "A station, a research station, hidden in the upper atmosphere of one of the planets. Hidden, where no one could find it. The research station I used to run. Look at the time stamp." She pointed; seventeen years ago, almost to the day.

Seventeen years ago. A station the Preacher had operated from.

No. No.

Everyone at the table was staring at me; even Mohammed and Sho, who didn't understand the implications of the text glowing on the screen. Such a little thing—just a string of numbers—to mean so much. To carry so much *weight.* "Esa," Jane said slowly. "Calm down."

I looked at her with wild eyes, my jaw clenched tight, my knuckles white as my hands gripped the table. I didn't remember standing. I *also* didn't remember levitating every single object in the room that someone wasn't currently sitting on, but I'd done that, too. My powers got tricky when I got upset.

"Is that the place, Preacher?" I asked, trying to force my voice to be calm, trying to force *myself* to be calm, missing by miles.

"Esa, you shouldn't—"

"*Is that the system where I was born?*"

The Preacher nodded, once.

I dropped the furniture with a crash. Looked slowly at Sho, a dawning feeling of horror sinking into my gut like a stone. "I don't think this is about *you*, Sho," I told him. "I don't think it's about you at all."

For a moment, no one spoke; no one was even willing to look at each other. We just stared at the table, or the walls, trying to process . . . this. "It is the first entry," Mo said finally, bending over another machine, following the map further back—but there was nothing. "The records go no further. There may be more information to be had once we can translate the language, but this particular . . . mission, this crusade he's on, whatever it was that made him *start* hunting the gifted—it started there. On Katya." With me.

"Okay. All right." It took a great deal to rattle the Preacher. This was a great deal. "Jane—here's what we're going to do. We'll bundle Esa and Sho onto Scheherazade; you'll have to give over control of her systems to Esa—"

"She won't have to *give over* a damn thing," Schaz put in on the comms; now that she was aboveground, she was free to listen in to our conversations again. "I'll be happy to take Esa and Sho wherever they need to go. Don't talk about me like I'm not here, Preacher."

"We don't have time for your nonsense, ship," the Preacher snapped. "Scheherazade will take Esa and Sho back to Sanctum; Jane, you and I will take Shell to Valkyrie Rock." "Shell" was what the Preacher called her ship; the name—such as it was—came from the fact that unlike the rest of the Justified, the Preacher hadn't let our engineers install an AI into her craft. She operated it herself, plugging her intelligence directly into its network of operating systems. For all intents and purposes, when Shell was in motion and the Preacher was on board, the Preacher *was* Shell, and vice versa. "Between the two of us, we can . . . *learn* what this thing wanted with the children. What he started on Katya." She hadn't even mentioned that the Cyn *might* be carrying a solution to the pulse—this new information was enough to make even the Barious disregard what he might represent.

Seventeen years hunting gifted children. Seventeen *years* of the chaos he'd sown on Kandriad, of the Vyriat girl, dead in her cage on his ship. And it had started with me.

"Bad idea." Mo shook his head.

"It's the *only* idea," the Preacher responded hotly.

"Then find another one." Mo reached out and tapped—hard—against the Preacher's carapace. She took a step back, stunned: I couldn't remember the last time *anyone* had touched her like that.

"Right there." Mo nodded at the place where he'd rapped his knuckles against the Preacher's metal skin. "Right below there, in point of fact."

"My power system? What the hell does that—"

"Your power system, fueled by kinetic motion and tiny solar reflectors dotting your skin, *stored* in a fusion battery inside of your chest."

"Oh, fuck." Jane was staring at the Preacher's chest now as well.

"So?" The Preacher glared at them both. "That's how Barious operate; I don't understand what it—"

"*You cannot be anywhere near this threat*, Preacher," Mo said forcefully. "The Cyn manipulates *energy*. He does it from afar, and no shielding can stop him; we've *seen* this, on the vids Jane brought us from Kandriad, and Valkyrie Rock. If he wants to reach into your chest and turn you *into a bomb*, he will do that thing, and you will be *powerless* to stop it."

The Preacher stared at him for a moment, in mute shock; she'd clearly never thought of her machine nature as a liability before. At this moment, it was. The energy that flowed through organic beings was probably too diffuse for the Cyn to manipulate—if it wasn't, surely he would have done so by now, or at least we would have heard stories from the few legends that survived of the Cyn who had populated the Golden Age—but *actual* electricity ran through the wiring that made up the Preacher's veins. If the Cyn wanted to rip that energy straight from her body and feed it back into the battery into her chest until she went up in a miniature version of the blast that had consumed the factory city on Sho's homeworld, he could, and there would be nothing she could do to stop him.

"You *must* return to Sanctum," Mo said again. "Other Justified forces may well be on their way to the rally point around Valkyrie Rock shortly—you can tell them of what we have learned when you cross their path, make sure there are no Barious among their number, but you yourself *must* get as far from this . . . thing . . . as possible. And you must take Sho with you." He looked at the young Wulf. "I believe Jane promised him new legs. It's time someone kept that promise."

"And Esa," the Preacher said mechanically. "If this thing is . . . focused on her, somehow, none of us should be in the team that tries to subdue the Cyn. We should *all* head back to Sanctum—"

"Not me," Mo shook his head. "I'm staying here."

"If the assault on Valkyrie Rock goes poorly, and the Cyn gets off—he knows what trajectory we took from that system," Jane said to Mo. "He can track us here. You shouldn't risk that, Mo."

"This world is where my search has taken me, and this world is where I shall stay."

"Don't be an idiot; that's—"

"All I can be is as God made me."

"Yeah, which is apparently *an idiot*. You were the one who told us what this thing was capable of, and now you—"

"I'm going," I said. I had to raise my voice to be heard, so I shouted the next sentence: "I'm *going* to Katya. Preacher, you take Sho back to Sanctum. Jane, if you want to go with them, I'll take Scheherazade on alone, if I have to."

Jane shook her head. "That's not an—"

I'm *done* waiting around," I snapped back. "I'm *done* sitting on my hands, just as much a captive here as the Cyn is on that fucking asteroid. I'm going to find out what this . . . this *asshole* learned there, what it was that made him *start* all this: I'm *going* to find out why he was there *three months* after my birth. The rest of you can do whatever the hell you like."

"Don't be a fool, Esa," the Preacher snapped. "If you truly want to revisit that . . . place . . . wait and do so from a position of strength, not when—"

Sho: "If Esa needs my help, then I will go as well. I will not abandon my sister. Not when she needs me the most."

That hit me; I hadn't expected it. A few tears ran down my face before I could stop them. "Sho, you *can't*," I told him, kneeling beside his chair. "God, I love you for offering, but you just can't. You should go back to Sanctum, get your legs fixed up—"

"And who will channel energy into your telekinesis?" he asked simply. "If the Cyn escapes Valkyrie Rock somehow, or if there are *more* of his kind, claiming that station: *energy* is all he has feared, all that has worked to even slow him down. If it comes to a fight, you'll *need*—"

Whatever he might have said next was interrupted as alarms started blaring from Mo's cobbled systems, loud enough to drown out everything else; the same "vessel on approach" alert we'd heard when Shell had been making her entrance into the atmosphere.

More Justified? Not the force from Sanctum, perhaps, but if Marus or Javier or another operative had been close enough to get our message—and done the same thing the Preacher had, ignored the directive to mass outside of the nebula surrounding Valkyrie Rock and traced the signal back to its source again—maybe that would explain the alarm. If we were lucky.

I only had time to put that thought together in my head, though, before *another* one of Mo's screens turned bright red, and suddenly my attention was drawn to motion, not on the monitors at all, but out the open doorway instead—a line of fire, streaking down through the lavender sky, pieces splintering off as it crossed in front of the twisting planetary rings: an object falling from orbit, disintegrating as it broke apart on reentry.

Someone had just shot down one of the war satellites. More were falling, even as we watched. I'd thought it would have taken a dreadnaught to break through that defense network, but we'd be able to see a dreadnaught hanging in orbit: this wasn't *that*. All the same, though, it *was* an assault—more satellites were falling, streaking the sky with bright plumes of fire.

Whoever was coming, it wasn't the Justified.

CHAPTER 15

Jane was the first to speak, the first to wrench her attention from the impossible sight of the war satellites crashing down, the Jaliad defenses—defenses that had protected this world for centuries—being torn down, one by one. "We need to go," she said. "We need to go *now*."

Sho tried to object. "We don't even know that it's him, we don't know—he was *trapped*, we don't—"

"Of course it's him, of fucking *course* it is," Jane snapped. "After everything else that's happened . . ." She just shook her head. "Preacher, take Sho. Get to Shell. Esa and I will take Mo and get to Scheherazade—"

"I am *going* with Esa," Sho put in again.

"Actually—no. you're not." The Preacher wasn't one to mince words. She just leaned over and pulled Sho out of his chair, throwing the struggling Wulf into a fireman's carry and making it look easy in the process; it was tempting to forget how much strength there was in her slim metal frame.

"Dammit, no!" Sho shouted, beating at the Barious with his fists.

"Sho—it's all right," I told him, reaching out to still his hands. "Go to Sanctum; that's where you belong. I'll see you again."

"You promise me?" There was something very much like despair in his voice, the fur on his cheeks streaked with tears.

"I promise you." I didn't even hesitate. Jane always said that she wouldn't make promises she wasn't sure she could keep. I *would*. I fully intended to keep this one, and if I couldn't—that would be the Cyn's fault, not mine.

Then they were gone, the Preacher vanishing in a blur of metal limbs, moving as fast as she possibly could—which was damned fast.

Meanwhile, Mo—for no apparent reason—was ripping up floorboards. "Those satellites have defended my refuge here for *decades*," he said, sounding more *annoyed* than anything else, his voice still relatively calm for a man tearing apart a priceless luxury villa, about to be threatened by a being from legend. "How is he bringing them down with *one ship?*"

"How the hell does he do *anything?*" Jane answered, checking the action on her rifle. "How did he get off the Rock, how was he tracking gifted children?" She shook her head. "It doesn't matter—not right now. He doesn't have to bring down *all* the war satellites—as soon as he's cleared an approach path, he'll be on his way to us: he tracked our trajectory here from scans on Valkyrie Rock, just like *we* tracked *him* from Kandriad, and he'll be able to track the broadcast signal to the tower, same as he used our comms to track us on the Rock. We need to—"

Except he wasn't on his way; not anymore. The villa shook as a craft flew overhead, its passage close enough to be felt in the boards underneath our feet. Whoever was coming to visit—and we all knew who it likely was— they were already here.

Mo finished ripping up the floor, and reached deep into the recess he'd uncovered, pulling a weapon out from the hidden stockpile inside. Not the antique ballistic hunting rifle he'd been using to bring down our meals every day—that one was still leaning against the wall—but instead a massive gauss rifle, bigger than any I'd ever seen, so big I doubted Jane could have even lifted it. Maybe not even the Preacher—the damned thing looked like it should have been mounted on a shuttlecraft rather than used as an infantry weapon.

"Go," he said to us, getting up off his knees and setting the weapon on his shoulder like it weighed nothing. "I'll greet our guest."

"Mohammed, god *damn* it—" Jane followed him out to the deck overlooking the ocean. I did the same.

It was the Cyn's ship that was hovering over the beach, maybe half a mile away. How was that *possible?* I'd set off a bomb in its fusion core. Even if whatever strange material the ship itself had been made of had been able to shrug off the damage from the blast, the drive should have been left in tatters. There was no way he'd been able to fix it. No way.

Except there was pretty compelling evidence that he had, in the form of the ship, battered but flying, just hovering in silence perhaps a half mile down the beach. He'd had nothing but *time* on Valkyrie Rock, time and material both; I supposed I shouldn't have been surprised he'd managed to break out of the prison we'd left him in.

I shouldn't have been surprised he was capable of *anything*.

"You need to *go*, Jane," Mo said, already setting up his rifle, laying the barrel across the railing of the deck. "You need to go *now*. If you wait around, he'll stop you from reaching Scheherazade. Go get to your ship and get out of here."

"We're not leaving you behind, Mo. That's *not* an option."

"Fine. Then come back and *get* me. But do it with a ship capable of burying that creature in laser fire. He'll have to disembark if he wants to search the villa; I'll keep him pinned on the beach long enough for you to get to Schaz."

Jane's jaw snapped shut on whatever objection she was about to make; that was actually a pretty decent plan. It had worked once, back on Kandriad, after the nuclear blast—it could work again.

Down the beach, motion: a hatch had opened, and the Cyn emerged from his ship, back in his suit of metal, his wings spread wide, his thrusters firing, keeping him airborne for a moment. Then the thrusters cut, and he dropped to the sand below, the razor-pinioned wings folding in behind his back. And then he started walking.

Not running. Not *flying*. Just . . . walking. Down the beach. As though he knew we were watching.

Mo tapped something under his jaw, some ancient implant; when he spoke again, his words boomed out over the surf as though he were speaking through a loudspeaker. "Hey," he said to the distant creature. "Go find a different beach. This one's mine." Not giving anything away—not letting the Cyn know that Jane and I were here. He might as well have been some vagrant, squatting in the abandoned villa, just warning off another vagrant from encroaching on his turf.

The Cyn didn't play along. *"Twice now, you have interfered with my hunts."* Once again, the voice came through our comms—he could sense the Justified encryption active on the channel's frequency, didn't buy Mo's facade for a moment. *"You will not be allowed to do so a third time. I have received . . . new orders. A new . . . communion."*

New orders? So he *did* answer to someone else—there was some sort of command structure in place, a threat we knew *nothing* about. But how would he have reached out to them, how—

Valkyrie Rock. Of course. The asteroid itself must have had a hidden broadcast antenna, left over from its days as a mining operation, strong enough to penetrate the nebula; locked on board, the Cyn must have . . . reckoned with Charon, somehow, and gained access. We'd come to Jalia Preserve to send a message; the Cyn had sent one of his own.

And received an answer.

"Last warning," Mo said again, flipping open the cap on the rifle scope. He knelt behind his weapon—railings meant for Reetha were about hip height on a Mahren—and took aim. He tapped under his jaw again, and said to Jane and me, without the voice amplification: "The same for you two. Go. Now."

Our comms crackled to life. *"Give them to me."* It was all the Cyn said, in response to Mo's warning; it was all he needed to say. Sho and I—gifted, both—were his targets. *"Give them to me, now, and the fires will take you . . . quickly. That is what the goddess desires."*

"We'll come back for you," Jane told her ex-partner, ignoring the psychopath being psychotic into our comms. "Just . . . keep him busy, Mo. Don't take him head on. I'll let you know when we've reached Schaz; you can hide in the villa then. Get him lost in that maze; buy yourself time. We'll pick you up from the other side."

"I don't think there will be any hiding. Not from a devil like this." The Cyn was still stalking down the beach, picking up speed, his metal talons scraping through the wet sand and the surf, his metal armor gleaming under the azure sun. Mo adjusted his aim, tracking the approaching figure, then said once more: "Go."

Jane nodded reluctantly, put her hand on my shoulder. I reached out for Mo, then let my hand drop. There was nothing I could do. We made our way back toward the door—we'd do what Jane had suggested, exit the villa from the back then break for the jungle, where the Cyn wouldn't be able to see us—and I'd almost followed Jane inside when I stopped, and turned.

If the worst happened, I couldn't let my last words to Mohammed be me delivering an ultimatum he hadn't deserved. "Mo," I asked him. "Do you believe today?"

He smiled slightly, his face still pressed into the rifle. "Look at what lies before me, little one," he said. "Not just the villain stalking toward us—a villain I get to delay, a villain I will thwart, in order to protect my friends—but all the wonder and the beauty of this planet, a world returned to a state nature never could have created it in, yet still, in the acts of unbelievers and the callous powerful, it remains a testament to the glory of Allah." Beyond him, the chains of the planet's rings rose up out of the sea like majestic towers, sweeping above us through the heavens even as the fire from the fallen satellites faded into the lavender glow of the sky. The shimmering sun glittered on the water of the ocean, and the breeze was out of the jungle, carrying the smell of sun-warmed vegetation and morning dew and *life*.

And down the beach toward us came the Cyn, running now, his wings beginning to spread out again—he was getting ready to launch himself into the air.

"Yes, Esa," Mo said, pulling back the bolt on his rifle that would energize the powerful magnets within. "Today I believe. Now *go*." The Cyn's wings snapped into a locked position, and he ducked low, preparing to take flight.

Mo fired before he could.

The thing about a gauss rifle that size—firing *rounds* that size—was that eventually, the bullets became less "projectiles" than "explosives." The projectile wouldn't tear through the Cyn so much as rip everything around its impact zone apart in a massive detonation of force, like being at the center of a tornado. And even if the zealot out of ancient fairy tales *could* absorb or deflect ballistic energy on a scale like that: he wasn't going to see this shot coming.

Jane and I still didn't wait around to see how he survived it. We knew he would. He always *did*.

We made for the jungle.

CHAPTER 16

We made it out of the villa and in among the trees without looking back. We just ran. Mo would hold the Cyn as best he could—keep him pinned down with rifle fire until we could reach Schaz, get aloft, then swing around and pick him up. All we could do was move faster, to use the window of time Mo was buying us.

We pushed our way through the underbrush, looking for the path back to the overhang where the ship waited; ordinarily, we could have just called Schaz to our position, but the thick canopy of tree cover would prevent her approach.

We ran.

It was shortly after we found the trail back to the clearing that the comms came to life again: Mo and the Cyn, taunting each other across the open ground of the beach. "The rulers of this world vanished into history, my friend, and this place is all they left behind." Mo's tone was almost conversational, polite, even as he presumably reloaded his rifle and tracked his target through the scope. "Whatever you're trying to achieve, you might ask yourself if it's *worth* all of this violence. Ultimately, you will meet the same fate."

The Cyn ignored the larger question Mo was asking—ignored it, or couldn't even comprehend it. "*I know they are here,*" he replied, his voice whispering in my ear, and now that I knew what he was, what he was made of, it was impossible not to hear a crackling undercurrent of energy in the words, as though they were spoken by fire itself. "*You will tell me where they are hiding.*"

"If you wish to ask me something, by all means—leave your cover behind. Come and ask. I will have an answer ready for you. But I suggest that you prepare yourself: you might not like the form that answer takes."

"*If you test yourself against me, you will be found wanting—I can promise you that.*

You still do not understand. Mahren. Humanity. Wulf. Tyll. There is no difference. All any of you are is a virus. Contaminating us, corrupting us. Interfering with what we always should have been. You should have worshipped us. Instead you infected us. So we withdrew, to quarantine. Let you infect each other instead."

"Several thousand years of the exchange of ideas between species; several thousand years of knowledge, of art, of *hope*, passed from person to person across the galaxy, and that's all you can see? An infection?" I could almost see Mo shake his head, even as I leapt over a twisting tree root and clambered my way up a hill. "No wonder you have no compunction against taking innocent lives. You do not understand what is lost—from those you kill, or from yourself—every time you do."

"What is lost is always secondary to what is gained; there is always a price to be paid for the exercise of will, and I pay it gladly. My will belongs to her, and I will become whatever it is she needs of me."

"Blind loyalty. Always a fearsome trait. One that destroys both, eventually."

"Destruction is what I am. She has made me the vessel of her wrath, and that wrath now falls upon you. Submit to her will."

"I submit only to the will of Allah and to his prophets, peace be unto them. And I very much doubt you are one of those. The cruel imitation of an angelic form you wear notwithstanding, I have very rarely met a being I was so sure stood so very distant from God."

"There are no gods; no prophets. No mercies. There is only—"

Another rifle shot crashed through the comms, loud enough that I could hear it through the jungle as well. I guess their conversation was over. Or at least, shifting its nature to something more base, more aggressive. The instinctual reversion to violence. A hundred years searching for God, and Mo would still answer an assault with an assault. He'd been a soldier much longer than a pilgrim.

Jane was just a little ways ahead of me; she hauled herself up a rocky outcropping, turned, and gave me a hand to scrabble up as well. "Keep moving," was all she said, but there was something in her eyes—having to listen to Mo taunt and delay the thing that had come to kill us: it was taking its toll. Grief was written on her face, but the thing behind her irises wasn't pain—it was fury.

We would get Mo out of this, the trap he'd sprung that had been laid for us. And if we couldn't, there would be hell to pay. Whatever goddess the Cyn kept going on about wouldn't be enough to save him from us.

We ran on, among the massive trunks of the great trees, the day suddenly growing brighter as the sun finally passed beyond the twisting rings that looped the planet, and we came out of the shadow of their chains.

Ahead of us, the roar of an engine—a ship, starting up. We could make out Shell, rising above the canopy, hell-bent on the stars. The Preacher and Sho had gotten out. At least they were safe. The whole point of all of this, where it had all started, had been to get Sho to Sanctum. We'd achieved that now. All the rest was just fallout and survival. I said a brief prayer that they'd make it home—I don't know who or what I prayed to, but I did it anyway.

Sho deserved better than this endless hunt Jane and I were locked into, first chasing, then fleeing, from the Cyn—whatever the creature's "crusade" *was*, ultimately, Mo was right: it would end badly. I just hoped we could survive it.

We kept moving, the ground rising steadily under our feet—the overhang was in the foothills of the mountain range that lay just beyond the sea. It was almost funny: all I'd seen of this world, Mo's stretch of pristine beach and the azure forests, and it was such a little part of it, just this one stretch of jungle between the mountains and the oceans, and what lay on the other side of the peaks was something entirely different, some different forest, some wildly shifted biome. Yet whenever I thought of this place, I'd see cerulean canopies, tranquil turquoise seas. That had been what this world was to me.

The place where I'd met Mo, Jane's former partner, and perhaps her oldest friend. God, I hoped it wasn't also the place where Mo died for us. We were going to save him. We were *going* to.

We reached the clearing where Schaz had returned after finishing her soak and dropping off the Preacher; she was already warmed up, ready for flight, ready for us to board. We pelted up the loading ramp, heading right for the cockpit, Jane sliding into the pilot's chair, me behind the gunnery controls. "Take us up, Schaz," Jane said, flipping the switches above her head, "we're going right back to that beach, we're going to punch a hole through that *thing*, and we're going to get Mo off of this rock. He can look for God somewhere else."

"Jane, we shouldn't—"

"Don't argue, Scheherazade, just *do* it. We—"

"You need to *listen*, Jane. Mo sent me this." She began playing an audio packet, one Mo had transmitted privately to her. I was watching Jane's face as it played. I *saw* it crumble and come apart as she realized—from the first few words—what he was going to say.

"Red." In the background of the message, we could hear the whisper of rain; he'd recorded these words the night before—before we'd even known the Cyn would arrive. "If you're listening to this, it means your enemy has appeared, has escaped your trap, and I've chosen to engage him while you and Esa escape. In order to get you to do so, I probably would have told you to come back for me. But you can't. My time in this universe is up. It has been, I think, for quite a while.

"Part of the reason I began my search was that I knew I *should* have died, back with the others, when we set off the pulse. I survived because of you. Because I knew I had to, to keep you alive, and because you *made* me. You never were one to surrender. But sometimes, Red—sometimes surrender is the only way you can win.

"To reach us here, your enemy will have to have carved a path through the war satellites; however many remain will respond to such an assault by gathering directly *above* any threat that has entered the atmosphere. And then they will open fire. A quicker ending than, perhaps, I deserve—and hopefully an ending for your nemesis, as well.

"This is the last thing I'll be able to do for you, Red; the last gift I can give you. Now you need to take everything you learned from me, and you need to forget it. Move beyond it. Don't pass all our violence, all our sins, along to that little girl sitting at your side. I made you better than me. You might not see it; I do. Now you have to make *her* better than *you*. That's how this works. People, I mean. It's the *only* way it works. It's the only way we can achieve anything. We hold back our failings, and pass on what righteousness, what little grace we've managed to grasp.

"Red—Jane—I love you like a daughter. That is where my grace has always lain. I'm sorry I used you the way I did, when we first met. I always wanted to say that; now I have, and I can go in peace. Or, hopefully, not in peace at all. My search for God not withstanding, I always knew I wouldn't die in my bed. From the day I set down on this world, I always knew this place would be my Aeliadh Hill. There are worse worlds upon which to die.

"Run, Jane. I'll hold him here. Run, and let the ancient hate of the Jaliad take us both down. That seems . . . a fitting end. *Alaykumu as-salām*, my child. I will see you again."

There were a few more seconds to the message—just the fall of rain, echoing in the background, filling Schaz's interior—and then the recording cut off, and the ship was silent around us.

For a moment, Jane simply sat in her chair, hunched over, a look of pure *anguish* on her face, a kind of pain I'd never known a human face could project. She didn't breathe for a moment, the loss was so intense.

Then she took a gasping breath in, and she grasped Scheherazade's controls. Said nothing. Just lifted us off, out of the forest, flying toward the mountains, away from the stretch of the ocean and the curve of the shoreline, even as above us the firmament turned to flame, the long-silent weapons systems on the Jaliad's satellites of death coming online.

We barely cleared the firing solution, the sun and the rings and the ocean and eventually the entirety of the sky obscured by the descent of arcing laser fire. Beneath us, the heat—the pure *force*—of that rain of ruin would be tearing apart the villa, blasting the sand of the beach to glass, setting the forests aflame, boiling the oceans. Killing all the fish and the deer and the animals Mo had lived on, had lived with. Killing everything that lay beneath the satellites' distant orbit.

And somewhere in all of that fire, somewhere in all of that screaming torrent of glowing, burning light, there was the Cyn, and there was Mo.

Jane took us up into the atmosphere, the rings passing nearly close enough to touch, the satellites still pouring flame down onto the surface of the world, ancient weapons from a long-dead reign, brought back to life by an even older hate. A hate I could not understand, a hate that meant nothing at all as far as I knew, yet had apparently *started* with me.

Wherever this *fucker* had come from, we knew where he'd been. And we were going to find out *why*. It had cost Mo's life to escape the Cyn's trap—there had to be a reckoning for that. And as for the Cyn himself—maybe a being made of energy could survive a rain of that much fire. Maybe not. I sure as hell didn't know. But if he *did*—if he came after us again—I knew this much: I was done running.

I'd rip him apart with my bare hands. I'd rip him apart with my bare *mind*. Jane, the Preacher, Mo—they all kept talking like it was my responsibility not to carry on down the bleak, cruel paths they'd all three walked. But as far as I was concerned, the one thing all of them had proved to me was that walking roads like those: that was just part of being alive.

Maybe it hadn't been, once. It was now. Those paths were the only ones left, to any of us. And if the Cyn was to be mine, I'd show him what I was capable of, now that he'd forced me into hate. Because I did hate him now. He'd *earned* that.

And when I met him again, he'd reap the rewards.

ACT
FOUR

CHAPTER 1

We saw Shell vanish into hyperspace just as we hit the upper atmosphere; a blink, and then the Preacher and Sho were gone, fading into the stars. Mutely, Jane put us on another vector, set our course. We sailed past the twisting rings of Jalia Preserve V, the satellites still firing downward, the light of their blazing rain reflected in the shards of ice trapped within the glittering circlet, making a whole curve of the band of debris seem to glow, as if the rings themselves were alight with some cosmic inner fire.

We leapt into hyperspace as soon as the engines had cooled and we were clear of the world's gravity well.

For a time, Jane and I said nothing. Just sat in the cockpit, unmoving, neither one of us even willing to take the few staggering steps back to the living quarters. Scheherazade didn't even try to break the silence. For a moment that seemed strange—her first instinct in situations like this was always to try and cheer us up, to focus our thoughts elsewhere—until I remembered that she'd known Mohammed as well, that he'd been around when Jane had "raised" her. Schaz, too, was mourning her friend.

"Can I ask you something?" I said the words when I finally stopped crying, said them to Jane, who wasn't crying at all, just staring out the viewscreen at the stars pouring past, her face lit by the glow of the instrument panels, something truly frightening there—not hate, just an emptiness, a kind of desolation of all feeling. Like she was shutting herself down.

She shook it off at the question. "Go ahead," she said, the words flat, hollow, like she didn't much care about speaking them, one way or another.

"Why did he call you 'Red'?" I asked.

She actually smiled at that, just a little bit, an almost autonomic response, disconnected from how she truly felt. "I'd almost forgotten," she said, so softly I didn't think she was talking to me at all.

"Jane?" I prompted her again.

"Way back when, when I first joined the Justified—when Mo first inducted me—it was . . . a whole new world to me. Maybe not quite as different as it was to you; this was before the pulse, so at least I wasn't dealing with new technologies, just new . . . ideology, new approaches, a new way of thinking about how life was meant to be led, what the . . . *purpose* of all of it was. All I knew was the strict dogma of the sect I was raised in, and even if I'd rejected those concepts—long before Mo recruited me—they were still how I *viewed* the world, because they were the only lens I'd ever had.

"The Justified changed all that. So the very first thing I did—well, maybe not the very first, but the first . . . choice I made, on my own, for myself, unbound by the old strictures—was to reject the world I *used* to know, to cast it off, by doing something the elders in my old sect never would have abided. Something I never would have considered in my old life, because it never would have been *possible*. Whether I believed or not—in their rules, in their strictures—everyone *around* me did, so I'd always had to follow. It was . . . a simple thing, just a little act of rebellion, a rebellion against old men already dead and gone, but still . . ."

"What was it?"

"I dyed my hair red," she said. "Chopped half of it off, and dyed the other half—and not just ginger, or auburn, or any natural human color, but I mean *red*, I mean bright, *screaming* crimson. Red like laser fire. It would have been enough to get me exiled in my old life, if not straight-up executed. Artificial changes to our appearances were completely forbidden.

"I knew it wasn't against the rules in the Justified, but you have to remember: to *me*, it was still something terrifying, something shocking. Mo just took one look at me when he saw it, then said: 'Looking good, Red. Now come on; you took so damn long in there we're gonna be last on the chow line.' And that was it—that was all anybody ever said about it. But from then on, that was what he called me."

"Your great act of rebellion was to dye your hair?"

She eyed my shorn scalp. "We can't *all* massively change our appearance just because we've been setting our hair on fire, Esa. Plus, you look a good deal better with that cut than I ever did with mine chopped down—it *really* didn't suit me. I only did it because I wasn't supposed to, after all. I looked . . . I looked pretty terrible, truth be told." She almost laughed at my expression, then cut it off before she could. "What? Come on, kid—I was young once too."

It was almost impossible for me to picture, but I tried to smile anyway. "How long did you keep it that way?"

"I changed it every few weeks, just to . . . again, just because I could, I suppose. Ask Marus about it sometime—when he first met me, I had a purple mohawk. He says that's still how he pictures me, when I'm not around to contradict the image."

"Is that why . . . the sect you used to belong to. Is that why you and Mo always disagreed? About his faith?"

She nodded. "Faith—religious or otherwise—was used to justify so many of the sect wars. Faith in a species' supremacy, or in a particular type of governance, or social system. Faith in . . . the history of the galaxy is full of people killing each other over the *stupidest*, most unimportant details of how or why they worship, what name they called god. I only knew belief as a way to justify extremism. That's the world I was raised in, after all. So once I was free of that, I took a hard shift in my views, in the other direction. Over the years, especially after we did . . . what we did, Mo began to drift back to the faith of his childhood, toward the answers Islam promised him. I could never understand. I was . . . cruel."

"So he left, to look for God."

"At least partially because his partner didn't have any interest in helping him in his search. I didn't drive him away, Esa—I've never believed that—but I didn't do anything to convince him to *stay*, either. In the decade after the pulse, we were all so . . . so lost. Mo stuck around for a while, I don't remember exactly how long, but once I'd decided that I couldn't run counter-ops anymore, that I was going to serve by tracking down the next generation instead . . . He made his peace with the idea of leaving, and then he just . . . he did that. A great many Justified—former Justified—did the same.

"By the time you met any of us, we'd all figured out how to live with what we'd done, with what the *pulse* had done. But there are plenty who couldn't.

Mo's response was actually one of the less-extreme decisions made in those years."

"Jane . . . he loved you. His leaving . . . it didn't mean that he didn't."

"I know that," she said quietly. "I just wish that he'd known how much I loved him back."

"He knew."

"That's kind of you to say."

"Jane?"

"Yes, Esa?"

"*I* love you."

Something like shock passed over her face, briefly, despite the fact that it wasn't like it was the first time she'd heard me say it; ultimately, though, for all her claims of having abandoned who she was in her old life, I think there was still a part of Jane that would always belong to the ascetic, war-obsessed sect she had been born in, one I was learning, more and more, had given no priority to the bonds between people, preferring instead the theoretical bond between a person and their god. That part of Jane never expected *anyone* to love her, because she'd spent the first few decades of her life being told that no one *should.*

"I love you too, Esa," she said quietly.

"And even if you decide to quit the Justified and go haring across the galaxy, looking for God or whatever else—I'll still love you. But you already know that, don't you?"

She nodded, slowly. "I suppose I do."

"Then Mo knew you loved *him.* It's that simple."

"I loved him, and he loved me, and I still got him killed."

"*No.*" Even I was surprised by the force with which the words escaped me. "The *Cyn* did that, Jane. The Cyn is who gets all the blame for that—*all* of it, a hundred and ten percent of it." I'd meant it when I said the same thing to Sho; I meant it now. "And we're going to go to where I was born, and we're going to find out what the hell he wants with me, and *if* he survived all of that back there, *if* he's still alive, we're going to use the information we learn on Katya against him, somehow. Cure for the pulse or not—we're *going* to make him pay. Because I love you, and you loved Mo, and I was starting to love Mo too, and if someone hurts the person we love, we hurt them *right the fuck back*. You taught that to me."

Jane nodded, softly. "All right. All right, Esa. You're right."

"I usually am."

"I wouldn't go that far."

CHAPTER 2

We didn't talk much over the next few days, just rested, and trained, and tried to prepare ourselves for whatever might come next, each in our own way.

I spent some of that time continuing to hone my newfound ability to manipulate energy with my telekinesis; I was gaining more and more control, and spending less and less time setting my hair on fire, when a question occurred to me.

"Schaz?" I asked, dropping myself into a seat at the kitchen table, exhausted by my latest round of juggling fireballs. Yes, I meant that literally.

"Yes, Esa?" Schaz replied politely.

"Did you ever finish your analysis on that mask I stole from the Cyn's ship?"

"I did; I didn't learn much. Is there something in particular you wanted to know?"

How to kill the son of a bitch, for good, but I doubted Schaz could tell me *that*. Instead, I laid out my thought process, just to see if the idea tracked once I said it out loud: "The Cyn can scorch flesh, melt metal. Its footprints leave decking blistered. But the armor it wears—it's immune, somehow. If it wasn't, it would just melt right off when the Cyn strapped it on."

"No different than how the skin of its ship is seemingly immune to laser fire and the blast of the bomb you set in its interior."

"Exactly. But how can something be . . . 'immune' to energy? If we were talking about matter, it would just be a question of tensile strength, of thickness and density—a bullet won't penetrate something significantly stronger than the force generated by its velocity and weight. What's the equivalent for being 'immune' to the Cyn?"

"*Our* shielding absorbs the heat and energy of laser fire by vibrating at the same frequency as the incoming laser blasts; perhaps the Cyn's armor does the same thing?"

"Can something made of matter *do* that? Vibrate like that?"

"It's certainly *theoretically* possible. The mask is still in my analysis lab; let me see what I can learn, and I'll get back to you."

"Are you on to something?" Jane had been listening, to the back half of the exchange at least: she'd just entered the kitchen from the cockpit.

I lifted my hand, shifted it back and forth. "If we can learn why the Cyn *doesn't* damage its own armor, I figured maybe we can learn what *will* damage it. It couldn't pass through the energy barrier Charon threw up in front of it on Valkyrie Rock, so it's not able to simply *ignore* electricity or laser blasts, but we unloaded on it with Schaz's turret, back on Kandriad—and again, with the satellite fire on Jalia Preserve."

"Which may have killed it."

"And may *not* have. And even if it *did*, we have no guarantee that was the only Cyn out there. If there was one, there might be more." I could still hear the Cyn's voice in my head—"*a new . . . communion.*" That was what he had said.

"We don't know that another would be hostile."

"And we don't know that it *wouldn't*, either. Are you, of all people, counseling me *not* to be prepared in case they are? 'If something might try to kill you, you better be ready to kill it right back.' You taught me that, like, *super* early on. I think it might have been just the fourth or fifth 'rule number one' that you taught me."

Jane nodded, taking a seat across from me. "So even if the laser grid on Jalia Preserve *did* kill it, you want to know *why*, when Schaz's lasers *didn't*."

"If it's just a question of overwhelming it—if it has some natural defenses against energy, the same way our skin is a natural defense against minor levels of force—then okay, we can *do* that. But it came flying out of a *nuclear blast*, Jane. I think what's more likely is that Cyn are *entirely* immune to certain *types* of energy, the same way humans can, say, be completely immersed in water with no ill effects, but you couldn't say the same if we were completely immersed in hydrochloric acid."

"Really," Schaz added, "it wouldn't take a *complete* immersion in hydrochloric acid to ruin a human's day. Just a minor immersion would do the trick."

"And that's my point. If *we're* 'immune' to water, but not acid: what's the equivalent for a Cyn? Are they immune to certain levels of heat, and light, but not others? Are there certain vibrational frequencies that their natural . . . natural . . ."

"Vibration," Jane supplied.

I frowned at her. "I know, but I already said 'vibrational,' and I didn't want to repeat myself."

"Schaz has a thesaurus programmed in, if you'd like to ask her."

"Shut it. You know what I mean. X-rays can't penetrate lead. If the Cyn's armor is the equivalent of whatever sentient energy the Cyn is made of— the lead to their X-rays—maybe knowing what they *can't* scorch through will give us a lead as to what *can*."

Jane narrowed her eyes at me over the table. "You don't just want to know how to kill him," she said. "You want to know how to *hurt* him."

"I mean . . . I want to know how to kill him, too. I figured that was implied."

"If you think this is a way to . . . *force* him to tell us how he consumes pulse energy . . . I think we both know that ship has likely sailed. Mo was right. We *can't* take him alive. He's too dangerous."

"It's not about that, Jane. Not anymore. I just need to know how to make him *hurt*."

She was looking at me closely, her gaze impenetrable. "This is a dangerous path you're walking, Esa."

"And having Mo die on us wasn't? Going up against him blind the way we have been *isn't*? If an army of those *things* shows up on Sanctum's doorstep, like the Pax did, we need to know how to deal with that, Jane. Of all your 'first rules,' like eighty percent of them boil down to 'be prepared.' I'm not saying I *want* to torture the son of a bitch, I'm saying if we *have* to, I want to know *how*."

"If it comes to that—"

"Don't give me some speech about how 'if it comes to that, you'll take the lead,' Jane. This is *my* choice, *my* cost, and if that's what I have to pay, then I will pay it *gladly*." I said the words with something almost like savagery behind them, and I think Jane, at least, believed me, but even as they escaped my mouth I heard a voice in my head, as clear as if he'd been sitting behind me: *"You don't mean that. You won't torture a sentient being, not just to lessen your own grief, not even if you think it's necessary to save someone else. You're better than that. Mo wouldn't want that. Not for you."*

Shut up, Sho. I'm doing this to protect *you.*

Shaking off the quiet voice of my conscience that apparently now sounded like the young Wulf pup we'd been tasked with protecting, I held up my hand in front of Jane, snapped my fingers. I'd taken to wearing a pair of metal rings on my thumb and forefinger that, when struck together, could generate a spark; now I willed that spark to be under *my* control, let it bloom and spread until I was holding a spike made of frozen lightning above my hand. There wasn't *much* energy there—I could *control* the flow of energy now, to a certain extent, but I couldn't *generate* it—but it still proved my point. "I'm the one that's going to be able to match him, Jane. Not you. I'm the one that's going to be able to *hurt* him."

Jane just stared at me for a moment, then shook her head. Asked softly: "Have you ever considered the notion that what the Cyn is doing—taking the gifted, starting from where you were born—that it's all some sort of self-fulfilling prophecy? Outside of some vague nonsense about a goddess and a destiny, we don't know *what* it believes; the fact that a being *made* of energy wants to capture a pair of gifted children who can *manipulate* energy has the ring of correlation to it, at the very least. Maybe *all* of the missing children— the children he's taken—maybe they were all similar, their gifts related to energy somehow."

"Or he's after me—after *us*—because I represent a threat," I posed an alternate option.

"Also possible," Jane agreed.

"In that case, I'm not going to *not* learn about my powers just because he might want me to. 'The more you hunt something, the more it learns to hunt you back.'"

Jane frowned at me. "Who taught you that?"

"Mo did," I said quietly. "He said it when I asked him why he varied his hunting grounds every day. If this Cyn thinks I'm its prey, well then, maybe it's time that fucker learned that prey can fight back too. Especially when cornered."

Jane sighed, shook her head. "You know I agree with you," she said.

"Then why the hell are we arguing?"

"Because I *shouldn't* agree with you. The Preacher—she thinks that—"

"I know what she thinks," I said levelly. "You two have voices that . . . carry, you know." I left out the part where I'd had to actively work to overhear their private conversation.

"I'm . . . sorry, Esa. You shouldn't have had to—"

"I know what Mo thought too. And you. You think you're getting old, that you're not just training me to be your partner, that you're training me to replace you, to be *better* than you. But Jane, I don't want to be *better* than you; I can't imagine greater praise than being *just like* you."

Jane shook her head. "If you think that, then I really have kept you too sheltered from the things I've done."

"Bullshit. You've always done what you had to do. To survive, and to protect the Justified. That's the math; nothing else matters." The little voice in my head—the voice that sounded like Sho—could go shove it. What I might have *wanted* didn't matter, not when set up against the cost of what would happen if I *didn't* act.

Again, Jane shook her head. "You can't think about people—you can't think about yourself—in terms of *math*, Esa. There's a cost to our actions—a cost to ourselves—that can't be . . . quantified, can't be laid out in columns or in rows. Mo thought it was a kind of . . . of spiritual deficit he racked up, serving the Justified; I just call it a conscience, or lack thereof. I won't let you *kill* yours purely in the name of survival. If you go too far down that road, you're no different than the Pax, no different than this Cyn. For all we know, all the wrong he's done—that all balances, in his head. As he sees *his* 'math.'"

I stared at her for another beat, then had to look away. Maybe she was right; maybe there were still lines I wouldn't cross. Maybe I was just pretending there weren't because I was angry, and underneath all that, because I was *scared*. Terrified.

But all the same, if I could learn how to hurt the Cyn, I would.

"Anyway, don't plan on retiring just yet," I told her, shifting the conversation to a different note. "You're still a pretty spritely hundred and eighty-three, after all; you've got plenty of good years ahead of you."

She almost laughed at that. "Goddammit, Esa, I'm not—wait." She'd finally caught on. It had taken her long enough. "Every time you say that, you drop a year lower."

"Yep."

"Are you just dropping a year every single time you make that joke, in the hopes that eventually you'll *actually* hit my correct age, and I'll have to admit it?"

". . . Yep."

Something quirked at the edges of Jane's lips; a smile. "Joke's on you, then," she said. "I don't actually have any idea when I was born. Even *I* don't know how old I am, Esa."

"Seriously? Bullshit. How can you not know *that*?"

"The wars were different. The worlds were different. And it was a long time ago."

". . . Your childhood kind of *sucked*, huh?"

"That's one way of putting it, yes."

CHAPTER 3

In a way—a terribly ghoulish way—the pall Mo's death cast over the interior of Scheherazade was almost useful to me. It meant I could focus on hating the Cyn for what he'd done, that I could focus on the notion that we were headed for our destination to learn why *he* had gone there, what *he* had learned that had set him on his path of bloodshed and misery.

Otherwise, all I would have been able to think about was that we were about to set foot in the place where my parents had died.

I didn't know much about them: they'd been scientists, studying the pulse, working with a primarily Barious sect of which the Preacher had been a member. Unlike the other gifted children out in the galaxy—children like Sho—my gifts hadn't come about randomly, as some evolutionary response to the radiation of the pulse; they'd come about because my mother had been accidentally exposed to a super-concentrated dose of pulse radiation, when she was carrying me in her womb. That dose had killed her, and my father as well.

That had happened on the station in Katya—where we were bound.

The Preacher had told us she'd abandoned the station almost immediately after my birth, that as far as she knew, the rest of her former sect had abandoned it as well, shortly thereafter. She'd fled with me to my homeworld, knowing that eventually, because of the high dose of radiation I'd received so young—and therefore, the high likelihood that I'd develop powerful next-generation gifts—someone would come looking for me, to use me either as a weapon, as the Pax had wanted to do, or to further their studies of the pulse, the way the Justified had. In a very real way, she'd used me as bait, trying to lure those who knew more about the strange cosmic event that had rendered the Barious "infertile," or close enough. So—yeah. That was one reason she and I weren't exactly on the best of terms these days.

I understood; I did. For the Preacher, studying the pulse and studying her people's slow-motion genocide was all the same thing. The life of one child— even a child she felt responsible for—was nothing next to that responsibility. And she *had* come to love me, in her own way. But it was still hard to square the years I'd spent, in the orphanage, desperately wondering who my parents had been, with the fact that the Preacher had known, had been a quiet presence in my life, but had never *told* me, had never tried to give me the family I'd desperately craved.

And now we'd learned that the Cyn had been seeking information on my birth as well, at the behest of whatever "goddess" he served. It seemed like everything came back to that, eventually—came back to Katya. Everything I was, everything I'd become since then: Jane's partner, at least a halfway decent fighter, even the children I'd helped, working at her side—none of it seemed to matter. My life would always be defined by *others* who knew more about what had gone on at that distant, hidden station than I did.

Mo had died because of something that had happened to me quite literally before I was born. Something I had zero control over, whose only remnants were the gifts it had given me and the circumstances of my life defined by the losses I'd suffered that day, losses I wasn't even aware of. Everything I *was*—and wasn't—stemmed from the system we were approaching, in one way or another.

So when we dropped out of hyperspace, I was already sitting in the cockpit, ready for anything. What I got was a perfectly normal system, unremarkable in every way.

I mean, it's not like I'd expected something different—some glowing portal to an alternate dimension in the place of a sun, or the ruins of some ancient civilization broken to pieces in orbit around one of the planets. The whole *reason* the Preacher's Barious sect had built their station here—Odessa Station, the Preacher called it; the place that had given me my name, in an abbreviated and differentiated form—had been that Katya *was* a wholly unremarkable system, the last place anyone would think to look for them.

There was an inner ring of rocky worlds, none terraformed, none particularly rich in useful minerals; a thick belt of comets formed a river of ice through the middle of the system, interesting as an astronomical curiosity, perhaps, but not actually of any scientific value; three outer gas giants, each with a smattering of moons, none of which had anything to recommend them either.

My heart was still in my throat as Schaz scanned the system, looking for the hidden station.

"You all right?" Jane asked me quietly, sensitive as always to my moods.

I nodded, not trusting myself to speak.

"Hmmm. Strange. Our destination is not at the coordinates the Preacher gave us," Schaz said. "It *should* be in a low orbit around the second gas giant—the blue one, there." She pulled up a close-in view of that particular world, without even a name, just a scientific designation: K1401-AG492Z5B. Its "surface," inasmuch as gas giants really had one of those, was a rippling sea of mist and storms, incredibly slow-moving hurricanes inching their way through the low gravity of the indigo atmosphere.

"I'm taking us in closer," Jane announced. "Schaz, plot the orbital coordinates the Preacher gave us; let's see if we can find where Odessa Station went off track." She looked sideways at me, reached out to touch my wrist, briefly. "Breathe, kid," she told me. "Just breathe."

I did that—hadn't realized I *hadn't* been.

We approached the world at sublight, the starfield passing by on either side of us. At some point, my parents had seen this same view, on their approach to the station where they would spend their last years: at some point, the Cyn had as well, tracking me—or the Preacher's sect—to this location, seventeen years before I'd known he even existed.

"Hmmmm. That *might* be the problem," Schaz said.

"What's up?" Jane asked her.

"Remember what the Preacher said about the station's first line of defense?"

"A minefield in the upper atmosphere, sure."

"Yeah. It's not there."

"She said the mines were cloaked; maybe we should—"

"She also gave us the cloaking parameters, Jane—I'd be able to spot them if they were there, even if they *were* cloaked. They're just . . . gone. The Cyn must have brute forced his way through them with that astoundingly ugly ship of his, the same way he pushed through the war satellites in orbit over Jaliad."

"So why would *that* make the station shift its orbit?" I asked.

"Another defense mechanism," Schaz said. "A kind of quarantine purge. Intended to destroy the research the Barious were doing there, before someone else could get to it. According to the schematics the Preacher sent, if the minefield was breached, the station was supposed to drop down into the gas giant and flood itself with atmosphere. The stuff's not dangerous, per se: primarily nitrogen and xenon, some oxygen, traces of helium; nothing you'd want to fill your lungs with for long periods, but perfectly breathable, actually. However, exposure to unregulated atmosphere like that would still ruin the *experiments* being performed on board; the atmosphere carries a static charge, and most of the work was being done in a sterile station and in zero gravity for a reason. An atmospheric flood would also make the station approach trickier to manage."

Jane frowned at the viewscreen. "Give me an overlay of the prior orbit," she told Schaz; obediently, Schaz calculated, and suddenly there was a shimmering line on the cockpit window, a path for Jane to follow: the former orbit of Odessa Station. Jane swept Scheherazade into the same flight path the station would have taken, scanning the slowly churning surface of the storms below as we went.

"There," Schaz chirped, zooming one of her cameras in on a tiny silver speck in the misty sea underneath us, a metal island half-sunk into the depths of the slowly shifting atmosphere.

We'd found it.

Only the highest towers of Odessa Station were visible; the rest was hidden in the clouds of mist and storms. It looked like nothing more than a shipwreck, just the tops of the masts sticking clear of the sea, except in this case the "masts" were steeples of steel and minarets of latticed alloys, probably containing the labs themselves, built away from the body of the station in case something had gone wrong.

"Odd again." Schaz murmured.

"What's up?" Jane asked.

"It's sunk into the atmosphere, but it should have descended even *lower*. As I understand these schematics, part of the purpose of the descent defense mechanism was to eject the station's computer core, deep enough into the gravity well that it would smash to pieces on the core of the world below."

"And?"

"And they're not *deep* enough for that. K1401-AG492Z5B—"

"We can just call it 'K one four,'" Jane said dryly.

"As you like. K14 has very weak gravity; again, part of the reason the station was built here was so they could orbit low enough to not be seen, whilst still maintaining zero-gravity labs in parts of the station. The station is currently *not* low enough to have ejected its AI core with enough force to have destroyed itself."

"You're telling me their AI might still be intact?" I asked, my heart hammering in my chest. Another being—next to the Preacher—who had *known* my parents, who had been present at my birth.

"I'm telling you that the AI was not destroyed in the manner of Odessa Station's built-in defense mechanisms," Scheherazade temporized.

"If you had to guess?" Jane asked her.

"The Cyn forced its way through the minefield, got on board, and gained access to the AI systems fast enough to prevent the discharge of the core," Schaz said. "That would also explain why the third step in the quarantine protocols—the overloading and discharge of the fusion reactor—also didn't occur."

"You're telling me it might have power?" Jane was taking us on approach, skimming over the top of the seas of azure mists; as we closed on the towers of the station, lights began to appear—in portholes and on radar masts, the "wreck" of the station suddenly lit from within, the illumination shining up from the depths of the atmospheric ocean it had become half-drowned in. With those lights cut on—likely triggered by our proximity—I could see the shadowy outline of the station below the "waterline" of the fog, a massive metal structure built out from the central fusion reactor, silent for decades, now slowly returning to life.

"I'm telling you it might have power," Schaz agreed, somewhat unnecessarily.

CHAPTER 4

Jane slowly pulled us into a loop, descending into the atmosphere of the gas giant a good bit away from where Odessa Station was sunk into the mists. That way we'd be able to scan for a docking bay or at least an umbilical on our approach.

As we sank into the fog, Schaz's engines caused the atmosphere around us to glow with reflected light, a different shade of blue from the slow eddies that surrounded us. "Can you raise the station's AI?" Jane asked Scheherazade.

"I've been *trying*," Schaz replied, somewhat testily. "He's not answering. Nobody's answering."

"We're never lucky," Jane muttered, mostly to herself. Down in the atmosphere, the station was invisible again—we could see the pinpricks of its distant lights through the murk, but other than that, we might as well have been surrounded by the deep blue nothingness of the gas giant on all sides.

Until we weren't. Something *rose* out of the depths of the storm around us, something *massive*, coming up on our port side; my first thought was that it was a goddamned dreadnaught, hiding deep in the mists, except it was even bigger than that, and none of Schaz's sensors went off, no alarms sounded— the only reason we knew it was there was that Jane had cameras scanning all around us.

"What the fuck is *that*?" Jane swore, swerving the ship away from the . . . whatever the hell it was. It had no running lights, like a ship would: no portholes glowing from within, no blinking proximity-warning indicators. More than anything it looked like a goddamned mountain, like we were approaching *it* rather than the other way around, except in place of a rocky surface it had clean, straight lines and razor-sharp edges; there was no broken stone or craggy peaks, just . . . metal, a massive precipice of metal rising up from the mists below us. It hung motionless for a moment, the fog eddying around it, then slowly descended, until it was like it had never been there.

"What the fuck is what?" Schaz asked innocently. "You really don't have to swear at me, Jane, I'm scanning on all—"

"What do you *mean*, what the fuck is what?" Jane was doing her best not to screech; she wasn't being at all successful. "You almost ran us into a goddamn . . . a goddamn . . ."

"Jane, I promise, there's nothing *down* here; just the station in front of us. I'm not picking up anything at all on my scans."

As if to give lie to her words, the obelisk rose up from the depths again, the pillar almost *floating* up from the fog like a cork bobbing in water in slow motion. It was on our starboard side this time: we couldn't even tell if it was the same one, or if there were dozens down there, hundreds, rising and falling in the misty sea. I pressed my face right up next to the camera—I couldn't be sure, but I could have sworn there was *writing* on the side, massive carved letters in a language I'd never seen before.

"She can't see them," I whispered. "Schaz can't see them at *all*."

"Schaz, check your damn camera feeds," Jane swore. "There are . . . *things*, fucking *things*, coming up out of the atmosphere below us."

"Jane, there's *nothing*—I'm reviewing the camera footage now, there's just the atmosphere and the storms. Slightly higher static charges than usual, yes, but beyond that—"

"They're forerunner relics," I told Jane, breathless. "They *have* to be. That's why the Preacher's sect built the station here—they thought the pulse had come from the forerunners, the lost species that built the Barious. They weren't just studying the pulse; they were studying those . . . those whatever the hell they are."

"Why wouldn't the Preacher *warn* us about them?" Jane growled. "We almost plowed into the side of one, for fuck's sake."

"Because she was expecting the station to still be in orbit, not down here in the atmosphere. If Schaz couldn't sense them and we weren't *looking* for them, we never would have found them at all. I guarantee you that they're deep enough in the atmosphere you can't *see* them from above." Another one of the massive obelisks rose, then fell, back into the mists; there was *definitely* writing on this one.

"She still should have told us."

"It's the Preacher, Jane. She keeps secrets out of habit. Honestly, she's worse than you."

"Thanks, Esa. Thanks so much." Ahead of us, the station was finally visible through the blue atmosphere; two of the obelisks rose and fell, nearly in tandem, on either side of it, but it was like they were avoiding it on *purpose*. They had to be—otherwise, it was inevitable the station would have been smashed to pieces by one of the rising pillars at *some* point over the last seventeen years.

"Why is there *always* weird shit." Jane wasn't really talking to me—it wasn't even a question, just a tired statement. "Can't just find the station, dock at the station, copy its logs and be on our way; oh, no. That would be too goddamned *easy*. It has to be sunk in an atmosphere and surrounded by ancient *obelisks* of unknown origin, unheard of on tens of millions of surveyed worlds."

"That's actually not true," Scheherazade put in. "I mean, theoretically— if you *are* seeing something that I'm not seeing—"

"Unless you've somehow fucked up the oxygen mix coming out of life support and we're both hallucinating, we're *fucking seeing this*, Schaz—"

"I'm saying if you *are*, that would match the obelisks found in the Oberon system, the ones uncovered by a Culda survey team about a thousand years ago, deep in the seas of liquid methane. No one ever knew what they were, just that modern technology didn't even recognize their existence. They were destroyed in the sect wars a couple hundred years later—the whole world was, a casualty of the Crimson-Cardosi conflict—but there is precedent for—"

"Just . . . just . . . just get us to the station, Scheherazade. Save the history lesson for later."

"You're the one at the stick."

"I am indeed." Jane had cut our speed back significantly when the obelisks had first appeared; now, she rerouted a little more power to the engines, and we floated again through the indigo mists, the massive stone pillars— Monuments? Tombstones? The cores of some ancient computer system that operated on some kind of dimensional wavelength we couldn't comprehend?— rising and falling on either side of us, soundless even in the ocean of fog that *should* have carried the noise of their passage.

Odessa Station loomed above us, its lights muted by the atmosphere. "There's an open docking bay on the third level from the bottom," Schaz informed us. "See? I can still see things." The last came out in a defensive mutter, Schaz's version of speaking under her breath.

"Yes. Thank you, Scheherazade. Any luck raising the station?"

"None. I don't think anyone's home."

"If there are lights, there's power—if there's power, that means at least *some* systems are running. Can you interface with their network?"

"Not yet; there's no wireless envelope for me to interface *with*. I don't know if that's on purpose, built into the station's design to keep them hidden, or if something's gone wrong inside. Once you dock, though, you should be able to hardwire me into whatever's left of the system. If the AI is still present, I'll be able to contact them from there. If not, depending on the level of damage, I *might* be able to take direct control of the remaining programs myself."

"You get to upgrade from a ship to a station," I told her, smiling weakly. "Hell of a promotion."

"I prefer my ship, thank you," Schaz replied primly. "It's taken a long time to get it just like I want it, and I like being *mobile*. Winding up stuck here, floating alone in this gas giant—that is *not* how I'd choose to spend eternity."

"There's the docking bay." Jane was craning her neck to look upward as the metallic structure of the station rose slowly past our window, all interlaced metal piping and bulkhead walls lapped by the mist. The open bay doors came into view, and Jane eased us inside, guiding Schaz through the shifting fog, the glow of our engines lighting the interior of the ingress tunnel that was otherwise pitch black.

"Welcome to Odessa Station," Jane said.

CHAPTER 5

Unlike the docking bay on Valkyrie Rock, the bay on Odessa was a massive hangar, wide enough to accommodate numerous ships at once, even vessels significantly larger than Scheherazade. Being that we were the only craft within, it was hard not to feel dwarfed by the sepulchre-silent space, our tiny ship all alone on the wide-open platform meant to hold a dozen craft of Schaz's size.

Jane and I took all our guns. We weren't expecting trouble, but given that we weren't expecting anyone at *all*, there was no reason not to.

We emerged from Schaz's interior into the relative dimness of the hangar; there was emergency lighting, but that was it: the huge floodlights built into the ceiling were still dark. "There's a hardwire access panel, there." Jane pointed at one of the walls, picking up the necessary machinery on her HUD.

I remembered when I'd first left my homeworld, and been so *excited* by the concept of spaceflight. I was still excited—I still got a thrill every time I saw a new world, every time Schaz took us out of atmosphere and the stars spread around us like a curtain of shimmering light—but I'd also gotten used to the fact that living on and around spaceships meant a lot of *work*: good, old-fashioned manual labor, not really all that different from what I'd done in the settlement back home, when the kids from the orphanage had been loaned out to whatever farmer needed help at harvest time.

It took Jane and me a bit to first wire a heavy cable into the access panel, then feed the cable into a nearby extender so we could push that extender across the empty bay—one of its wheels squeaked terribly; I guess nobody had been around to oil the thing in a while—then stretch *another* cable from the extender into Scheherazade's exterior port. After *that*, we still had to find the nearby hangar control room—up a flight of spiral stairs, through a sealed door that I had to breach with my teke—find an emergency generator, find a spare fusion *battery* for the emergency generator, wire the generator into the hangar controls, and divert the power conduits to the access panel we'd wired Schaz into so the relays would open up. Only once all that was done did she have access to Odessa Station's internal network.

Come, see the galaxy, learn about exciting electrical engineering and *lifting* heavy things.

"Took you long enough," Schaz grumbled—through the speakers in the bay, this time, rather than through our comms, which I guess was progress. Jane made a rude gesture at her through the hangar control window. "I saw that," Schaz said, sounding vaguely offended. "Wait—I *saw* that. I'm patched into the hangar's programming directives. Camera feeds, too. Apparently."

"Anybody in there with you?" Jane asked.

"That would be a negative," Schaz replied. "The table's all set but nobody's home, and the kitchen . . . door . . . is . . . locked."

"I . . . don't know what that means," I said.

"You really shouldn't try to metaphor, Schaz," Jane added. "You're not actually very good at it."

"I am too; shut up," she replied, a little reproachfully. "Don't be rude. What it *means* is that the AI core *was* purged, purposefully. Not damaged or destroyed, but *removed*, intact. Standard practice for a decommissioning."

"Except that the station *wasn't* decommissioned," Jane pointed out. "And if the core wasn't ejected, then whoever breached the minefield and came on board must have taken it with them when they left."

"That would follow, yes," Schaz agreed. "But the good news is, that means I *will* be able to get access to station systems; there's no one else inside to fight me for them. The *bad* news is—"

"I thought we already covered the bad news," I interrupted.

"Well, there's more bad news," Schaz replied, somewhat testily.

"There always is," Jane sighed.

"The *bad* news is," Schaz just powered through, "the former inhabitant of this network locked pretty much everything down on their way out. I have MelWill's intrusion programs, which are a ways past the firewalls the sect here could build, so I will be able to push through eventually—it'll just take some time."

"Do you have access to the hangar, at least?"

"I do—and since *someone's* broken the hangar control-room door servos, it's kind of a din in here, what with all the alarms." I stole a guilty look at the door in question, still halfheartedly trying—and failing, repeatedly—to slide shut. I hadn't *meant* to break it, but even though I'd learned a great deal about my teke in the last few weeks, fine motor control still wasn't exactly my strong suit. "In the meantime," Schaz continued, "have some light." One by one, the big floods cut on in the ceiling above; from up in the control room, we could suddenly see all the way to the end of the hangar in either direction, what felt like miles away. This was . . . a *really* big station.

"Can you get us access to the AI core?" Jane asked Schaz. "If we can get in there, maybe we can . . . expedite the process of giving you full control."

"I'll have to get into the tram system first—unless you want to find your way through the station through several hundred miles of looping, twisting maintenance access shafts," Schaz said, somewhat archly. "I don't have access to mapping data for those areas, either, so you'd have to pick your way through blind." I shuddered slightly—the concept of crawling through cramped tunnels *again*, after what I'd found in the center of Valkyrie Rock, was most definitely *not* an appealing one.

"We'll wait for the tram, thanks," Jane told Schaz dryly.

"A wise decision. All right—from here, I have to cut through the outward sensor node in order to get to tram system controls—no, it doesn't make any more sense to *me* how the Barious laid out this network. Let me just shift . . . the intrusion program . . . over to. . . . *ALERT ALERT ALERT ALERT unidentified craft on approach unidentified craft on approach unidentified*—"

"Tell me that's just us, Schaz; tell me it's still reading *our* approach," Jane begged.

With what sounded like actual effort, Schaz stopped shouting alarms at us. "Negative," she replied. "*Two* ships on approach, descending into the atmosphere of K14 now. I don't have exterior cameras up yet; just radar."

"What's the *size* of the contact?" Jane was asking even as she and I hauled ass back down the spiral stairs, sprinting across the docking bay toward Scheherazade. If it *was* the Cyn—if it had, somehow, managed to survive the rain of fire on Jalia Preserve and then *somehow* followed us here—at least we'd have access to Schaz's turrets if it tried to take us on in the hangar.

"Ah—smaller vessels, smaller than me," Schaz said; Jane and I didn't stop sprinting, but we slowed our pace a bit. Whoever was on approach, it wasn't the Cyn.

"Can you contact them? Or at least ping them, see if you get a response?"

"I *told* you, I don't have all of the station's systems online yet, and that includes communications—"

"Do you have *your* systems, Schaz? Plugging you into Odessa didn't *remove* your control over your *own* comm system, did it?"

"Oh. Right. Yes. Hold on." A moment, as Jane and I reached Scheherazade's side; we both leaned against her bulkheads, getting our breath back, our hearts pounding in our throats. "Oh! Hello! Hi! So good to see you!" Whoever the hell Schaz was talking to, she sounded *delighted*; I suppose that was a good sign.

We weren't inside, so we couldn't hear whatever response the two ships outside made to Schaz, but we could still hear her reply: "Yeah, watch out for those, they're . . . no, *I* couldn't see them either, but Jane and Esa both swear there's something . . . I know, I kind of thought they were messing with me at first too, but—no, no, I'm sure it's not—come on, Var, Jane wouldn't *do* that to us, and you know it."

I let out my breath in an explosive release. "Bolivar?" I asked Schaz, cutting into her conversation. "That's *Bolivar* on approach?"

"Bolivar and Khaliphon, as well," Schaz reported, still sounding just as pleased as punch, like she'd been throwing a fancy dinner party and been a *little* disappointed at the guests who had shown up, only to find two late arrivals at the door. "Apparently they were both following our signal back to Jaliad, got redirected here by the Preacher, and met up en route. Both of them dropped what they were doing to come help us out: isn't it *nice* to have friends?"

Jane was grinding her teeth again; I put a hand on her shoulder, and grinned weakly. "She means well," I told her, and then started laughing.

With actual, physical effort, Jane restrained herself from shouting at her ship. "Open a channel to Bolivar, please," she said into her comm.

"Of course, boss! Javier's actually been broadcasting for a bit now; you're just not inside, so you're not in range of my internal speakers—"

"And you *couldn't forward that signal to the docking bay?*"

"Oh. Well. Yes. In my defense—I've been a ship for a very long time. Getting used to being a ship *and* a station both is taking some getting used to."

"*Schaz*—"

"Transferring Javier's signal now," she said hurriedly, and then both our comms *and* the hangar speakers were suddenly broadcasting Javier's voice. "Jane, Esa, this is Javier—Can you read? Repeat—Marus and I are on approach, making our way past these . . . whatever the goddamned hell these monoliths are. If you're there, please respond. Jane, come on, just—"

"Hi, sweetheart," Jane said. "We're here—we're okay. My ship is just an idiot. It's good to hear your voice."

Javier laughed. "And yours," he said then, as he shouted into another channel: "Marus! I got them! They're on board!"

"Hi, Javi!" I said, not willing to let Jane have all the fun. "How's it going?" I know, it was kind of stupid, but I couldn't help it: I was glad to hear his voice.

"Hi, kid," he replied; I could hear him grinning. "I'm good, like always; more to the point, how are *you* doing? It sounds like you've had a rough few weeks."

"Been better," I replied. "But I can channel energy through my teke now, so, you know. That's . . . cool."

"The approach is simple enough," Jane told Javier, ignoring me completely. "The obelisks down in the mists *seem* like a navigational nightmare, but we think they're avoiding contact on purpose; how big, floating mountains *have* a purpose is a question for another day."

"Yeah, we've noticed that too—Marus closed Khaliphon with one, to try and scan some of that weird writing on the side, because of course he did." As an explorer and cartographer, Javier tended toward "look, don't interact" when it came to new discoveries; as an intelligence operative, Marus's inclinations were always a bit more . . . active. "It actually *moved away from him*, even though Khaliphon himself still couldn't sense it. Weird shit. Anyway, we're both coming up on the hangar ingress now—we'll see you soon."

"Sounds good," Jane replied. "And Javier?"

"Yeah, sweetheart?"

"Thanks for coming."

"That's what I'm here for."

I triggered my comms off. "For that," I whispered to Jane, "and so that you can use him as you will, mostly to satisfy your *massive* appetite for—" She glared at me, and I sniggered, looking away. I hadn't realized *how* tense I had been, until the arrival of our friends had broken that tension like a fever. Schaz was right—it *was* good to have friends.

CHAPTER 6

Given that—out of absolutely necessity—I *had* managed to break the airlock seal on the control-room door, just a little bit, Jane and I were forced to retreat to the interior of Scheherazade as the hangar airlocks cycled to allow Bolivar and Khaliphon entrance to the station.

Parked together on the gleaming metal deck, the three ships were a study in contrasts: if Scheherazade was a knife, her vestigial wings like the curved guard sweeping forward from the hilt of her engine, then Bolivar was an arrowhead, smaller and lighter than Schaz, his exterior studded with all sorts of sensors and probe-launchers for Javier's mapping duties. Khaliphon was smaller and sleeker than either ship, built for stealth and insertion—unlike Bolivar, he *did* possess wings for agile atmospheric flight, but they were retractable, folded up against his body when he was maneuvering in the void, then expanded as he approached atmosphere. It was a design decision Schaz was constantly needling him over, given that she felt his Reint designers had settled on a compromise choice rather than sticking to their proverbial guns on one path or the other.

Javier and Marus descended almost as soon as the airlocks had cycled again; they were about as mismatched a pair as could be, Javier tall, good-looking in a rakish, just-rolled-out-of-the-cockpit kind of a way, Marus slight even for a Tyll, possessed of a kind of preternatural stillness that contrasted even more with Javier, who *always* seemed to be in motion, even when he wasn't. Jane and I emerged from Scheherazade to meet them, and I gave Marus a hug as Jane granted Javier a significantly more . . . enthusiastic greeting.

"I suppose it must be strange for you, to be in this place," Marus murmured softly as he released me. "Whatever it is you need, Javier and I are here for you, Esa. I want to make sure you remember that."

"Thanks, Marus. I'm . . . I feel like, yeah, it's weird, a bit. But it would have hurt a lot more a couple of years ago. I lost something in this place, true, something I didn't even know I had to lose when it happened. But I've made myself a new family now."

"Pretty much through sheer force of will, yes." He smiled at me.

I shrugged. "It helps that I had a wise old uncle to guide me through." I patted his green-skinned hand, matching his smile with my own.

"I'm not that much older than Jane," he protested.

"She doesn't actually know how old she is. She told me that earlier."

"Well, I know how old *I* am," he retorted, "and it's not old enough to not object to being called 'old.' I'll take the wise bit, though. Happily."

"Fine. I should tell you . . ." I paused. Maybe it should have been Jane to say it, but she was occupied, and he deserved to know. "I know you served with Jane, back in the day. I take it that means you served alongside Mohammed, as well."

"I did, yes. Though 'beside' might be a stretch; the work the two of them did was . . . associated with my own, much in the same sense that the work you two do *now* is linked to mine, but we were rarely in the field together. I passed intelligence on to their division; they acted on it. The lives they took doing so—that weight was on me, as much as them, I admit, though I much prefer the way we do things now, when I can claim at least *partial* credit for the lives you're saving." He studied my face again. "Esa—the Preacher told us what happened; she scanned Scheherazade before she jumped to hyperspace, knew that he didn't get on board before the weapons systems defending the planet fired. I know he's gone. I'm sorry you had to suffer through that."

Just the kindness in his voice, the sympathy, was enough to bring the moment welling back up inside me; I stuffed it back down, and kept myself from crying again. "I'm sorry you lost your friend, Marus," I said in reply.

He sighed. "That's the thing about getting 'old,' as you put it: you reach a certain point where, unfortunately, you have to learn to make your peace with that aspect of life. Mo's search for his God was always quixotic in nature—I sometimes wonder if he *was* looking for answers, or if he was really looking for one last fight. One final *good* battle, where he could feel he was on the side of the angels again. Setting off the pulse bomb robbed him of that feeling, of the security he'd always felt, serving with the Justified. I believe, if he made the choice he did, it was because *you* granted him that sense of righteousness again. I'd thank you for that."

It meant the world to hear Marus say that, but it *also* meant I was about to start crying, yet again. "Thank you," I told him, then turned to Jane and Javier. "Do I have to find a bucket of water to throw on the two of you?" I shouted, more to give myself something *else* to talk about than for any other reason. "You can make out later; we've got work to do!"

Given that her *mouth* was somewhat occupied at the moment, Jane replied with a two-fingered salute, one Javier had taught me had been *particularly* rude among the sect she was born into. Of all the other vestiges of that life Jane had left behind, it was funny what still clung to her like barnacles on the hull of a boat, invisible beneath the waterline of her personality.

"I've managed to get basic structural readings from the sensors," Scheherazade put in. "The station's still sinking into the atmosphere, its orbit decaying day by day. We're not in any *immediate* danger, but a year from now it will be entirely beneath the sea of atmosphere, and once that happens, some of its automated propulsion systems *will* short out, and its descent will begin in earnest."

"What about internal sensors?" Jane asked her, finally breaking away from Javier. "Do you have any readings there?"

"Basic integrity only, so far," Schaz replied. "The superstructure of the station has multiple structural failures, ranging from minor to severe. Also, several of the station bulkheads—more, the lower down you get—have been breached, and several of the emergency airlocks have failed. I'd say roughly a quarter of the station is flooded with atmosphere."

"Is that affecting the fusion reactor?" she asked. "Is that why power's so spotty?"

"In parts, yes," Schaz said. "It's also because the reactor was supplemented by solar panels, which, currently sunk beneath the fog, are operating at . . . less than optimal efficiency."

"You mean they're doing fuck-all in this soup," Javier translated, his tone dry.

"I mean pretty much that, yes."

"The bulkhead breach, the structural damage," Marus said. "Can you tell *what* caused it?"

"I do not have access to those records; they may be locked behind a firewall I haven't breached yet, or they may have been purged completely, along with the station's AI. Based on the orbital decay of the station, though, I can tell you *when* the damage occurred."

"Seventeen years ago," I said quietly.

"You are correct," Schaz acknowledged.

Of course I was. The Cyn had been here before, and he'd fucked things up, just like he always did, like a force of nature, a hurricane that returns to calm shores again and again and again, tearing down whatever the natives have built in the interim.

Jane, as always, tended toward the paranoid. "You have internal sensors online?" she asked.

"Some of them, yes."

"Can you scan for life forms? Energy-based life forms, in particular?"

"There's no way he somehow survived Jaliad, then *beat* us here," I protested. Jane just raised an eyebrow at me, and I regretted the words almost as soon as I said them. At this point, ruling out *anything* concerning the Cyn was dangerous—and just because *he* might not have beat us here didn't mean he might not have cohorts remaining, cohorts who perhaps had never left.

"I can assure you a Cyn—the one we've tangled with, or any other—is not on board," Schaz said. "There are, however, several divergent scans in one of the higher laboratory facilities, up in the towers."

"Life signs?" Jane asked, her hand going to the butt of her gun.

"Corpses," Schaz replied succinctly.

Apparently the station hadn't been fully abandoned by the time the Cyn arrived, shortly after my birth. More lives to put on his butcher's bill.

"We'll start there," Jane said. "Can you map us out a route?"

"With some of the structural damage, it may take some doing; the tram system appears to be entirely nonfunctional."

"We can breathe the local atmosphere, right? So you can take us through some of the breached airlocks."

"You can, but you can't so much breathe *void*, and some of the higher airlocks in breach were still above the atmosphere line when they failed, leading to cascading decompressions. I'll find you a safe route, Jane, it may just require some travel time. Calm yourself." She paused. "Would you like some tea while I'm calculating?"

CHAPTER 7

We didn't take Schaz up on the tea. Javier and Marus were already geared up; unlike Jane and I, their positions among the Justified—cartographer and intelligence gathering, respectively—didn't take them into heavy action *quite* as often as our escort duty did, but it was still a dangerous universe, and they knew how to defend themselves.

Both of them wore body armor laced into their clothing, just like Jane and I did—Javier's under a battered leather jacket, Marus's woven into the tactical gear he wore under a loose saffron robe, a typical Tyll accoutrement. He'd discard the robe the second we hit trouble, and knowing Marus, it was likely laced with electronic countermeasures or smoke grenades or something, to cover an escape.

As far as armaments went, Javier wore an ancient long-barreled shotgun slung over his back, and a semiautomatic pistol in a shoulder holster that was the missing triplet to the twins under my arms; Marus carried a brace of submachine guns, both outfitted with permanent suppressors, a necessity given the clandestine nature of his operations. We weren't expecting combat, but we were in unknown territory, so we acted as though an attack were imminent.

Though what good our ballistic weapons were going to do against the Cyn, if he showed up and decided to start wrecking shit, I wasn't sure.

After Schaz calculated our route, Jane lined us up at the ingress point out of the hangar, a maintenance shaft leading down to the lower levels. Consciously or not, she'd already started taking charge of our little impromptu exploration, taking point herself with Schaz's route laid out in her HUD, putting me next to allow me free reign with my teke if we hit something heavy, Marus third, and Javier in the rear, I think as much to curtail his natural curiosity as to put his shotgun in a position to cover anything coming at us from behind.

"Here we go," Jane said finally as she popped open the access panel.

We filed down the ladder, and started into the innards of Odessa Station.

The route wasn't quite as bad as Schaz had implied—though that may have been simply because she was guiding us around the more damaged sections of the station—but it still involved a great deal of what *felt* like backtracking, heading half a mile down one section of corridors, only to climb down another floor, backtrack a *full* mile, picking our way through long-silent machinery, then to climb back up and retrace the same mile yet again.

Most of what we saw was either typical space-station machinery—if you've seen the inner workings of life-support systems and gravity generation on one station, you've pretty much seen them all, and for whatever reason, my work with Jane seems to take us through station support machinery a good deal—or anonymous corridors, some of which were flooded with the cyan fog of the planet below, the shifting mists just slightly heavier than the station's generated atmosphere, meaning it hung low around our knees, making it feel more like we were wading through a slow-moving river than passing into a cloud.

I tried not to think about the notion that my parents had perhaps walked these halls, the parents I'd never met, the parents I didn't even know what they *looked* like. It didn't matter—they were where I came from, genetically speaking, but that was just biology; my *real* family was close by, the three people willing to brave a dying station sinking into the storms of a gas giant just because I wanted answers. I concentrated instead on moving forward, sometimes using my teke to clear our path, forcing open sealed doorways or widening already-existing breaches in bulkheads so that we could pass through, following the low river of fog as it wended its way through the interior caverns of the station.

"All right," Jane said, turning to the rest of us as she neared a sealed door. "Good news is, we're almost there."

"That *is* good news," Javier agreed. "Why do I feel like you didn't turn around just to tell us that?"

"Because you're an observant fella sometimes," Jane replied dryly. "The laboratory with the signals bouncing back from Schaz's scans is on the other end of this tramway tunnel. The bad news is, that *particular* tunnel is just below the water recyclers that feed into the fusion core's coolant systems, and sometime in the last decade or so the recyclers sprung a leak."

Marus sighed. "How bad is it?" he asked.

"Schaz isn't sure; she doesn't have internal sensors in the tramways," Jane said. "Based on her scans, it's not entirely flooded, since it's still draining *out* somewhere, but we *are* all going to get wet."

I was finally going to get to go for my swim after all. Hooray.

"Great," Marus said. "Spelunking. My favorite hobby."

I almost laughed. "That's not a real word," I told him. "You just made it up."

"Did not. It means cave diving. Well, cave exploring, actually."

"Why wouldn't you just call it *that*, then? Also"—I nodded at the sealed doors—"not a cave."

"Close enough."

"Come on, guys, we've all done something like this before," Javier said. "Nobody here's allergic to *water*."

"*I* haven't," I pointed out.

"Well then, welcome to the wide, wonderful world of spelunking through a manmade cave system, Esa."

"*Still* not a word."

"Keep in mind," Jane told us all, "it's pitch black in there. It was a *tramway*— nobody but maintenance was ever supposed to be inside, so there wasn't ever much lighting, and what there *is* has been shorted out by the water."

"Oh, for fuck's sake," Javier sighed. "Can you share your HUD mapping data?"

"We don't have mapping data; just blueprints. No sensors in there, remember? Schaz is extrapolating the flooding based on coolant levels and the higher operating volume of the recyclers on the floors below, where the draining liquid is getting soaked back up."

"Well, it's already been kind of a foggy day around here," Marus said, gesturing with a smile at the blue atmosphere hiding our boots. "Might as well add some artificial rain to it."

"I just didn't want you to say I didn't warn you," Jane told him.

"Well, now you did. Esa?" Marus nodded at the door.

I reached into the interior machinery with my mind, getting my "fingers," otherwise known as the edges of my teke field, in between the sealed doors. I braced myself mentally—since yes, Newtonian physics still applied to quantum state telekinetic force, in a kind of fucked-up way—then started pulling the doors apart, steadily applying more force until the machinery inside the walls gave and the panels shifted back into their housing, releasing a small rush of water that washed into the mists already lapping at our knees.

"Here we go," Jane said, cutting on the light built into her tactical vest; she didn't need it, not with her HUD, but neither Javier nor I had low-light implants, plus the lighting would make the footage from her body cameras easier to study, if for whatever reason we needed to do so later on. Even with the added illumination, we still couldn't see much within—falling water arcing in streams from the pipes above and the rain-slick walls beyond, and that was about it.

"Look on the bright side, kid," Javier whispered to me as Jane started descending down the stairs. "At least you don't have to wait for your hair to dry."

"Speaking of which," I whispered back. "Did I tell you that I figured out how to control energy with my *mind?*"

"You mentioned; that sounds *awesome*. Wait—does that mean—"

"Yep! I can grow my hair back out now. *I am so excited by that.*"

The metal stairs went down into the slick of water below us; it was impossible to tell how deep it was, the lack of light and the shifting layer of misty atmosphere on *top* of the water just making it seem like we were descending into an actual river. Jane had already sunk up to her knees, and she was still going, but when it was about waist-high on her, she stopped. "I think I found the tram line!" she called up to us, feeling at something with her boot.

I breathed a small sigh of relief. I wasn't the world's *best* swimmer, especially carrying about forty pounds of combat gear—including my weapons—and I didn't really *want* to have to try and swim the length of the tram tunnel to our destination.

Jane was holding her rifle above her head, despite the fact that all of our guns were designed to fire wet, and our ammunition was sealed against exactly this sort of scenario. I wasn't sure where she'd picked up that particular habit, or when she'd carried a weapon antique enough to *not* have that kind of sealing, but I followed her lead, raising Bitey up out of the water as I waded in.

Cold.

I think the fact that I couldn't *see* actually made it colder, as well as giving me the impression that something was always *inches* away from swimming past my legs, despite the fact that I *knew* we were the only things living on the station. It *also* didn't help that I was the shortest of the group, a few inches shy of Marus, which meant where the water hit Jane at about the middle of her ribcage, I sunk down damn near to my shoulders. For a second I thought I'd just keep dropping—that I'd inadvertently stepped off of the stairs and into a recessed walkway or something, and the water was significantly deeper here than the scant few feet away where Jane was wading—but then I touched down against the metal decking below us, my raised arms still barely clear of the water.

"All right, let's go," I told Jane with chattering teeth. "I'm *freezing.*"

She didn't say anything, just nodded under the curtain of falling water that was spattering her face. She started forward, moving deeper into the impromptu river that snaked its way through the abandoned station, pushing her way through what had once been the connective veins of Odessa. The constant flow of liquid from above us—and the fact that it was draining *away* somewhere below—meant that, while there wasn't quite a *current*, there was still a lot of motion and flow, and I had to work to keep my footing, focusing on just following the shifting beam of Jane's guiding light as it reflected off the arcs of water jetting down from the breaches above and the clouds of mist surrounding us.

It wasn't my favorite bit of exploration ever. Still better than Valkyrie Rock, though.

CHAPTER 8

We pushed our way through the slow churn of the dark river; thankfully, no one lost their footing and went for a swim. Finally, we could see more illumination around a bend in the tram tunnel—a flickering *something*, there, then gone, seemingly at random. We came around the corner in darkness, Jane's light playing against the rear of a tram car, thrown off the track and nearly on its side in the water; we'd reached the laboratory station.

Wading past the long-silent vehicle, Jane pulled herself up out of the river, through the mists rolling off the edges and onto the tram platform; whatever the light we'd seen had been, it was gone now, and there was just the darkness and the beam of Jane's flashlight, filling the abandoned station and the still trams.

Javier pulled himself up as well, then bent to help me; I'd only just gotten out of the water—shaking myself like a dog—when the burst of light came again, almost blinding to eyes that had *just* gotten used to being surrounded mostly by darkness. "Contact!" Jane shouted, the word followed almost immediately by two cracks of her rifle, the flash of her muzzle flare blending into the new light, lending a strobe-like atmosphere to the empty station.

"Or not," Javier told her, still bent over to help Marus climb out of the murk. "Congratulations, babe: you just killed a ghost."

"False alarm," she admitted, lowering her weapon, and I swear to god she actually sounded a little disappointed.

The gunshots were still echoing down the tunnel, the sharp, fading pops breaking the constant sound of the waterfalls behind us. I turned to look at whatever the hell she'd been firing at—before then, I'd been too disoriented by the darkness.

The light was coming from a low holographic pedestal, rising just above the thick mist that still eddied around our knees. It was projecting the image of a Barious, standing on the projector, an automated greeting for arrivals stepping off the tram—an ancient recording. She was speaking, yet not saying a word: the projector's audio system must have shorted out.

Not just any Barious, either: it actually took me a moment to recognize the Preacher without all of her late-life additions. This had been recorded before she'd taken various combat damage and replaced pieces of her chassis with whatever detritus she could find that could be welded into the advanced alloys that made up her skin; before she'd changed out her optics from microscopic calibrations to more combat-useful scans. The Barious standing on the pedestal was worlds away from what the Preacher had been in my first memories; this was who she had been *meant* to be, a scientist, a leader, welcoming visitors to her sect's laboratory deep in the hidden reaches of space.

"What a difference a couple of decades makes, huh?" Javier asked, his thoughts echoing my own. Behind the holographic image, the two bullet holes Jane had left behind smoked faintly—I thought there might have been something subconsciously telling in the fact that she'd shot at an image of the Preacher before she'd realized it was a hologram.

"Yeah, it's a blast from the past," Jane said sourly. She'd stowed her rifle, and had knelt before the panel that would give us access to the sealed blast doors leading deeper into the lab; she popped the metallic cover free with her knife as she trained her flashlight on the inner workings, digging through the wiring. "Say goodbye to the Preacher, Esa," she told me. "Our cameras have recorded the projection anyway; you can remind her when we get back to Sanctum of what she *used* to look like. Meantime, I'm going to have to short out that thing to redirect power to these doors; not even *you* can haul open something this thick." She jerked back from the panel as a shower of sparks emerged from the wiring; the system didn't seem to like her digging around inside with a soldering kit. "Whatever they were doing in this lab, they did *not* want anyone getting in without permission."

"Or whatever was inside getting *out*," Marus added, shaking himself off as he, too, emerged from the river and the mist.

"Wait," I whispered, ignoring the two of them, still staring intently at the image shifting before me. Then, almost screaming: "*Wait!*"

The hologram wasn't of the Preacher anymore: it had shifted to project a Vyriat instead, her facial tentacles waving a greeting. Then the image became a tall Wulf, dressed in a lab coat, and then another Barious, just like the Preacher, still shiny and undamaged by the outside world. One by one, different faces appeared, scientists and researchers, smiling and greeting those who stepped off the tram.

The projections were cycling through the various team members who had worked in this lab: the lab run by the Preacher, the lab where the Cyn had dragged the dead from the station, and thus, the lab where his goal, whatever it had been, had been hidden. "Just wait," I whispered again, something I barely recognized in my voice, something almost like agony. My eyes were locked on the projections; I don't think an interstellar tug could have pulled me away as the flickering hologram cycled, then cycled, then cycled again.

Another Wulf, this one with gray-shot fur.

Two more Barious, their expressions somber.

Another Vyriat, then a Reetha, the base of the projector rising up slightly to make the shorter species even with whomever might have been emerging from the tram.

Another Barious, then another.

A Tyll.

And then—

And then—

I swallowed, made a strange, low noise in the back of my throat, caught somewhere between grief and awe, the sound almost *begging*, somehow. I was weeping, the tears mixing with the water still clinging to my face from the river we'd left behind as I stared up into the gaze of the newest team member projected onto the holographic platform, a face I'd never seen before that was nonetheless incredibly familiar, a face looking down at me with a gentle smile.

I had my mother's eyes. I hadn't known that.

Now I did. The eyes looking down on me were the same ones that I'd seen looking back from every mirror I'd ever passed, from every photograph or vid that had been taken of me at Sanctum. They matched the kind smile on the figure's lips—the same expression I wore at times myself, not the one that came out when I was *trying* to smile, but the one I saw sometimes out of the corner of my eye in a reflection, the one that just *happened*, instead, when I was truly happy. My mother had worn that smile well, and easier than I did.

The hologram kept shifting in and out of focus as the fading machine kept trying valiantly to fulfill its long-unneeded purpose, my mother's face shifting in and out of a blur, looking down at me with the same hazel eyes that had always felt like an anomaly in my own makeup, not quite a match for my dark brown complexion or my kinky, tightly curled hair. They fit her face better, I think.

She wore a lab coat and held a tablet in one hand, the other raised in greeting; I stood before her, soaked and dripping and bedraggled, dressed in ratty castoffs and combat armor, holding tightly to the grip of a gun. We couldn't have looked more different; we couldn't have looked more the same.

Then she was gone—the hand I hadn't known I'd raised to try and touch her face pushed through the image of the Barious who came next, and then the projector flickered out again and I was left alone in the dark. Suddenly I was leaning against the wall behind the projector, leaning and sobbing and almost screaming, but not quite, the sound more *keening* than that, filling the station around us with a banshee wail.

Then Jane was holding me, and Javier, and Marus. They pulled me down to the slick tile of the station floor and just *held* me, let me spend all my grief and all my pain in that wailing, keening scream as they held me tight and refused to let me go. The projection returned, bathing us all with light, cycling through the team members again—still facing us, the projector's sensors orienting the image still functioning—and when the ghostly image of my mother returned again, I looked up at her from the embrace of my family, and my sudden grief was spent, gone as fast as it had come.

"At least now I know," I whispered to them. "At least now I know what she looked like. I have that now. I didn't before."

"Our cameras caught it, kiddo," Javier said to me, his hand on the back of my head. "We'll get you a printout, to keep with you. You don't have to lose her again."

"Thank you. I'm . . . come on." I shook my head, smiling now, through the tears and the mist; we were packed so tight the motion brushed me up against all of them at once. "You guys can let me up now. I'm good. I'm good."

"I'm not. Good lord, I'm still crying." Marus wasn't lying; he was wiping tears from his face. You'd think a hard-as-nails, do-whatever-it-takes intelligence operative wouldn't be that susceptible to powerful emotion, but nah. Marus was a big old softy, one of the most empathetic people I'd ever known.

"Schaz is ready to open the door, Esa," Jane told me. "Are you—"

I nodded, even though I was still staring at the projector—it had just cycled off of my mother's image again, back through the majority Barious of the rest of her research team. "I'm good," I said again, and it actually felt true. "Let's get in there. Find out what that glowing bastard *wants* with me."

A sharp electrical crack, and a flood of sparks showering through the mists, originating from the panel Jane had been working on; then the holograms cut off abruptly, and the overhead lights began to shift on instead, even as the door started to groan. I stood—we all did—and we lifted our weapons.

My mother had been a scientist. I was something else. I didn't know quite what that *was* yet—not exactly a soldier like Jane, but not the leader or guiding light the Preacher expected me to be, either—but whatever it was I would eventually *become*, right now, the answers we sought lay in my past, not my future.

Time to step into the lab where I'd been born.

CHAPTER 9

We left the low, shifting mists behind as we stepped through the door, this area of the station still having been sealed off; Schaz sealed it up again behind us, and suddenly the corridors got a great deal quieter, the sound of falling water having been a near constant for the past twenty minutes or so. Jane started forward again, her footsteps the only noise echoing against the corridor walls, but she didn't make it very far before she stopped, and held out her hand.

She was facing another door; I raised up Bitey to my eye, shrugging my shoulders as I did, very purposefully trying to shut down the powerful emotions—positive and negative both—that had overwhelmed me moments before. No, we weren't *expecting* a fight, but the fight you weren't expecting would kill you just as fast as the one you were prepared for; usually even faster. Another one of Jane's maxims.

"What have we got?" Javier asked Jane from the back of the line.

"Some sort of common area in front of us," she said. "Not a lab, but maybe a kind of gathering place. It's an atrium, multiple stories tall; a fair amount of dead plants. The labs branch off of there, including some sort of factory floor on the top level, reaching farther back into the spire." She wasn't picking all this up from her HUD—station walls tended to be sealed against exactly the sort of differing-spectrum scans that would have let her see straight through the doors if they'd been made of wood instead—so Schaz must have been relaying camera feeds to her from the interior. "It's fairly dark inside, but what I'm picking up . . . it's not good."

"The dead are in there?" Marus asked. I'd almost forgotten that was what had brought us here—not the fact that this had been the lab where my parents worked, but that this was the lab where the Cyn, for whatever reason, had gathered those who had still been on-station when he attacked.

"They're in there, somewhere," Jane agreed. "I can't see where."

"Only one thing to do, then," Javier said, gesturing with his shotgun. "Open it up."

Jane nodded, and touched the access lock. The door hissed open—still enough power for that, apparently—and we stepped out into the wide open space before us.

Once it probably would have been beautiful, the terraced upper levels designed to flow gracefully down, wide spiral stairs linking each avenue. Much of the empty open area near the top of the atrium had been given over to canopies of large trees from multiple worlds, growing up from the well-tended gardens that made up much of the common area below. A place of greenery and life for the inhabitants of the sterile labs, a kind of arboretum, a place of calm and depressurization where they could remind themselves of what they were working for, what they were trying to save.

Except now, all the trees were dead, their bare branches snaking upward like skeletal hands reaching up from tombs, and most of the cunningly re-cessed lighting was either outright depowered or at minimum malfunction-ing, flickering on and off and lending the shrouded paths that wound through the gardens a kind of sinister aspect. Too, here were the first telltale signs of combat: splintered bullet holes in the tree trunks, bloodstains in various spe-cies' shades on the ground, a few blackened patches in the gardens or on the paths where they'd tried to use explosives to slow the menacing figure that must have seemed to have stepped out of their nightmares.

Still no bodies, though.

"Forward?" I asked Jane, still holding Bitey to my eye.

"Forward," she nodded, and did just that, still following the tracker that would lead us to all the dead.

I'll give whoever had designed the atrium this: they'd done a bang-up job mimicking a natural landscape. The paths actually rose and fell slightly, like a real landscape would, and here or there they carved around large boulders or other "natural" obstacles, giving a winding, kind of pleasantly aimless feel-ing to the actually rigidly designed walkways through the gardens. Of course, the effect was somewhat ruined by the long-dead trees above us and the shell casings littering the ground that we had to carefully step over.

The flickering lights only amplified my quiet unease with the place, and

I wasn't the only one: I could see Jane's hand tighten on the combat grip of her rifle as well. The experience was just too similar to our trek through Valkyrie Rock, except there, the bodies had been *everywhere*, not just gathered in the central bonfire. Here, the Cyn had made sure to put them *all* in the same place, even though, as far as we knew, he'd never planned to return here—hadn't done so in the seventeen years since he'd arrived—and had never intended that anyone else find whatever grisly tableaux he'd left behind, either.

We came up another rise in the path below us, and as the walkway curved, slightly, we could see around one of the large, dead trees, to a truly *massive* specimen of timber that was likely the exact center of the atrium, reaching all the way to the ceiling and spreading its now-dead branches out in all directions. I couldn't even tell what species it might have been, though, because my attention was stolen by the fact that the huge tree was *also* where the Cyn had left all the bodies.

They had been *hung* from the branches; they had been nailed to the trunk. They'd been chained or tied or otherwise attached *somehow*, making the titanic tree seem more corpse than wood. Even for a being of infinite energy and with terrible reserves of patience, it must have taken hours; there were dozens of bodies, at least. And that wasn't even the most disturbing part.

The organic species' faces were missing, just like with the bodies we'd found on Valkyrie Rock—burned straight off, I'd imagine by the Cyn's grasping hand, no different than the palm-print he'd left on Jane's shoulder as a memento of her scuffle with him back on the asteroid. Human or Tyll or Vyriat, it made no difference; he'd grabbed them around the face with one hand and pressed *inward*, until he was scorching bone. Desiccated and almost mummified by seventeen years in the climate-controlled atmosphere of the station, the mouths of the withered corpses all hung wide below their blistered faces, each ruined visage more disturbing than the last.

The majority of those he'd tied to the tree, though, weren't organic at all; they were—had been—Barious, just like the majority of faces projected from the hologram outside had been. Odessa Station had been operated by a majority-Barious sect, after all. Almost to a unit, the Barious had died the same way, their chests burst open, the fusion battery that operated as their "heart" turned into a live grenade buried in their metallic skin. He hadn't melted the Barious's faces, though I'd imagine he could have; he burned hot enough if he chose.

Instead, he had given them *masks*.

Each and every one of the synthetic race that had been hung from the tree wore finely detailed, well-crafted masks, strapped to their metal faces with wire. The macabre decorations resembled humans, and Wulf, and Tyll, and Klite—almost every organic species was represented, adorning the Barious dead. Not just with cheap party masks, either: these were almost *lifelike*, the fake skin supple—god, I hoped it was fake skin—the glassy eyes carefully attached, each hair an individual strand among thousands. I'm fairly sure that where there were teeth, hinted at behind some of the lips—fully visible in a few, where the metallic mouths had been stretched out in a mocking simulacrum of screaming—the teeth were *real*. Each mask would have had to have been crafted individually, by hand, then carried from the Cyn's ship all the way here; even if the tram had still worked at that point, it would have been a haul. That was a *lot* of effort to go to for his . . . art. For whatever the hell this was.

What in the *fuck*? What in the *hell* was the point of all this?

"What in the fuck . . ." Javier and I apparently had roughly the same thought process. "This . . . this doesn't . . . this makes no sense."

"Welcome to our last few weeks," Jane told him, though in truth, this was well beyond even the Cyn's somewhat inexplicable actions as we'd encountered them before. This went well beyond burning corpses, or even triggering a nuclear detonation: this was . . . *purposeful*, not intended for his enemies, not intended for us. This had been for *himself*.

He'd enjoyed it.

"It's laid out, very specifically," Marus said, staring up into the branches of the tree. "No two species set next to each other; none allowed to touch. This wasn't just random, meant to strike fear in whomever saw it—this was . . . it was a design. Had a purpose."

"This motherfucker's purpose is to be crazier than a bag of cats," Jane told him roughly. "Don't go looking for meaning in it, Marus—that's a black hole, there's no light at all beyond that pull."

Marus shook his head, though, stepping closer—off the path, onto the twisting roots of the tree where they emerged from the once-carefully-tended

earth. The empathy in him earlier, the deep reserves of feeling that had allowed him to share my pain: it *also* allowed him to peer into the mind of
the . . . *being* . . . that had done this. "He removes the organic species' faces
because he doesn't *want* them to have identity—they don't *deserve* it, haven't
earned it. The masks on the Barious serve almost the opposite purpose; it's a
mockery, an indignity, an insult. Despite what *they* perceive as the great dif-
ferential between themselves and the other species, to him, they might as
well be organic. He is as far beyond them not *just* as they are beyond us, but
so far past what *they* are that the difference between them and us is minis-
cule, meaningless. He doesn't *like* that Barious think they're so far evolved,
so purpose-built; he wants to remind them that *he* is the superior being, the
supreme creation of the cosmos, not them."

"Great," Javier told him. "He has a psychopath's pathology. Wonderful.
Did we really need to *know* that? I mean, couldn't we have pretty much
guessed it by the trail of bodies he's left in his wake?"

Marus turned, gave him an apologetic smile, which only served to make
the grisly scene more morbidly terrifying. "Sorry," he said. "Occupational
force of habit. Psychological profiles can be *very* useful, in my line of work."

I swallowed, still staring up at the gallows tree. "Yeah, I'm with Javier and
Jane on this one, Marus," I said. "Crazy motherfucker is crazy—that's about
all I need to know. He came here for a reason, and . . . *whatever* the fuck this
is, whether it's a monument or an offering or a morbid goddamn re-creation
of his primary school art-fair project, I doubt very much it was actually his
purpose here. Can we move on from the murder tree, please?"

"Esa's right," Jane nodded, sweeping the area with her HUD, the light
playing up one of the spiraling stairs. "The fighting leads into some of the
labs up on the third story, up past the factory floor—they were falling back,
defending something, likely his goal. That's where we should head."

Javier shut his eyes for a moment. "Of course it had to be on the third
story," he said.

"What's the problem?" I asked him.

"That means we have to go up the stairs. And the stairs go up right past
that fucking thing." He nodded at the tree again. "We've been here all of two
minutes, and I've already had my fill of looking at the terrible corpse tree,
thank you very much."

CHAPTER 10

We made our way up the stairs, level by level, past the gruesome icons that the Cyn had made out of the dead. At the third landing, the atrium opened up yet again, the top floor stretching out past the walls below, the ceiling continuing up—another wide-open space, this one bounded on one side by the atrium itself and on the far end by a long window, stretching all the way across the wide expanse. The window was just a few stories above the shifting fog below, looking out over the roiling sea of clouds that made up the atmosphere beyond us. It was like we were on an oceangoing ship, staring out at the tempest-tossed waves.

I couldn't figure out what *use* the scientists had for all that space—the various equipment and gear scattered across the level, empty tables and what looked like generators didn't seem to fit with the larger pieces of machinery: it was as if it had been half laboratory space, half factory floor. Most of the machinery was trashed, ruined—there had been real fighting here, where they had made their last stand, melted metal and holes in the floor from explosions.

Still: didn't matter. The Cyn's goal hadn't been here, either: once he'd dispatched the defenses on the factory floor, he'd continued on to another set of doors, just off the floor proper. We could tell by the trails of blood. I peered in through a window beside the entranceway; a medical center of some sort.

I think we might have *literally* been looking in on the room where I was born. Where I'd been born, and where my parents had died.

We entered the medbay; the central console within had been damaged by an explosion. Whether that had been from the Cyn himself, or whether it had been a last ditch effort by the defenders of the station to destroy whatever it had been that he had come for, I wasn't sure. Jane echoed my thoughts as she studied the damage, and said, "It's a link to the dedicated server for this complex—information even the central AI couldn't access. They compartmentalized their information. Good for them." Jane always admired paranoia.

"Didn't work, though." Marus knelt by an access port on the damaged machine; the lock on the door had been melted off. We all knew what did that. "Looks like he wired in, here."

Jane was already busy stretching a wire from another console in the wall to the breached port below, plugging Schaz into the laboratory mainframe. "This is great and all," Schaz told her as Jane wired her in, "but I can't *see* anything. The power to the servers is down. If you want me to find out what he was after, you're going to have to restore power to the server room."

"I saw it, on the second level," Javier said. "I'll go."

"Be careful," Jane told him.

He grinned. "Quiet as a mouse," he promised.

I watched him go, stepping out of the lab as he descended again past the tree of corpses, then I turned; I didn't want to look at that macabre sight anymore. That left me staring across the factory floor and out the wide window instead, to the sea of azure fog below as it rolled past. There was a storm building, circular patterns rotating faster and faster in the atmosphere, like looking down at a whirlpool—arcs of lightning flashed across the surface of the mist, a web of electrical discharge jumping from cloud to cloud.

Jane came to stand by me, put her hand on my back. "You okay?" she asked.

I shook my head mutely, rubbing my arms, still shivering from the drenching I'd taken as we'd made our way through the flooded tram tunnel. When we'd been pushing through the rest of the station, I didn't have to think about it, the fact that *this* lab, our goal, was where the research my parents had been doing had killed them, the very science that had given me my gifts poisoning their bodies and stealing away their lives. If parents were meant to protect their children, my mother had done so in the most literal way possible, her womb filtering out the lethal dose of pulse radiation that was slowly killing *her*, while still leaving my own physiology irrevocably changed.

Had she *wanted* to get pregnant? They'd kept it a secret from the Preacher; she'd told me that much. Was I the product of a long-deferred wish? An accident? Some kind of fucked-up research project, my mother *intending* to expose herself and her fetus to the radiation she was studying? My father hadn't been in the holoprojector's imagery, the team members whose recorded visages greeted new visitors to the lab: there hadn't been a human male among them. Had he *not* been a member of this project? If so, why had *he* been exposed to the same levels of radiation my mother had? Maybe he just hadn't been high-ranking enough to be displayed as the face of the project; maybe he'd been a maintenance tech or the janitor or something, and had only been poisoned when the research had gone wrong and he'd tried to save my mother. That was romantic enough. I could almost even believe it.

"No, Jane," I answered her question. "I'm pretty fucking far from okay."

She nodded, like that was about what she had expected. One thing I liked about Jane: she wasn't about to pitch me some platitudes, I wasn't going to have to listen to "time heals all wounds," or "that which doesn't kill us defines us," or "how we're born is not who we are." Of course it didn't, of course it does, and it sure has a fucking impact. But Jane knew that just as well as I did, and she *knew* that I knew, and she wasn't about to try and convince me otherwise just because I was *sad*. I was standing within the laboratory that killed my parents; of *course* I was sad; what the hell else would I be?

Instead, she just stood beside me, her hand on my back, just a *presence*: there if I needed her. There just to remind me that she was there. Sometimes—most times, maybe—words weren't the comfort people wanted them to be, but just physically being nearby, being *with* someone, that was what actually helped.

I appreciated it.

"Javier got the servers up and running," Schaz told us over the comms. "I'm in."

Jane rubbed my back, then returned to the medbay; I followed, despite being pretty much *done* with this place. All of a sudden, I didn't really care why the Cyn had come here, what he'd butchered all these people for—Jane had been right, and so had Mo. He'd done it because he was fucking crazy, a zealot and a lunatic: there was no other explanation that would change those base parameters. He'd done it because the voices in his head had told him to, and he thought those voices were his god, and that hearing them *made* him a god, and so the lives of others meant nothing next to his own desires.

Mo's faith had driven him to search the cosmos for a voice he couldn't make out any longer, a voice that came from inside himself rather than from some distant figure always just out of reach. This motherfucker had always heard that voice loud and clear; he just hadn't understood that it wasn't God at all, just his own madness.

"What have you got?" Jane asked Schaz. I knew the answer wouldn't be anything I wanted to hear.

I was right. "It's . . . I don't think it's a good idea to—"

"Just tell us, Schaz," Jane sighed. "We know it's going to be bad."

"It's bad, yes, but what I'm saying is—"

"She doesn't want to say it where I can hear," I said suddenly; after three years, I knew when Schaz was being evasive, mainly because she was crap at it.

"Esa, sweetheart, that's not—"

Jane was looking at me when she spoke. "Just say it, Scheherazade," she commanded her ship. "She can take it."

Schaz sighed. "He was after *her*," she said.

Jane scowled; that wasn't much of an answer. "What does that *mean*? He's been after her this whole time, or at least, after gifted kids like her; it was something he learned inside *those servers* that put him on that path. That's what we're looking for: what painted the target on her back?"

"That's not—I mean he was after her even *before* he came here. I don't know why. But what he *took*: it was *her*."

Something cold dripped from the top of my spine to puddle at its base. I'd known it wasn't going to be something good. "When I was . . . born," I said softly. "They took a genetic profile of me, didn't they?"

"That would be standard hospital obstetrics procedure," Marus nodded. "To tailor your nanotech suite against hereditary diseases and the like." I'd never actually *received* that nanotech—like vaccines, a child's suite of minia-ture medical machines was implanted in stages across the first few years of their life. Given that by then the Preacher had already taken me and run, all the way to a world where medical nanotech had been pretty much a myth, I hadn't had mine implanted until I'd been taking my courses on Sanctum, preparing to work as Jane's trainee and partner while she healed from the injuries she'd taken during the fight with the Pax.

My eyes fluttered shut; suddenly I didn't *want* to be staring at this lab anymore, the medical center where I'd been born as my mother had died. "And that's what he took," I whispered. "My genetic profile."

"Your profile," Schaz confirmed, her voice miserable. "Your tissue samples, your genome sequence, and your MRI scans. More. All of the medical information gathered on you after your birth, and there was a *lot* of it—the doctors here were scientists first, after all, and you were . . . an anomaly."

I couldn't help but ask. "Why?" He was crazy, that's why.

"I don't know. I'm . . . I'm so sorry, Esa. I can't imagine how . . . *invasive* it must feel, to know that he has that information."

Fuck it. Fuck *him*. I was more than my biology; I was more than my gifts. I assumed that's what he had been after—that like the Pax before him, he'd wanted to see if he could *copy* my abilities somehow, the abilities I hadn't even known I had yet, that wouldn't manifest themselves for more than a decade after my birth. His ability to manipulate the energy of his own body was dangerous enough; matched up with telekinesis, he'd be unstoppable.

But if that *had* been what he was after, it hadn't worked. We hadn't seen him use telekinesis, not once over the past few miserable weeks. So fuck him twice: once for stealing my genome, and once more for being a failure.

And another couple dozen times for all the lives he'd destroyed.

"Fine," I said, nodding, trying to seem assertive. "We know what he was after, and we know he didn't accomplish *shit* with it. Can we get the hell *out* of this place, now?"

Jane nodded. "Yeah," she said. "That seems—" She stopped as a low rumble echoed through the lab, strong enough that we could *feel* it through the decking under our feet. The entire station was vibrating for some ominous reason.

We ducked out of the medlab, staring out the window: sure enough, the view of the storms rising out of the sea of azure fog was *listing* to one side. Something had just gotten fucked in the station's orbit.

Jane touched the comm bud underneath her ear. "Schaz?" she asked.

"I think we have a visitor," Schaz replied.

CHAPTER 11

What the hell was *that?*" Javier asked, coming back up the stairs.
Jane held out a hand to forestall him, still talking to Scheherazade.
"Can you see—"

"I don't have cameras up throughout the interior, but based on the exterior sensors I *do* have active—and based on the fact that none of them picked up a craft on approach—I can only guess that a stealthed ship just rammed the station, not far from here. Based on the amount of force with which it hit and the parts of the structure that it displaced—"

"It's him," Jane said.

"It's the Cyn," Schaz agreed.

"Schaz," I interrupted. "Did you ever finish running that secondary analysis of the mask I took off the Cyn's ship? Trying to figure out how to match the . . . the wavelength, the vibrational frequency of his energy signature?"

"It's almost done. I've had to redistribute some of my processing power—"

"Fucking distribute it *back*. I need that frequency, *now*. How long?"

"Well, now that I can apply some of Odessa's dormant RAM to my—"

"How *long?*"

"Five minutes, tops."

"Do it." I cast about; of *course* none of us carried energy weapons. We were all used to being prepared to fight on pulsed worlds, which meant adding lasers or other energy-firing guns to our arsenals—the sort of thing that would be eaten up by pretty much *any* level of pulse radiation—would have been rarely useful at best, and we'd all phased them out. Not that those would do any good anyway even if we *did* have them on hand; outside of a dedicated, fairly advanced armory, something better than what Schaz had on board, we wouldn't have been able to reprogram their munitions to match the vibrational frequency of the Cyn anyway.

So where else did we have access to an energy output that we could manipulate, that we could use to—

Intention shields. Our *shielding* was a form of energy. But its frequency was set, the day of its installation. It couldn't be reformatted without—

Oh, god. I knew what I had to do. I *really* didn't want to do it.

"Do we know where on the station he . . . landed?" Marus was asking. "How much time do we have?"

"Not far from here, but I'd bet good money that the flooded tramway would be a more difficult hazard for him than it was for you," Schaz told him. "What with the 'being made of energy' and all."

"Could we fall back *into* the river?" Javier asked. "Use it for natural—"

Jane was already shaking her head. "What happens when you introduce an electrical current to a body of water?" she asked Javier.

"Oh. Right." He grinned almost sheepishly.

The station shook again, the view of the cloudy sea out the curved window seeming to *roll*. "He is on his way," Schaz added, somewhat unnecessarily.

"Marus," I told the Tyll spy. "I need you." Oh, I hated this plan. "Jane, Javier—buy us some time. Five minutes. If you *can*, peel some of his armor off. But don't, you know—"

"Don't get killed." Javier nodded, checking his shotgun one more time before throwing me a grin. "Don't worry, Esa—that's pretty much my theme song."

I frowned at him. "I don't know what that means."

"It's a reference to vid programs, they . . ." He trailed off, then turned to Jane. "Have you *really* not exposed her to, like, *any* culture at all? What do you two *do* during long hyperspace jumps?"

"We train. And this is *not* the time," she hissed back.

"Just hold him off," I said to them. "Marus, back into the medlab, now."

Jane reached out, caught me by the arm. "You know what you're doing, right?" she asked me.

I gave her a wan smile. "No," I said. "I'm winging it. I am *totally* out of my depth."

"Well, good of you to admit it," she sighed. "We'll get you the time you need. I led him on a chase around Valkyrie Rock for nearly an hour; I can buy you five minutes."

"In an hour, Odessa Station may well be sunk entirely in the atmosphere and on its way to the bottom of this world's gravity well," Schaz reminded her. "The pressure won't be enough to prevent *me* from taking off, but this station was never designed to survive *any* kind of atmospheric descent beyond its current depth. Exposure to much more than the barest of atmospheres and it will begin crushing itself."

"Just like the *Ishiguro*," Jane said, mostly to herself.

"God, don't remind me," I told her. "Now *move!*"

I watched her and Javier just long enough to see them approach the stairwell—Jane speaking low to Javi, likely giving him the benefit of whatever she'd learned in her cat-and-mouse flight from the Cyn back on the asteroid station—and then I turned to Marus, who was waiting patiently, his robe already shed: ready for a fight. "You said something about the medlab?" he asked.

I nodded, and we both retreated within. I cast about for a moment, digging through the available supplies—overturning trays, pulling open drawers—until I found what I needed; an access port to the station's systems, otherwise known as Scheherazade, and a single scalpel. I tested the edge of the blade against my thumb, then immediately regretted it, and not *just* because of the pain: watching the bright line of blood rise up through the surface of my skin was a chilling reminder of what I was about to ask of Marus.

"You've got the steadiest hands of all of us," I told him, flipping the scalpel and handing it over grip first. "Six fingers and all that."

"Esa?" He didn't like the expression on my face. "What are you about to ask me to do?"

I took a deep breath, then turned away from him, gripping the edge of the counter as tightly as I could. "I need you to cut open my neck," I told him. "Peel back the muscle tissue." Staring at the far wall and trying my damnedest *not* to anticipate the descent of the scalpel and the *feel* of it slicing into my body, I took a series of deep breaths, trying to calm myself. Based on the churning in my gut, I was failing pretty miserably. "I need to give Schaz access to the intention shield wired into my brainstem. It's just at the top of my spine," I reminded him helpfully, just in case he needed a refresher on human anatomy. "Once you've found it, run an access line from the station network port into the shielding unit itself."

"You have a plan," he said quietly. That was the *other* reason I'd wanted Marus to do this, rather than Javier or Jane—they would have asked questions. So long as Marus thought *I* knew what I was doing, he'd be willing to follow my lead. He'd give me the benefit of the doubt.

I hoped I deserved it.

"I have a plan," I agreed.

"Let me find some anesthetic."

I shook my head. "We don't have *time*, and I don't know if anesthetic would interfere with my ability to control the shield. We can't risk it."

"Esa—this is going to hurt. A great deal."

"I *know* that. Just—"

He cut into my flesh with the razor-sharp scalpel. He'd only prompted me to say something—even if that something was about how much *pain* I was about to be in—so that I had been thinking about my response, rather than concentrating on the sensation of my muscles being parted and the blood that was flowing freely down my back, soaking into my body armor.

I struggled not to scream; managed to at least choke it down to a whimper. The *pain* was bad enough, but Jane had taught me how to deal with pain, how to suppress it, or at least drown it out—what really got to me was the *feeling* of Marus probing with the metal blade of the scalpel *inside my body*. It made me want to puke.

My arms were trembling, struggling to hold me up against the counter—a very specific part of me wanted to turn around and *fight*, because I was under *attack*, something was causing me *pain*, and why wasn't I *doing anything about it*. I forced that part of me low, into the pit of my stomach; it wasn't any good, it was of no *use*, not here, not now.

Marus kept cutting. The tiled walls of the medbay began to shake and split; a spiderweb of tiny cracks burst free of the mortar and the porcelain, like something had hit the tile from the other side, *hard*. Marus didn't pause in his work, but he asked, "Was that the Cyn?"

"No," I ground the words out, "that was me." I needed to keep a tighter grip on my teke, or my autonomic responses were likely to break Marus's arms in an attempt to stop him from doing what I'd asked him to do. "Keep going."

Beneath our feet, the station shook again, and I could hear gunfire; somewhere behind us there was a bright flash, one I could only see reflected in the cracked tile of the wall I was staring intently at. Javier and Jane must have found the Cyn, or the Cyn had found them. Either way, we were running out of time.

Marus kept cutting.

CHAPTER 12

"Got it," Marus said, dropping the scalpel with a clatter and expertly applying gauze and medical tape to the upper and lower extremities of his incision. "I'm wiring you in now."

"Schaz, have you got the . . . *godfuckmaargghhh.*" The sounds that came out of me disintegrated into guttural growling as Marus threaded the cable through my sliced-open skin, past exposed muscle tissue and nerve to the tiny black box at the top of my spine. "Rewire my intention shield," I panted to Scheherazade when I could speak again, not unclasping my hands from their death grip on the cold counter, not even to wipe away the string of spittle hanging from my lips. "Reformat its vibrational frequency to match the Cyn's."

"Esa, that will—"

"*Fucking do it!*"

The shield was wired directly into my nervous system; that was what let me control it with a thought, what let me control it unconsciously. When I saw an enemy raising their gun toward me, the shield would snap into place, blocking all incoming fire from that direction. In order for that to work, not only did the unit have to "trick" my cerebellum into thinking that *it* was part of my muscular system, it was also wired directly into my neural pathways—it siphoned off tiny pieces of energy from my own bioelectric field in order to charge.

Which meant Scheherazade rewriting the intention shield's control system felt a whole hell of a lot like someone was running an electrical current through *all* of my dense muscle tissue *and* my entire nervous system at the same time. Every single nerve ending I had, every single part of my body: they all felt like they were on fire.

I did vomit this time; I couldn't help it. That was part of why I'd chosen the counter to cling to—there was a sink right in front of me. Then it was done, and I was panting, still holding on to the cold metal for dear life, and Marus was removing the wire from the back of my neck and spraying me down with clotting foam—the cool gel would harden in the wound, stopping the blood loss immediately, and my own nanotech would start working on repairs.

"Oh, god," I moaned. "Ohhhh, god." The shield was rebooting; it would take a moment, and in the meantime its connection to my nervous system was flooding my brain with all sorts of strange sensations. "I taste *copper.*"

"No, that's likely just blood dribbling out of your sinus cavity," Marus said with a shaky laugh, his hand on my shoulder giving me a squeeze. "Go ahead and rinse your mouth out."

My comm buzzed to life. "Esa, Marus—he got *past* us," Jane panted, a sliver of pain in her voice. "Those fucking *wings* of his—"

A crash, just behind us—*right* behind us. I tried to turn, but the pain had been too overwhelming, I was too weak, and Marus had removed his hand from my back, the only thing that had been holding me upright, as it turned out. I slipped on the floor and almost fell, caught myself on the counter again. I couldn't see anything but the floor beneath me—the thought of moving my head, of asking the muscles in my neck that had just been sliced open to *work*, made me want to puke again.

The sound of Marus's submachine guns opening up was deafening in the small room, even with his suppressors attached, and I still couldn't even *see* what was happening. The bursts didn't last long, though, and then *something* had knocked me to the ground, my grip on the counter finally pried away. Biting down on a scream, I managed to turn my head; my body still wasn't *obeying* the way I wanted it to, the shield's systems reboot scrambling my reactions, my responses.

And I *needed* to be able to respond.

The Cyn was just outside; he had Marus pinned up against the outer wall, right beside the doorway, Marus's guns both smoking ruins on the floor. All I could see of my Tyll friend was a single six-fingered hand, grasping at nothing past the doorframe—convulsing, mangled, ruined. The Cyn had *exploded* the rounds still in the guns' magazines while Marus was gripping the weapons. "Marus . . ." I tried to whisper, but I still couldn't move, even as I *watched* the Cyn retract the armor from his free hand and reach up with the glowing fire of his skin to grip Marus around the face.

"Defilers," he whispered, even as Marus began to scream, beating at the Cyn's armor with his ruined fists. The Cyn wasn't burning his face off all at once; he was *slowly* increasing the temperature of the hand that held Marus's head pressed against the wall. He *wanted* Marus in agony. *"This galaxy has never belonged to you, yet you spread and you scheme and you gnaw at its worlds like vermin."*

I tried to gather my teke, tried to do *anything*, but there was nothing I could do; I was still too weak, still gripped by muscle spasms. He was going to *kill* my friend, right in front of me, he was going to *torture* him to death, cause him so much pain that his heart would explode, and I was going to have to watch. No. No. *No.*

God, the *smell.* Marus's skin was beginning to scorch and char; smoke spread from between the Cyn's outstretched fingers, smoke that had just been *Marus.* He wasn't just screaming anymore—he was *keening*, a sound of utter agony unlike anything I'd ever heard. And it was coming from my *friend.*

"Your reckoning is coming." The Cyn had pressed his mask right up to Marus's face, right behind his own hand, as though he wanted to *whisper* to him, even though his voice was coming through our comms, not through any vocal chords that he possessed. The snarling, impassive visage of steel stared with its dead eyes at the damage his grip was doing, even as he whispered: *"The rise of the fallen empire will begin, built upon the corpses of those who sought to supplant it, and there is nothing—"*

I swallowed all my pain, swallowed all my fear, pushed past the convulsions of my nervous system and the lingering dizziness of the blood loss. I *used* the adrenaline pouring into my bloodstream to force my teke to snap into place, and I *grabbed* at the Cyn's armor with it, grabbed him by one of his partially retracted wings, ripping him free of Marus and hurtling him backward as hard as I could.

Which was pretty hard. He went through the far wall, all the way across the wide open area that made up the factory floor, and he didn't come out.

Tears that I couldn't feel were streaming down my face as I forced my body to work, scrambling in a crouch to Marus's side; I didn't even know that I could stand, and I didn't want to risk it—I just needed to get to him. He was terrifyingly still, crumpled on the floor up against the outer wall, but he moaned softly as I reached out and touched him; he was still alive.

His hands were ruined, and his face was one terrible wound. I think . . .

I couldn't entirely tell through the damage, but I think both of his eyes were just . . . gone. The Cyn had boiled them out of his skull, superheating their own vitreous fluid around them until they'd just *popped*.

Panting, I reached down and dragged him back into the medbay, scrabbling behind me until I found the half-used bottle of medical foam he'd just used on my neck. I sprayed down the wounds on his face, careful not to block his airways, then used what was left on his hands. He was already slipping into *cort*, an autonomic Tyll reaction to severe trauma—like a medically induced coma, only a natural occurrence in his species.

Part of me wanted to seal the door, to huddle in the medbay with Marus and shut off the lights, whimpering in the dark. I knew the Cyn wouldn't be dead—if the laser fire from a war satellite hadn't stopped him, throwing him through a wall wouldn't stop him. But the impulse to just *hide*—a mammalian holdover from the days when we weren't anywhere *near* the apex predator of our homeworld, and pressing against the back of a darkened cave to pray that whatever *thing* stalked the shadows beyond would just *go away* was our best hope for survival—was almost overpowering.

Almost. Jane and Javier were still out there. My intention shields had been rewired, the energy that coursed through them the same as what made up the Cyn's body; by using my teke to twist the defensive energy of the shield into an offensive blow, I could *hurt* the motherfucker now, if I could get close enough. And he'd just done his damnedest to kill Marus, had maybe crippled him for life. All the kindnesses Marus had done me—not just saving my life on occasion, but the *little* ones: introducing me to my greatest guilty pleasure, romantic literature from the Reetha golden age; making sure there was a gift waiting for me at Sanctum when Jane and I returned from a long run and the anniversary of my official induction into the Justified had passed us both by; reminding Jane to restock Schaz's supply of Tyllian fruits because she didn't like them—too sweet—and I did.

He'd held me, just an hour ago, when I'd seen the face of my mother for the first time and actually *felt* my heart breaking, a worse pain by far than what I'd just gone through under his steady hand. And the Cyn had ruined him.

I was going to make the bastard pay for that.

CHAPTER 13

I got to my feet, using the counter for balance, ignoring the smell of Marus's charred flesh and my own sick that choked the medbay air. I willed my limbs to stop trembling; willed my spine to straighten; gave myself just a moment to let my heartbeat stop pounding, *forcing* it to a slower drumbeat instead. There are limits to what you can accomplish just by doing your damnedest to *want* it to happen, but those limits are further out than most people think, especially when you have nanotechnology coursing through your bloodstream and telekinesis to stiffen your limbs.

For the briefest of moments, I thought about the Pax: their soldiers had a device built into their armor, one that could inject them with various chemical compounds at will. I wouldn't have objected to a cocktail of *something* at the moment, something beyond the adrenaline already pouring into my system. But, no: I was on my own. And *fuck* that, anyway. I had everything I needed to tear this motherfucker apart. I was my own goddamned weapon.

I stepped through the medbay door and sealed it behind me, locking Marus inside.

There was a bright flash in the darkness beyond the hole the Cyn's passage had made when I'd smashed him through the wall; then another. He must have been trapped by falling rubble, was disintegrating it piecemeal to pull himself out. The flashes were getting closer—he was almost clear.

As I watched, gashes of light appeared in the dark hole itself: the tears in his armor where Jane and Javier had managed to expose his energetic skin. He stepped through and spread his wings, taking a monster's posture, a silhouette of predatory form: a stance purposely designed to remind the beings he hunted of the winged apex predators that had terrified their ancestors on most of their homeworlds.

I stood opposite, waiting for him to make the first move. As far as I knew, of the various threats that had tormented early humans, a giant raptor hadn't been among them. But every second he postured was one more I had to get my breath back, to reexert control over my own body. The motherfucker could try to scare me all he wanted with brute-force base psychology and animistic shadow puppets; I was beyond being scared. I'd moved right into furious instead.

One way or another, I was going to tear him apart.

"*You think I have come to claim you,*" he said, and as always, despite the fact that he was well over a hundred feet away, the words sounded as though he were whispering them into my ear as he manipulated our own comms against us. "*You think if you can hide in the dark, you will somehow be beyond the fire's reach, beyond her reach. You are wrong. You look now upon the last face you will see before your fall; you look now upon your end. You will be sundered; you will be shattered. You will be severed from the very—*"

I reached up, very deliberately, and deactivated my comms. There was not a single thing he had to say that I gave a shit about.

He didn't like that, hadn't expected it: took a single step forward. I didn't move. When he saw *that*, he reached up and carefully removed his mask, the snapping connections behind it creating a small cloud of steam around his head as he dropped the metal visage to the floor, revealing the *no*-face he hid beneath it: no eyes, no nose, no mouth, no features, just a swirling void of light and fire with the vaguest semblance of form hidden within.

I already knew what he looked like; that didn't shake me either.

He raised his arms above his head, the action stretching his wingspan out to full; more posturing, and I was getting sick of it. So I reached out with my teke—echoing the motion of my mind with both hands—and I grabbed at the tops of his wings, at the highest point, then I pulled straight *down*.

I ripped his wings right the fuck *off* the rest of his exoskeleton, then I cast them aside, the steel throwing up sparks as they slid across the floor.

Try flying now, you motherfucker.

He raised up his hands—he might have been roaring with anger, but I couldn't hear it, not with my comms deactivated, his only method of communication to create vibrations in radio waves that I couldn't sense—and retracted the palms of his armor again, revealing the indigo glow of his not-quite-flesh. It began to swirl; he was preparing another burst of energy, to try and blast me apart. I readied my teke to catch it, just like I had on the asteroid, except I'd been training, and this was going to end very differently than that little debacle—it was going to end very poorly for *him*, he just didn't know it yet.

Except he never got a chance to try; the roar of a shotgun echoed across the wide room, and the Cyn was thrown forward, his armor hitting the ground with a clatter as he dropped, revealing Javier, standing behind him. He must have been crawling through the rubble, trying to finish the Cyn where I'd put him down, then lining up his shot when the asshole was distracted.

I started forward, almost at a run. Javier pumped another round into the chamber, fired again into the Cyn's back before he could start to stand. The ammunition in his cartridges wouldn't pierce the heavy armor, but the *force* was still keeping our hunter on his knees. Javier racked in another round, then tossed the shotgun across to me, over the Cyn's form—he didn't have an angle on anything other than armor, but *I* did. I caught the flung gun and raised it up to my shoulder, aiming directly at the Cyn's exposed face—more specifically, at the cowl of his exosuit *behind* his face—and fired the shell at almost point-blank range.

The pellets didn't strike the Cyn at all—they passed right through his energetic form as though through flame—but I'd been aiming *through* him, at the interior of his armor. The rounds ricocheted throughout the metal casing, doing all kinds of damage to the internal systems of his exosuit. I worked the pump, then put another round down through his head; I tried again, but the chamber was empty.

"Jane?" I asked Javier, tossing the shotgun back to him.

"Binding her wounds. She'll be along." He was reloading the weapon as he spoke, both of us still staring down at the kneeling enemy between us. "In the meantime, you wanted this asshole out of his armor? Then your wish is my command. Let's—"

The back of Cyn armor split open, all at once, right between the sparking stumps of the wings, and the Cyn *flowed* out, moving like gravity had no effect on him. Before either Javier or I could react, he had spun and smashed his glowing arm into Javi from the side; thankfully, Javi's shield had been raised, and it converted the energy from the Cyn's blow into kinetic force, instead, meaning Javier went flying.

He smashed through the corpses hung on the great tree, then fell, followed by a dozen or so of the dead knocked loose from his passage.

The Cyn swapped targets in an instant, came right at me. *God*, the motherfucker was quick. I danced backward, away from the lashing blows of his flowing limbs, in close quarters now, which is where I'd wanted to be, yeah, but I hadn't had *time* to prep my intention shields, and—

"*Esa, get clear!*" Jane's voice cracked across the open area like a whip; we turned to look, the Cyn and I both. Standing just inside the medbay, she'd seen better days; whatever the brief fight between her and Javier and the Cyn had been like, it had taken its toll. Her guns were gone, to where, I didn't know, and it took me a moment to register *why* she wanted me to break off: she was standing on a chair, holding something up just under the emergency sprinkler system on the lowered ceiling of the medical lab. "*This is for Mo, you son of a bitch!*"

A lighter. That's what she was gripping in her hand; the lighter she *always* carried, for when she wanted to smoke one of her nasty fucking cigarettes.

She snapped the flint; the flame sprung out on the first try. Jane never used anything other than utterly dependable tools, even when it was just the thing she carried to feed her nicotine habit. The sprinkler system cut on immediately in response to the presence of the teardrop of fire.

What *did* happen to a being made of energy when it was introduced to a veil of falling water? We were about to find out.

CHAPTER 14

The Cyn's reaction was immediate, and *spectacular*. His being was stretched, spattered, the energy that made up his body trying to pull itself along every single drop of water all at once; it was like he'd become a pointillist projection of himself, whatever field or thought process he used to control his form overwhelmed by the natural inclination of energy to travel through a conductive fluid. If it hadn't been so goddamned *terrifying* it almost would have been beautiful, in an abstract, avant-garde kind of way.

For a brief moment, I saw something else through the downpour—I *thought* I saw something. Something quite literally at the heart of him, something revealed as the energy that made up *most* of his body was stripped away and pulled apart. There was something there, something *not* energy, something firm and real and made of organic matter, a kind of pulsating organ at the center of where his chest used to be: not a brain, not a heart, not *anything* I recognized, but *something*, all the same. Then it, too, was gone as he tried to *shift* himself out of the flow of water, back toward the stairway and the arboretum, where the sprinklers hadn't been triggered.

Jane staggered off the chair toward me. I retreated in her direction, deeper into the downpour; there was strength in numbers, even if she could barely stand on her own. A blistering burn spread across one of her arms, and even as the water from the sprinklers washed over her I could see blood, pooling and spilling from a nasty gash on her side. I let her lean against me as she emptied a canister of medical foam into the gash, then I slipped her one of my handguns. She checked the action—of course she did—then we both turned to watch the Cyn as he slowly *drew* himself back together, just on the other side of the veil.

In the middle of the fighting over Sanctum, during the war against the Pax, I'd watched one of the enemy frigates pulled into a black hole, part of the natural defenses of the Justified's home system; this was like *that*, only in reverse, pieces of the light and heat and energy that made up the Cyn's form drawing themselves together as he passed beyond the reach of the falling water. Kneeling on the landing of the stairs—even freed of his armor, he still took a bipedal form; two arms, two legs, feet and fists and a head at his extremities—he glared at us, safe from him behind the protective wash. He *almost* had a face this time, but not quite.

"He's talking again," Jane told me, still leaning against my shoulder, slightly. She frowned, even through the pain. "You really ought to have your comms on."

"Why the *fuck* would I care what he has to say?" I growled. "He *hurt* Marus, Jane. Bad. He's already slipped into *cort*."

"I know, Esa; I saw." She was holding her comm nub as she spoke, so the Cyn couldn't hear us. "Javier, too—I saw him fall. Bolivar checked his vitals— he's alive, but he's busted up. A few broken limbs, a concussion. If the Cyn figures that out and goes after him, tries to finish him off, we're going to have to follow. *That's* why you should listen; we *need* to keep him up top."

I growled again—a mean rumbling sound I could actually feel in my chest, too afraid and angry to actually make words—but I triggered my comms back on all the same.

"*—purity of my people, the purity of our beliefs, and we knew one day that a cataclysm would come, that your kind would only ever race toward your own destruction. But the old gods could no longer protect us, not from the new galaxy you had created. So we found a* new *god, ready to manifest, to be. And as she commands, so do I obey.*"

"You've killed *thousands of people* chasing me down," I screamed at him through the water. "Do you even know *why*?"

"*Because she commanded it.*" He had stood again, his form complete, rebuilt from its passage through the downpour. "*My salvation lies in her deliverance.*"

"Any salvation that requires the lives of innocents isn't fucking worth it," Jane told him, glaring across the open space, through the sprinklers' wash. "It isn't *salvation* at all. You're being used. Like every other goddamned idiot in the sect wars; you're no *different*. You were handed a gun and told the only difference between right and wrong was that your side was one and your enemies the other. And you never thought to question that because it meant everything you *did* was right, and that horrible thing at the heart of you—the thing that *enjoys* doing what you do—it meant you could *indulge* that thing, that you could fulfill your psychotic need for bloodshed, secure in your moral superiority." She shook her head. "It's not your obsession with this 'goddess' that's made you a monster, and deep down inside, you know that. She just gave you a reason to let the monster *out.*"

I held my own comms silent. "Are we entirely sure that this 'goddess' isn't just in his head?" I asked her.

"Oh, not at all," Jane replied, just to me. "I think he's just a fucking lunatic, but pointing that out isn't likely to help."

"And baiting him *is*?"

Instead of answering, she looked up at the sprinklers; one by one, they were starting to shut off. Whether that was because the fire was "out," or because the pipes above were just running dry—after all, a not-insignificant portion of the station's water supply was now flooding the tram tunnels we'd taken to get here—we didn't have much longer. The Cyn was moving now, stalking back and forth just on the other side of the falling water, waiting for his moment to strike.

"We will return what you started," he swore at us, discs of energy forming, then dissipating in the palms of his hands—the Cyn equivalent of clenching and unclenching his fists, I supposed. *"The goddess's call grows stronger and stronger, day by day; the return is inevitable. It will be summoned from the beyond, and it will pull the organic species back to where they belong. In the filth, in the dark, huddled against the return of the light."* He spat the last word, even though he had no mouth to spit with.

"What the fuck is he even talking about?" I asked Jane, but she had an expression on her face, a terrible one, something that went beyond the pain of her injuries or fear for Javier and Marus.

"The pulse," she whispered. "He's talking about calling back *the pulse.*"

Of course he fucking was.

His species was immune to pulse radiation—could *subsist* on it, if our conjectures were correct. The Cyn had fled civilized space over some long-forgotten disagreement with organic beings; apparently, they—or at least whatever splinter sect *this* asshole belonged to—had spent the last several hundred years convincing themselves they were an inherently superior species to the life forms they'd left behind, even though it was the Cyn who had fled, not us. It was frighteningly plausible that the coming of the pulse must have seemed like an act of their new gods—punishing those who had driven the Cyn away, rewarding his people with a goddamned banquet of strange radiation—and so now, at the whim of his "goddess," he was gathering gifted children, just like the Justified. Only rather than training their gifts to *protect* worlds against the return of the pulse, he was planning on using them to *hasten* its return instead.

I didn't know if that was possible; the metaphysics of the pulse were well beyond me. But even if it wasn't, he was clearly willing to kill a whole hell of a lot of people just to get at the gifted, just to *try*. Except apparently I'd proved myself too recalcitrant for his liking, and now I was just another target to be wiped out, so that the Justified couldn't use *my* gifts in defending against the very threat he wanted to summon from the black space beyond the edge of the galaxy.

It was studying the pulse that had exposed my pregnant mother to the concentrated dose of radiation that had given me my gifts; it was because of the Justified's role in the pulse that the Pax had come to our doorstep. And now this. Everything always came back to that one fucking moment, a century gone and still defining the lives of every single sapient creature on every settled world spinning.

We will return what you started. That's what he'd said. Had he just meant the organic species? No—and if he'd thought his gods were behind the pulse, he wouldn't have said it like that either. Which meant he *knew* it was the Justified that had brought the pulse into being, and he *still* thought it was the will of his goddess. Because he was a goddamned maniac.

"Water's almost gone," Jane told me. "Did you get your weapon rigged up? The one you think you can hurt him with?"

"I did," I said, "but I'll need a clear shot, and I'll need to close the distance."

She cast a quick glance behind us, at the mechanical detritus that littered the wide-open space between the landing where the Cyn stood and the wide window showing the bright blue clouds of the gas giant outside—clouds that had risen closer since the last time I looked, the station's slow descent inevitable at this point. "Pull back," she said. "Find cover back there somewhere. I'll draw him in. We'll ambush the motherfucker."

I shook my head. "*You* don't have anything you can hit him with," I told her. "Just let me—"

"Not negotiable, Esa. Schaz," she raised her voice, "kill the lights."

Immediately, the water-soaked central area was plunged into darkness—the only illumination at all was coming from the incandescent Cyn himself, and the vaguely luminous clouds of the atmosphere behind and beneath us, reflecting the glow of the distant star. Trapped in the darkness between those two blue poles—bright azure radiance from the Cyn, a softer, turquoise bloom from the gas giant that, combined with the water still falling from the sprinklers, made it seem like the entirety of that side of the station had sunk beneath a sea—I had no choice but to follow Jane's lead, and I slunk back toward the heavy detritus of the factory area as Jane did the same.

Out the wide window, the storms rising up out of the planet's atmosphere coursed just under the misty surface, bolts of lighting bathing the machinery in brief brighter bursts of illumination.

In the other direction, the last of the sprinklers cut off, nothing refracting the light of the Cyn now—our enemy's path to us was clear.

Jane and the Cyn squared up against each other, Jane holstering my pistol somewhat awkwardly in her belt, and drawing a *knife* instead. What the hell she thought she was going to do with that, I had no idea. She was beaten, she was injured, she was *still* bleeding, even through the application of medical foam, but all the same, she faced down the glowing zealot who thought he was serving a god, and she *grinned* at the motherfucker.

"You want to get to her, you go through me," she said, raising her blade. "That's the deal; that's how this works. Simplest thing in the universe."

The Cyn formed those discs again in his hands; this time, instead of fading out, they stayed in place, spinning and radiant and almost certainly deadly. "*Death,*" he corrected her, his voice still a whisper in my ear. "*Death is the simplest thing in the universe.*"

"I know. That's what I just said." She held the knife forward and beckoned him with its edge. "Come and get yours, you son of a bitch."

CHAPTER 15

The Cyn lunged forward, going from his motionless stance to a dead run in nothing flat; Jane faded backward as he flung his energy discs toward her, his wrists *snapping* at the last possible instant to make the projectiles curve, their flight paths harder to predict. She dodged them anyway, ducking just slightly to the left as one carved through the air barely an inch from her face, then *vaulting* to the right, over the second. She was firing her—my—handgun before she'd even landed, emptying the magazine so fast I was afraid it would jam; she *knew* the bullets wouldn't hurt him, but it didn't matter—it wasn't harm she was after, it was *distraction*.

"Scheherazade, *now!*" She screamed the words even as she scrambled for cover behind one of the larger pieces of silent machinery—not cover from the Cyn, but on the other side instead, cover from the wide window at the back of the massive room.

A shadow, through the turbulent light cast by the twisting clouds of the storm, and then Schaz was *there*, just outside, hovering in place, her guns spinning up. "Stay away from my *crew*, you giant electric son of a *bitch*," she said—almost politely—and then she was firing.

She used ballistic rounds first: shattered the window entirely, and there was a roaring rush of air as the atmosphere inside the atrium and the atmosphere of the planet tried to reach an equilibrium. The Cyn was *pulled* forward, closer to Scheherazade, off-balance for just a moment, and that moment was all Schaz needed to swap off the machine guns and onto her forward lasers, the stuttering fire brilliant and bright as it seared crimson through the room and punched right *through* the Cyn, drowning the interior of the factory level in fire.

She'd reset her laser banks to the same vibrational frequency as the energy that formed the Cyn's "body"—the same trick I'd been trying to use, except instead of the relatively mild output of my intention shields, she was hitting him with a ship-to-ship laser battery, enough energy in those bursts of light and heat to tear through blast-resistant hulls.

The lasers punched through the Cyn, again and again—I hoped that, wherever Javier was below us, he wasn't getting charred by the reflected blasts hitting the far side of the atrium—and the glowing figure stumbled to one knee, but he still wasn't *down.*

"Schaz, he's got some kind of *organ,* at the center of him!" I called out. "Hit him *there,* target the—"

It was too late. The Cyn was already reaching out, *through* Schaz's firing pattern. She blasted his arm off, and it just re-formed: her big guns didn't have the kind of keen accuracy needed to target the one tiny piece of his mass we needed to hit. We were lucky she was accurate enough to mostly contain her fire to an area *around* the Cyn. Even as the lasers tore through his energetic flesh, I could *feel* him reach out, the sensation uncomfortably close to how it felt when I reached out with my telekinesis.

"Schaz, get out of here!" I screamed.

She reacted immediately, trained and programmed to respond to commands from Jane or me in an instant; the barrage cut off and she was gone, ascending up past the upper limit of the window, and just in time, too. If the Cyn could have forced his way through her shields—and that was exactly what he'd been trying to do—he could have grabbed hold of her fusion core, triggered an explosion inside her bulkheads, exactly the same thing he'd done to the dead Barious who hung from the tree in the atrium except on an entirely different scale: the blast likely would have killed *all* of us, possibly even the Cyn, though I doubt he would have cared.

That must have been what he'd done on Kandriad: if there had been a dormant fusion reactor in the factory complex, it would have given him exactly the fuel he would have needed to trigger the nuclear detonation, once he ate the pulse around it and brought it back online.

Still, Schaz's attack had served its purpose: he was weakened now, piecing himself back together again, the torn shreds of his luminescent flesh twisting like radiant ribbons that swam through the darkness as they re-formed his being, and his recovery was going much more slowly than the re-formation we'd witnessed after we'd caught him in the sprinkler system's deluge. The glow from his limbs and chest was significantly less bright than it had been, almost cloudy in places; however it was that he created the energy that made up his form, it wasn't limitless—nothing was.

Jane didn't wait for him to put himself back together. She lunged.

She was going for the organ in the center of his chest; we could see it again, just the edge of it, but his energetic "skin" was sealing around it, fast, and she knew her window of attack was limited. I pushed off the ruined—and slightly on fire—piece of machinery I'd been using for cover, trying to reach her, to join her, to *help* her, but I had been significantly closer to the window when it shattered than either of them had, and the rush of the station's atmosphere being sucked outside had pulled me far out of position.

I wasn't going to make it in time.

The Cyn didn't have a weapon; he didn't *need* one. Schaz had done too much damage for him to spend his energy forming projectile attacks, but his very *limbs* were his weapons, and Jane had no way of blocking them as she closed—her knife would have just passed right through. The two of them were locked into close-quarters combat, Jane evading the Cyn's blows by ducking or turning or simply shifting her center of gravity just enough to let his attacks pass her by, the Cyn laser-focused on the edge of the knife in her hand. He *knew* that was the only way she could hurt him, that anything else she threw was just a distraction, trying to open him up for a killing blow.

There was no way I could close the gap between me and the two combatants as they danced around each other in a ballet of motion and light; I was just too far away. That meant I had a choice: I could draw my pistol, try to target the strange organ in his chest myself, or I could reach out with my teke, try to grab the Cyn directly—a risk, but I'd proved that I could hold his projectiles, so maybe I could hold *him*, rip open his wounds, give Jane a better angle of attack. Taking the shot with the handgun meant aiming at a target smaller than a human head, a target constantly in motion, and Jane would be well within my field of fire: if I missed, I might not just miss the Cyn, I might put the bullet right through her.

I chose, left my pistol hanging under my arm, and reached out with my gifts instead.

I knew as soon as I touched him: I had chosen poorly.

If grabbing the Cyn's projectiles had been like holding a searing-hot coal in my hand, this was like plunging my entire *arm* into a vat of molten metal; there was just too *much* energy, an entire fusion reactor's power output contained within his form. The backlash was a physical thing—I was thrown backward, and only smashing into one of the abandoned pieces of machinery stopped me from being flung out the gaping window Schaz had shattered with her barrage. I hit, hard, and dropped to the deck, barely conscious.

Conscious enough to watch, though. I was coughing red droplets of blood onto the wet floor, well beyond doing anything useful; farther away from the fight than when I'd started, and in no *shape* to be of any help anyway, but I could still *see* them, their combat like a play of light and shadow as Jane tried to cut open the being who shone like a star.

She was ducking and weaving through his flurry of defensive blows, the melee seeming almost like some form of obscure theater: neither of them making contact, just feinting and sweeping through the darkness lit only by the glow of the Cyn's own luminous skin. Jane was holding the knife in a backhanded grip tight against her chest, looking for her moment: when it came, it would come fast, there would be a split second, less, where she'd be able to exploit it. So she fought, and she watched, and she *waited*.

It came.

She saw the opening even through the lashing glare of his limbs: he'd extended a punch just a *hair* too far, shifted the crackling light of his body to do so, creating a gap in the energy field of his chest that revealed the pulsating organ inside, the thing that was neither heart nor mind but might have been something of both. Hesitation was never part of Jane's makeup—she struck as soon as it was visible, folding the motion into the sweep of her own defensive movement, as if that single attack had been what she'd been building toward all along. The knife plunged into his chest, sparks flying off the blade as it entered the energy that made up the Cyn's body, diving for the beating *thing* at the heart of him.

It missed the strange organ by millimeters, or less, as he shifted just *slightly* to the right.

And she was open to a counterattack.

He hit her, hard, right in the chest. I think he was trying to punch his fist right *through* her, but she still had her intention shield raised; just like when the Cyn had hit Javier, the shield converted the attack into kinetic force

instead, but there was still a *hell* of a lot of force, and Jane went flying backward, toward the shattered window and the storms beyond.

I tried to grab her, but she was just moving too *fast*, and before I could
reach out with my hand *or* my teke she was gone, sailing out into nothing,
hanging for just a moment in the upper atmosphere before vanishing into
the lightning-laced clouds of the gas giant below.

"Schaz, *grab her!*" I screamed, praying that Scheherazade could reach her
in time. If she couldn't, Jane would have a long, long, *long* way to fall.

I saw Schaz dive past the window; she plunged into the azure clouds where
Jane had disappeared, the churning storms of the atmosphere now nearly
level with the tilting, sinking space station. As the swirling fog swallowed
the ship up, there was a brief instant where I could still see Scheherazade's
form, illuminated by a flash of lightning that struck her shields. Then nothing.

Schaz was gone; Jane was gone; Marus and Javier were both badly hurt.
And I was alone with the Cyn.

CHAPTER 16

The shattered window had finally sunk beneath the storm; the blue clouds spilled across the slick deck, a low fog swallowing and reflecting the light of the Cyn as it stalked across the factory floor, looking for me.

I slid backward, soundless, tracking his motion by the glow that spread through the shadows. A burst of lightning lit the room, and the whole station shook: the lower levels might even now be crushing themselves apart as the gravity of the gas giant pulled at the depths of Odessa.

"Don't be afraid, child." The menace in his voice was a tactile thing, belying the intention of his words. *"It is not your fault you were born as you were. This is simply your fate, coming to find you. The way of all matter is entropy; the way of all flesh is to fear the inevitable. The pain will be fleeting, and then you will be as you were always meant to—you will be not. Your purpose was only ever to—"*

Jane had told me to keep my comms on, because that's what she would have done: always a soldier, reading her opponent, always keeping an eye on the tactical ground, the psychological lay of the land. I switched mine off again. I didn't need to hear his threats. I already knew he was here to kill me, and I was already plenty afraid.

Letting him feed that fear served nothing. He'd kill me if I was afraid or not; the fear would just make it easier. I needed to *not* be afraid. Needing a thing didn't make it so. But my fear was a part of *me*, a reaction, and I could control it, the same way I controlled my teke, and so little by little, I pushed it down—didn't banish it, but locked it away, made it quiet. The others were gone; I was alone. It was up to me now.

I was huddled behind a ruined stack of useless mechanical detritus, blood flowing freely from a nose I wasn't even sure *when* I'd broken; ignoring the sticky wash for the moment, I reached out and started pulling myself up onto the unstable pile of wiring and plating, moving up out of the rolling fog handhold by handhold until I was crouched on top of the scrap, well above head height. I looked down and out, across the factory floor—the Cyn was hunting me, and I was hunting him. But only one of us was lit up like a fucking glow stick.

That made the Cyn easy to find, a bright figure in the dark, searching for me among the still monuments of the broken machinery and the torn-apart decking where Schaz's fusillade had ripped across the factory floor. Maybe he was still whispering threats, *probably* he was still whispering threats, and a good soldier would have listened, would have shouted back arguments and insults, tried to throw him off-balance.

Jane was a good soldier; consciously or not, just like the Preacher had said, that's what she was teaching me to be. But I *wasn't* a soldier, and I never would be—there was something different inside me, something that wouldn't ever be able to see the world that way. Besides, I'd seen what the Cyn did to soldiers. They didn't last. Soldiers of the sect wars, soldiers of the old orders—they were what he had trained *himself* to fight.

If I wanted to beat him, I needed to be something *new*, something different, something he couldn't see coming. A force of nature, a creation wholly of *this* galaxy, not the old orders he'd built himself to bring down. The pulse and the power and the purgatory worlds where I'd been born and raised: they were all a whirlwind inside me, a whirlwind trying to coalesce into something *else*, something he'd never seen before. Looking down on him, hunting me—he never looked up, assumed I'd be crouched low somewhere, trying to use the creeping fog for cover—I knew what that new thing would have to be, what I already *was*, and had just never known the name for.

I dove into the rad-soaked worlds, into battlefields and war-torn cities and the chaos of the new; the Cyn and the Pax and all the other threats of this clawing, terrifying universe didn't faze me at all, because all of their power and all of their violence would never be able to stop me. The glowing figure below wasn't going to stop *me*. He might have been able to stop a leader, a leader like the Preacher wanted me to be, because all leaders failed, eventually. And he might have been able to stop a soldier, a soldier like Jane was trying to train me into, because that's what he *did*. But I wasn't either of those things, nor any of the others he might have expected, fighting old wars begun on older worlds, the same worlds that had created whatever long-ago schism that had twisted inside the Cyn until he became the zealot I saw before me, willing to do anything to satisfy his hate.

I was different from *all* of that. I had a *purpose*, and I had a will, and I used whatever tools at my disposal I needed to in order to fulfill that goal: to take those chosen from the chaos of the post-pulse universe and to ferry them safely to where they could change the galaxy, for the better. *That's* what I was, that's what the whirlwind inside me was telling me I'd long ago become, even if I hadn't known it: a thing that saved the children of the pulse, that *delivered* them, even out of the chaos of war.

I was a goddamned valkyrie.

And not one he knew how to fight.

I took a slow, even breath, ignoring the taste of my own blood as I watched the Cyn stalk below. I narrowed my eyes and summoned my intention shield into being; didn't focus it on the threat before me—focused it on *myself*, instead. I reached out with my teke toward the edges of the shield—took the shimmering, vibrating energy and *narrowed* it, pulling it into place, manipulating the current until it was concentrated, not covering the whole front of my body like normal, but compacting it instead, locking it into place like a sheath. For a moment, the energy leapt against me—this was *not* where it was meant to be, and it wanted to rebel, to fulfill its purpose, but I held it down, wrestled it into submission by will and by the strength of my gift, forcing the energy of my shield through the channels of my telekinesis, and then it was done: I had my weapon.

My hands and arms were covered by a faintly shimmering field of blue, matching the rolling fog *and* the azure fire of the Cyn beneath me, held in place by my gifts. I pressed one thumb up against my broken nose; blew the blood out of my sinuses so I could breathe again, then pushed, hard, *into* the pain, until the break was reset. I spat the resulting wash of blood from my mouth, and wiped it off my lips, the crimson sizzling against the electric field of my shielded, teke-enforced gauntlets.

Somewhere in all of that, the Cyn had seen me, or heard me; he was staring up, out of the fog, his swirling no-face raised to stare at me. I stared back, my expression just as blank as his—no hate, no fear, no pain—and I raised up my fists.

I'm sure he was saying something—something about my death and my destiny and how linked they were and how fucked I was. He knew *nothing* about what I was. But he was about to find out.

Another crack of lightning spat through the storm that was even now flowing into the factory floor from the broken window—I think it was *just* outside the station itself, the electricity drawn to all that falling metal. The Cyn flinched back from it, just a little bit—a being made of energy was especially attuned to electrostatic discharges, I suppose—but I didn't.

I dove forward instead.

CHAPTER 17

I hit him hard and fast, and I didn't let up.

He hadn't expected it—not even when he'd seen my arms, wreathed in the crackling energy of my intention shield like a street fighter's knuckles wrapped in the tape and barbed wire of my telekinetic gifts. The first hit was *absolutely* clean, heavy with the drop of my descent, and if he'd been made of flesh and bone it would have broken his motherfucking jaw, but he wasn't, and he just staggered back from the force and the crackling discharge, the void that was his face shifting and flickering. I didn't give him time to react.

I shifted my shield to the sole of my boot and kicked him in the chest with a motion almost like a *stomp*; as he reeled back from that, I spun the electricity around my form like I was wreathed in ribbons of light, using my teke like a hurricane pull until the glow was focused along my left arm, shrouding it in pale fire from the shoulder down. I closed with him, landing two hits, quick, both in his face—first an elbow, then a backfist—then I spun the light again, this time to cover my right hand and left leg, driving an uppercut into the center of his form, then catching him on the back of the neck with the same hand to force his head downward and meeting his descent with a rising knee.

I stepped back to let my intention shield recharge, but I never dropped my stance.

If the Cyn had been human—organic—I would have expected him to be coughing, wheezing, spitting blood and maybe teeth; he didn't quite do that, but he dropped to one knee, the places where I'd hit him discolored like bruises on his energetic flesh. He didn't gasp for air—he didn't breathe—but instead just looked up at me, his lack of a face unreadable, almost certainly a glare, and whatever he might have been saying at that moment, threats or ultimatums or begging, I just didn't give a fuck.

As soon as my shield was charged, I hit him again.

My first attacks had surprised him; now he was in the game, throwing fast blows of his own. But I wasn't Jane—my defense wasn't just a dodge, because I had the energy of my shields and I could shift them where I liked, and so long as I *knew* where he was throwing I could not only block his strikes, I could *hurt* him where he connected. He came away from that exchange even worse off, suffering not just from my attacks, but also from the strikes he'd landed against my shifting shields. If he'd been organic, I imagined those must have felt something like punching a solid wall.

I hoped they fucking *hurt*.

He tried to focus his will, to launch a projectile at me; before he could even fire it off I reached out with my teke and took the energy *away* from him, stretching it and shifting it and making it fit *my* needs instead, until I was holding a shield of light in one hand, round and flat like some ancient centurion. Then I took that shield, and I proceeded to bash it into his face as hard as I could before wrapping my leg in defensive energy and kicking outward, putting teke force behind the blow.

The kick connected; for each action there is an equal and opposite reaction, and I flew backward into a controlled reverse somersault, landing on my knees, as he went crashing through half a dozen pieces of collapsed machinery before sliding to a stop, his glowing form marking a trail through the fog. He was leaving traces of himself everywhere he hit, like spatters of luminescent blood.

Come on, motherfucker. Stand up. Stand *up*. We're not done. You hurt my friends. You hurt my *family*. You killed tens of thousands of people to get to me, maybe more over the years as you hunted my kind: here's what you wanted, standing right in front of you, *beating the everloving shit out of you*. Here's what you asked for—here's what you were *looking* for, what you *stole* from this place, come back to fucking haunt you. Your goddess wants me? Here I *fucking am*. Now stand the fuck *up*, you son of a bitch—stand up and see if you can *take me*.

He obliged.

A beam of light like a laser cut through the darkness; his next attack. Still holding the energy shield I'd made out of his last projectile, I knelt behind it, crouching my body behind its barrier, and as his laser hit its surface I shifted my defense slightly, using the shield to reflect his beam back toward him. It cut through the fog and swept directly toward his head—he only realized what was happening a moment before he decapitated himself with his own attack, and the light flooding from his hand shut down undramatically.

I hadn't reflected *all* of the energy he'd just poured at me, though—and I hope it cost him, I hope every single joule of electric power he'd poured into that beam felt like it had been ripped right from his strange and pulsating heart. Some of it I'd kept back, held to myself, and it had *hurt*, and I'd done it anyway, because sometimes pain was necessary, sometimes pain was what you had to *eat* in order to win.

I started charging at him, and as he prepared new projectiles I flung his own energy back into his face, first the shield—hurled on its edge like a discus—then the rest that I'd gathered, lobbed as twin orbs of light. He blasted the shield out of existence; tried to do the same with the arcing orbs, but they were as much light energy as anything else, and as the resulting flash blinded him—apparently with eyes or without, if your entire sensory input revolved around energy, bright things were still bright—he reeled back.

It was just for a moment, but long enough: I was already closing the gap, and I smashed my teke into the ground beneath me, the added momentum sending me sailing over his head. I lashed out above me as well, smashing a teke battering ram into the ceiling, reversing and adding to my momentum— that sent me hurtling toward him like a cannonball, barreling down from above and behind, where he'd expected me to hit low and from the front.

I had just a moment to wrap myself in teke and energy, and then I hit him so goddamned hard I carried us both *through* the decking below, into the labs beneath us.

Away from the reflected light spilling off the atmosphere through the window, the only illumination was the Cyn's azure form and the focused glow of my intention shield that wrapped around my body like an extension of my mind. We slammed through the laboratory walls; I was *using* his own energy like a battering ram, forcing him to spend himself to break through the barriers. Finally, I leapt free—he staggered to his feet, and I just hit him again.

As we clashed in the darkness, it was like bolts of lightning meeting in a void. He was still *trying* to fight, but I'd realized something very early on:

maybe once, a long time ago, he'd trained to fight other Cyn, other enemies that could meet his electrified form, but he'd spent the last seventeen years—maybe even longer—hunting organic beings instead, beings he didn't have to fear, beings he didn't have to *defend* against, beings he could kill with one hit, and not even a *clean* hit.

I'd spent the last three years training, every day. Training to fight for my life, training to fight through pain, training to fight through fear. I was *better* than he was.

Of course, Jane had been as well. But she couldn't *hit* him. I could.

My only weakness was that every few moments I had to spring backward to let my shields recharge, and he *still* wasn't recovering as fast as I was. He tried to press his advantage during one such break, coming at me with what he *thought* was a fast combination, but I'd trained with Jane and Criat and Sahluk, better fighters all, once you took his natural advantages out of the equation; I simply ducked low under the flurry of blows, my palms to the floor, then stabbed at him with an arc of energy that rose off of my back like a razor-edged tail, my gifts giving me the telekinetic approximation of a Reint physiology.

Match *that*, you asshole.

He doubled over against the intensely focused blow, that much energy striking such a small target that it must have felt like a gunshot; I straightened up even as he went down, using the moment to coat the fingers of my right hand with absolutely *all* of the energy my shield had left. Before he could recover, I *reached* into his neck with those electrified fingers and I ripped his head right off his goddamned body, scattering its fading light into the darkness that surrounded us.

I won't lie: that was pretty fucking cathartic.

He dropped to his knees, headless, his being flickering in and out of focus, the energy that made up his body barely able to maintain his form now, and there it was, my target: the organ at the center of him, all that was left of what had once been the organic beings the Cyn were so goddamned sure they'd evolved right past.

I didn't have much energy left in my shield at all—I'd pushed it well past the point of recharge with that last attack, compensating for the incredible storm of power that made up his flesh—so I drew my knife instead. I was

wrapped in darkness now, the light of my shield gone, and the Cyn was trying to stand, a glowing-fading being of light in all that black.

He took a staggering step toward me, still trying to re-form his head; I
don't know if that was involuntary reflex or what, but it was drawing even
more of his being away from his chest, revealing more of my target. I siphoned
what little of my shield I had remaining into the palm of my off hand, a single pool of light in the darkness, and held the knife out in front of me in my
right, weaving the blade in patterns slightly serpentine so that even if he *could*
see me, he wouldn't be able to predict the strike. Just like Jane had taught
me: don't let the enemy see you coming.

That was all I had—the knife in my hand and three years of training by
the most dangerous, most formidable badass I had ever known. And I was
going up against a deathless thing of energy and fire. Fucker didn't stand a
chance. I'd seen his heart now—or the closest thing he had to one. I didn't
know what it *actually* was, that pulsating, slime-soaked organ beating in the
center of his chest, suspended in the energy of his form like a planet in a
void of crackling light, but it didn't matter: all I had to do was get a knife
through it. Nothing can survive a blade in a major organ, not if you can sink
it deep enough. Stab once, and you're done: Jane had taught me that, too.

He came at me with a lumbering strike, desperate to land one last blow
that would turn the tide of the fight, almost pathetic in its predictability. I
slid to one side, let it pass, then jammed my shielded palm up under his jaw—
drove his re-forming head back and up, exposing his chest further as the
energies of his being pulled taut—and I sank the knife hilt deep into the meat
at the heart of him, the piece he wanted to pretend didn't even exist.

He screamed into the silence; I *felt* it, even with my comms cut off, a
ghostly reverberation, like a wail from another world. For a moment, we simply stood there, me holding his head up with my hand under his jaw, pushing the blade deeper into the organ that kept him alive, him convulsing, the
echoes of that scream still broadcasting through every audible frequency he
could access. Pulses of light and tongues of flame rose outward from his form
as he struggled to hold on to voluntary control of his being—struggled, and
lost. The dark laboratory was bathed in shifting hues of fire, azure and crimson and orange, until I gave the blade one final twist.

Then he was gone—fled, routed, retreating through the torn-up lab around us like a lost bolt of lightning, desperate to be anywhere but close to me. He found the exit, staggered through and went out, and up; I stayed where I was for a moment, panting. I wasn't in any rush to catch up with him—he'd taken the knife *with* him, still sunk into that organ. He was dying now. It was only a matter of time.

Plus, I was pretty done in. *Shit*, that had taken it out of me. And to top it all off, with the Cyn gone, I couldn't see a *god* damned thing in all the darkness.

I *really* needed to get a HUD installed.

CHAPTER 18

Eventually, I found the door out of the labs on the second floor, made my way back up the stairs, through the curtain of mists rolling off of the upper level like a waterfall of fog. That's where I found the Cyn, kneeling in the shattered window, staring out into the storm, dying.

Good.

I triggered my comms on as I approached; I could hear him . . . not breathing, exactly, but transmitting random waves of static, the Cyn version of a death rattle. Over the broken glass of the window and the atmosphere beyond, we could see the bright, shining light of the system's sun, a single crescent of a dawn. The last one he would ever see.

I picked my way through the ruined factory floor, over the torn-up decking and past the ancient, silent machinery. Behind me were the bodies that still hung from the gallows tree, a grisly reminder of all he had done. I checked the pistol underneath my arm, made sure there was a bullet in the chamber. Then I approached.

I stood behind him for a moment, watching the light slowly fade from his being; he was on his knees, and that wouldn't last for much longer. His extremities were . . . fading, as the organ at the center of him lost its ability to feed the energy that gave him form. His feet and hands were already gone. The rest of him would soon follow.

All the same, I commanded him: "Turn."

A long, drawn-out burst of static in my comms, and then he did so, slowly, still on his knees. He'd pulled the knife free of the organ in his chest—it lay before him; I could see it through the mists as he turned, almost like an offering to some distant god held captive in the rising light of the day.

He stared up at me, holes beginning to form in the blank nothing he called a face, his very being dissipating, finally a victim to the entropy he'd claimed to exist beyond.

"*So,*" he said, and there was nothing in his voice—no weakness, no anger, no pain. It was the same haughty tone of command, of *surety,* that he'd always used. I'll give him that: even in the face of the end of his existence, an existence that stretched back who knows how long—I had no idea if Cyn even aged—he showed no fear. A zealot to the end. "*You braved your own fall. Managed to ascend, instead. I was wrong.*"

"I don't know what that means," I told him. "I don't know what *any* of it means. What did you want with me—what did you want with *any* of it?" My voice was rising, and I knew it was pointless, I *knew* he wouldn't answer, but I didn't care. "Why did you attack this place—why steal the data on my birth? *How* do you eat the pulse radiation? Is it you—or those like you, those that share your beliefs, your sect—that have been stealing gifted children before the Justified can reach them? What have you been doing with them? Is this goddess of yours *real,* or just some figment your people have conjured, a lie you've all agreed was necessary? If you've been looking for *me* all this time, why didn't you show up sooner? Where have your people *been?* Are you the last of them, or are there more? If there are more, are they all like *you?* Why did they leave in the first place? If they can *all* eat away at the pulse, why keep hiding after it appeared? Why *torture* and *murder* to get what you want when you've already *got* something more precious than any level of violence? *How could you kill so many people?*" I don't know when I'd started screaming at him, but that was the question at which I finally stopped, just stood before him, panting, gasping for air, like I was the dying one.

Slowly, the nimbus of light that was his head twisted and shimmered, until finally he had features of his own: eyes for me to stare at, lips to speak—or at least borrowed ones. It was my own face that looked back at me, the expressions I recognized from the mirror reflected instead in the Cyn's skin made of fire. "*You have your destiny,*" he told me, "speaking," now, with my lips, even though the words still came from the comm bud in my ear. "*I had mine. Mine, it appears, ends here. I believe . . . I believe I have fulfilled it. Earned my end. Set you your path.*"

"And it took the deaths of *thousands* to do that?" I asked him. I don't know when I'd raised up my pistol, pointed it at his face, but I had, and my finger was inside the trigger guard, tightening around the trigger itself. All the dead flashed before my eyes, on Kandriad, on Valkyrie Rock, the girl in the cage, Sho's mother, in the tunnels. Mo.

The steel of the gun's grip was cold in my hand. God, I *wanted* to shoot him, even if it wouldn't do any good—even if he was dying already. All he had done. "You psychotic, self-absorbed *fuck*. How is your destiny—how is *mine*—that much more important than all of those that you tore away? How fucking *dare you* say that this was worth it?"

"*Because it means . . . it means you can challenge her now,*" he said, his features struggling to hold their form, his nose running like wax, dissolving back into the heat and light of his head. "*And that's all she ever wanted. To be able to prove . . . to prove her own worth. And when she cuts you down . . . and when she finally transcends . . .*" His eyelids—mine—fluttered, his expression one more of ecstasy than of agony, as though in the grip of some awesome revelation.

Staring at that slavish devotion, I felt nothing more than disgust; I came back to myself, the gun still trembling in my grip. My questions, the answers I was desperate for—they didn't matter, not any more than his own need for closure, for deliverance, did.

Past his kneeling form, in the atmosphere of the planet, I could see motion, and not just the storms: we were low enough now that I could make out the distant shadows of the strange obelisks, rising and falling in the fog like hints of ancient leviathans in a misty sea, lost to time. Whoever had built them, why—none of that mattered. All they were now were monuments. Whatever gods they had been raised to venerate, whatever machine they'd been meant to power—all gone, the obelisks all that were left, waiting to be discovered by beings like us, beings that had no idea what their significance once had been. As one day Odessa Station might be, lost and crushed in the gas giant that was swallowing it up.

Whether we acted for gods or ourselves or in the name of some ideal, ultimately it was the actions *themselves* that mattered, that we would be judged by. Regardless of whether it was some higher being that had set him on the path of bloodshed and chaos he'd followed all his life, or if he simply needed to believe that, *he* was the one who had chosen to walk it.

I lowered the gun.

In some ways, taking that final shot might have been a mercy; he was dying, the fires of his very being flickering out. But that wouldn't be *why* I'd be doing it—I'd be doing it because I hated him, and that was all. One more life on the altar of my own conscience, one more life I'd taken out of this universe that would never come back. Even a being as brutal as he was still unique, individual, even if just by the resolve and *dedication* he'd shown to his own hate.

I didn't shoot him, because Mo wouldn't have wanted me to. Not to save the Cyn, who would be gone soon enough, but to save myself. Violence haunted Jane; it had haunted Mohammed, right up until his end. There had to be another path. For myself; for Sho; for our generation.

There had to be another way.

My "face" was almost entirely gone from the Cyn's glowing features now; he could barely hold his body together. In the wash of the dawn pouring over the edge of the planet, spreading toward us over the tops of the distant storms, he looked more ghost than being, translucent and fading as he knelt in the mists. Even still, he saw me lower the weapon, saw the resignation on my face, and the fires in his own shifted, just a bit. I couldn't read the expression, didn't really try. I was beyond trying to understand him. But still: I had to ask. One last time.

"Tell me," I said simply. I wasn't begging, nor was I threatening—didn't draw the gun again, not when he'd already realized I wasn't going to fire. I just didn't see the *point* of it. Of any of it. "What you do—*how* you do it— you could save . . . so many. The pulsed worlds. The Barious. I've *won*; give me that, at least. Tell me how to save them. *Let me save them.*"

He shook his head, once. "*You cannot save the damned.*" The words were almost sorrowful, as he spoke them. Then he leaned backward—the last of his features vanishing in the dying fires of his face—and he fell. Dropped backward from the window ledge and into the abyss below, his fading form indistinguishable from the blue glow of the lightning-streaked clouds, vanishing into the deep nothing of the storm.

I stood in the light of the new dawn, and stared at the point where he had vanished, stared for much longer than it had taken him to disappear.

Then I holstered my gun, and went looking for my friends.

CHAPTER 19

I still couldn't raise Jane or Scheherazade—I *hoped* that was just interference from the storm lashing up against the station. I checked on Marus; he was deep in *cort*, so I headed back down the stairs, through the swirling atmosphere still spilling over the factory level, to see if I could find Javier. He found me, instead; he was pulling himself up the stairs, tread by tread, muttering a slow string of curses under his breath. An impressive feat for a man with a shattered ankle and a broken arm.

It helped that he'd dosed himself with a fair bit of morphine from his emergency medical kit.

He took one look at me, standing on the landing above him, then grinned. "You got the fucker," he said, making it a statement—I guess he figured if I was standing there with my guns holstered, rather than running or shooting or dodging energy blasts, then the fight was over.

"I got the fucker," I agreed, helping him to his feet. Well, foot, anyway. "He's *super* dead."

"Good girl. Well done, and all of that. Jane? Marus?"

"Marus is up top, in one of the labs; he's hurt . . . pretty bad, Javier. He's slipped into *cort*. Jane got thrown off the station. Schaz went after her."

"Right. Okay." He took a deep, shuddering breath as we made our way—slowly—back up the stairs, his arm over my shoulders. "Schaz'll get to her. Don't worry. In the meantime, we need to get the hell out of here. I don't know how much longer this place will last." As if to punctuate his words, the station around us gave a groaning, twisting kind of a sound, the pressure of the atmosphere beginning to bend and compact the rigid superstructure.

Javier activated his comms and reached out to Bolivar and Khaliphon both, told them to get themselves out of the docking bay, to come and meet us at the shattered window. I didn't know why *I* hadn't thought of that. It had been a long day. Week. Month. However long it had been—I honestly wasn't sure anymore.

By the time we made it back up to the factory floor—and it took a while; Javier was barely up to limping, and he was significantly heavier than me, not to mention taller, making it somewhat difficult for me to be much help supporting his weight—we could see the sweep of a spotlight, playing through the mist. It wasn't Bolivar or Khaliphon, though; Schaz had returned, and Jane stood on her lowered ramp, crouched behind the hidden .50 caliber machine gun inside the airlock.

She shifted the barrel toward us as we came into view; Javier held his shotgun up over his head, though since he'd been using the damn thing as a crutch, the action *almost* made him slip and fall again, which would have been . . . bad. Jane relaxed on the gun. "You got the fucker," she shouted across the top of the rolling fog.

Javier just pointed at me, using the finger of the hand still wrapped around his shotgun; Jane grinned. "Well done!" she shouted.

Yes, yes—everybody was very proud.

Together, we got Javier on board Scheherazade—he was so doped up, he passed out almost as soon as we got him to a chair—and then Jane and I went back for Marus. We could worry about transferring everyone back to their respective ships later—for now, we pretty much *all* needed medical attention, and it would be safer to have everyone on the same craft. Jane was careful—even gentle—as the two of us lifted Marus, Jane taking most of his weight. "He'll be all right, Esa," she told me softly. "We've still got Tyll compounds on board that can supercharge the *cort*."

"He'll be scarred for life," I told her. "He was only here for *me*, and this . . . his *eyes* . . ."

"He will," she agreed. "The eyes . . . the doctors at Sanctum should be able to fit him with prosthetics. He won't be able to infiltrate pulsed worlds anymore, but he *will* be able to see again. And that guilt—it's not yours to carry. You didn't *do* this to him, and you made the one who did answer for it. Marus was here for you, yes, but he was *also* here because the Cyn was an enemy of the Justified, and that's what we do—we *fight* the enemies of the Justified, and we protect the next generation. Marus will just have to find another way to go about that. He was due . . . due for something like retirement anyway. Whether he'd admit it or not, he was getting too old for intelligence work."

"And you?" I asked her. "I heard you and Mo talking, you know. Back on Jalia Preserve. About how you feel . . . about how you think there's only so much longer you can do this."

She shook her head as we struggled up the ramp, Marus still held between us. "Come on, Esa. I'm never going to take a teaching job at the university; I'd be shit at it. You know this."

"You really wouldn't."

"Well, I'm not going to, regardless. *This* is what I do. Like it or not, kid— you're stuck with me." We'd made it into Schaz's living quarters; we strapped Marus down to the medbay table and let Schaz's medical protocols take over. Jane and I retreated back to the ramp, staring out through the shattered window at the torn-up factory floor where we'd waged our war against the Cyn. I should have felt something—anything—looking out at the rolling fog still pouring inside the station, taking what would be my last glimpse of the place where I'd been born before it was swallowed up by the gas giant's atmosphere, lost to the depths along with the hidden monuments of the ancient race.

I didn't. Maybe I would, later, but for now, I was just too goddamned tired.

"I was born here," I said, just a basic statement, more because I *felt* like I should say something than because I actually had anything to say.

"Well, at least you didn't die here, too," Jane said. Jane wasn't . . . great . . . at expressing her emotions. "Esa. It doesn't matter."

I turned to her. "What?"

"Whatever—any of it. All of it. Why the Cyn wanted you. Why he was studying your birth. Whatever the hell his 'goddess' is, or wants. If she's actually out there—and that's a big fucking 'if'; I'd still lay odds on her being the creation of a diseased mind and nothing more—but if she *is*, we'll deal with her when she comes, just like we would any other threat. Ultimately, all this chaos, all this pain . . . we got Sho out, Esa. We got him back to Sanctum. We did our jobs."

"And the Barious?" I asked softly. "The 'cure' for the pulse?"

"If we can save the Barious, we will," she agreed. "And maybe we can learn something, from the Cyn's data, from his maps. But the pulse . . ." She shook her head. "This is our universe, now, Esa. This is what the galaxy is. Saving those—*helping* those who are just trying to survive in it . . . *that's* what the Justified do. What the Justified were always supposed to do. *That's* what matters."

"That's what matters." I echoed the words, and I tried to believe them.

"It's *all* that matters." She looked out, across the station, as the light of the dawn cut from behind Scheherazade, making the fog of cyan mist still spilling across the combat-ravaged laboratory glow like it was lit from within by incandescent fire. "So take one last look"—she nodded at the place where I was born—"and say your goodbyes, and don't think about the Cyn, or whatever the hell he was after. Don't think about the pulse, and don't think about what comes later, what happens next: think about your parents, instead. Think about your mother."

I tried, and for just a moment, I succeeded. The broken machinery and the rolling fog faded away in my vision as I slowly closed my eyes, and it wasn't just the hologram we'd seen at the laboratory entrance that came into my mind's eye then: that was *part* of what I saw, but I saw more than that too, not just glowing lines of light, but an *actual* face, a woman of flesh and blood smiling down on me, holding me, supporting me when I was too tired to stand. What I'd always wanted.

It took a moment for me to realize what I was looking at, the face I'd inadvertently called up in my mind's eye; not the face from the hologram at all, but an entirely different woman, the woman who'd *actually* done her damnedest to keep me alive, to keep me safe, to keep me happy and sane and free—who'd taught me what she thought I'd need to know, and struggled to hold the rest back, to rein in her darker impulses so they wouldn't creep across the bond we shared and settle into me. She hadn't always been successful, but maybe she didn't always need to be; so long as she let me make *my* own choices, let me decide what was wrong and what was right, I could take that darkness, use it as a tool, and maybe keep it from consuming me— the same way she always had.

I laced my fingers into Jane's own, and squeezed her hand. All we'd been through, together. All we'd *seen.* A hundred suns rising over worlds so different I could hardly believe they were all in the same galaxy—suns whose light was diffused by thick canopies of blooming trees, suns hidden behind shimmering shields of atmospheric energy, suns of orange or red or blue or green. The sun on Jalia Preserve, rising up past the twisting arches of the rings circling the planet; the sun descending behind the abandoned, crumbling factories of Kandriad, its light finding every tear and hole in the metal structures and making tiny pinpricks of brightness within their darkened facades. The glow of the dawn striking the mists on the factory floor before us, making a sea of shimmering color, a veil of beauty even in this damaged place. So many sunrises; so many worlds. And we weren't nearly done.

We weren't *nearly* done.

"Let's get out of here," I told Jane. "We've still got more stars to find."

ACKNOWLEDGMENTS

Writing a sequel is like staring at a horizon: you have to look beyond the point at which you can see no further—the point where the first story finished, what was up 'til now "the ending"—and ask yourself, "What's out there?" It's a trickier question than you might think, to find a way to push past the boundaries of the first book—otherwise why do it at all?—while still staying true to the spirit of the characters and the universe. And attempting to answer a question that tricky requires a great deal of help . . . so let's get to the thanking!

We'll start off with the repeat customers, and neither this particular story— nor its author!—would be the same without my family: Robert, Nancy, Sean, and Summers Williams, as well as the extended Williams branches, Ken and Maxine and Steve. The same is equally true for the Barnacastle side (deep breath, there's a lot of us): Jack, Marsha, Jeff, Jenny, Jeffrey, Johnny, Susan, James, Ryan, Riley, and Kai (welcome to the family, Kai! We're a bunch of lunatics, but you knew that—you married one!). And as always, I've reserved a special place here for Daniel and Janna, not just because without them, I would have lost my mind a long time ago, but because of the work they did bringing Presley, to whom this book is dedicated, into the world. (Okay, so Janna did most of the work.)

I could also spend pages and pages thanking the friends and coworkers without whom I never would have been able to answer the question above— "What's beyond the first one?"—but I want to thank a specific batch in particular, this time around: Joanne Howard, Kathleen Wylie, Kate Waters, Norah Madden-Lunsford, Sam Baine, Dani Mason, Maggie Jones, Kirby Quinn, and Addison Rees, otherwise known as the crew keeping the lights on at Little Professor in Homewood while I was working on *Chain*. Yes, guys: every single conversation we had over the course of the autumn and winter of '17,

I was building this story in the back of my head, and snatching inspiration right and left from you all to do so. All of you are in this book, in one way or another.

On the professional side, the indomitable will and good-natured advice of my agent, Chris Kepner, are absolutely what make all of this possible, and I'll never be able to properly express how grateful I am, and continue to be, to him. It also helps to have not one, but two publishers working to make sure a rough manuscript becomes a polished novel: on the Tor end, everything starts with Devi Pillai (who endured innumerable phone calls and emails, patiently waiting for me to catch up to where she already knew this manuscript should be) aided as always by the incomparable assistance of Rachel Bass; the contributions of LJ Jackson, Liana Krissoff, and Deirdre Kovac also cannot be overstated. On the Simon & Schuster UK side, Anne Perry is the one ruling with an iron fist (that's . . . not even remotely true; I only put it in here to make her laugh), but similarly, the talents of Harriett Collins and Richard Vlietstra help make the strange, terrifying concept of the British market an entirely welcoming place.

And last but certainly not least—Sara Glassman, always the first person to read any draft of anything I write (and the first person to get text messages that say, "What the hell is the word I'm trying to think of? Read my mind, please!"): Sara helped to shape everything about this novel, from scope to characters to narrative to setting, everything from the smallest details to the overarching themes. When I write anything, and I imagine the reaction of the reader, it's usually Sara's reaction I'm trying to conjure.

The larger point of all this thanking people: a book doesn't just come from nowhere, and it certainly doesn't come from the author alone. Without the talents, influence, and support of all the people I've just named (and plenty more, as well), this story never would have come into being at all—and it certainly never would have made it into bookstores and libraries (and computer banks, I suppose) across the world. I never assumed I would get to write a sequel to *The Stars Now Unclaimed*: the fact that so many people worked so hard to make sure that I could—and that it became the best novel it could possibly be—is something that I can never repay them for; words, for once in my life, have failed me.

So I'll close by simply saying this:

Thank you, everyone—and thank you, reader, most of all. Thank you for reading, thank you for caring—if you made it this far, I hope Esa, Jane, and the rest mean as much to you as they do to me.

Now let's find out what's over the next horizon, together.

Drew Williams
November 08 2018